Joan Jonker was born and bred in Liverpool. Her childhood was a time of love and laughter with her two sisters, a brother, a caring but gambling father and an indomitable mother who was always getting them out of scrapes. Then came the Second World War – a period that Joan remembers so well – when she met and fell in love with her late husband, Tony.

For twenty-three years, Joan campaigned tirelessly on behalf of victims of violence, and her first book, *Victims of Violence*, is an account of those years. She has recently retired from charity work in order to concentrate on her writing. Joan has two sons and two grandsons and she lives in Southport. Her previous bestselling Liverpool sagas have won her legions of fans throughout the world:

'Your sense of humour and knowledge of the old Liverpool is unsurpassed by any other writer' Judy Down, New Zealand

'Your books are fantastic' Jill Gibas, Slough

'Wonderful characters and humour' Mrs Ivy Decks, Essex

'When I'm low and feeling sorry for myself . . . all I need is to pick up one of your books . . . and I'm soon feeling better' Marion Carver, London

'Absolutely wonderful' Jean Bowers, Canada

D0784334

When Wishes Come True

JOAN JONKER

headline

First published in 2003
by HEADLINE BOOK PUBLISHING

First published in paperback in 2004
by HEADLINE BOOK PUBLISHING

10 9 8 7 6 5 4 3 2 1

ISBN 0 7553 0319 9

Typeset in Times by Avon DataSet Ltd,
Bidford-on-Avon, Warwickshire

Printed and bound in Great Britain by
Clays Ltd, St Ives plc

Headline's policy is to use papers that are natural, renewable and
recyclable products and made from wood grown in sustainable
forests. The logging and manufacturing processes are expected to
conform to the environmental regulations of the country of origin.

HEADLINE BOOK PUBLISHING
A division of Hodder Headline Limited
338 Euston Road
London NW1 3BH

www.headline.co.uk
www.hodderheadline.com

To Clare Foss, Sherise Hobbs and the staff at Headline,
and to Darley Anderson and the staff at his agency,
for their kindness, friendliness and encouragement
over the years.

A big hello to my readers and friends

I hope all is well in your world.

There is a treat in store for you with *When Wishes Come True*. It's a little different from my other books, but I promise you will love it. Our heroine is a young girl who will capture your heart, as she has mine.

With a mother who shows her no love and thinks she is a cut above their neighbours, Milly's life is far from perfect. Then she is befriended by the woman next door and her two mates, who bring love and laughter into the young girl's life. There are a lot of surprises ahead for Milly, her new friends and for my readers. I suggest you hurry through your housework, make yourself a cup of tea, choose the most comfortable chair and put your feet up. But don't forget to have a box of tissues handy. I went through two while I was writing this book.

Take care.

Love

Joan

Chapter One

1925

'Just look at this one, walking up the street as though she owned it.' Aggie Gordon was standing on the bottom step of her two-up-two-down house, talking to her next-door neighbour, Rita Wells, when she saw a familiar figure turn into the street. 'Miss Hoity-Toity... she gets on my bleeding nerves!'

'Ah, come on, Aggie, she doesn't do us any harm,' Rita said. 'I don't know why yer feel so strongly about her, she can't help it if she's down on her luck. She's in the same boat as all of us, without two pennies to rub together.'

Aggie pulled a face and folded her arms under her bosom. To say she was well endowed in that department would be understating it, she was enormous. 'Aye, but we don't all walk down the street with our noses in the air, do we? Stuck-up madam! She wants taking down a peg or two. And if she ever looks sideways at me, I'll clock her one.'

Rita turned her head to see a slim, attractive young woman who walked with a straight back and an air of confidence. She'd lived in one of the houses opposite Rita and Aggie for a few years now, but hadn't made any friends. Her seven-year-old daughter Amelia wasn't allowed to play with the other children in the street either, which caused most of the neighbours to say the woman was a stuck-up cow who thought she was too good for the likes of them. 'If she wants to keep herself to herself, Aggie, then that's up to her, she's not hurting anyone. It's the

1

young girl I feel sorry for, she hasn't got one friend in the street. She's a nice little thing, too!'

'How d'yer know that when she's not allowed to speak to anyone 'cos her bleeding mother thinks we've all got fleas?' Aggie shook her head and her many chins danced. 'Ye're daft, you are, Rita Wells, yer never see the bad in anyone.'

'While you, Aggie Gordon, are never happy unless yer've got someone to pull to pieces. Yer haven't spoken more than ten words to Mrs Sinclair, but yer can't stand the sight of her. I'm glad I'm a friend of yours, 'cos I'd sure as hell hate to be an enemy.'

Aggie's head wagged from side to side, sending her layers of chins flying in all directions. 'And why haven't I spoken more than ten words to Her Ladyship? Because every time I see her she looks down her nose at me, as though I'm a bad smell.'

'That's probably because she knows ye're always pulling her to pieces. Yer've got a voice like a foghorn, Aggie, they should use you when there's a fog over the Mersey to guide the ships in. Unless Mrs Sinclair is deaf, she must hear yer calling her fit to burn and wonder why. The poor woman lost her husband in the war so yer should have some pity for her, having to bring her daughter up on her own. She's never done you or me no harm, so for heaven's sake leave the woman alone and pick on someone who can stick up for herself.' Rita chuckled. 'Me, for instance, 'cos I could hit yer back.'

Aggie's laughter was loud. 'You! I could knock yer into the middle of next week with just one of me fingers.'

At that moment the woman who was the target of Aggie's criticism happened to turn her head before inserting her key into the lock. When she saw Rita nod her head, she nodded briefly in return before opening the door and stepping inside. Once the door was closed behind her, Evelyn Sinclair leaned back against it and sighed. How she hated this mean little house in the mean little street, where most of the neighbours were coarse and vulgar.

Particularly the little fat woman opposite, whose language was that of a fishwife. The only person in the street she ever had any conversation with was the woman next door, Bessie Maudsley, and on the odd occasion she had exchanged nods with Rita Wells opposite.

Evelyn pushed herself away from the door and hung her coat on a hook in the tiny hall before entering the living room. There, she pulled out one of the wooden chairs from the table and sat down. With her chin cupped in her hands, she took a deep sigh. Just looking around the room filled her with despair. There were no mirrors on the walls, no pictures, and no ornaments on the bare sideboard. When she went into the kitchen to make herself a cup of tea, she would find the pantry almost bare. It wasn't because she was lazy, and spent her days gossiping like a lot of the women in the street. She had found herself a job in the office of a firm of solicitors in the city centre, and worked there five hours for four days a week. But her job was really a junior's: running errands, making cups of tea and filing the correspondence of the two solicitors who shared the practice. The wages were low, barely enough to pay the rent on this house and buy what food she could to feed herself and Amelia. New clothes were out of the question, and a fire in the grate a luxury.

Evelyn dropped her head into her hands. What a far cry this was from what she had been used to. Then, as she often did, she closed her eyes and let her mind go back over the years to when she was nineteen. She was an only child, and lived with her parents in an eight-roomed house. Her father ruled her and her mother with a rod of iron. She wasn't allowed to invite friends to the house, nor accept invitations to visit theirs. But on her nineteenth birthday her father reluctantly agreed that she could go to an afternoon tea dance to celebrate, on the understanding that she was to refuse any requests from strange men to take to the dance floor. She had thought how stupid it sounded to say she could go to a dance but must not take part, but daren't voice her thoughts or she would have been sent up to her room and told to stay there until Father said she could come down for her meal. So she promised she would not dance, and that she would be home by six o'clock. She would have promised him anything, just to get out of the house and be able to act her age.

Her office friend, Gwen, had loving parents, and as a result was more sure of herself and more outgoing. When they met up that Saturday afternoon, she linked Evelyn's arm and grinned. 'First day of freedom, eh?'

'Hardly a day, Gwen, it's two o'clock now and I've to be home by six.'

'You'll not set any hearts on fire in that dress, Eve, it's positively old maiden auntish! Have you nothing more glamorous in your wardrobe?'

Evelyn shook her head. 'You don't know my father, he's so old-fashioned. I'm lucky to be here at all, never mind worrying about my dress.'

'Then I'm going to put powder, rouge and lipstick on your face, and I'll do something with your hair. Otherwise you'll never be noticed.'

So the Evelyn who walked out of the ladies' powder room of the Adelphi Hotel was very different from the one who'd walked in. Not that she wouldn't have attracted many a roving eye without the make-up because she was tall and slim with dark brown hair, enormous brown eyes and a flawless complexion. But whether it was the make-up or not, the friends barely had time to sit at one of the small round tables before a man appeared in front of them, his hand outstretched, and addressed Evelyn.

'May I have this dance?'

She looked scared. She was about to stutter that she had never been to a dance before when Gwen said, 'Of course you may, my friend would be delighted. Go along, Evelyn, I will be all right, I can see some of my friends waving to me.'

So Evelyn, for the first time in her life, found herself in the arms of a man. And what a handsome man he was! Tall, slim, well dressed, with jet black hair and laughing eyes that were constantly changing colour from hazel to dark green. When he spoke his voice was that of a well-educated person and very pleasing to the ear. 'Are you always so shy? You don't have to be afraid of me, I won't eat you.'

'I'm not afraid of you, I'm afraid of standing on your toes! You see, I've never been to a dance before and I'm nervous in case I make a fool of myself.'

'No one as beautiful as you could possibly make a fool of themself.'

And that was how their romance began. After the dance was over and Evelyn could see Gwen was with company, she agreed when her partner asked her to sit with him at another table. She may as well make the most of this opportunity, she thought, there may never be another. When he asked she told him her name, where she lived, and about the father who was very strict but who provided a nice comfortable home for her and her mother. Then the man, oozing confidence and looking at her with more than interest in his eyes, told her his name was Charles Lister-Sinclair. With a smile, he said, 'I work for my father who is far from strict and keeps me in the lap of luxury. He is also very generous in allowing me as much free time as I wish. So I hope to see much more of you in the very near future.'

Because she was smitten, Evelyn took a chance and arranged to meet him in her lunch hour the following Monday. She had never dared defy her father before, but she did so want to see Charles again, and if she had to tell lies to do so, then so be it. When she met up with Gwen in the cloakroom later, she was so excited the words poured from her mouth. 'I'm meeting him on Monday, Gwen, and he's taking me to lunch. I find it unbelievable I've met such a handsome and charming man on my first day of freedom!'

Gwen raised her eyebrows. 'You do know who his father is, don't you?'

'No, except that Charles said his father spoiled him.'

'You are so innocent, Eve! Don't you know anything about the social life of this city? Charles is one of the most sought-after, eligible young men in Liverpool. There are literally dozens of mothers chasing him for their daughters. He would be quite a catch for any girl, with his good looks and charming manner, quite apart from the fact that his father is one of the richest men in the city.'

Evelyn gaped. 'He never said! Except that his father was good to him.'

'No, he wouldn't brag about his wealth, that's what is so refreshing about him. Not like some of the young bloods I've met at parties who think because their families are well heeled they should be welcome in any virgin's bed.' Gwen grinned when she saw the look of horror on her friend's face. 'Don't worry, Charles isn't like that, he's a perfect gentleman. And if you can hook him, Eve, then you'll be the envy of every young female of marriageable age, and that includes myself.'

'I didn't know you knew him? You never said when he came over to ask me to dance.'

'I've seen him around many times, even been to parties where he's been a guest, but I wouldn't profess to know him well enough to introduce him. Anyway, it's time for you and me to go our separate ways, so I'll say "Sweet dreams", and I shall look forward to hearing what happens on Monday. I presume you will not be telling your father?'

'You presume right, Gwen, I'm not going to say a word. If I did, I wouldn't be allowed out of the house.'

Sitting at the dining table later with her mother and father, Evelyn was praying that her father would question her about the dance. But it was her mother who, unknowingly, came to her aid.

'Were there many at the Adeplhi, my dear? Do tell us what type of person freqents these places?'

Evelyn nodded. 'Yes, quite a few people, Mother, and some of the dresses on the young ladies were absolutely delightful.' She saw the familiar frown crease her father's forehead and hoped her little plan would work. 'I only knew Gwen, of course, but she did introduce me to one of her male friends.' She turned her head. 'I wonder if you know the Lister-Sinclairs, Father? Gwen said they are a very well-known family.'

The frown disappeared like magic, and his eyes widened in surprise as he lowered his knife and fork. 'I don't know them personally, but everyone locally has heard the name. They are a very well-known family, wealthy and much respected in the business world. Cyril Lister-Sinclair has many interests, and is probably the richest man in the city of Liverpool.' He coughed behind one curled fist before asking, 'And the son was at the dance, you say?'

'Yes, Father, and seemed very personable.' Evelyn could tell her father had taken the bait. 'Quite friendly with many of the people there.'

Herbert Wilkinson looked across at his wife. 'Perhaps I have been doing our daughter an injustice, Gertrude, by not allowing her to attend these dances. Don't you agree?'

'Oh, yes, Herbert, now we know the cream of local society attends them, we can rest assured she is in good company. Would you like to go next Saturday? If your father gives his permission, of course.'

Evelyn's plan was working beautifully. She had bargained on this being the reaction from her parents, who were both tight with money and would be delighted if their daughter married a rich man. 'Oh, I don't think I want to go again, Mother, I would feel like a poor relation. You see, I couldn't compete with the fashionable dresses and high-heeled silver shoes all the ladies were wearing. I really felt like a wallflower in this drab dress, and wouldn't want to go through that again.'

'Oh, I'm sure that, under the circumstances, and because we want you to mix in the right circles, your father would give you an allowance to buy suitable clothes. We can't have our daughter looking less attractive than the other ladies. Aren't I right, Herbert, when I say you will give Evelyn an allowance for some new clothing?'

'Of course, my dear.' Herbert Wilkinson was what you would call a sombre man who seldom smiled, and had never been known to laugh aloud. But right now he was positively beaming. He had a good job and was well paid, but he was a greedy man; not content with being well off, he wanted to be wealthy. And now, perhaps, through his daughter and her newfound connections, he could well find himself on the way to riches and social acceptance. 'When we've finished our meal we can discuss what is needed so that Evelyn can mingle with the best in society as an equal.'

True to his word, if against his better judgement, Herbert handed over four white five-pound notes. That it pained him to do so was obvious from the length of time he held on to them before Evelyn finally whipped them out of his hand. 'I need at least two dresses, Father, I'd be ashamed to wear the same one week after week. Then there are silk stockings, shoes, a band to wear around my forehead and some jewellery . . .'

'Your mother has plenty of jewellery you could make use of. It's only lying in a box on her dressing table, it would be an absolute waste of money to buy more.'

'I'll see, Father, when I go to the dance on Saturday. I will take more notice of what is in fashion then, but meanwhile I can get advice from Gwen. She is very up-to-date on fashions as she attends many dances and parties.'

And so Evelyn's social life began. She had never known such freedom and, dressed to kill, was thoroughly enjoying herself.

Wherever she went, Charles Lister-Sinclair went too. They saw each other every day and visited each other's houses. Herbert Wilkinson and his wife made a great fuss of Charles, but on visiting the Lister-Sinclairs, Evelyn found that while Charles' father was friendly with her, his mother was distant and didn't even try to hide the fact that she wasn't pleased with her son's choice. When Evelyn mentioned this to Charles, he laughed and said any girl he took home would not be made welcome by his mother who doted on him. Her only child, she wanted to keep Charles under her wing until he was older, and only then would she find a suitable wife for him. Evelyn continued to be pleasant to Mrs Lister-Sinclair. It didn't bother her that her friendliness wasn't reciprocated because she knew Charles was besotted with her, as she was with him.

A rattling against a pane of glass in the window brought Evelyn down to earth. It took her a few seconds to get her thoughts together, then she jumped from her chair. This was her daughter home from school and she hadn't even thought about what they were going to have for a meal. It wouldn't be much because there was nothing in the house.

'I've been knocking for ages, Mother.' The seven-year-old girl hadn't inherited many of her mother's features, but she had learned to copy her expressions and mannerisms. 'I was beginning to think you had gone shopping or were working late.'

'I was tired after a busy day, Amelia, and must have dropped off to sleep. I've nothing in for our tea because all I have in my purse is a sixpenny piece, and that has to last until I get my wages on Friday.'

Amelia knew they were poor, her mother was always telling her so, and it made the young girl too old for her years. She didn't worry, though, because all the girls in her class at school were poor, and some of the boys in the street had no shoes on their feet. 'I could go for a pennyworth of chips, Mother, and we could make sandwiches with them. We could do the same tomorrow, that way your sixpence would last until Friday.'

'You need bread to make sandwiches, dear.' Somewhere at the back of Evelyn's mind a little voice was telling her she shouldn't burden her young daughter with their money worries. But another little voice, a trouble-maker, was saying that if Amelia had never been born then Evelyn would still be living a life of luxury, being waited on hand and foot by servants. And it was this voice that made her so bitter inside because her life had been reduced to living in this two-up-two-down house, with no money for the fine clothes she was used to. Not even enough to buy food or provide ha'pennies for the gas meter. So she found it hard to feel any sympathy for the little girl who wouldn't remember the good times, and who, if she was allowed, would be happy to associate with the common-as-muck people in their street.

'You could try the baker's, they usually sell it off cheap when it gets near to closing time. It's probably bread from the day before, and stale, but it would be filling and better than nothing. Perhaps you could get a small loaf for a penny, and with a pennyworth of chips we could make sandwiches and keep the hunger at bay.'

'Ooh, that's a good idea, Mother, I'll go there first.'

Evelyn passed the small silver coin over. 'Keep tight hold of that, in case you lose it. And if any of the women in this street are in the baker's, don't let them hear you asking if they have any stale bread. Come out of the shop and wait outside until they've gone. I don't want the whole street to know our business.'

'Yes, Mother.' Amelia placed the silver coin in the centre of her palm and closed her fingers over it. 'I'll keep tight hold of it. And if there's no one in the shop that I know, I'll give the woman behind the counter a big smile when I ask if they've any stale bread. You never know, Mother, I might get a large loaf for a penny if I'm nice to her.'

'Make sure you speak correctly, and don't run down the street, it isn't ladylike.'

'Yes, Mother.' The girl turned towards the door. She was mixed up inside because the other children at school made fun of her for talking so 'posh'. She didn't know about the children in this street because she wasn't allowed to play with them.

As soon as the door closed on her daughter, Evelyn held her head between her two hands and she went back to her memories of days gone by.

Chapter Two

It was 1914 when war with Germany broke out, and Charles wanted to join the Army right away. He said it was the duty of every able-bodied man to fight in defence of his country. He wouldn't be persuaded by Evelyn not to be hasty, but much to her relief Mr Lister-Sinclair pulled a few strings and Charles was classed as being involved in important war work. He wasn't happy about it, thinking he would be thought a coward, but gave in to his father's wishes and his mother's tears. So he and Evelyn continued to enjoy dances, theatres and eating out in the best hotels. Charles still had feelings of guilt, though, and every time he saw a man in uniform felt like a coward. He couldn't live with that. So when the war had been raging for eighteen months, without telling his parents first, he enlisted in the Army. With his education and background, he entered as a Captain and was sent for training in a camp just north of London so was able to get home regularly. Then, after a few months, he came home on a three-day pass to tell his parents and Evelyn that talk in the camp was rife that they were being sent overseas very soon, and he didn't know when he would see them again.

Cyril Lister-Sinclair showed no emotion, but there was fear in his heart for his son. Every day there was news of thousands upon thousands of young men being killed. As for Charles' mother, she wailed uncontrollably, and as there was nothing Charles could tell her that would calm her, he took Evelyn's hand and they stole away to find somewhere quiet and peaceful where they could have some privacy. This was impossible in either of their homes, so Charles suggested they take his car and drive out to one of the nearby country lanes. There was little petrol in the car because it was very hard to come by, but he felt sure that what he had would take them a few miles.

Dusk was falling as they sat with their arms entwined, wondering if they would ever see each other again. Charles rained kisses on Evelyn's face and promised to write to her every day, but that was little comfort to her, and tears trickled slowly down her face. 'Don't cry, my dearest darling.' Charles pulled her closer. With her body pressed against his, he could feel a stirring inside him. He tried to resist the urge, but need took him beyond the point of no return. Evelyn was taken by surprise at first and tried to pull away, but the thought that in a few days he would be going off to war caused her to cease her resistance. If she spurned him now, he would go away thinking she didn't love him, and she couldn't bear that.

When his passion was spent, Charles was full of remorse. 'Oh, I am so sorry, my dearest, what have I done to you? I have disgraced myself and am so ashamed I throw myself on your mercy. You will forgive me? Remember, I love you so much I couldn't help myself. But we'll get married on my first leave, I promise. In fact, I travelled up today with another officer and he told me he was getting married tomorrow by special dispensation. Apparently if a soldier is being sent overseas, he and his fiancée can be married by special licence . . .'

'But I can't get married so quickly,' Evelyn protested. 'I haven't a wedding dress to get married in!'

'My darling sweetheart, you don't need a wedding dress to be married in a registry office! All you need are two witnesses, and I'm sure that will be no problem.' Charles was warming to the idea. 'I'll drive you home now and ask your father for your hand in marriage. If he gives his consent, I'll go and tell my parents. My mother will probably have a fit of the vapours and faint, and I don't think Father will be too pleased. I'm sure both of them would like a big, extravagant, high-society wedding for their only child, but I'll remind them there is a war on and many people are doing things they wouldn't normally do. I'll bring them around, I always do, then I'll meet you in the city centre tomorrow and buy you the engagement and wedding ring of your choice.'

Evelyn's parents were delighted. What a feather in their cap for their daughter to have landed such a good catch! And they didn't mind at all that the wedding was going to be a registry office affair, for, as Charles said, there was a war on. When their future son-in-law had left to break the news to his own parents, Mr Wilkinson was so full of good will towards his daughter he pulled her chair nearer the grate and, taking the tongs from the companion set, placed three extra pieces of coal on the fire before rubbing his hands with glee.

However, the news wasn't so well received at the Lister-Sinclairs' home. As Charles had predicted, his mother reacted by falling back in her chair and lifting the back of one hand to her forehead. Her other hand was holding a fine, soft linen handkerchief edged with lace, which she waved at her husband while in a tearful voice demanding her bottle of sal volatile fearing she would faint. With a deep sigh, Cyril rang for the maid. He loved his wife, but did wish she had some backbone instead of always behaving like a child. He wasn't too pleased with the news his son had brought either, having always thought that when his only child married it would be the wedding of the year in their social circle. But the sight of Charles looking so handsome in his Captain's uniform, and the knowledge that in a few days his beloved son could be facing the enemy, was enough for him to keep his views to himself.

'Father, would you make some enquiries on how to go about obtaining a dispensation and special licence?' Charles asked. 'You're so much better at getting things done quickly than I am. And I'm meeting Evelyn in town tomorrow to buy the rings.'

Cyril nodded. 'I'll make a few phone calls in the morning and get what information I can. But you will only have two full days, and I can't imagine having the necessary papers completed in that time.'

'Two days and a half, Father. My train doesn't leave until one o'clock on Thursday.' Both men turned their heads at the tinkling of the silver bell which Mrs Lister-Sinclair kept on her side table. They watched the maid enter the room, and heard her being told her mistress would like to retire as she was feeling quite light-headed. When his wife had left the room, leaning heavily on the maid's arm and sobbing as though her heart was breaking, Cyril asked if there was anything else he could do to help his son.

Charles leaned forward, resting his clasped hands on his knees. Gazing down at the floor, it was a few seconds before he spoke. 'This is frightfully forward of me, Father, and I would understand if you refused. But I would be so grateful if you would buy a house for Evelyn and me, as a wedding present. While I'm away she could be making it into a home for when the war is over and I'm back with her again. I really would like to know we had a place of our own, it would give me something to look forward to.'

Cyril was thoughtful for a few seconds, then sighed. This was a far cry from what he'd wanted for his son. 'I know there are one or two suitable houses empty in Princes Avenue. This confounded war has caused many people to move to the country. If that's what you want, I will certainly set the wheels in motion. You know I love you dearly and would move heaven and earth to make you happy. Everything I have will be yours eventually, and I'll be so proud when you take over the reins.'

'Thank you, Father, you are very kind and I admire and love you in return. When the time comes for you to retire – which I trust will not be for a very long while – I will do my best to make you proud of me. But if meanwhile you could settle Evelyn in a house, and look after her welfare, it would take a weight off my shoulders.'

Again Cyril was thoughtful for a few seconds before saying, 'I will purchase a house, furnish it, and make sure Evelyn has everything she needs. But I do think it would be best if I had my name put on the deeds. Only as a precaution, in case you came home and found you didn't like the house. You would have no ties to the property then and could look for another you think you would be happy in, and where you would like to raise your children.'

Charles lowered his head to hide the flush of guilt. 'Thank you, Father.'

So the following day, while Charles and Evelyn strolled down Church Street towards the jeweller's, their arms linked and their eyes gazing lovingly at each other, Cyril Lister-Sinclair was trying to arrange their wedding. After many phone calls, and taking advantage of his standing in the city, he managed to extract promises that the papers needed would be ready at five-thirty on Wednesday. Then, making a telephone call to the registry office, he was told they were booked solid for the whole week. However, when he mentioned his name and used a little persuasion they agreed to fit his son and fiancée in at half-past-eleven on the Thursday morning. No amount of coaxing would make the registrar's secretary change her mind about this. There were so many servicemen wanting to be married, she had to be fair to them all. Mr Lister-Sinclair was lucky she'd managed to fit his son in at all.

Charles didn't let his disappointment show, for he knew he was lucky being able to marry before going back to camp. But it would give them only an hour and a half in which to get married and then head for the train station where he would catch the one o'clock train. There was no time to invite friends or even let them know, and both sets of parents declined to attend on the grounds that the whole affair was too rushed. Charles' mother said wild horses wouldn't drag her there because it was so degrading that a son of hers was being married in a registry office – oh, the shame of it! And when the Wilkinsons heard the Lister-Sinclairs were not attending, they made the same excuse. If Charles' parents had been going, they would have jumped at the chance of meeting the man who would soon be almost like family to them, and who they were hoping would help them up the ladder to social acceptance and wealth.

So the young couple were married with Evelyn's friend Gwen, and Oscar, a friend of Charles, acting as witnesses. They made a handsome bridal pair, with Charles looking handsome in his Captain's uniform and Evelyn in a fashionable short beige coat, a lighter beige cloche hat, and carrying a posy of flowers. It was a quarter-past twelve when they came out of the registry office, leaving them tight for time. Charles hailed a taxi and they reached the station with just enough time for last embraces, tearful kisses and vows to love each other for ever. Then Evelyn, accompanied by Gwen and Oscar, was waving goodbye to Charles through the steam and noise of the train taking him away.

Charles' father kept his promise to his son, and two weeks after the wedding Evelyn received a telephone call from her father-in-law asking her to meet him at the house in Princes Avenue which he felt sure she would like. And he was right, because she loved the wide avenue, with its three-storey red brick houses. The one he'd bought was handsome with an imposing entrance hall and a wide, curved staircase. Magnificent furniture graced the rooms on the first two floors of the house. What excited Evelyn the most, was that this was her means of getting away from her grasping parents. Cyril said he would give her a very generous monthly allowance and would also pay for the services of a live-in maid as the house was far too big for her to live in alone. In the days that followed, Evelyn had never been so happy in her life with her newfound freedom and very comfortable life style. The allowance from her father-in-law was three times what she'd earned at the office, and as he paid all the bills, too, she saw no point in working and gave in her notice.

Gwen was the only visitor to the house, for Evelyn discouraged her parents from visiting. But she didn't feel lonely, she revelled in the unaccustomed luxury and in being waited on by the maid, Eliza. Charles had been gone eight weeks, and although he had written to her from the camp before his unit was shipped out, she hadn't heard from him since. She wasn't particularly worried because Gwen had told her letters were taking months to get through, and because Evelyn was so content with her life of luxury, she gave little thought to anyone but herself and how lucky she was. Until the morning she experienced a feeling of nausea, followed by vomiting. It was only then she thought back and realised she'd missed the last two periods.

She took to her bed, telling Eliza she had a headache and would ring if she needed her. That she was with child she never doubted, but she didn't want a child, not now when she was enjoying the good things in life. Then, gazing up at the decorative ceiling in the huge, richly furnished bedroom, an idea formed in her head. She didn't want a child, she didn't feel in the least maternal, but perhaps that was the very thing that would make her mother-in-law warm towards her. If Evelyn was carrying her son's child, surely they would become closer – friends even? Of course they would, a grandchild would put a different complexion on their relationship. Feeling light-hearted in anticipation of now being taken into the bosom of the wealthiest family in Liverpool, Evelyn slipped her legs over the side of the bed and reached for the telephone on the ornate bedside table.

With the ear-piece in one hand, she was ready to dial when she gave a low cry and quickly changed her mind. Her face drained of colour, she sat back on the bed. How could she tell Charles' parents she was expecting his baby when officially they had never slept together? And she couldn't lie to them about it because they knew the young couple, with their friends, had gone straight from the registry office to the train station. Evelyn would have lied through her teeth if it would have got her out of this trouble, but no amount of lying would help her now. It was all Charles' fault, she should not have let him have his way with her. Her temper high now, Evelyn had no one to take it out on but the maid. So she pulled on the velvet bell cord. When Eliza entered the room she was ordered to draw the curtains as her mistress had a headache, then she was to fetch up a pot of strong tea.

It was Gwen who first remarked on Evelyn's expanding waistline and fuller face. 'Would I be right in saying someone has been doing things no respectable woman should?'

Evelyn's face turned crimson, but she tried to talk her way out of an embarrassing situation. 'Are you not forgetting I'm a perfectly respectable married woman?'

'Come off it, Eve,' Gwen drawled. She was quite happy to see her friend looking uncomfortable because she was tired of hearing how rich the Lister-Sinclairs were, and how wonderful life would be when Charles came home, and how they would always be giving lavish parties. 'Don't forget it's me you're talking to, and I know you too well to fall for any balderdash. If you are pregnant, then Charles can't possibly be the father. So come on, out with it, who have you been dallying with?'

Evelyn knew it would be no use pretending, she was in trouble no matter which way she turned. 'It *is* Charles' baby! I was stupid for allowing him to have his way with me before we were married.' She had the grace to blush. 'I felt sorry for him with him being sent overseas, and now I don't know which way to turn. I never see my parents, which is the way I want it, but what am I going to say to my father-in-law when he comes? He's due any time now with my monthly allowance, and you were quick enough to notice so he's bound to.'

'I imagine you'll meet some hurdles, Eve, because how can you prove it's Charles' baby? Mrs L.S. doesn't like you to begin with, so she's bound to cause problems.'

'Charles will soon put them straight when he comes home. And I hope that's soon because it's very embarrassing for me. Do you think I should explain to my father-in-law when he comes, tell him the truth? Or should I wear something that doesn't make it obvious and hope that the war will soon be over?'

Gwen shrugged her shoulders. 'That's up to you, Eve, I can't advise you.' She got to her feet. 'I'll have to go, I'm off to a cocktail party with Oscar. His parents are almost as wealthy as the Lister-Sinclairs, but I don't think I'll be letting him have his wicked way with me. Not until I have a wedding ring on my finger.' She swaggered towards the door. 'You take care, darling, and I'll call next week for the latest news.'

Evelyn eyed her coldly. She would have expected at least some show of sympathy or helpful suggestions from her friend. 'I'll let Eliza show you out.'

When her father-in-law called a few days later, Evelyn was wearing a loose dress, and as Cyril passed the money over without making any comment, she thought her weight gain had slipped his notice. He never stayed long to chat so there was nothing unusual in his making an excuse not to sit down. But as Evelyn followed him down the wide hall, she ventured to say, 'I've been expecting a letter from Charles, I thought I would have heard by now.'

He turned to face her. 'Any letters, or correspondence of any kind, would come to me. You see, when Charles joined up, he wasn't thinking of getting married and put me down as next-of-kin. There has been no word from him since he left, but I will inform you if there is any news.' He reached the front door, smiled at Eliza who was holding it open for him, then placed his hard high hat on his head and walked down the path to where a horse and carriage stood waiting for him. Without a backward glance he climbed into the carriage and gave his groom instructions to move away. His mind was very disturbed on the journey home as he hadn't failed to notice the loose-fitting dress which wasn't his daughter-in-law's usual style. That combined with the filling out of her face were signs of a woman with child. But it couldn't be, he was being bad-minded. However, in the weeks that followed doubt niggled at the back of his mind. If she was with child, it couldn't be his son's. She must have cheated on Charles.

Cyril waited another four weeks before calling on Evelyn again with her allowance. The door was opened by Eliza, whose usual smile was missing. The girl looked uncomfortable. 'The mistress asked me to apologise for her absence, Mr Lister-Sinclair, but she is feeling unwell and has taken to her bed. But she did say you could safely leave any messages with me and she would see you next month.'

Cyril stepped into the hall and handed his hat and gloves to the wide-eyed maid. 'Tell your mistress I insist upon seeing her, and will wait in the drawing room. And please ask her not to keep me waiting as I have another appointment.' The maid did a little bob, placed his hat and gloves on the huge carved hallstand and scurried up the stairs while Cyril made his way to the drawing room. He didn't have long to wait for Evelyn was afraid of displeasing him. As soon as she walked through the door he knew his fears were well founded. Despite her loose-fitting dress, the filling out of her breasts and face were a sure sign. Although Evelyn had a large silk handkerchief trailing from her hands, it couldn't hide the swell of her stomach or the apprehension in her eyes.

'I won't beat about the bush, I have an appointment and can't stay long.' Cyril nodded to the hands vainly trying to cover her stomach. 'I think you have some explaining to do. It is very obvious you are carrying a child, and it is also obvious my son can't be the father. So I think an explanation is in order.'

'But it *is* Charles' baby!' Evelyn lowered her head in shame as she told him what had happened three nights before she and Charles were wed. 'I am telling the truth, Mr Lister-Sinclair, and Charles will verify that when he comes home. I should not have succumbed to his advances, I know that now, but he was going away so soon I couldn't deny him.'

Cyril reached into an inside pocket and brought out an envelope which he placed on the table. 'I will continue to pay you until my son comes home. If you are telling the truth I will be saddened by the actions of both of you. If you are telling lies, I will have no pity for you or your child, and you will leave this house as you entered it. There would be no further allowance and no further communication between you or any member of my family. I won't, for the time being, discuss the present situation with my wife as she is longing for her son's return and I will not add to her worries.' He nodded curtly and walked towards the door. 'I will in future hand the envelope in to Eliza. I will not enter this house until my son comes back from the war. If you take my advice, you will be more frugal with your money for the time being, and save what you can. The day might not be far off when you will have need of it.'

Evelyn was afraid now of a time coming when all this wealth and comfort was snatched away from her, so she became miserly with money. If she was thrown out of here she would have nowhere to go, her parents would disown her. But still she clung to the hope that the war would end soon and Charles would come back home and put things right. However, it wasn't to be. When she was seven months pregnant, Cyril came to tell her he'd had a telegram from the War Office to say Charles had been killed in battle. 'As I told you, Charles had put my name down as next-of-kin, and that is why the telegram was sent to me. My wife is absolutely distraught and I must get back to her.'

'But what about me?' Evelyn cried. 'It is his child I'm carrying, you've got to believe me! You can't throw me out on the street, not in my condition.'

'You may stay until the baby is born, then you must look elsewhere for a house. Anyone could be the father. Please send a note a few weeks after it is born and I'll come and check that you have made arrangements to move. I might possibly allow you to take some of the smaller pieces of furniture and other items. Send the letter with Eliza and impress upon her that she must not hand it over to anyone but myself.' With a curt nod, Cyril was gone.

When Evelyn went into labour she would have been lost if Eliza hadn't run for her mother, who had delivered several babies in the street where they lived. Evelyn had not dared attend a hospital, nor had she booked the services of a midwife. All because of her pride, in case word had gone around that the woman calling herself Mrs Lister-Sinclair was carrying another man's baby.

She may have been unlucky in many things, but she struck lucky with Eliza and her mother. They were very efficient, and the mother in particular seemed to know exactly what to do. Evelyn was in labour for only five hours, there were no complications. She screamed throughout the birth. Afterwards there was relief on her face, but no thanks on her lips. She was used to being waited on by now and could not see why she should thank a servant who was being paid to look after her. Eliza's mother didn't like her at all, thought she was a proper snob, but because she was her daughter's boss, she kept these thoughts to herself. Besides, she was being paid a pound for delivering the baby and that would keep her family for a week. So as she placed the baby in Evelyn's arms, she kept her voice pleasant. 'What are yer going to call her, Mrs Lister-Sinclair? Have yer got a name for her?'

'I've always liked the name Amelia, so that's what I intend to call her.'

Eliza, who would have loved to cuddle the baby, said, 'Oh, that's a nice name. She'll get called Milly at school.'

Evelyn nearly bit her head off. 'Her name is Amelia, and woe betide anyone who calls her Milly.' She looked down into the child's wrinkled face, then pushed the sheet aside. 'Take her away now, I'm quite exhausted and wish to rest.'

Eliza's mother was named Dora, and right now Dora was looking at Evelyn with disgust on her face. 'That baby needs to be put to yer breast. It needs feeding.'

'Feed a baby?' Evelyn looked at the woman as though she'd gone mad. '*I* am not going to feed the baby. Now take her away. Perhaps tomorrow when I feel a little stronger.'

'That baby needs feeding at once, yer can't feed her just when it suits you.' Dora didn't care whether her daughter got the sack, she wasn't going to stand there and listen to this selfish bitch. 'If yer won't feed her, yer'll have to get a wet-nurse to do it or I'll bring a doctor in to yer. I brought that baby into the world and I'll not stand by and see it die just because you can't be bothered. Make up yer mind before me and Eliza walk out and leave yer to get on with it. And then it would be God help you and the baby!'

One look at the angry face looking down at her had Evelyn asking, 'What is a wet nurse?'

'It's a woman who has just had a baby herself, but who has enough to milk to feed another. There's a few of them around here.'

Evelyn found this thought distasteful and shuddered. But one look at Dora's face told her she would be well advised to take heed of this woman; the last thing she wanted was to have a doctor call. A doctor who would perhaps know her in-laws. 'How would I go about getting one of these wet nurses, and would she be clean and decent?'

Dora shook her head. For all her posh talk, this woman was as thick as two short planks. If it wasn't for the baby she would have walked out and left her to get on with it. She'd soon learn the hard way, when the baby began screaming with hunger. Besides, Dora wasn't about to leave without a pound note in her hand. 'She would be as clean and decent as you are, madam. And the need is pressing, so yer'd better make yer mind up quick.'

'What would this person charge, and how often would she come?'

Dora wasn't going to let this spoiled woman off lightly. If she couldn't be bothered even to hold her new baby, let alone feed her, then she could pay handsomely for someone else to do it. She was living in the lap of luxury, while the wet nurse would be selling her milk to put food in the bellies of her family. The usual price was twopence for feeding a child three times a day, but there was nothing usual about the circumstances here. 'It will be two pence a time, and yer'll need her three times a day. During the night yer'll have to feed the baby yourself, and that'll get yer used to it. If yer have the nurse for a week, yer should be used to the baby by that time and be able to manage for yerself.'

Evelyn's eyes narrowed. She dreaded the thought of having to feed the baby herself, but she didn't want to part with any money to pay someone else to do it. 'But that is sixpence a day – three shillings and sixpence for the week! Surely if the woman is desperate for money she'll do it for less?'

Dora was really getting on her high horse now. Who the hell did this woman think she was? 'If yer don't like the terms, then forget it. Wet nurses are in great demand, they're not crying out for work. So I'll leave yer to sort something out yerself.'

'No! I would be grateful to you if you would arrange for one of the nurses to call as soon as possible. And as I'm sure you're wanting to get home now, I won't keep you.'

Dora's jaw jutted out. 'I'm not leaving here without the pound yer owe me for delivering the baby. And the wet nurse will want paying in advance, so have the money handy.'

At the end of the second day, the wet nurse, Minnie, waited until she had the sixpence in her hand before telling Evelyn she wouldn't be coming back. She made an excuse about someone in her family not being well, but it was a different tale when she called at Dora's.

'I'm not going to be treated like a piece of dirt by anyone, I'd rather starve first. God help the baby, 'cos she's a lovely little thing and doesn't deserve to be lumbered with a mother like that. She's an unwanted child, that's sticking out a mile, and will never know a mother's love. The only one that stuck-up bitch thinks about is herself. She treats your Eliza like a slave. Sent the poor girl into town today to buy a cradle so she won't have to have the baby in bed with her. And she wrote down on a sheet of notepaper that the cradle must be of the best dark mahogany, with carving. But what's the good of a lovely cot when there's no love for the baby in it? Her own flesh and blood and anyone would think it had leprosy.'

Dora nodded. 'She's a stuck-up bleedin' cow, that's what she is. But I'm worried about the child. D'yer think I should get another nurse for her?'

Minnie pulled a face. 'That's up to you, queen, but if yer take my advice yer'll leave her be. Left on her own, she's going to have to feed the baby because her breasts are full of milk and she'll be in agony if she doesn't. It may take her a while to realise that, I don't think she's got a bleeding clue about being a mother, but she'll soon catch on when the baby's screaming and she's in pain. That's when she'll start putting two and two together.'

And Minnie was right. Evelyn hated the task, and at times hated the baby for making it necessary, but for her own comfort she fed Amelia whenever both felt the need.

Four weeks after the birth, Eliza was sent with a letter to inform Mr Lister-Sinclair. It was another two weeks before he visited, and he spent several minutes gazing down into the cradle before asking, 'Have you been successful in finding a new house for yourself and the baby?'

'I haven't been out since Amelia was born, I haven't felt strong enough.' Evelyn didn't want to leave this beautiful house and the allowance that went with it, so she begged. 'Please believe that Amelia is Charles' baby. I swear that is the truth.'

Once again Cyril looked down into the child's eyes. They seemed to be looking straight at him. 'This baby bears no resemblance whatsoever to my son. Not in colouring, not in one single feature. In my eyes she was conceived out of wedlock and is therefore an illegitimate child, thanks to the immorality of her mother.'

He sighed, for he was not a cruel man at heart. But he was hurting so much from the loss of his son, and this woman was adding to the hurt by tarnishing the dead man's reputation and bringing discredit to the Lister-Sinclair name. And she had never loved his son, Cyril knew that now. His mind went back to the day he'd called to tell her he'd received a telegram saying Charles had been killed in action. She didn't even flinch, just stared at him as though the person he was talking about was a stranger to her. No tears, no outpouring of grief, no word of sorrow for the man she had married and professed to love. She hadn't even asked where and how her husband had been killed. Her only thought was of what was going to happen to her. She didn't even go into mourning, wearing widow's weeds, but was always colourfully dressed when he called. Nor had she ever expressed sympathy to him and his wife for their loss. It was as though Charles had never existed in her life. The only person Evelyn

27

cared about was herself. No, she'd never loved his son, it was his money she'd loved.

'I do not want this child to bear my son's name,' he told her now, 'and if I find you have put Charles' name on the birth certificate as being the father, I will take legal action against you.' He turned, hesitating momentarily before walking away. 'There is a property letting office in Moorfields. They are a good firm and I suggest you try them.' He nodded curtly. 'Goodbye.'

The next day, after feeding the baby, Evelyn left Eliza in charge and went into the city. She soon found the letting office in Moorfields and asked for information on six-roomed houses. The clerk gave her a list of addresses, saying the rent of each depended on the area in which it was situated and the condition of the property. After listening to Evelyn's cultured voice, he recommended two that she should try first. They were in a good area, and as they were in sound decorative order, she could move in straight away.

From there, Evelyn went to order a pram to be delivered the following day. Then it was time to head for home before the baby started screaming to be fed. Once satisfied, Amelia settled down and would sleep for at least two hours, so Evelyn set off to look at the two houses. She wasn't very happy about having to move to such a small place, but was afraid the Lister-Sinclairs could make her life unpleasant if she didn't agree. One of the houses had a small front garden, and looking through the letter box and the windows, it seemed clean and bright. So she took the tram down to the letting office, was told the house was three shillings and sixpence a week, and was asked to pay two weeks in advance. She told the clerk she was a war widow and that her name was Mrs Sinclair. When the forms were filled in, she received a rent book and a set of keys.

Evelyn hated the house. It seemed so poky after the one she had grown used to. Nevertheless, having had to give Eliza notice, she found it impossible to clean and feed the baby, and keep up with the other washing and ironing, shopping and cooking. As she had no idea of the value of money, she bought the best of everything, even though she had no money coming in. It didn't take her long to fritter her savings away. When she'd been in the new house a year she had to pay her first visit to a pawn shop. Over the next year, all the expensive ornaments, pictures and mirrors, brought from the house in Princes Avenue, found their way into that shop. She was too naive to realise the pawnbroker was only giving her a fraction of what the items were worth, and she would never have the money to redeem them. She lived from day to day in a dream world, thinking that somehow she would be taken back to the riches and wealth she loved so much and which she thought she deserved. She never blamed herself for her situation, it was always the baby who had ruined her life.

One day as she sat at the bare table, she thought of the empty larder and her empty purse. There was nothing left for her to pawn except the rings on her finger. She knew they were very expensive because she'd been with Charles when he bought them. The wedding ring she'd have to keep or people would think she was an unmarried mother, and common sense told her the engagement ring would be better sold to a jeweller than to a pawnbroker. It was a beautiful ring with a huge diamond in a claw setting. She had to get a good price for it because the money would have to last a long time. She couldn't take it back to the shop it was bought from because they had known Charles. So she found another well-known jeweller's, and for once stood her ground and refused the fifty pounds she was initially offered for it.

'My husband paid four hundred pounds for that, and you offer me fifty? That is nonsense and you know it! I shall try elsewhere and am sure I'll get what the ring is really worth.'

She was right, of course, as the jeweller was well aware. 'What price were you expecting to get for it, madam?'

'At least half what my late husband paid for it.'

The man removed the glass from his eye. 'I'm sorry, madam, but you won't get that from any jeweller. It is after all secondhand which lowers its value considerably. I would be prepared to give you one hundred and fifty pounds for it, which would leave me a very thin profit margin.' He passed the ring back over the counter. 'But perhaps you would like to try one or two other shops?'

Evelyn didn't have time to try other shops, she'd left Amelia playing with a rag doll in her bedroom. The child was three now, and sensible for her age because Evelyn was very strict with her. She had been warned not to leave the room, and wouldn't dare disobey her mother. They never had visitors, nor were they friendly with the neighbours. The women to either side had held out the hand of friendship to Evelyn the day they'd moved into the house, offering to mind the child while she got her furniture sorted out and was settled in. But all they had received in reply was a frosty stare, for she regarded them as being of a lower class than herself. They'd shrugged their shoulders and given up on her. Even now, after three years, she would pass them in the road without a glance. They felt sorry for the little girl because she was seldom taken out for a walk in the fresh air, even though there was a park nearby with swings which all the local children used. Except Amelia Sinclair.

'I'll take what you are offering, and would like to complete the transaction quickly, as I really must get home to my child.'

As Evelyn pushed the white five-pound notes into her handbag, her mind went back to the time she was getting as much money in her monthly allowance from Mr Lister-Sinclair. And she'd had no bills to pay out of it so it mostly went on clothes. She sighed as the tram came to a halt and she stepped on board. She would have to be very careful with this money, it would have to last until Amelia was old enough for school and she herself could look for work in one of the offices in the city centre. She had thought many times that she should be entitled to a pension from the Army; with Charles having been a Captain it would probably be a decent one. But she was afraid that with his father being down as next-of-kin, he would probably be notified if she put in an application. It was years now since she'd had any contact with the Lister-Sinclairs, or her own parents who had disowned her for blackening their name. Nor had she seen Gwen or Oscar, but that didn't worry her because she'd hate them to know of her drastically reduced circumstances.

Amelia was holding the rag doll to her chest when Evelyn opened the bedroom door. 'I'm hungry, Mother, can I have some bread, please?'

'Yes, and I've got a treat for us. I bought some boiled ham, tomatoes and a nice crusty cottage loaf. And we'll have real best butter on the bread.' Evelyn found nothing strange in talking to her three-year-old daughter as if she were a grown-up, or that in return she was called 'Mother', not Mammy or Mummy. 'I've also bought a cream sponge cake for dessert, so we are eating well tonight. But it's only because it's a special occasion, so don't expect it every day. I'll have to be careful with money.'

Despite her good resolutions, with money in her purse Evelyn could not resist the finer things in life, and in eighteen months the money she'd got for her engagement ring had dwindled to a few pounds – not enough to send her daughter to a high school in six months when she'd be five. The thought of any child of hers attending a corporation school filled her with despair. Neither could they stay on in this house because the rent had gone up over the years to four shillings a week, and it was such a draughty place it took two bags of coal a week to keep it warm. So once again Evelyn had to lower her sights, and was forced to move to a working-class area, with street after street of two-up-two-down houses occupied by families who were lucky if they saw a square meal once a week. There was a lot of unemployment there, dozens of men chasing after every vacancy. They would turn their hand to anything to put food on the table for their families, but life was hard and poverty was rife. Evelyn, with her knowledge of another lifestyle, hated it, and looked down her nose at everyone. The only person she felt sorry for was herself. Her misfortunes were not her fault, she decided. They were the fault of Charles for going away to war when he didn't have to, and of Amelia for being born.

Once again a knocking on the window had Evelyn shaking her head to clear it of the memories. She pushed her chair back and, wiping her eyes with the heel of her hands, opened the front door to her daughter. There was no smile or greeting for the child, she just turned on her heels and walked back to the chair she'd vacated.

Amelia's face was aglow as she followed her mother in, forgetting to close the front door behind her in her excitement. 'Mother, you'll be very pleased with me!' She put the newspaper-wrapped parcel containing the chips on the table, plus a large tin loaf. 'I walked up the street with Miss Bessie from next door, and she said I was very clever for getting a large loaf for a penny.'

The slap was delivered so quickly, and with such force, it shocked the young girl who looked bewildered as she let out a cry before putting a hand to her cheek. The cry of pain was loud enough for Bessie Maudsley to hear as she rooted in her bag for her front door key. Bessie was a small, wiry woman, who seemed to do everything at the double. A spinster, she'd lived alone in the house next door since her parents had both died in their fifties. She had a job as a seamstress and worked five and a half days a week. The pay wasn't much, but there was only herself to worry about and she managed fine. She was fond of her young neighbour who, to her mind, was too old in the head for her years, and wasn't allowed to enjoy her childhood like the other kids in the street. And if she thought for one minute that Lady bleeding Muck was going to give the girl a thrashing, she'd be in next door like a shot. So she stood with her door key in her hand and listened.

Unaware that the front door was still open, Evelyn raged at her daughter who couldn't understand why she'd been smacked for doing what her mother had asked her to do. 'How dare you discuss our affairs with the neighbours when I have told you so often that you must not have anything to do with them? They are not our kind and I will not let you bring us down to their level.' Poking a finger in her daughter's chest, she growled, 'Now do you understand what I'm saying, or do I have to knock it into you?'

Over my dead body, Bessie thought, rushing to knock on the open door. But she remembered to be careful what she said in case young Amelia suffered for it. 'Is everything all right in there?'

It was then Evelyn noticed the front door was still open, and hissed, 'You stupid child, you didn't close the door behind you!' Then her expression changed from one of anger to one of sweetness and light which didn't sit well on her face because it was so obviously false.

'Oh, hello, Miss Maudsley! Of course everything is all right. My clumsy daughter here bumped into the table and hurt herself, but it was nothing serious.'

Bessie stared her out. 'I'm sorry if she hurt herself 'cos I'm fond of yer daughter. I'll no doubt see her tomorrow and I can ask her meself how she is.'

With that veiled warning she turned back to her own front door. She'd be keeping her eyes and ears open in future, for she wouldn't trust that two-faced villain as far as she could throw her. Apart from thinking she was better than anyone else in the street, she had that sly look about her and obviously wasn't to be trusted. Now Bessie didn't care what her neighbour did, she could pretend she was the Queen of England if she wanted, it was no skin off Bessie's nose. But when it came to a child being ill treated, well, that was a different kettle of fish. She'd not stand by and see any youngster punished when they'd done nothing wrong. She'd mention it to Rita over the road, ask her to keep an eye out during the day while she herself was at work. The queer one next door was sly and needed watching.

Chapter Three

Rita Wells happened to glance out of her front window and saw Bessie Maudsley standing on her front step with her arms folded. The table had been cleared after their meal, the dishes washed and the two boys were out playing. Her husband Reg was reading the *Echo*, which was a ritual with him every evening and the one luxury he had in life beside his pint every Saturday.

'Bessie's standing at her door watching the world go by. She's probably glad of the fresh air after being stuck behind a sewing machine in a noisy factory all day. So, seeing as I've cleared up and everywhere is tidy, I think I'll go over and have a natter with her.' Rita jerked her head back and tutted. 'Don't look at me like that! Anyone would think I was Cinderella and had told yer I was going to a ball in a glass carriage, the sour face on yer. I wouldn't care if it was a case of yer missing me to talk to, but yer never open yer ruddy mouth until yer've read the paper from front page to back page. All I ever see is the top of yer head, and that's not interesting enough to keep me in. So whether yer like it or lump it, I'm slipping across to while away half-an-hour with Bessie.'

Reg lowered the paper to his knees and spread his hands. 'I haven't opened me flaming mouth! If yer want to go and have a talk with Bessie, then by all means do so.' He was a tall, broad man with black hair who loved his wife and kids dearly. He had a sense of humour too. 'As long as ye're back in time to make me a cup of tea and put me slippers on.'

Rita patted the top of his head. 'I'll be back long before yer bedtime, sunshine, I'll only be half an hour. Unless Bessie has some exciting news for me, and then yer can make yer own tea and put yer own flaming slippers on.' She got to the door and turned with a puzzled expression on her attractive face. 'Ay, yer haven't got no pair of slippers.'

'I wondered when the penny would drop.' He gazed at his wife's bonny figure, curly mouse-coloured hair, and round happy face. It was a lucky day when she'd come into his life. 'Go on, love, yer deserve a break. But give us a kiss first.'

'Pucker up then, don't leave me to do all the work.' Rita bent to kiss him and found herself being pulled down on to his knee. 'Ay, now come off it, Valentino, don't be going all he-man on me. Not when I could be missing some juicy gossip.'

'How can Bessie have any gossip for yer when she's been out at work all day? You and Aggie see more of the neighbours than she does.'

'I know that, soft lad, it was supposed to be a joke. Anyway, I'm off, and I'll see yer when I see yer.'

As Rita crossed the cobbles, she was hoping her next-door neighbour Aggie wasn't watching through her window. She liked Aggie who had a heart of gold and was always the first to help in time of trouble. Her only fault was she couldn't control her tongue. If there was anything on her mind, she came out with it, regardless of the consequences. If she took a dislike to anyone, she let them know in no uncertain terms. But if she took a liking to yer, she'd move heaven and earth to do you a good turn.

Bessie smiled. 'Hello, girl, where are you off to?'

'Nowhere, I've just come to keep yer company and have a natter.' It was Rita's turn to smile. 'And if yer believe that, sunshine, then yer'll believe anything! I'm here because I'm nosy. No, I'm not going to call meself nosy! Let's say I'm curious about what was going on next door.' She kept her voice low. 'I saw yer going to the door, and I heard yer shouting in, but I couldn't hear what yer said. Has Her Ladyship been up to something or were yer just being neighbourly?'

Bessie stepped back into her hall. 'Come in, girl, before the whole street gets nosy about what ye're doing standing on me step.'

When Rita followed her friend into the living room, she nodded. 'Yeah, yer still keep it like a little palace. Yer should have got married, sunshine, and had a load of kids, 'cos yer'd have made a wonderful wife and mother. Still, yer know the old saying: If yer've none to make yer laugh, yer've none to make yer cry. There's times I wish I'd never got married, even though I love the bones of my feller and the two boys.'

'Go 'way, yer'd be lost without them.' Bessie waved to a chair. 'Sit down and take the weight off yer feet.' She sat down opposite. 'This is to go no further, girl, especially to Aggie. Not that I've anything against her, she's a good mate, but yer know she can't keep a thing to herself. And knowing how she feels about Mrs Sinclair, this would be right up her street. So, least said, soonest mended.

'Anyway, I walked up the street this evening with young Amelia, who was really excited 'cos she'd gone to the baker's and they'd let her have a stale loaf for a penny. God love her, she said her mother would be very pleased with her.' Bessie shook her head sadly. 'Her mother was pleased with her all right . . . so pleased she gave her a smack across the face that I could hear as I was looking in me bag for the door key. So yer can imagine it must have hurt the poor lass if it was loud enough for that. Anyway, Her Ladyship mustn't have known the front door was open, and gave the girl down the banks for telling the neighbours their business. It went something like this.' Bessie put on a posh accent, looking comical as her mouth did contortions. ' "How dare you discuss our affairs with the neighbours when I have told you time out of number that you must not have anything to do with them? They are not our kind and I will not let you bring us down to their level. Now do you understand what I'm saying or do I have to knock it into you?" '

Rita gaped. 'Well, the cheeky sod! There isn't a woman in the street who isn't a better person than she is. They mightn't have much money, and their clothes might be threadbare, but by God, they love their kids. They have a happier life than poor Amelia, 'cos it's sticking out a mile her mother has no love for her.' She tutted. 'The cheek of the woman to say we're on a lower level than her! Who the hell does she think she is?'

'I was blazing meself,' Bessie said, 'but because I thought she might give the girl another smack, I kept me face all innocent like when I knocked and asked if everything was all right. And yer wouldn't have thought she was the same person, she was all smiles then. Well, what passes as a smile for *her*. I think a good belly laugh would kill her! Anyway, I felt like having a real go at her, the two-faced so-and-so, but I thought better of it because of the girl. I wouldn't want to get her into more trouble. The queer one made an excuse, said her clumsy daughter had bumped into the table and hurt herself. Well, as I've told yer, I didn't want to cause any bother because I could hear the child sobbing. I was as polished as Her Ladyship, said I hoped her daughter hadn't hurt herself badly but no doubt I'd see her tomorrow and could ask her then meself how she was. That was by way of a threat, and I hope it sank in 'cos I'd be in there like a shot if I thought the kid was being ill treated.'

'D'yer think she's all right in the head?' Rita asked. 'I mean, what makes her think she's better than any of us? Oh, I know she talks and acts posh, but that could all be put on! If she's from monied people, she wouldn't be living in a two-up-two-down, would she? I've always thought there was a bit of a mystery about her, ever since she moved into the street. I wouldn't say that in front of Aggie, I always stick up for the woman when me mate's pulling her to pieces, but I can't help thinking there's something weird about the airs and graces she puts on. And she wants reporting for the way she treats her daughter. The poor kid has no fun at all, she's missing her childhood years.' Rita let out a deep sigh. 'God knows, they're not children for long, they should be allowed to enjoy every minute of it while it lasts. And playing rounders or tag or going on the swings doesn't cost nothing, so why doesn't Mrs Sinclair let Amelia be her age and play out with the other kids?'

'I haven't got no answer for yer, Rita, 'cos I've spent hours trying to puzzle her out meself. The clothes she wears are years old, but yer can tell they were very expensive when she bought them, and she does look after them.' Bessie gazed up at the ceiling before coming to a decision. 'I'm going to tell yer what I know about her, but yer have to give me yer word that it isn't repeated to anyone, not even your Reg, although I know men don't tittle-tattle like women.'

Rita made a cross on her chest. 'On my honour, sunshine.' A smile crossed her face. 'Anyway, me and my Reg don't spend our time in bed telling tales, we've other things on our minds.' The smile became a chuckle. 'And it's not what ye're thinking either, Bessie Maudsley. Our conversation before turning our backs on each other usually consists of me asking him what he'd like for dinner the next day, and him telling me to blow the candle out.'

'Yer've got a good man there, Rita, he's one of the best in the street. But let's get back to Her Ladyship next door. You won't have noticed this because she always uses the back door but she's forever on the cadge. It's bread, tea or milk, things like that, and it's usually twice a week. It's been going on since the week she moved in, and she doesn't come herself, she sends Amelia. I got fed up with it after a while, thought she had a bloody cheek and felt sorry for the kid who looked terrified. So when I was asked to lend them sugar one day, I wouldn't give it to the girl, said I'd carry it for her and give it to her mother myself. I followed her up the yard and into the kitchen. That's how I came to go in the house and found she had little in the way of furniture but what she had was pure solid mahogany, the likes of which you and I would only ever see if we walked up Bold Street and looked in the windows of the posh shops there. She's only got a couple of pieces, mind, but enough for me to think that somewhere along the line she's known a better life.'

Rita leaned forward, her eyes wide and her voice angry. 'Are yer telling me that she's been borrowing off you all these years? You, who has to work hard to keep yer own head above water? She's got some nerve, she has. All la-di-dah, but she sends her kid out the back way to scrounge off yer?'

Bessie shook her head. 'Not now she doesn't, girl, 'cos the day I took the sugar to her, I told her straight that anything she borrowed must be paid back, in full, every Saturday when she'd her wages. So, while she still borrows, I make sure I get it back. If I didn't, I'd tell her to find herself another sucker. But I'm fond of Amelia, she's a good kid with a lovely nature.'

'It's a shame,' Rita said. 'The kids all make fun of her because of the way she speaks, and there's nothing she can do about that now. I know it's not her fault, but yer can't blame the other kids because she's different from them.'

'Nobody is blaming them, girl, certainly not me. But before I go and put the kettle on to make us a cuppa, let's finish off the business with next door.' Bessie laced her fingers together. 'Now all the information yer've had off me tonight came with a price attached. I've never told anyone before, and you know, girl, I'm not a gossip. But I told you because I want a favour off yer, and that is, will yer keep yer eye out for Amelia? I know yer can't see right into their living room, and I know her mother won't let her play out, but with yer living opposite yer might just see something that makes yer think the girl is being badly treated. And if yer do, I want yer to tell me. Oh, I know it's none of my business, but the kid has nobody else with her welfare at heart so

I intend being a busybody and keeping an eye on her. Obviously I can't do it while I'm at work so that's why I'm asking you to do it as a favour for me.'

'Of course I will, particularly now I know that woman's capable of hitting the child for nothing. She certainly wouldn't get away with it if I saw her. I'm on nodding terms with her, much to the disgust of Aggie, so I might try and take it a bit further, to where we pass the time of day. I'm not saying she'll co-operate, or that we'll become bosom pals, but it's worth a try. In any case, I'll keep an eye out, sunshine, yer have my word on it. And now, if it's not asking too much, will yer go and put that ruddy kettle on? Me tongue is hanging out!'

Next door, Evelyn was still seething. Betrayed by her own daughter! Now everyone in the street would know their business and be laughing because they were living on stale bread. She had worked hard to teach Amelia how to act like a lady, to enunciate her words and be careful not to associate with the poorer class of people who lived in the street because one day they would be back where they belonged, with people of their own class. She never told her how or when this would happen, and would never admit to herself that it was only a dream. She was so wrapped up in herself, it hadn't occurred to Evelyn that while she could keep Amelia away from the children in the street, she had no control over her during school hours. Never once had it entered her head that, for all her teaching and dire warnings, she couldn't control every one of her daughter's waking moments. Nor had she sensed that her child was very confused and unhappy. She was forced to have one personality at home to please her mother, then to become someone different at school. The one she attended was for the children of working-class parents, some of them living in abject poverty, and Amelia quickly learned she must speak like them if she didn't want to be pushed around and laughed at. At school she spoke with a working-class Liverpool accent, while at home she spoke as her mother wished her to.

Now and again, in her head, Amelia questioned her mother's attitude towards her. She knew Evelyn wasn't the same as the other mothers in the street, who hugged their children as they set off for school, and laughed as they played games with them. She wouldn't say what she thought out loud because it would only bring forth a tirade from her mother, but inwardly she wondered why she was never kissed, or loved like all the other children. She did try to do everything she was told so her mother would love her, but no matter how hard she tried, she never received a word of praise or affection. Young as she was she knew this wasn't fair, and wished she was allowed to mix freely with other children instead of having to be careful of every word that came out of her mouth.

'Well, young lady, are you going to apologise?' Evelyn bent to poke the girl in the chest. 'I want you to say you are sorry over and over again until I say you may stop. Now do as I say.'

The injustice of it brought tears to the back of Amelia's eyes. 'But I haven't done anything wrong, Mother, so I don't understand. I only did as you asked, why should I be punished for it?' She rubbed the cheek that was still tender from the smack she'd received. 'You hurt me.'

'Don't you dare answer me back! If you continue to disobey me then I shall have no alternative but to smack you again. And I can assure you it will hurt you much more this time. Now, I want to hear you saying you are sorry.'

Amelia had never answered her mother back, nor questioned anything she was told to do. But a little demon in her head was telling her now that if she didn't stick up for herself she'd never be like the other children in the street. 'Miss Bessie thought I was very clever, and I think I was too! I told her you would be pleased, and she said she would be if someone got her a loaf for a penny.'

The mention of their neighbour's name had a sobering effect on Evelyn. She relied on Miss Maudsley to help her out when she was desperate, without a penny in her purse. And she hadn't forgotten the little woman's remark about seeing Amelia herself tomorrow, and asking her daughter if she was all right. But she wasn't going to give the child the satisfaction of seeing her weakening or she would soon become out of control. 'I am tired – too tired to argue. So instead of the chastisement I had in mind, I will instead send you up to your room where you will stay until the morning.'

Amelia was glad to get out of the room and away from a mother she could no longer understand, and who, more and more, was beginning to frighten her. So she took the stairs two at a time. Instead of going into her own little room, which was at the back of the house, she entered her mother's and went straight to the window to look down on the street where boys and girls were playing, shouting to each other and having a fine time. Oh, how she wished she could join them. She pulled aside the net curtain for a better view, just as one of the boys on the opposite pavement looked up. He stared at her for a while, then smiled and waved. There was no return smile or wave because Amelia had quickly dropped the curtain. She would really be in trouble if her mother knew she was looking out of the window, never mind having one of the street children smiling and waving at her. But when her mother didn't come running up the stairs to give her another ticking off, the fear subsided and Amelia felt a warm glow. That was the first time since she'd lived in the street that one of the other children had smiled at her. Mostly, when she was going and coming home from school, a gang of girls would walk behind her and shout and make fun of her.

Stepping over the floorboards she knew would creak, Amelia made her way to her own bedroom and lay on the bed staring up at the ceiling, which was badly in need of attention. It had once been white, but now was a dirty colour, with cracks everywhere and plaster peeling off and falling like snowflakes on to her bed and the lino-covered floor. But although she was staring at the ceiling, she wasn't seeing it. She was thinking about the boy who had waved and smiled at her. He lived opposite, next to the house where the fat woman lived. The woman her mother said was the most common, ill-bred person it had ever been her misfortune to meet. But Amelia thought the woman looked a warm and happy person, who always had a smile on her face. She did talk loudly but there was no harm in that. It didn't matter how noisy you were, if you had a smile on your face. The boy's mother was nice, she always let on when she saw Amelia. There were two boys. The one who had waved was the smallest, so he must be the youngest. He was a big lad, though, and Amelia guessed he'd be about nine or ten. They were lucky to have such a nice mother who was always hugging them, even in the street.

Amelia sighed. She was seven now, but it was her birthday in a few weeks and then she'd be eight. Not that her mother would even mention her birthday, she never did. Not even a card to celebrate a new year of her life. She'd never had a birthday party, never even been to one because she wasn't allowed to have friends. Another deep sigh. If she ever got married and had children she'd love them to bits, would always be hugging them and kissing them better when they hurt themselves. But that was a long time off, and until she was old enough to look after herself she'd have to put up with the life she had.

It was Evelyn who opened the door to Bessie the following day. 'I've just called to see if Amelia is better? You know, after the accident she had?'

'Oh, she's fine, Miss Maudsley, a storm in a tea cup. She banged herself, but she was as right as rain half an hour later.'

Evelyn was standing four-square in the centre of the step, and Bessie thought, Oh, aye, she doesn't want me to see the girl.

Which only made her more determined. 'Let's have a look at her then, I'm not going to eat her.'

Grinding her teeth, and wishing she was in a position to tell this nosy little woman to go away and stay away, Evelyn called, 'Amelia dear, come and say hello to Miss Maudsley.'

'Hello there, sweetheart,' Bessie said. 'I was expecting to see yer in bandages, like a wounded soldier. But yer look fine to me, as pretty as a picture.' She raised her eyes to Evelyn. 'She seems to get taller every time I see her. How old is she now?'

Amelia saw her chance and took it. 'I'm seven now, Miss Bessie, but in three weeks I'll be eight.'

Bessie pretended to look surprised. 'Well, I never! It's my birthday in three weeks as well! What date is yours on?'

A smile lit up Amelia's face. She knew she had an ally in their neighbour. 'Mine's on the eighteenth, when's yours?'

'I don't believe it! Talk about coincidence isn't in it! Mine is on the eighteenth, too! Except, of course, I'm forty odd years older than yer. Well, well, how about that!' Bessie beamed at a very irate Evelyn. 'Ay, would yer let Amelia come to me for a birthday tea? Just her and me, like, for a little celebration. I've never got anyone to celebrate me birthday with, being on me own, so if yer've no objection, Mrs Sinclair, can I expect her to come to mine for tea on the eighteenth? It would give me something to look forward to, and I can make some fairy cakes and jelly creams.'

Evelyn was trying to think up an excuse for refusing, but Amelia could see how her mother's mind was working and begged, 'Please, Mother, say I can? I've never been out on my birthday before.'

Afraid of any more home truths coming from her daughter, Evelyn gave in. 'Just this once, Amelia, and only because it's Miss Maudsley.'

Bessie kept the smile on her face, but inside she was thinking that this woman must think she was stupid if she expected her to fall for that. There was no way she would have agreed to the request if she'd had nothing to hide. She was a queer one, all right, but now she'd agreed to Amelia having a birthday tea with her neighbour, then that's how it would be. Mind you, she'd had to tell a white lie because her birthday was months away. But to see the pleasure on the girl's face was worth the prayers she would say in bed tonight.

Reg Wells watched his wife run her hand over the maroon chenille cloth she'd just put on the table. There was an affection-ate grin on his face as he saw her stand back, her head tilted, to run a critical eye over the cloth and make sure it was perfectly straight before taking a glass bowl from the sideboard and setting it in the middle of the table. 'Yer should have been in the Army, love, yer'd have made a good sergeant.' He himself had served a year in the Army when the war was on, and was one of the lucky ones who'd come home. 'Mind you, ye're nicer-looking than any sergeant I've ever seen, and yer don't put the fear of God into me.'

'It'll take me a while to figure out if that was a compliment or an insult.' Rita tapped her chin with one finger and looked thoughtful. 'Is it a compliment to say I'm nicer-looking than a man, and that I'd have made a good sergeant? Oh, I need help from another woman on that, so I think I'll nip over to Bessie's and ask what she thinks.'

'Over to Bessie's again! Why don't yer take yer bed over there?'

'It's yer own fault, sunshine, yer asked for it.' Rita turned her head to hide a smile. 'If yer'd said I was nicer-looking than any woman yer'd ever seen, well, I think I'd have been suggesting we had an early night in bed. But being likened to a man . . . it's just put me off.'

'Excuses, excuses! Ye're a fine one for wriggling out of things, Rita Wells. But if this nipping over to Bessie's for a natter becomes a regular habit, I'll start thinking yer've got a fancy man and yer make that yer meeting place.'

Rita's head went back and her chuckle was loud. 'I should be so lucky, sunshine! And wait until I tell Bessie that yer think she's running a brothel, she'll die laughing.'

Reg's chair was creaking as he rocked back and forth. 'Tell her if she is, love, I'll be one of her customers, as long as I can choose me own wife to slink into one of her bedrooms with. At least I wouldn't have to beg, or wait until yer were in the mood.' The creaking of the chair grew louder. 'I don't think good-time girls ever have headaches.'

His wife pretended to be outraged. 'Well, it just shows the way your mind works, that does. Anyway, clever-clogs, good-time girls get paid, or haven't yer thought of that? And if yer were to pay me, well, I'd make yer the happiest man in the street. Yer'd be guaranteed to go out of this house every morning with a spring in yer step and a smile on yer face.'

Rita placed her arms straight and stiff by her sides, then spread her hands out to give a short exhibition of the dance she'd heard was all the rage in the dance halls: the Black Bottom. She'd never seen it, and was only going by hearsay, but whether she'd got it right or wrong it was enough to please her husband.

'See how lucky yer are, sunshine, being married to a good-time dancing girl?' She reached into the glass bowl for the front-door key. 'Entertainment over now, I'm off to see me mate what lives across the street. I won't stay long.' She reached the door, then turned. 'I'll mention to her about her letting the house be used by women of the street – she might think it's a good idea. If it took off, she'd soon be rolling in money and could pack her job in.'

There was no surprise on Bessie's face when she opened the door because she'd seen her friend crossing over. 'Come in, girl,

I've got a bit of news for yer. But yer probably saw me talking to next door, did yer?'

Rita plonked herself on the couch, then put a hand to her heart. 'I cannot tell a lie, sunshine, 'cos God might be listening. Yeah, I did see yer, and yeah, I'm glad yer've got a bit of news 'cos I could do with something to liven me day. And when I've heard your news, I'll tell yer the idea my feller has for yer making yerself a bit of money so yer can retire.'

Bessie's eyebrows shot up. 'If he's got an idea how to make money, why doesn't he make some for himself?'

'It doesn't work like that, sunshine, I'm afraid. But you start and I'll explain later what Reg has in mind. It won't half surprise yer.'

'Ooh, er, yer've got me wondering now. Why don't you go first?'

'I couldn't stand the excitement, that's why, sunshine, me heart would give out on me. So, off yer go.'

'I hope God isn't listening because while I was standing next door I committed two sins. I told a bare-faced lie, and I had bad thoughts. Still, they were in a good cause, and I'm sure God will take that into consideration. Anyway, I knocked next door on pretext of asking how Amelia was after she'd hurt herself. It was Her Ladyship who opened the door, and she tried to get rid of me quick by saying her daughter was fine. But I wasn't going to be fobbed off, so I asked if I could see Amelia.

'She called the girl to the door and yer'll never guess how devious I was! I said Amelia seemed to get taller every time I saw her, and asked how old she was. Then, although I could tell the queer one was wishing I'd go and drown meself in the Mersey, Amelia took advantage of what I'd said, and told me she was seven now, but would be eight in a few weeks' time. That's when I started to lie me head off. I asked her when her birthday was, and when she told me the eighteenth of next month, I made a great fuss by pretending that was my birthday as well. Honest,

Rita, I deserved a prize for me acting. I invited Amelia to come and have tea with me on her birthday, saying I'd never had company to celebrate mine with before.'

Bessie pushed a hand through her greying hair. 'Honest, girl, I've had a ruddy good laugh about it. While I was frying meself an egg for me tea, the tears were blinding me I laughed so much. Anyone would think me and the girl had rehearsed what we were going to say. I could see her mother was blazing, but she didn't have a leg to stand on when her daughter said she'd never been out for tea on her birthday before. And when I said I would make some fairy cakes, and jelly creams, I bet Her Ladyship was wishing I choked meself on them.'

Rita was sitting on the edge of the couch by now. 'Yer don't mean to tell me that Miss High and Mighty agreed to let the girl come here for a birthday tea?'

'There was no way she could refuse without insulting me, was there? If she had refused, I'd have asked her if my house wasn't good enough for her.'

'Well, that certainly is a piece of news. They must have lived in the street for three or four years now, and that's the first time she's allowed the girl to mix with us riff-raff. Yer've worked wonders there, sunshine, and I'm glad for Amelia's sake she's got you to look out for her.'

'It's a start, isn't it, girl? Who knows what will happen in the future? Yer know they say big trees from little acorns grow, all yer need is patience. So, we'll just have to wait and see what happens.'

'I'll get a birthday card for her,' Rita said. 'I'd buy her a present, but yer know what the money situation is, we're living from hand to mouth like everyone else in the street. I'm just about keeping our heads above water.'

'There'd be no point in buying her a present anyway, girl, 'cos she wouldn't be able to take it home. Her mother would make her throw it right in the bin, then wash her hands thoroughly before touching anything. A card would be nice, though, she could leave it here if she thought she'd get into trouble.' When Bessie sat back in a chair, she was so small her feet didn't touch the floor, and as she couldn't wait to hear what Rita's husband's idea was, she wriggled to the edge of the chair and leaned forward. 'Well, yer've heard my news, so what was it Reg told yer to tell me?'

'Will yer promise not to throw that cushion at me?'

'Why would I do that? Ye're not expecting me to get a cob on over what your Reg said, are yer? When have yer ever known me to really lose me temper with you? Other women in the street, yeah, but never you.' Her eyes narrowed. 'D'yer think I won't like it?'

'Like it? I hope yer laugh yer ruddy head off, Bessie, same as I did. Yer see, it all started when I told Reg I was coming over here, and he asked me why I didn't bring me bed 'cos I was spending a lot of time here and he was beginning to think I had a man on the sly, and your house was our meeting place. Anyway, that's how it started, and I'll tell yer the rest as long as yer promise we'll still be mates afterwards?'

Children playing in the street, and neighbours standing at their door having a jangle, all looked over to Miss Maudsley's house when the roars of laughter began. The children stopped playing, and the women stopped talking, as wave after wave of merriment reached their ears. And, laughter being contagious, it wasn't long before everyone else had a smile on their face too. Bessie Maudsley's mood was contagious. It cheered them up, and brought a little sunshine into their lives.

Chapter Four

Evelyn stopped briefly outside the building in Castle Street where she worked, and glanced at the gold lettering on a first-floor window which read 'Astbury and Woodward, Solicitors'. Then she mounted the steps, pushed open the heavy door and hastily climbed the flight of stairs facing her. She was a little late this morning as she'd missed the tram she usually caught, and unless she could sneak in without meeting either of the partners she would receive a glare to reprimand her for her tardiness. But she was lucky. The only person she saw was Miss Saunders, secretary to the senior partner, Mr Astbury.

'I'm sorry I'm late,' Evelyn said, hanging her coat on the carved coatstand. 'I'm afraid I missed the tram and had to take a later one.'

Mildred Saunders, a woman in her late-fifties, had been with the firm since she was eighteen years of age. She was plain, a spinster who still lived with her aged mother, and although always neat, to Evelyn's mind she was dowdy. 'You're only minutes late, and I'm sure that on this rather special day, Mr Astbury would excuse you.'

'Why is this a special day? Is it Mr Astbury's birthday?'

'No, but he has made up his mind that at the grand old age of seventy it's time for him to retire. He will be staying on for two weeks for the new partner to acquaint himself with the clients he will be taking over.' Mildred Saunders was usually prim and proper, always working with quiet efficiency and seldom indulging in conversation with Evelyn or the other female member of staff, Janet Coombes, secretary to the younger partner, Mr Woodward. But today she seemed different, and was wearing a smile as she spoke. 'As I've worked with Mr Astbury for so many years, and am used to his ways, I feel I'm too old to begin with a new partner and have decided to retire at the same time.'

'Is there someone ready to take over?' Evelyn asked. 'And if so, do you know him?'

Mildred nodded. 'Mr Astbury's nephew is taking over. He's coming in today so you will meet him. He is also an Astbury, Philip, and is leaving his present firm to take up the position here. I have met him, he seems very pleasant.'

Evelyn couldn't help herself from asking, 'Is he a young man, then?'

'I would say mid-thirties, but I'm not very good at guessing a person's age. He has several letters after his name, which takes years of exams, so he's certainly no younger.' Mildred fixed her gaze on Evelyn for a few seconds. She had never taken to the woman somehow, but couldn't put a finger on why. There was little known about her except that she was a widow, her husband having been killed in the war. One really should make allowances for her, and help her if it was possible. 'I believe you told me once that before you married you worked in an office and were skilled in shorthand and typing?'

'I did some secretarial work, like shorthand and typing, yes, but that was some years ago. I would be very rusty at it now.'

'It wouldn't take you long to get your speed up,' Mildred said. 'You'd be surprised how quickly it comes back to you. I only mentioned it because they will be taking on another secretary when I leave, and I thought you might be interested. It would mean a rise of five shillings a week which should be an incentive. I'm sure it can't be easy living on an Army pension.'

'No, it isn't.' While Evelyn spoke slowly, her brain was working overtime. An extra five shillings a week . . . just think what she could do with it. The only drawback, was it meant she would have to work an eight-hour day for five days. The office didn't open on Saturdays. It would be awkward with Amelia, but she couldn't say this because she had never told anyone here that she had a daughter. 'Thank you for telling me, Miss Saunders, and for considering me suitable. I will certainly give it some thought, and if I think I can make up for all the lost years, and not be a hindrance, then I would love to apply for the position.'

'Why don't you slip into my office while I'm taking dictation from Mr Astbury? I'll be with him for half an hour, and in that time you could practise your typing. If anyone asks for you, I'll say I've asked you to do some filing for me.'

'You are very kind, Miss Saunders, and I'll definitely take you up on your offer.' Evelyn had already made up her mind she wanted the job if only for the rise in status it would bring. She'd manage somehow with Amelia, the girl was quite sensible and reliable. She could have a key and let herself in after school and make herself tea and sandwiches.' May I use some of the office paper?'

'Yes, of course.' Mildred was wondering now whether she should have kept the news to herself for a while longer, as Mr Woodward's secretary Janet had already met Mr Astbury's nephew at a social event and taken quite a fancy to him. In fact, she'd talked about nothing else for a week afterwards. He was good-looking and a bachelor, which made him fair game for the unattached Janet. If she knew there was a possibility of gaining the position of secretary to a young man with film-star looks, she would move heaven and earth to secure that position. Janet had told Miss Saunders he'd gone out of his way to smile at her, but neglected to add that he'd smiled at every woman in the room. At least all the young and pretty ones. 'Please don't discuss our conversation with anyone, Mrs Sinclair. I only mentioned it to you because I thought you would be interested in the promotion,' said Mildred nervously.

'Which I appreciate. And I assure you it will not be mentioned elsewhere.'

Sitting at Miss Saunders' desk later, with the typewriter in front of her, Evelyn felt a little nervous. Not about the fact that she would be leaving her daughter on her own for a couple of hours every night, she would get around that somehow. The girl was quite capable of looking after herself and surely wouldn't come to any harm. Besides, she would benefit from her mother working full-time as they wouldn't go hungry any more. No, Evelyn was nervous about passing the interview if she applied for the post. She would surely be asked about her speeds at both shorthand and typing, and it wasn't something she could lie about. It would be almost impossible to get them up to the required speed within two weeks. The shorthand she might manage perhaps, for this she could do at home every night by asking Amelia to recite poems or repeat what she'd been up to at school that day. But how could she hope to impress at an interview if she could only have half-an-hour's practice on a typewriter two or three times a week?

Evelyn sat up straight and shook her head to clear it. She had a chance now to try her hand again at something in which she was once very proficient. Why not take full advantage instead of wasting precious time? After fifteen minutes her fingers were losing their stiffness and she was remembering how the letters were placed on the keyboard. When Miss Saunders came into the office later, she raised her eyebrows in surprise for the keys were clicking away quite quickly.

'Very good, Mrs Sinclair, I'm quite sure that within the two weeks available, you will be well up to speed.'

Evelyn smiled with pride at the compliment. It made her more determined than ever. After all, a new job could quite possibly change her whole life. Get her out of the rut she was in and back amongst people of her own class.

'I hope you won't think it very forward of me, Miss Saunders, but I would be grateful if you'd allow me the use of your office, and typewriter whenever possible,' she said. 'I would need to practise very hard to make a suitable applicant for the position which you say will soon be available.'

'My office will be free after our lunch break, Mrs Sinclair. Mr Astbury is writing to all the clients who have retained him over the years. He wishes to let them know personally that he will be leaving and to thank them for their loyalty over the years so I imagine his dictation will take at least an hour. You are more than welcome to make full use of my office then.'

Mildred Saunders hadn't realised until now how happy she would be to retire. She would have more time to devote to her mother, and even enjoy a limited social life herself. She would never have retired while Mr Astbury still worked, but both of them now deserved a more leisurely kind of life, and she could see herself sitting in the garden on a sunny afternoon, with her dear mother, enjoying a pot of tea. How blissfully happy she would be.

Evelyn tutted when her finger landed on the wrong key and the word on the paper came up as 'would' instead of 'could'. 'I really am very stupid,' she muttered. 'I should know better by now.'

'We all make mistakes, even the best of us.'

She spun around, her face crimson. 'I'm sorry, I didn't hear the door open and you've taken me by surprise.' The man standing inside the door was tall and slim with pale brown hair and bright blue eyes. He was dressed in a suit of the finest tweed, an expensive shirt and silk tie, and wore an air of confidence that was so obvious you felt you could stretch out your hand and touch it. It was a long time since Evelyn had seen a man dressed in such fine attire, or one who was so very attractive. She pushed her chair back. 'If it's Miss Saunders you wish to see, I'm afraid she's taking dictation from Mr Astbury. If you will tell me your name, I will let her know you are here.'

'There's no need, I've just come from my uncle's office where he is keeping Miss Saunders very busy dictating dozens and dozens of letters.' Philip Astbury leaned against the frame of the door, a man at ease with himself. 'I was on my way to see Mr Woodward when I heard someone in here calling themselves stupid. I wasn't listening at the door, it was ajar and I couldn't fail to hear. I was rather curious to see this stupid person.' He moved away from the door and approached her with hand outstretched. 'Philip Astbury, delighted to meet you.'

Evelyn took his hand. 'Evelyn Sinclair.'

'I will be joining the firm as of today, but will not be taking over completely from my uncle until he retires in two weeks. In the meantime I shall be looking and learning, and making myself familiar with the files of our clients. And you, Evelyn Sinclair, what is your position here? Oh, and is that Miss Sinclair?'

She shook her head. 'I'm a widow, my husband was killed in the war. And I'm more or less the junior here because I do the menial chores. I came back to work to give my life some meaning. I was wallowing in self-pity for too long and allowed myself to lose contact with all my friends. Consequently my social life was non-existent. At least coming here every day gives me a reason for getting out of bed. I don't work full-time at present, but that may change in the near future.'

'And would it be presumptuous of me to ask why you think you are stupid?'

Evelyn lowered her eyes coyly, remembering how Charles had found this habit very endearing. 'It's a while since I sat behind a typewriter and I was calling myself stupid for having forgotten the position of all the keys. I had no idea the door wasn't closed properly or that I would be overheard. I'm not actually stupid, just finding it rather strange. But that's something I can easily overcome, and I am determined to do so.'

Philip had an eye for a pretty face, and found Evelyn very pleasing to look at. A bachelor of thirty-three, he had many women friends, but with him it was a case of love them and leave them. He led a very enjoyable life as a single man and no woman had yet been able to lure him away from it. 'I hear Miss Saunders is leaving the same time as my uncle, and haven't had time as yet to ask if they have found a replacement for her?'

'I really don't know.' Evelyn didn't want to pass on any information in case he repeated it to Miss Saunders. If she lost the trust of the older woman, she may also lose the chance of filling the vacancy. 'I only found out an hour ago that Mr Astbury was retiring, and it came as a great surprise. It was an even greater surprise to hear Miss Saunders was retiring too, but having been secretary to your uncle for so long, and being so used to his ways, I imagine it would be difficult at her age to adjust to starting afresh with a new partner.'

'So with whom am I going to have the pleasure of working? I hope it is someone pretty, and not an ogre with two heads.'

Evelyn thought it would be to her advantage to leave the room before this conversation became too personal, and questions were asked that she would have difficulty in answering. 'It's time for our morning break so if you're going to see Mr Woodward, I will bring in an extra cup of tea for you. And would you prefer a digestive biscuit or a cream?'

'That rather sounds as if I'm getting my marching orders.'

'Not at all!' Evelyn was beginning to think that here was a man who was so sure of himself he expected every woman to fall at his feet. But she felt sure this wasn't the way to attract his attention. 'I am not in a position to give anyone their marching orders. This is Miss Saunders' office, lent to me only until she has finished taking dictation.' She took the paper out of the typewriter, folded it in two then pushed her chair nearer to the desk. 'I really must make the morning tea, I'm sure the partners and their secretaries are feeling thirsty.' She squared her shoulders and held her head high as she passed an astonished Philip, who wasn't used to being dismissed in such a manner. 'I will see you in Mr Woodward's office. It has been most pleasant talking to you.'

'Yes' he agreed, 'a pleasure indeed.'

Philip and his uncle were having their lunch in the State Hotel when the younger man asked, 'Uncle Simon, have you anyone in mind for my secretary?'

Simon Astbury raised his thick white eyebrows. 'I presumed you would be bringing your present secretary with you. I'm used to hearing you singing her praises.'

'She is very efficient, I must admit.' Philip decided a little white lie was called for. 'However, the other two partners feel she will be needed for the new man they are bringing in to fill my position as she is familiar with our clients. And as I have given so little notice of my departure, I felt it would be unfair of me to deprive them of such an efficient worker. You must admit, Uncle, a good secretary is jolly hard to find.'

'Then we must be quick about finding a replacement for Miss Saunders as we are both leaving in just two weeks. I'll have a word with her when we get back, perhaps she knows someone who would fit the bill.' Simon picked up the heavy linen napkin and patted his lips. 'Miss Coombes is very punctual and efficient, but she is settled in with James and I'm sure he wouldn't want to share her.'

'What about Mrs Sinclair? I was talking to her while you were busy and she seems to have had a decent education. She is certainly articulate.'

His uncle showed surprise. 'Mrs Sinclair is an office clerk, she does not have the qualifications to be a secretary.'

'You do surprise me,' Philip said. 'I walked into Miss Saunders' office after leaving yours because I heard the click of a typewriter and wondered who could be in there. I found Mrs

Sinclair sitting at the desk, typing. She stopped immediately so I couldn't say for sure how fast she was. But I'm surprised you didn't know this, Uncle Simon? She's obviously far too intelligent to be a mere clerk.'

Simon looked at his nephew under his thick eyebrows. 'And of course she is very attractive too, is she not?' He shook his head. 'Don't you tire of constantly moving from woman to woman? Would you not like to settle down with a good wife and raise a family?'

'Good heavens, Uncle Simon, are you trying to spoil my lunch for me?' Philip laughed, for he and his uncle were very close and dear to each other. 'I ask a question about a member of your staff who is, I admit, very attractive, and it leads directly to my settling down and getting married. Oh, *and* raising a family.'

'You are incorrigible, Philip,' Simon Astbury said, a smile on his thin, lined face. 'Anyway, I know very little about Mrs Sinclair apart from the fact that she's a war widow. Perhaps Miss Saunders would be the best person to whom to direct your questions. She probably knows more about the woman's qualifications than I do. And in the meantime, could we forget the office and enjoy our meal in peace? It isn't often I have a companion to talk to over a decent meal and a glass of excellent claret. So indulge an old man and forget your pursuit of the opposite sex for the next half-hour.'

Philip feigned shock. 'Half an hour, Uncle Simon, surely not! That's an eternity.'

'You mark my words, young man, the day will come when one of the pretty girls you pursue will trap you in her net. And I hope I live long enough to see it, it would give me great pleasure.'

'I'll see if I can arrange it, Uncle, but didn't you suggest a while ago that we should eat our meal in peace? It will soon be time to return to the office.'

* * *

'Miss Saunders, may I have a word with you in your office?' Philip knew that Mrs Sinclair was in his uncle's room filing away some correspondence and wanted to take advantage of her absence. 'I won't keep you long from your work.'

'That's all right, Mr Philip, the letters I have to type practically all read the same so I don't have to keep checking my notes.' Mildred led the way into her office, and when Philip was inside, closed the door. 'How can I help you?'

'It concerns my secretary.' He sat down and crossed his legs. 'Uncle Simon was under the impression I was bringing my own, but two of us leaving the firm at once is a little too much. It would be inconsiderate of me to leave my previous partners short-staffed. After all, I've been there for ten years, and we have always worked in harmony. I would not like to walk out leaving any bad feeling. Which means I have to find a new secretary before my uncle retires.' Forever the ladies' man, he added, 'Of course, you would have been ideal, but alas you too are leaving. Which leads me to ask for your help. I do hope you don't mind my taking advantage of your experience?'

Mildred was old enough to want to retire, but not too old to succumb to the charm of such a handsome young man. 'Not at all, Mr Philip! If I can help then I will be more than happy to do so. What had you in mind?'

'I met a young woman in your office this morning. Her name, she told me, is Mrs Sinclair. She was busy at the typewriter at the time, and I took her to be a senior secretary. But Uncle Simon tells me she is merely a clerk and not experienced enough to take over from you. In fact, he was of the opinion that she was unable to type. So I thought I would seek out someone who has the welfare of this firm at heart and ask for her opinion.' His lopsided grin, as he'd expected, had her going weak at the knees. 'Do you think Mrs Sinclair, given a little time, is capable of following in your footsteps?'

'Oh, I couldn't say with any certainty, Mr Philip, that wouldn't be fair to you. But she worked in an office before she was married, and was qualified then in both shorthand and typing. She admits she is rusty now, after so long, but I allowed her to use my office this morning, and was quite pleased with her speed on the typewriter. Not up to the standard required, mind you, but she could well pass a test in a few weeks.' Mildred thought she'd better include the other female member of staff in this conversation too. 'Miss Coombes mentioned that she would be happy to serve both you and Mr Woodward for the time being. And she suggested that as your uncle has the heavier workload, with her experience, it would be best if she stayed with your uncle and his replacement, and the new secretary could work for Mr Woodward.'

There, Mildred told herself, no one could accuse her of not passing on the message as she'd promised. But she hadn't promised anything else. 'I don't think that would work, frankly. I believe a new member of staff would be better placed with a new partner, so they could learn together how the office has been run under Mr Simon. We had a system, understood each other, and have worked in harmony for more years than I care to remember.'

Philip remembered flattery always worked for him. As he was intrigued by the very attractive war widow, he now flashed his best smile. 'It would solve all our problems if you could stay on, Miss Saunders. My troubles would be over then, I think we would work well together. But I understand your desire to retire, and am in agreement that you have earned the right to enjoy some freedom now. You have served my uncle well, our whole family agrees, and we are grateful to you.'

Blushing like a schoolgirl, Mildred was indeed delighted by such praise. 'It has been a pleasure to serve Mr Simon. In all the years we have worked together there has never been a cross word. I shall miss him, and miss coming to this office every day too. But no one can go on for ever, Mr Philip, age catches up with us all eventually.'

'Nonsense, Mildred! You don't look a day older than you did ten years ago. I have watched Uncle Simon grow older, but you never seem to change.'

It was the first time the blushing woman had been addressed by her first name since she came to work for the firm, and she lowered her head to hide her embarrassment. 'Now you know that's not true, Mr Philip, the mirror in my bedroom tells me otherwise. But it's nice to be flattered by a handsome young man.'

Philip left his chair and sat on the edge of the desk. 'Sit down, Mildred, and let's discuss this further. I want the take-over from Uncle Simon to go smoothly so that our clients are not inconvenienced. In other words, in the next two weeks I have to learn everything I need to know. Now, can we go back to Mrs Sinclair? I know she is at present filing away copies of letters to and from clients which I hope means she is familiar with the filing system and able to put her hand on any correspondence I may need? Am I correct in thinking this?'

Mildred nodded. 'Oh, yes, she is very competent. You will never find a file or a letter out of place. She is always able to put her hand on anything she is asked for. And she is familiar with the working of the office, which it would take a newcomer several months to get used to. There are many points in her favour, I have to say. She is always neat, never a hair out of place, and quite capable of answering the telephone politely and welcoming clients to the office. In fact, several clients have commented on her style and deportment.'

'Both qualities which are an asset to the firm, would you not say?' His uncle's secretary was eating out of Philip's hand by now, and nodded enthusiastically. So he pressed the case he was quite sure he would win. Mrs Sinclair's looks and manner had appealed to him, and he intended to become better acquainted with her. Miss Saunders was being very co-operative, and he was sure she would add her weight to his intention of making Mrs Sinclair his secretary. If she didn't, then he would seek permission from the uncle who would deny him nothing. One thing he was certain of: Janet Coombes would never get close to him. She may be an excellent worker, but he didn't find her in the least attractive. He'd only met her once socially and then she'd been all over him, practically drooling. Philip liked a challenge, he didn't want an easy conquest, there was no thrill or fun attached to it.

'Well, what do you think, Mildred?' he asked, knowing it made little difference what the older woman said for his mind had been made up since Evelyn had walked out of the office, saying indifferently, 'It has been most pleasant talking to you.' He had immediately told himself that this was a challenge he couldn't resist. 'I think we should give her a chance, rather than taking on a new member of staff. After all, she has been here for a couple of years and deserves to be considered. And I'm sure that while you are here, you will continue to offer her all the help you can.'

'You have my promise that my office will be at her disposal for at least an hour in the mornings and an hour in the afternoon.'

Philip stepped away from the desk and ran his fingers down the immaculate crease in his trousers. 'I don't think Mrs Sinclair should be approached by me or your good self. Uncle Simon is the obvious one to interview her. That's if she's interested in taking up the position, of course. Perhaps she has a private income and doesn't need any extra money?'

'Oh, I'm sure she will be interested, Mr Philip, I don't think she has any private income. She is as careful with money as she is with her clothes. She never mentions a family, so I have always presumed she lives alone. Never talks about her dead husband either, but of course the reason for that may be that she finds it too painful.'

'Then I'll ask Uncle Simon to go gently with her. On such a delicate subject as her late husband, I'm sure he will be very understanding.' Philip put a hand on each of Miss Saunders' shoulders, sending shock waves down her spine. 'You are a brick, Mildred, and I am indebted to you for your help. I hope our plan works, for I would hate to take over from my uncle while working with a secretary who knows nothing of the firm or its clients. At least Mrs Sinclair can hold my hand and show me where everything is.'

Mildred was wishing she was twenty-five years younger. She hadn't been bad-looking then, and might have stood a chance with Philip. Then she mentally shook her head. He was a playboy, not likely to be content with a nice, down-to-earth girl who would keep a good house for him. He would find that far too dull. Playing the field was more in his line. 'I won't say anything to Mrs Sinclair, I'll wait until she tells me, and then I'll act as though the news is a complete surprise.'

Philip squeezed her shoulder again. 'How lucky my uncle has been to have you to care for him all these year. Never a worry about correspondence going astray or words mis-spelt. He has been truly blessed.'

And Philip's words were sincere, for he was very fond of his uncle and had been told over the years how this dear lady made sure his working life was made easy. Always a hot drink when he arrived at the office on a winter's morning, and never a draught allowed to reach his desk. Philip bent to kiss her forehead. 'Thank you.'

After leaving a tearful Miss Saunders, he made for his uncle's office. He rapped on the door with his knuckles and called, 'It's only your beloved nephew, Uncle Simon, so you don't have to hide your snuff box.'

Simon Astbury tried in vain to hide a smile. 'You cheeky young whippersnaper. Wait until you reach my age, then you too will have to make do with whatever pleasures remain to you.'

Philip pulled out a chair facing his uncle across the shiny dark mahogany desk. 'Thank you for the warning, Uncle. I shall have to make hay while the sun shines, don't you agree? I intend to experience as much of life as is humanly possible, and I reckon I have at least thirty years left to do it in.'

'And with the grace of God you may, my boy. But try to pack everything into the time allotted to you and you may find yourself worn out before you reach the age of fifty. You can never have your cake and eat it.'

'I intend to do my damnedest, Uncle, but I will remember your words when I reach the grand old age of fifty. For now, I want to talk to you about engaging a secretary. Do you have the time to spare?'

Simon took off his spectacles and laid them on the desk. 'I will always make time for you. What have you in mind?'

Chapter Five

'Well, Mrs Sinclair, in two weeks' time you will be working as my secretary. Meanwhile I hope to find out a little more about how my uncle's office has been run so efficiently for the last twenty or more years.' Philip had caught up with Evelyn as she was leaving Miss Saunders' office after telling her why Mr Simon had asked to see her. 'I am quite looking forward to the experience, as I hope you are?'

'Like yourself, Mr Astbury, I have quite a lot to learn in the next two weeks, and think perhaps I would rather answer your question after that. If I wasn't so out of practice in taking dictation, I would feel much happier about my abilities. As it is, I have to admit to being a little apprehensive.'

Evelyn was feeling quite flustered by the way he was staring her out, but she was determined not to show it. He was very sure of himself, almost cocky, and she didn't intend to add to his inflated ego. 'I am not used to this feeling, I am usually so sure of myself. But I'm going to put that down to the surprise your uncle sprang on me. The last thing I expected was to be offered the position of secretary. It's a position I last held before I was married and, without wanting to sound boastful, I really was very good at my job then.'

She didn't want him digging too deeply into her past, and tried to step around him. But he was quick to put himself in her path. 'Oh, and where was this job you were so good at? In the city centre, was it?'

'I'm a private person, Mr Astbury, not one to gossip about

myself or other people. My private life is my own, and I wish to keep it that way. I hope you will understand and respect my wishes?'

'Ah, well now, Mrs Sinclair, that has made me very curious. Two or three children hidden away, and a man friend perhaps? Or is it one child and two men friends? I am really very intrigued now.'

'I live alone, Mr Astbury, and that is through choice. After my husband was killed in the war I became a recluse. Over a period of time my friends dropped off one by one, and for the last couple of years my social life has been non-existent.' Evelyn liked the sound of the life she'd just created, and almost came to believe it herself. But she mustn't let herself be carried away. 'May I pass now, please? If I want to be proficient by the end of two weeks, I am really going to have to work hard on both my typing and shorthand speeds. Miss Saunders has kindly offered the use of her machine, but shorthand I'll have to practise at home. Something we shall both benefit from.'

He watched her take her coat from the stand and said, 'I forgot, you only work until four o'clock.'

Evelyn slipped her arms into the sleeves of the coat. 'Just for today and tomorrow. On Monday I start working full-time.' She was fastening the buttons as she walked towards the door. 'I'll see you tomorrow, goodbye.'

Philip stood still for a few minutes after she'd disappeared through the door. And under his breath, he muttered, 'It's going to be fun breaking *her* in.'

He might have thought differently if he could have read Evelyn's mind as she skipped lightly down the stairs. For while he saw her as an attractive woman whom he would eventually add to his long list of conquests before moving on to the next, she saw him in an entirely different light. She saw him as a way out of the rut she was in, and a way back to the life she believed she deserved. A wealthy husband and a life of luxury. She'd known it would happen some time.

Evelyn's spirits were high, her mind filled with excitement and pleasure as she sat on the tram on her way home. She had no doubt it was Philip Astbury who had talked his uncle into offering her the position of secretary, which meant he was more than a little interested in her. In fact, he hadn't hidden the fact he found her attractive. But he was so sure of his ability to charm any woman, she knew he was the love them and leave them type. Because of this, and because she really needed him in order to change her life, she'd decided the way to keep him interested was to play it very cool. And she would do, until she had him just where she wanted him. She didn't want a short fling, she wanted a lasting relationship which would lead to marriage and her step back up the social ladder to all the trappings that went with wealth.

It was only when she turned into her own street that her spirits fell and she stared reality in the face. How could she ensnare a rich man when she lived in such a poor neighbourhood, amongst people of the lower class? Philip Astbury would take one look at the street and turn tail and run. And what about Amelia, how could she hide the fact that she had a daughter? And how was she to manage working full-time when it would mean the girl being on her own for two hours every night when she came home from school?

As Evelyn walked down the street, looking neither to left nor right, she began to have dark thoughts about her daughter. If it wasn't for Amelia, she wouldn't be living like a pauper. She would still be a member of the Lister-Sinclair family, enjoying the sort of lifestyle that only their sort of money could buy. She would have had to pretend she was heartbroken over Charles being killed, of course, and gone into mourning for a few months. It would have been a small enough price to pay for a lifetime of being waited on hand and foot. The truth was, she hadn't mourned him at all. She was sorry he was dead simply because it had cost her so dearly. But she could be a good actress when necessary, and it would have been worth it for the reward. It could well be that with Mr Philip she'd have a second chance of the good life . . . if only she didn't have the drawback of a daughter nobody knew about.

When Evelyn reached her house she could see the two women who lived opposite out of the corner of her eye, but was in no mood to acknowledge their presence. If they had nothing better to do than stand jangling all day, what a sad life they led. They'd never know what it was to walk into the Adelphi on the arm of one of the wealthiest men in Liverpool, wearing clothes that were the height of fashion and had cost a fortune. Well, she was going to do her very best to get away from this tiny house in this narrow street full of common people. How she'd do it, she didn't know right now, but she vowed that as soon as Mr Philip began to woo her – as she had no doubt whatsoever that he would – then she would manipulate him until he was so crazy about her he'd do anything to keep her happy.

After hanging her coat up Evelyn sat at the table, wanting to clarify things in her mind. That her daughter would be in from school any minute meant little to her. She never cooked a proper meal anyway, it was only ever egg on toast, a sandwich or a pennyworth of chips from the chip shop. And for that they'd consider themselves lucky, for many a time all they had to eat was bread and dripping. Even if she'd had enough money to make dinner, though, she would have turned her nose up at the thought of soiling her hands peeling potatoes.

A knock on the door brought a frown to Evelyn's face. The girl was home. She would have to go to the chip shop again, there was nothing to eat in the house. When Amelia looked up at her mother she was met with a hostile glare. There was no greeting, but then she didn't expect something she'd never had.

She was left to close the door after herself, and when she entered the living room her mother didn't even meet her eyes as she said, 'Sit down, I have something to tell you before you go to the chip shop for our tea.'

Always afraid of doing something to upset her mother, Amelia pulled a chair out from under the table, taking care to keep the legs clear so they didn't get scratched. 'Yes, Mother?'

'I had some very good news at the office today, Amelia, which I am sure will make you feel proud of me. I was offered the position of private secretary to one of the partners. It is a promotion, which is an honour, and also brings with it an increase in wages.'

'Oh, Mother, that's wonderful news. When will you start this new job?'

'I am to begin learning on Monday, and start the job proper in two weeks. But I am in a dilemma, Amelia, and need to ask your advice.'

Her daughter was not used to being spoken to so softly, and young as she was, sensed her mother was putting on a show because she wanted something. 'I don't see how I can advise you, Mother, when you are far more clever than I am.'

'Perhaps advice was the wrong word, I should have said I need your help. You see, I would be working full-time, which means you would be back home from school two hours before I was home from the office. That is the only thing that stands in the way of my taking up a position of importance which would bring in enough extra money to make a difference to our lives. We wouldn't have to borrow any more, and there would be a vast improvement in the meals we eat and the clothes we wear. We wouldn't be rich, not by any stretch of the imagination, but we would be better off.'

'Mother, I can look after myself for two hours, you know I can! You need have no fear, I'll not come to any harm. Is that all that is worrying you, my being left alone for two hours?'

These weren't the words of a young girl, nor did she sound like one. But that was how Amelia had been brought up. She acted and spoke differently at school, knowing the girls in her class led a very different life from her. But she was too young to be in any position to change her lot. 'You can trust me, Mother, you know you can,' she said eagerly.

'Yes, I know I can trust you, but what are the neighbours going to think if they know you are left on your own for two hours, especially in the dark nights of winter? They will think I am a very wicked mother.'

This gave Amelia food for thought. She had forgotten the winter nights, and the prospect of sitting in the dark for two hours every day filled her with dread. She wasn't allowed to light the gas and there would be no fire in the grate to give out light so it would be pitch black. 'Could I not go into Miss Bessie's to wait for you? I think I would be afraid in the dark nights, Mother, with no fire to see by and not being allowed to light the gas.'

'What a silly child you are. Once you are in your own house, with the curtains drawn, what harm can come to you?'

'I am afraid of the pitch dark, Mother, which is what it would be.'

'How silly! The street lamp isn't far away, there'd be light through the curtains. I do *not* want the neighbours knowing my business, so if I am to take advantage of this opportunity you will have to learn that one can't have everything one's own way. If we are to have a more comfortable life, it will have to be earned – by you as well as by me. Now, do you understand me?'

Something in Amelia made her rebel. 'I do understand, Mother, but I don't want to be in a dark house on my own 'cos I'd be frightened. I'd rather stand outside and wait for you, then I wouldn't be scared because there're always children out playing.'

Evelyn was about to scold her daughter when a thought entered her head. If Mr Philip were to ask her out, something she confidently expected in the very near future, she couldn't refuse by making her daughter the excuse because she had no intention of telling him about Amelia. On the tram journey home, she'd made her plans very carefully. She would take things slowly, charm him into wanting more than she would give him at first. She needed him to become besotted by her, to desire her so much he would do anything for her. But all her dreams and desires would come to nought if he knew where she lived, and that she had a seven-year-old daughter. So she had to lead a double life, and for that she would need help.

'I'm surprised at your being scared, Amelia, but we'll have to find a way around it. What time does Miss Bessie get in from work?'

A smile crossed the girl's pretty face when she saw a glimmer of hope, but she quickly hid it for fear it would displease her mother. 'I'm not sure because she sometimes goes in at seven in the morning and finishes at four o'clock. I think she told me it depended on whether they have an urgent order to finish or not. I'm not sure what she meant by that, and I didn't like asking.'

'I wonder if she would be kind enough to mind you for two hours every night, if I were to pay her a shilling?'

The girl's eyes nearly popped out of her head. 'A whole shilling! That's a lot of money, Mother. I'm sure Miss Bessie wouldn't ask you for that much just to let me sit in her house for two hours each night. I could pay her back by running messages for her, or helping her with the dishes.'

'I think we should ask her first before we discuss it any further. She could possibly refuse point blank. If so, I would have to reconsider the situation.' Evelyn shook her head as though to dismiss the possibility of being turned down. She knew Miss Maudsley had a soft spot for Amelia, and it was to this she would appeal. 'I heard the front door closing a few minutes ago so I know she's home. If you will go to the chip shop for a pennyworth of chips and a pennyworth of scallops, I'll slip out the back way and put my request to her.'

Amelia jumped from her chair and stood by the table waiting to be given the two pennies. Chips and scallops, that was a rare treat. Being offered a promotion must have made her mother very happy. As soon as she had the two coins in her hand, she skipped out of the door and down the street. She could hear the other children out playing, but tonight she didn't envy them. And all the way to the chip shop she kept on praying that Miss Bessie would agree to mind her each day until her mother got home from work. If she had to choose between having a nice meal from the chip shop tonight, or Miss Bessie agreeing to what she was now being asked, then Amelia would starve tonight and live on the thought of the pleasure she'd have every night thereafter. For in their neighbour, she knew she had found someone who really liked her and would enjoy her company. And she wouldn't have to watch every word that came out of her mouth in that house, or be afraid to laugh out loud. Oh, it would be lovely.

As Evelyn walked up next door's yard, the smell of bacon frying wafted towards her. But although it made her empty stomach rumble, she wasn't jealous. In the not-too-distant future she would enjoy food only the rich could afford, things which Miss Maudsley and her cronies had probably never heard of. But of course she mustn't say anything to annoy her neighbour, she needed her now.

When Bessie opened the door she showed no surprise, she'd seen her neighbour pass the window. She wasn't particularly pleased to see Evelyn. She'd not long got in from work and was longing to sit down and eat the bacon, the smell of which was making her mouth water. She was wearing a floral wrap-around pinny that almost reached the floor, and which she'd been promising herself for months that she'd put a hem on to save her tripping herself up. But she wasn't a snob and didn't care whether her neighbour wrinkled her nose at the sight or not. 'Yer've just caught me making me dinner, Mrs Sinclair, so can yer make it quick before me bacon burns?'

'I'm sorry to call at an inconvenient time, Miss Maudsley. If you like I will call later when you are more prepared?'

Bessie pushed a strand of hair out of her eyes. 'Was it something important?'

'Yes, it is really.' Then Evelyn played her trump card. 'Important for me, and for Amelia. But I can see you're busy so I'll call back later.'

Had it not been for the mention of Amelia's name, Bessie would have told her to come back. Instead she opened the door wider. 'Come on in. I don't want me bacon to be ruined, but I'll make a butty of it and yer'll have to put up with seeing me eat it. I can't afford to waste good food.' She waved Evelyn through to the living room. 'Make yerself comfortable, I won't be a minute.'

While she was waiting, Evelyn looked around the room. She had to admit it was clean and polished, like a new pin. But the furniture wasn't up to her own standards, far too cheap-looking.

Bessie bustled through with a plate in one hand and a cup and saucer in the other. 'I won't offer yer a drink 'cos I know yer'll be having yer dinner soon.' She sat at the table and lifted the butty, which was very substantial and which her neighbour was mentally comparing to a doorstep. In fact, she was having trouble trying to stop her nose from wrinkling, which Bessie noted and found hilarious. What a snob Evelyn Sinclair was! Before taking a bite from the butty, she said, 'I don't mind yer talking while I'm eating, Mrs Sinclair, so don't let me stop yer. I'm too hungry to be polite and wait until yer've gone.'

These people were not brought up to be genteel, they had no manners whatsoever. This was the thought running through Evelyn's head, followed by one that said she must make sure her neighbour's lack of manners didn't rub off on Amelia. But right now it wouldn't do to offend the woman she was going to ask for help.

'Please don't think me forward, Miss Maudsley, and please don't hesitate to refuse what I am about to ask you if it is something you wouldn't want even to consider. But I'm going to ask a big favour of you.' She thought a little craftiness would help her cause. 'At least, it was Amelia who put the idea in my head for, as you know, my daughter is very fond of you.'

Bessie's eyes narrowed as she took another bite. This one was after something, the two-faced, stuck-up article. And she didn't have the nerve to come straight out with it, had to pretend she was asking for her daughter. She must think I was born yesterday, Bessie told herself. That I'm green around the gills.

'Yer can only ask, Mrs Sinclair, and I can only say yes or no. Which I will do, if yer'll tell me what it is?'

Evelyn laced her fingers and put her hands on her knees. 'I was pleasantly surprised today when one of the senior partners in the office where I work asked if I would like the position of private secretary to a new partner who is starting with the firm next week. It is obviously a great honour and brings a not insignificant increase in salary. It was only after the interview that I realised it would mean my working full-time, which would leave Amelia to come home from school and be alone in the house for two hours each night. That is something I couldn't even contemplate. The girl is only seven, after all, and couldn't be expected to stay in the house on her own on dark nights. So I was intending to tell my boss tomorrow that, sadly, I am not able to take up the position . . .'

Bessie could see what was coming, but she certainly wasn't going to make it easy for a woman who looked down her nose at everyone in this street. It was a wonder she'd sat down on the couch without flicking her handkerchief over it in case it was dusty. So let her sweat it out for a while. 'Ye're not taking the job then?'

'That is what I was telling Amelia when she surprised me by saying perhaps you would mind her for those two hours every night? I pooh-poohed the idea at first, but Amelia was so taken with the idea, she wanted to come and ask you herself. Of course I wouldn't let her do that, so I'm here instead. There would be recompense for your trouble, I wouldn't expect you to do it without payment. I thought a shilling a week would be appropriate.'

Bessie didn't reply for a while as she stared down at a tea leaf floating on top of her cup. Of course she would have the child, she would love to. And she knew jolly well the girl would be overjoyed. But although her first instinct had been to tell her neighbour to stick her shilling where Paddy stuck his nuts, a voice in her head told her she would be stupid not to take the money. She could use it to buy treats for Amelia because she had never seen the child with a bag of sweets in her hand in the three years she'd lived next door.

'I'm not always home before Amelia, it depends whether I start at seven or half-past. We sometimes have to pack orders, yer see, and they need to be on the cart by eight. Mind you, some of the women go in at seven all the time, so they can be home for their kids coming in from school. I could do the same thing.' She pretended to give the idea some thought, but it was only to keep the queer one in suspense for a while. Then she said, slowly, as though she wasn't really keen, 'I suppose we could try it for a week to two, see if it works out. I mean, I'm not used to having children in the house, and on the other hand, Amelia might not like sitting with an old woman every night.' Then she felt like a little bit of devilment, and came out with something she knew would fill her neighbour with horror. 'She would be better playing out in the street with the other children. I could keep me eye on her through the window, make sure she came to no harm.'

The colour drained from Evelyn's face, and Bessie, who held conversations with herself as people who live alone often do, told the frying pan later that night as she was washing the dishes that her neighbour looked so shocked anyone would think a doctor had just told her she dying, and only had minutes to live.

'Oh, I can't allow Amelia to play in the street, Miss Maudsley, not under any circumstances. Heaven alone knows what sort of diseases those children could be carrying, not to mention head lice. It is entirely out of the question. I will not subject my daughter to their lack of hygiene or their ignorance. And I must insist that you do not allow her to play in the street.'

How Bessie kept her temper she would never know. There wasn't a woman in this street wouldn't lay down her life for her children, and many of them were going hungry to give food to their families but never moaned about going without themselves. Family always came first. But if Bessie told Miss High and Mighty what she really thought of her, she'd be cutting off her nose to spite her face. The stuck-up snob might take the huff and say she had decided it wasn't appropriate to leave Amelia in her care, which would mean Bessie and the girl losing out on something they would both enjoy.

'If that is the way you want it, Mrs Sinclair, then of course that's the way it shall be. She is your daughter after all. So shall we start our trial period on Monday and see how it goes?'

Evelyn kept her sigh of relief silent. Although she'd meant what she had said about her daughter playing in the street, she knew she needed Bessie more than Bessie needed her. She hadn't the slightest intention of telling Mr Simon she wouldn't be taking the job, for his nephew was at the forefront of all her plans. And she wasn't letting the welfare of her daughter get in the way of those plans. If all else failed, the girl would have to be in the house on her own for two hours each night, whether she was frightened or not. In her twisted mind, Evelyn put the blame on Amelia for everything that had gone wrong in her own life.

'You are very kind, Miss Maudsley,' she said now, 'and I'm sure we shall both benefit from it. And Amelia, of course, will be delighted when I tell her the result of our conversation.' Evelyn got to her feet. 'I must go now, Amelia will be waiting for her tea. I want you to know I am very grateful, and hope our little arrangement is of mutual benefit. And I do apologise for calling when you were about to have your meal.'

'I'll see you out.' Bessie pushed her chair back and began to walk towards the front door with her. 'Tell Amelia I'm looking forward to seeing her. Oh, and remind her it's only two weeks on Saturday to our birthday party.'

But as Evelyn pulled on Bessie's arm it was herself she was thinking off, no one else. 'I'll go out the back way, Miss Maudsley, I don't want to be seen by the neighbours. Especially those two from opposite, who seem to spend their whole lives gossiping in the street. It's a pity they haven't got anything better to do. I do not want them knowing my business so, if you don't mind, I'll go out the back way.'

'Please yerself.' Bessie followed her through to the kitchen, and when she'd closed the door after her, muttered, 'Good riddance to bad rubbish.'

Then she went back to the table for the remains of her sandwich, and a conversation with the fireplace. 'I don't know whether to laugh or cry, I really don't. There's something wrong in the head with that bleeding woman. She's definitely not normal, yet the silly bugger thinks we're all mad and she's the only sane one! I mean, how does she think I can have her daughter coming here every night straight from school, and not one of the neighbours will see her and start asking questions? Is the silly bugger going to give everyone in the street a ruddy blindfold and insist they wear them?'

Then Bessie chuckled. 'She'd do her nut if she knew Rita is coming over tonight, and seeing as she's me best friend in the street, it's only natural I'll tell her me bit of news. She's bound to find out, living opposite, and she'd think me a fine friend if I hadn't let on. In fact, she'd think it was sneaky, and I'd agree with her. So Rita will be told of our little arrangement when she comes tonight, and sure as eggs is eggs she'll tell Aggie first thing in the morning. I'll tell them to keep it to themselves, of course, but I can't help it if they can't keep a secret. But I'd better not mention what her Ladyship said about the other kids having diseases and head lice, 'cos then they'd lynch her. I think Rita might laugh and see the funny side, but not Aggie. Aggie Gordon has a good sense of humour, but not when someone is saying her two children are diseased and lousy. She'd be over there like a shot, with all guns blazing, and if she didn't get an answer, she'd boot the ruddy door in. I don't want no trouble, so I'll be careful what I say and make sure me tongue doesn't run away with me. I don't like the woman, it's no use saying I do, she gets up me bleeding nose with her airs and graces – but I'd hate to see her getting her hair pulled out and losing her front teeth.'

Bessie chuckled and pointed a finger at the fireplace. 'That's the best thing about having a conversation with you, yer never repeat it. And yer don't use no bad language either.' She'd picked up her cup and saucer, put them on the plate and was carrying them out to the kitchen when she turned and looked back at the grate. 'Don't start getting big-headed, 'cos I'll still be taking me poker to yer in the morning to rake out the ashes. So behave yerself, and don't be spitting no live coals on to me hearth rug either.'

'Don't die of surprise, will yer,' Rita said, passing Bessie on her way in, 'but I've got a few biscuits to have with the cup of tea I know ye're going to insist on making. I hopped in lucky when I went to the corner shop for a gas mantle, and Sally was sorting the biscuit tins out. She was emptying the crumbs into a bag ready to put in the bin when I spotted that the tin next to the one she was emptying was the broken biscuit one, and there were some decent ones in there. So I acted daft and pretended I thought she was going to throw them away too! And although she said she wasn't mad enough, nor rich enough, to throw out nearly good as new biscuits, she did take pity on me eventually. God love her cotton socks, she picked a few of the best out and put them in this bag.' She waved a small paper bag in the air. 'So when we're having our cuppa, we'll raise our cups to Sally.'

'You're me second visitor since I got in from work, I'm getting to be very popular.' Bessie waited until her friend was seated. 'Only I didn't ask the other one if she wanted a drink 'cos I knew she wouldn't drink out of one of my cups in case it had a crack in it. And I bet she's never heard of broken biscuits in her life.'

As Rita passed the bag over, she said, 'I don't need three guesses for this one, sunshine, I'll lay odds it was the queer one next door?'

'Right first time, girl. But I'll bet yer'd never guess in a month of Sundays what she came to see me about.'

Rita rolled her eyes. 'She was on the cadge for something?' When Bessie shook her head, her mate racked her brain for inspiration, then said, 'Ooh, don't keep me in suspense, sunshine, me heart won't stand it. Come on, I'm all ears.'

Bessie pushed her chair under the table before striking a pose. She straightened her back, stuck her nose in the air, then laced her fingers across her tummy. And only being the size of sixpennyworth of copper, she looked so funny Rita was laughing before the little woman opened her mouth.

'I was honoured today when one of the senior partners in the office asked me if I would like the position of private secretary to a new partner who is starting on Monday. It is a great advance and brings a not insignificant increase in my salary.'

Unable to keep up the pose, Bessie burst out laughing. 'It's all right for you, Rita Wells, but I had to keep me face straight while she was going on, in that posh voice of hers, about how delighted she was. And d'yer know what was going through me head as she went on about it? Well, I was thinking that while not one soul in this street likes her, she doesn't see it 'cos she's too busy loving herself.'

'I'm surprised she told yer, sunshine, 'cos she never talks to anyone else. None of us knows the first thing about her, so how come she's suddenly opening up to you? She must be after something, so I'd watch out.'

'Oh, she was after something all right. I knew that as soon as I saw her passing me kitchen window. But what she was after suited me, so while I dragged it out for a while, I knew she was going to get her own way.' Bessie pulled the chair back out and sat down. 'I may as well sit while I tell yer the whole story. But before I start, I want yer to know I only let her carry on because of young Amelia. I'm very fond of that girl and think she leads a lousy life. Otherwise I wouldn't have let Lady Muck over the doorstep.'

Rita listened wide-eyed, clicking her tongue a few times. But she didn't interrupt until Bessie had finished. When she did open her mouth to give her opinion, she was asked to wait until they had a pot of tea on the table. Then they sat facing each other across the table with cups of tea in front of them and some biscuits in the saucers.

'She's done me a favour, girl, 'cos since they moved in I've wanted to make friends with Amelia seeing as she doesn't have any young friends. Not that I'm young, like, but at least I talk to her as I would a young girl, not as if to an adult like her mother does. I think we'll both enjoy being together for a few hours each night. It'll be a change for me to have young company, and I'll be able to take her to the park or round the shops, something her own mother never does. And she can't say she hasn't got time, 'cos she's in from work about the same time as me. Anyway, that'll all change on Monday 'cos she's working full-time then, and what the eye don't see, the heart don't grieve over.' Bessie put her cup down on the saucer. 'It goes against the grain with me, taking a shilling a week off her, and I almost told her what she could do with it. Then I thought of how I could spend it on Amelia, buy a few books I can keep in here for her to read, and a game of Snakes and Ladders or Tiddly-winks. She'd like those. I'd rather she had it than the mother who doesn't show any love for her. No hugs or kisses, no sign of affection even.'

'That's because there isn't any, sunshine,' Rita said. 'I can see a lot from our house, and it's not because I'm nosy but yer can't help noticing that she never sees the girl off to school, never stands at the door to give her a kiss or shout after her to tell her to hurry home. They'd only been living there a couple of months when I started to notice those things. I've never said anything to anyone 'cos it's not my worry, but I'd say that woman has no feelings, no emotions, and no love to give her own daughter. In fact, I doubt if she has ever known what true love is.'

'I've noticed all those things too!' Bessie was thinking of Amelia's happy expression when she'd been able to get a loaf for a penny. She'd been so sure her mother would be pleased with her, yet her only thanks was a smack across the face. 'That's why I want to show the kid all women aren't like that. I want to try and show her the love, affection and fun that every other kid in this street knows. They might not have any shoes on their feet, but by God, they know what love is. And laughter too.' Bessie looked surprised that she'd only just thought of this. 'D'yer know, Rita, I've never once heard laughter coming through the wall of that house. I think Amelia is afraid of her mother, afraid to look as though she's enjoying herself.' She banged one clenched fist on the table. 'By God, I'm going to change all that, starting on Monday. I don't care if I have to lie to the stuck-up snob, I'm determined to show that young girl what a real home is like.' She grinned. 'I'll keep God informed every night, and I'm sure He will be on my side.'

'Yer can count on me to be on your side as well, sunshine, I'll help all I can. And yer can take it from me, I'll be doing it willingly. And I'll have a word with God too, 'cos yer never know, an extra voice might add more weight.'

Chapter Six

It was Monday morning. Rita was waving her sons off when the front door to the next house opened and Aggie's eleven-year-old daughter Kitty stepped down on to the pavement, followed by her brother, ten-year-old Kenny. Close behind came Aggie, who never missed seeing her children off.

'The start of another week, eh, girl? The flaming time just flies over.' Aggie held on to the door frame for support as she carefully lowered her eighteen stone down the steps. 'You two better get a move on 'cos ye're a bit late this morning. Too bleeding lazy to get out of bed.'

'It was your fault, Mam, yer never called us.' Kitty wagged her head from side to side, a habit she had acquired from her mother. She also had her mother's features, plus her quick tongue and sense of humour, and was already showing signs of being plump. But woe betide anyone who dare mention this. 'It was you what slept in, so don't be trying to get out of it.'

Her brother pulled on her arm. 'Me mam made us a bit late, but it's you what's making us very late. Shut up and come on, otherwise the school gates will be closed by the time we get there.' As he dragged his sister down the street, he turned his head and appealed to Rita, 'Why do girls and women talk so much? They'll have the last word if it kills them.'

'You're a fine one to talk,' Kitty growled, trying to tug her arm free. 'When ye're out with yer mates, it's always your mouth what's going fifteen to the dozen.'

When Aggie let out a roar and pretended to run after them, shaking her fist in the air, her two children ran hell for leather. But they were both laughing, for they loved the bones of their mother who was warm, loving, and very funny. There was never a dull moment in their house for she never ran out of funny tales. Most of them she made up, but that didn't matter if it made them laugh. 'See yer tonight, Mam,' they both shouted, waving their hands over their head.

'God love them,' Aggie said, 'if they get the cane for being late, it's not because they overslept. It was the ruddy alarm clock, it's away to hell. I'll have to see if Sam can fix it tonight 'cos I can't afford to buy a new one.'

'I can always give yer a knock on the wall,' Rita told her. 'Our alarm clock has never let us down.' She crossed two fingers. 'It's bad luck to speak too soon, so forget I said that. But I'll give yer a knock, if yer want.'

'I'll wait and see if Sam can fix the clock. If he can't, I'll let yer know.' Aggie folded her arms which disappeared under her mountainous breasts. 'Ay, her over the road, Tilly Mint, she was out early this morning. I don't know what the time was, what with the bleeding alarm letting us down, but it can't have been more than eight o'clock, ten-past at the latest. That's early for her. And when the girl came out later, I felt sorry for the poor lass, she had a hell of a job closing the door. She tried pulling it with her two hands in the letter box but that was no good. Then she stood on tip-toe to reach the knocker and that failed. I'd have gone out to her if I hadn't been at sixes and sevens, trying to make the kids some toast before they went to school. I wouldn't let them go out on an empty tummy.' The bosom was hitched up higher. 'Anyway, Mr Bleasedale from the top of the street gave the door a good bang for her.'

'Aggie, I've got something to tell yer,' Rita said, 'although I really shouldn't.'

'Then leave it until later, eh, queen? There's half a pot of tea on me table, and I want to drink it before it gets cold. I can't afford to throw good tea away.'

'It's to do with Mrs Sinclair, and I thought yer'd be interested. So when yer find out, don't call me a dark horse for not letting on.'

It didn't take long for Aggie to decide, and she decided she didn't want to miss her pot of tea *or* the news her neighbour had. So she grabbed Rita's arm and pulled her up the steps. 'I think there's enough tea in the pot for two cups. And that way I've got the best of both worlds.'

'I suppose yer know ye're nearly pulled me arm out of its socket?' Rita bent over and then straightened the arm in question. 'The trouble with you, Aggie Gordon, is yer don't know yer own strength. Yer'd make a ruddy good prize-fighter.'

Aggie wasn't even listening, she was too busy laughing at what she had in mind. Opening a door in the sideboard, she brought out a china cup and saucer, and with a flourish put them down in front of Rita. Once she saw her good china was out of harm's way, she began to shake with laughter. 'Nobody has ever drunk out of that cup before, I've treasured it for the last ten years. But I suddenly had a flash, like lightning, of Her Ladyship's face. She was looking down her nose at someone as though they were the lowest of the low. And I thought that's how she'd look if yer were pulling her to pieces while drinking out of a mug what had dozens of cracks and chips in it. So tell me what the news is, and because of the dainty cup and saucer, I expect yer to speak proper posh.'

'How long did yer say yer'd had this cup and saucer, sunshine?'

'Ooh, easy ten years, maybe a bit more. It's the first and only time I've ever had anything so delicate, and I wouldn't use it in case it got broke.'

'And have yer ever washed it in all those years?'

'Of course I haven't. I've been frightened to touch the bleeding thing, never mind wash it. And you'd better be careful 'cos I'm never likely to get anything else so fragile and dainty.'

'Oh, I won't have to worry about being careful, sunshine, 'cos I've no intention of drinking out of a cup that hasn't been washed in ten years. It's probably thick with dust, and has had creepy-crawlies walking all over it.'

'Ay, ye're not half a fussy blighter, Rita Wells.' Aggie was laughing inside as she picked up the delicate white china cup that was decorated with tiny pink flowers. 'I'll give it a rub with me pinny if that makes yer feel better.'

Rita gasped. 'What! I'd rather take a chance on the creepy-crawlies than your pinny. God knows what yer've spilt on it, let alone wiping yer hands down it after yer've cleaned the grate out and scrubbed the step. So I certainly ain't going to drink out of a cup that yer've wiped on that filthy pinny, I'm too young to die. Put the flaming thing back where it's been for the last ten years and get me a mug with chips and cracks in.'

The cup and saucer were put back in the dark depths of the sideboard, and probably wouldn't see daylight again for another ten years. 'Fussy bugger, that's what yer are. And just because ye're afraid of creepy-crawlies, and yer've kept on about it for the last ten minutes, the ruddy tea in the pot is stone cold now. So whatever it is yer have to tell me, queen, after all that, it had better be good.'

Rita suddenly remembered she'd left her front door wide open. 'You put the kettle on and boil enough water to warm the tea up, while I go and close me front door. I haven't got anything worth pinching, but what's mine is mine and I don't want no one else having it.'

She was back within seconds and Aggie was just carrying the kettle through. 'I only put enough water in to cover the bottom but the tea will be weak. So long as it's wet and warm I don't care, it's better than a slap in the face.' She put milk in the mugs, poured the tea out and then plonked herself down heavily on a wooden dining chair. 'Well, go on, queen, tell me what all the mystery is about? Make it as interesting as yer can so it'll give me something to think about all day while I'm doing me housework and then when we're out shopping.'

'I'm afraid there's no mystery about it, sunshine, but I believe yer will find it interesting. And it's for your ears only. Is that understood?' Rita waited for her friend's reluctant nod for Aggie was hopeless at keeping things to herself. 'It's about Mrs Sinclair – she's got another job and it's full-time. That's why she was going out early.'

'Oh, aye, what sort of a job is that, then? How come she can get a job and half the men in the street are out of work? And it's not for the want of trying. They're out at the crack of dawn down to the docks, hoping to get a day's work in.'

'She's been promoted to private secretary to one of the big nobs at the office she works in.' Rita could see that didn't go down well with her mate, who couldn't stand Mrs Sinclair. 'And if yer start making fun of her, I won't tell yer any more.'

Aggie put a hand to her mouth and muttered behind it, 'I promise I won't laugh, girl, at least not until yer've gone. Then I'll laugh me bloody head off. She was a snob before, so what's she going to be like now? Will she expect us to curtsey to her and pull our forelock?' Her eyes narrowed to slits. 'How do you know all this anyway?'

'She asked Bessie if she'd mind Amelia for two hours each night, 'cos working full-time she won't be home until after six.'

'Bessie didn't agree, did she?' Aggie tutted when she saw Rita nod. 'She wants her bleeding bumps feeling! She does all the hard work while Miss Hoity-Toity walks around as though she owns the place? I know what I'd have done, I'd have told her to get lost and then thrown her out.'

'Oh, and would yer have thrown young Amelia out as well?'

'Of course I wouldn't, she's only a kid. Yer can't blame her for having a stuck-up madam for a mother. I feel heartily sorry for the poor blighter.'

'So does Bessie, and that's the only reason she's agreed to mind her. She really loves that kid, and she's not half looking forward to having her for those two hours. Don't forget, Bessie hasn't got no family. She'll show that girl more love than her own mother does. Already she's talking about playing Snakes and Ladders and Ludo, and taking her to the park so she can have a go on the swings. That will have to be kept quiet, though, 'cos the queer one doesn't like the girl to play with the children round here. As yer say, Aggie, she's a bloody snob, but that doesn't mean we have to take it out on young Amelia whose life is miserable anyway.' Rita knew how to bring her friend round to her way of thinking. 'Anyway, I told Bessie I'd give her all the help I can, 'cos I've felt really sorry for the poor mite since the day they moved in across the street. That will be my good deed, and I'm sure God will chalk it up to me.'

'Ye're a crafty sod, Rita Wells, yer must think I'm as thick as two short planks. I'm supposed to say now that I'll be delighted to help, aren't I? Just so I'll get in His good books up in heaven.' Aggie pressed her thumbs into the fat around her elbows, leaving deep hollows. 'The way I look at it, we've lived next door to each other in this street for about fourteen years or thereabouts and never really had a falling out. So what I say is, if yer've got good neighbours then hang on to them. Which boils down to me saying I'll help with the young girl, as long as I don't have to get involved with her mother, 'cos I know that sooner or later I'd end up flopping her one. Yer can tell Bessie I'm here if she wants me, and yer can also tell her I'll keep me gob shut. And now that little matter is settled to our mutual satisfaction, can I ask if yer have any influence in heaven?'

'No more than anyone else, sunshine, I just do the best I can in life. The only sin I ever commit is telling a little white lie, and

I'm sure I won't have that held against me. I believe God is very fair-minded.'

Aggie wrinkled her nose and swung her head from side to side, her chubby cheeks wobbling. 'It doesn't sound very promising, that, girl, 'cos it means yer can't put in a good word for me. What yer *could* do for me, and it won't cost yer nothing only a little breath, yer could casually bring my name up in yer prayers each night. That way He would get to know me.'

'Why don't yer say what yer want to in yer own prayers each night? It would be in your favour to do it personally.' Rita saw a blush spread across Aggie's face. 'Aggie Gordon, yer don't say any prayers, do yer? Well, shame on yer, that's all I can say.'

'I do say prayers, queen, cross my heart and hope to die. It's just not every night, like what you do.' Aggie put on the woe-begone expression which to her friend was a sign that excuses were on the way. 'Yer see, I'm so worn out by the time me head hits the pillow, I'm fast asleep before I know what's happening. It's hard going looking after a husband and two children, and doing the washing, ironing, cooking and shopping. I never seem to have a minute to meself.'

Rita tutted. 'It's no good moaning to me 'cos yer won't get any sympathy. Yer seem to forget I've got a husband and two kids, the same as you!'

Aggie injected a whine into her voice, which she was very good at and did for fun. 'Well it's like this, yer see, queen. You don't moan, so how can anyone give yer sympathy if they don't feel sorry for yer? Me now, I can put on a miserable face and a crying voice, and before yer can say Jack Robinson, folk are asking what they can do to help. Yer should try it, 'cos it never fails for me.'

Rita knew this was a load of rubbish, and thought she'd throw in some of her own to even things out. 'And you're daft enough to think people like yer and feel really sorry for the hard-done-by Aggie Gordon? That only shows how stupid yer are! Yer should hear what they're saying behind yer back. Calling yer fit to burn, they are.'

'Ye're only making that up, Rita Wells, 'cos yer know the neighbours like me more than they do you, and ye're jealous. And there's nothing worse than jealousy. I can't help it if I'm more popular than you are.'

Rita looked at the clock. Another five minutes of this comedy and then she'd better be on her way and get some housework done. But she'd make good use of the five minutes, she couldn't let her mate get the better of her. 'Yer live in a dream world, Aggie, a little world of yer own. If yer'd heard what Mrs Sloane said about yer in the butcher's last Thursday, it would have brought yer down to earth. Her and Mrs Johnson called yer for everything.' Rita spread her hands. 'I stuck up for yer though, sunshine, 'cos I couldn't stand there and let them pull me best mate to pieces.'

Aggie's arms appeared like magic from beneath her bosom to press upon the table. 'When did yer say this was, queen?'

'It was last Thursday morning, about half-eleven. I'm so sure of the day and time, 'cos I remember wondering how I was going to manage two days on the tanner I had in me purse.'

'Oh, yeah, I remember that now, 'cos I had a penny more than you did!' Aggie rubbed two fingers on each of her temples and closed her eyes, imitating the actions of a gypsy who came to the street about once a year to ask if she could read their fortunes for a penny. The women in the street had got together and said if she would only charge a ha'penny, then they'd all have their fortunes told.

Aggie began to groan. 'Oh, yeah, it's all coming clear now, I was standing next to someone – I can't clearly make the face out, but I think it's my neighbour and best friend . . . Rita Wells. We were in the butcher's together waiting to be served.' She frowned as though deep in concentration. 'But I can't see Mrs Sloane or Mrs Johnson, and I can't feel their presence. Oh, it's all fading now, my mind is going blank.' She fell back in the chair, seemingly worn out by the experience. 'Oh, I do feel drained.' Then a smile spread across her chubby face. 'That was good, that, wasn't it, girl? Passed a bit of time away.'

'Anybody listening to us would think we were two sheets to the wind, yer know that, don't yer?' Rita pushed her chair back. 'I'm glad I got someone as daft as meself for a neighbour 'cos it adds a bit of spice to me life. But I'm going to love yer and leave yer now, and get me dishes washed and the grate cleaned out. The washing has been steeping all night in the dolly tub, so the worst of the dirt will be out. I'll have a bash with the dolly peg for a few minutes, then rinse the clothes, put them through the mangle and have them on the line in no time. There's a bit of a blow out, so they should be ready for ironing tonight.'

Aggie put her hands flat on the table and pushed herself up. 'What time will yer be ready for the shops? Say half-eleven?'

'That's fine, sunshine, I'll give yer a knock as near to that as I can. And don't sit down again when I'm gone, get cracking on yer housework.'

Aggie stood to attention, as did her bosom, and saluted. 'Aye, aye, sir! Three bleeding bags full, sir!'

Over the years since her fall from grace Evelyn had made the most of the clothes she had. No one would have guessed on the Monday morning when she entered the office that her coat and dress were years old, and that she'd spent the weekend sponging and pressing them. She was an attractive woman, with an eye-catching figure. Buoyed up with newfound confidence she walked with the air of a woman who knew what she wanted in life and intended to have it. And adding to her feeling of well-being was the news that Mr Simon had decided that as Miss Saunders would be spending a lot of time in his office over the next two weeks, making sure that everything was up-to-date for his nephew to take over, her office could be assigned to Mr

Philip and his new private secretary. He would, of course, have to spend some time with his uncle, familiarising himself with those clients who were important to the firm, but several hours a day could be spent getting his secretary used to his way of working. Although Evelyn kept her cool exterior when told the news, she was gloating inside.

Philip Astbury was already in his temporary office when Evelyn opened the door. He was sitting in a leather swivel chair, smartly dressed as usual and wearing a satisfied grin. He jumped to his feet when she entered and waved to the chair on the opposite side of the desk. He was congratulating himself on being so lucky in having been handed such a stunning-looking woman to work for him. He was sure they were going to get on very well together. 'Good morning, Mrs Sinclair. My Uncle Simon has kindly given us the use of this office until such time as he and Miss Saunders finally retire. Jolly thoughtful of him, don't you agree?'

'Extremely generous.' Evelyn placed her handbag at the side of the chair, took her time over sitting down, and once seated crossed one slender leg over the other. It was done deliberately to catch his attention, and she smiled inwardly as she saw his eyes following the movement. 'We must show our gratitude by taking full advantage of his kind offer.' She bent down to take a note-pad from her bag. 'I have been practising my shorthand over the weekend and feel I have made real progress. Perhaps you would like to dictate a letter to an imaginary client, to test my speed?' She lowered her eyelids seductively and said softly, 'You see, I aim to please.'

'Oh, I have no doubt I shall be well pleased, Mrs Sinclair.' Philip sat up straight and leaned his elbows on the desk. 'So, this letter to an imaginary client. Shall we begin?'

Evelyn had her pencil poised in readiness. 'May I crave your indulgence, Mr Philip, and ask that you do not dictate too quickly? Otherwise I shall become very embarrassed and my hand will shake. Now, can I have the name and address of the client, please?'

His eyes shining with laughter, Philip said, 'How about my writing to a certain charming lady by the name of Evelyn Sinclair, to ask if she would do me the honour of having lunch with me today? I'm sure Uncle Simon would not be too upset if he were to lunch alone at his club, and it would give you and me a chance to get better acquainted?'

Although her heart was fluttering, and she would indeed be delighted to dine with such an attractive man, Evelyn let her head rule. To rush into anything would be completely the wrong thing to do with a man who was obviously very fond of getting his own way with the female sex. The thought of a nice meal in one of the finest restaurants was tempting, but Evelyn was aiming higher than a few stolen moments.

'I really don't think so, Mr Philip.' She met his eyes and held them. 'I think we should keep our relationship on a strictly boss and secretary basis.' Head bent slightly, and eyelids fanning her cheeks, she said softly, 'At least, for the time being.'

'Oh, and how long is for the time being? It could be anything from a moment to a year or more. Would you really be so cruel to your new boss?'

'That is the problem, Mr Philip, don't you see? It is because you are my boss that I must not be seen to be taking advantage of you by flirting. Perhaps when we know each other better we will be able to meet away from the office and the gossiping.'

'Is that a promise I can hold you to, Mrs Sinclair?'

Evelyn was very sure of this because she had lain awake in bed last night planning the whole operation. And so far it was working just as she had planned. 'Yes, Mr Philip, that is a promise you can hold me to. And I'll see if it can be arranged in the not too distant future.' Lifting her pad, she said, 'Now, can we proceed with the letter to the imaginary client, please?'

* * *

That evening, as she sat on the tram on her journey home, Evelyn told herself she must somehow find the money for new clothes if she was to make a real impression on a man-about-town like Mr Philip. His family were almost as rich as the Lister-Sinclairs, very well known in the higher social circle. The dress she had on today was dark blue, knee-length, and showed off her figure to perfection. It had cost a fortune when new, and she had certainly had her money's worth out it. She also had a deep maroon one, also well-cut and fitting her very well. But two working dresses were not enough; she really needed another two, at least. Her mind went to the large trunk in her bedroom which was filled to the brim with fine silk dresses, long and short, several silk and satin shoulder capes, feather boas, costume jewellery, shoes made of the softest leather, and several wide-brimmed hats. None of these had been out of the trunk since Charles had gone off to war, for with his death had come an end to her social life. Nothing in that trunk was any good for day wear, but she was sure there would be something suitable that she could wear to go out for an evening meal with Mr Philip. She'd go through the trunk tonight, after Amelia had gone to sleep. Thinking of her brought a frown to Evelyn's face. How could she get ahead in life when her daughter would always be holding her back? For Evelyn was under no illusion about her new boss. The admiration and desire in his eyes would soon disappear if he found out she had a seven-year-old daughter.

Evelyn saw her tram stop looming up, and made her way down the aisle to the platform. As she waited for the tram to come to a shuddering halt, she reminded herself that her daughter would be eight a week on Saturday, and was having tea with Miss Maudsley then. This gave birth to an idea of how she could manage an evening being wined and dined by Mr Philip. Stepping down on to the pavement, Evelyn told herself it would be simple enough to find an excuse for asking her neighbour if she would allow Amelia to stay with her until ten o'clock. After all, there would be no school the next day so the girl could have an extra hour in bed. Oh, there would be a way around it, she was sure. There had to be if she were ever to get out of the working-class rut she was in.

While her mother was thinking of ways to off-load her daughter on to her neighbour, Amelia was in Bessie's kitchen helping to dry the dishes. Her pretty face was flushed with laughter. Oh, the last two hours had been the happiest of her life! Miss Bessie was so funny, and it was a nice change not to have to worry about what she said. 'I can come tomorrow, can't I, Miss Bessie? We can play Snakes and Ladders again, and you won't have to let me win 'cos I know how to play it now.'

'Of course yer can come, sweetheart, it's been a pleasure having someone to talk to and laugh with.' Bessie handed a plate over to be dried. 'I usually talk to the fireplace, and though we get on fine, there's not much fun when yer never get an answer to a question.'

Amelia's chuckle filled the tiny kitchen. 'You don't really talk to the fireplace, do yer, Miss Bessie?'

She kept the smile on her face, but groaned inside. Already there were signs of a Scouse accent creeping into the girl's voice, and her mother would not be very happy about that. But Her Ladyship couldn't put all the blame on Bessie, for the girl had been telling Bessie about the friends she'd made at school, and how she played with them in the playground. It was a dead cert they all had accents you could cut with a knife. 'Don't lose that nice way of speaking yer have, sweetheart, or yer mother will think it's my fault and have me life. It's no good saying I'll learn to speak posh, 'cos I'm too old to change the habits of a lifetime even if I wanted to, which I don't. I believe everyone should be natural, and not try and change themselves to please other folk.'

'My friends all speak like you, Miss Bessie, and I do when I'm in school. Only not in front of my mother because she's very strict.'

Bessie took her hands from the soapy water and pulled the plug out of the sink. As she watched the water running away, she thought what a sad life this young child had. In a roundabout way, when they were playing board games, she had asked what games Amelia had at home. Her face as innocent as a new-born babe's, the child had answered that her mother didn't believe in games, they were a waste of time. She was set homework to do by her mother apparently, and not allowed to leave the table until it was completed and every question right.

'I think I heard the latch on the entry door open, sweetheart, so yer mother must be here for yer,' Bessie told her now.

The expression on Amelia's face changed completely, from a happy little girl's to that of someone afraid they are going to be reprimanded for doing something wrong. 'Don't forget to tell my mother I've been good, and ask if I can come again tomorrow?'

This was all that could be said before the knock came on the door. 'Come in, Mrs Sinclair,' Bessie called. 'Your daughter has been helping me wash and dry our dishes. I hope yer don't mind me giving Amelia some dinner, do yer? It just means me cooking a bit extra, but if you have any objection then I'll just give her a cup of tea and she can wait until you come home for her meal.'

No matter what Bessie had asked, Evelyn would have agreed. She needed this little woman, for she had no friends she could call on to mind her daughter. 'That is extremely kind of you, Miss Maudsley, and I do hope Amelia was gracious in her thanks.' Her voice was so sickly sweet, Bessie turned her head away. If it weren't for the girl, and her affection for her, she would have told this false, lying snob to go to hell.

'Amelia has been a pleasure to have as a guest. She is very polite, doesn't answer back or give cheek, and we get on very well together.' And for good measure, she added, 'And her table manners are impeccable.' That was a big word for Bessie, who felt like sticking out her tongue and telling Her Ladyship she wasn't the only one who could get her tongue around big words and know the meaning of them. 'If you still want me to mind her for two hours every night I'll be delighted, and I'll give her a meal.'

'You really are too kind, Miss Maudsley, and perhaps one day I will be in a position to repay your kindness.' For the first time, Evelyn acknowledged her daughter. 'You are a very lucky girl, Amelia, and I'm only agreeing to Miss Maudsley having you each night on the strict understanding that you behave yourself and do exactly as you are told. Do you understand?'

In a tiny voice, devoid of any emotion, she answered, 'Yes, Mother.'

Chapter Seven

It was eight o'clock when Evelyn told her daughter it was time for her to go to bed. Amelia didn't object. She was longing to lie quietly and go over all the things Miss Bessie had said and done, and the way they'd laughed at silly things her mother would only have frowned at. There had never in her life been a goodnight kiss or a hug, so after saying, 'Goodnight, Mother,' the girl climbed the stairs. She didn't run up them, even though she wanted to, for that would have brought a sharp rebuke, and she didn't want anything to spoil the day. And tonight she didn't shiver when she slid in between the cold sheets, for she had a hand over her mouth so her mother wouldn't hear her giggles. It had been so funny when Miss Bessie had told the fireplace to keep quiet and not to interrupt. And then she'd pretended it answered back, and said, 'Don't be so flaming cheeky, I won't tell yer again. Anyone would think yer owned the house, the way yer carry on.'

Downstairs, Evelyn told herself to wait half an hour to give her daughter time to go to sleep. Amelia wasn't allowed in her bedroom, and although she may have seen the trunk through the open door, had no idea of its contents. That was the way it would stay. The less the child knew about her previous life, the better. She had been told very bluntly that her father had been killed in the war and wasn't encouraged to ask further questions. What she didn't know she couldn't pass on, and that was how Evelyn wanted it. So, while Amelia was reliving every second of the time she'd spent next door, her mother was making plans for a future that would take her back to the good life she had known, and which she longed to regain.

Exactly half an hour after her daughter had gone to bed, Evelyn lit a candle and placed it in the middle of a saucer. Then she made her way quietly up the steep, narrow stairs, lit by the flickering flame. She stood on the landing for a few seconds, her ear to the door of her daughter's room. Satisfied the child was asleep, she entered her own bedroom and closed the door. Then she put the saucer on the floor near the trunk before taking a large, rusty key from the top drawer of the tallboy. At first she thought she wasn't going to be able to open the trunk, for over the years the lock had rusted inside too and she couldn't turn the key in it. It would have been easier if she'd knelt down to do it, and shown a little patience.

But patience was not one of Evelyn's virtues, and there was much tutting and clicking of her tongue before the key finally turned. 'Confounded thing,' she muttered when she lifted the lid and it creaked loudly. The smell of dampness was another irritant which had her wrinkling her nose. Not for a second would she take the blame for not having opened the trunk before now, so the clothes could be aired. But then, nothing was ever her fault. In her mind there were two people responsible for her present plight: Charles for being killed, and Amelia for being born. But she intended to turn her life around as soon as possible. And to do that she must put on a front. She had never allowed herself to become friendly with the staff of Astbury and Woodward, and they knew nothing of her circumstances, which was fortunate. So as far as Philip was concerned, she wasn't poor but a well-to-do widow who had the means to live comfortably without a man in her life.

The candle was too low to give much light out, so Evelyn carried a wooden chair from the side of her bed and placed it by the trunk. Then she set the saucer on it, and nodded as if to say that was much better and she could see what she was doing now. The first thing she touched when she put her hand in the trunk was a feather boa, and as she shook it out memories came flooding back. It was one of the first things she had bought with the allowance her father had given her. This, and much of the clothing in the trunk, had been paid for by him as he saw Evelyn as his passport into the higher echelons of Liverpool society. But things hadn't gone the way anyone planned when Charles was killed in 1917. That in itself hadn't upset Herbert and Gertrude Wilkinson too much, for their daughter was now a member of the Lister-Sinclair family and could still be their means of joining the ranks of the very rich. However, when they found out she was pregnant, believing her marriage to Charles had not been consummated, they blamed her bitterly and disowned her. She hadn't seen them since. Not that it worried her, for she'd never had any love for her penny-pinching parents. She had never made the connection, but now she was treating her daughter exactly as they had treated her.

Evelyn laid the feather boa on the lino and leaned into the trunk to see if there was anything fit for her to wear on an evening out with Philip. Fortunately she had kept her slim figure, so the clothes would fit, but were they good enough? Were they still fashionable or would they look dated? She hadn't been to a social gathering for eight years and didn't know if the fashions had changed greatly. She hadn't noticed much change in everyday wear, except in the length of day clothes. Nowadays women wore them anywhere between knee and ankle-length. Cloche hats were still in vogue, though, and she knew there were two or three in the trunk. But would they be fit to wear or would the moths have eaten into them?

Delving into the darkness of the trunk once more, Evelyn came up with a dress that brought a smile of triumph to her face. It was a long blue gown in the finest silk which was a joy to the touch. It had full-length sleeves which were slit from the shoulder to be gathered together into a cuff at the wrist. It was low-cut to back and front, to reveal her spine and the cleft between her breasts. She held the dress to her, as though welcoming an old friend, and whispered, 'Please don't let the moths have got to you.' She draped it carefully over one arm while with the other she reached into the trunk to search for the cape which had been bought to match the dress. When she felt the material in her hand, she felt like shouting for joy. It was impossible in the candlelight to tell if there were any moth holes in it, but light enough to see it was a beautiful, knee-length cape in the same material as the dress with a diamanté clasp at the neck.

Evelyn sat back on her heels. If these garments had stood the passage of time, they would certainly pass the most critical eye. She remembered walking down Bold Street with Charles and seeing them in the window of the most expensive shop in the city. She had stopped to admire them, and of course the outcome was the one she'd hoped for. Charles insisted he'd buy them for her, and half an hour later she was walking down the street with the cord of a square silver dress box over her wrist, and her head in the clouds. Charles had offered to carry the box but she would have none of it. The name on the box and its shape were exclusive to the only shop in the city to have a uniformed man standing outside to open the door for customers, and then wave their carriage or automobile down.

There was a deep sigh from Evelyn as she remembered the heady feeling of buying only from the best shops and dining in only the best hotels and restaurants. Having a man admiring you across the table, and knowing there wasn't another woman who could beat you for looks or style. And she could make it happen again if she had the right clothes to wear, and a good address to invite prospective suitors to. She smoothed the soft material of the dress and cape draped over her arm, and decided: I'll take them downstairs to try them on and see if they still fit. If I raise the gas, it may give me enough light to check for moth holes. If fate is kind, and the clothes are wearable, I'll put them on hangers and hang them outside the wardrobe in the hope of getting rid of the smell. Then at least I will have one stylish, attractive outfit to wear. And who knows what else the trunk may produce?

So many years had passed she couldn't remember what she had packed into it, and it was too dark now to have a really good clear out. Perhaps she could get up half an hour early tomorrow and begin her search, before her daughter was awake. She'd do it a bit at a time, when Amelia wasn't around.

Evelyn shivered as she slipped the dress over her head. The material was cold, and the smell of damp sickening. It still fitted her, though, and as she ran her hands down the sides, she prided herself that it clung to her figure. If there was no moth damage, the one way of treating it so it would come up like new, and without the smell, was to have it cleaned at the Chinese laundry. It would probably cost a few shillings to have both dress and cape cleaned, but that was a small price to pay. The increase in her salary would start from Saturday, and although she had to pay Miss Maudsley a shilling a week, she would still be a few shillings better off. More even, as her neighbour was going to give Amelia a dinner every night. And she had asked if she could do it, it wasn't as though she was doing it out of pity for them. No, it was more likely they were doing her a favour, for, after all, it must be a lonely life not having any family.

When she finally climbed the stairs to bed, Evelyn felt younger than she had for years and in a more pleasant frame of mind. She had decided on her new future, and not for a second did she think she would fail.

At the precise moment Evelyn was climbing the stairs, Philip was lying in the arms of a very pretty young woman, paying her sugary compliments and claiming she was the most wonderful girl he'd ever had the pleasure of meeting. And the young girl blushed at his compliments for, at nineteen years of age, she had never met up with a charmer before, and believed he was sincere in what he was saying. Had her parents known where she was, and with whom, they would have been horrified. Philip was at least eleven or twelve years her senior, and although he didn't have a bad reputation, he was well known by his close friends for playing the field. But the girl's parents would not find out, for although she was young and inexperienced in the ways of romancing, she wasn't stupid enough to tell them; she knew what their reaction would be. And she did so want to see Philip again, he was so interesting, amusing, and a real man of the world.

'And what is my lovely Charlotte thinking now?' he asked, his finger running down a cheek as soft as silk. They'd met at a soiree in the home of one of his friends, and as Charlotte was the youngest and prettiest female there, Philip had lost no time in making her acquaintance. With the drink flowing, and the many conversations going on in the room becoming louder, it was almost impossible to hear each other. So Philip had taken her hand, and making sure they weren't seen, had led her to the study where he knew it would be quiet and there was a very convenient and comfortable chaise-longue. Charlotte wasn't worldly enough to know that going into an empty room with a strange man might not be the thing to do. Philip had in fact no intention of going beyond the bounds of decency. His trouble was, he was a born womaniser and couldn't help flirting with a pretty young girl. Had she been older, or married but available and willing, then he might have been more daring and taken his chances. But he wouldn't deliberately court trouble, especially in the home of one of his best friends.

'My father is sending the car to pick me up at half-past ten,' Charlotte said. 'I don't want to go, but I'm afraid I must. But will you promise we'll meet again soon, Philip, so I have something to look forward to? I really would like us to be friends.'

As soon as a female began to get serious, he backed away. He had heard the phrase 'shotgun wedding', and he was looking for fun, not a married life of so-called bliss. 'I'm sure we'll meet up again, my love, we're bound to. Most of my friends know your parents, so I have no doubt we will see each other again in the very near future.' Philip swung his legs off the chaise-longue. 'It's almost ten-thirty now. I'll walk with you to the front door and see you safely into the car. We'll pick up your coat on the way.'

On the front step of the large house which was now brightly lit, Charlotte reached for Philip's hand. 'Promise you'll see me again very soon?'

'I'll try, my love, but I am not a free agent. I have a job to go to every day, and apart from the time I spend at the office, I often have to take work home with me. I still live with my parents and feel duty bound to spend some time with them. But I do have some free evenings, of course I do, and I'm sure that the next party I go to, you will also attend. Anyway, my lovely Charlotte, you are so pretty you will always be sought after by men nearer your own age and far more suitable than myself. I promise that if we meet again at a mutual friend's house, and I see you with a very handsome Romeo, I will not try to steal you away from him. So go now, my love, don't keep the chauffeur waiting any longer. And do give my kind regards to your parents.' He waited until she was safely in the car, waved her off, then breathed a sigh of relief when he went back into the house.

In the wide hall, brightly lit by a huge scintillating chandelier, Philip was met by his friend and host Nigel, who raised his brows and shook his head slightly. 'You're sailing close to the wind, old boy. She is far too young for you, and her father is very protective. So take care, my friend.'

'Nigel, my dear boy, I may be many things but stupid I am not. Nor am I a rotter. I didn't lay a finger on the girl, didn't even kiss her goodnight although she stood with lips pouted in readiness. And despite her pleas, I have not promised to see her again. Like yourself, I prefer someone nearer my own age who is responsible for their own actions.'

'Don't compare us, Philip, I happen to be a very happily married man. If Marigold had heard you say that, she would have raised hell with me and never let me out of her sight again.' Nigel grinned. 'And I would never leave you alone in a room with my wife, even though you profess to be my best friend.'

'Have no fear, old boy, I have my sights set on a very attractive older woman. She has worked for Astbury and Woodward for several years, and as Uncle Simon's secretary is retiring too, luck was on my side and I acquired this lovely vision for my personal secretary. She hasn't fallen for my charms yet, but it's early days. She may be testing me, playing hard to get, or maybe she genuinely doesn't fancy me. Which would be quite a let-down for me. She's tall, very attractive, with dark hair, liquid brown eyes and a curvaceous figure. So while I have Mrs Sinclair in my sights, I am not really interested in any other female.'

'Mrs Sinclair? You mean you intend to pursue a married woman?' Nigel was taken aback. 'Shame on you, Philip.'

'You have it wrong again, dear boy. Mrs Sinclair is a widow. Very little is known about her at the office, apparently, she's not the talkative type. All that is known is that her husband was killed in battle in seventeen, not long after they were married. I find the aura of mystery surrounding her both thrilling and challenging and have made a vow to woo her, solve the mystery and claim the prize.'

Nigel again raised his eyebrows. He was very fond of his friend, who was always good company and very loyal. But with the best will in the world, no one could say Philip was not a terror for a pretty face. 'And providing she allows you to woo her and win her, what then?'

Philip flashed the grin no woman could resist. Both old and young were captivated by it. 'Ah, well, I'm not looking that far ahead, old boy. At the moment I'm attracted and intrigued, but once I've won the chase, who knows?'

Nigel's wife Marigold came looking for him then. She was very much in love with her husband, but could see why so many of her friends fell head over heels for Philip. He really was an attractive devil. 'Oh, and what are you two cooking up? We have guests, Nigel, and mustn't neglect them.'

'I'm coming now, my love, but would you kindly lock all the good-looking, available women in the study, please, where Philip can't get at them? I'm just giving him a lecture on his womanising. It really is time he settled down and gave his parents the grandchildren they long for before they grow too old to appreciate them.'

'Now you go too far, Nigel.' Philip feigned horror. 'In one fell swoop you would have me married off to a sensible little woman who would set to and bear several children to keep my parents happy.' He put a hand to his forehead. 'The mere thought is enough to bring on a headache. Come on, be a good host and give your guest a glass of champers before he faints.'

Marigold linked his arm. 'I'll look after you while Nigel fetches you a drink. I'll introduce you to a merry widow who has pots of money and is looking for someone to lavish it on.'

Philip pretended to draw away. 'Oh, no, not another merry widow! Why do all my friends wheel me out whenever they're a man short? And I don't know why you use the phrase "merry widow", because they're usually wearing thick make-up to hide the fact that they're ancient. I know some young men have no objection to being kept by a woman old enough to be their grandmother, as long as the money and expensive presents keep coming their way. But I do not need the money or expensive gifts, nor am I a kind enough person to flatter an elderly woman by telling her she looks twenty years younger than she actually is. Let them grow old gracefully, that's what I say. So, Marigold, my darling, I'll have the drink but not the woman.'

'Why don't you tell her you already have a beauty in your sights, Philip?' Nigel said as they made their way towards the loud laughter and voices coming from the drawing room. 'I'm sure Marigold would love to pass on that piece of information, and revel in the disappointment on the face of every female guest.'

She squeezed his arm. 'Oh, do tell, Philip, is what Nigel said true?' Again she squeezed his arm. 'Can you hear the noise of laughter and people shouting to make themselves heard? Well, if I repeat what my darling husband has just said, the female voices will all fall silent and the men will have smiles on their faces as they gloat over the fact that at last someone has stolen your heart and you are no longer a threat to their wives, lovers and sweethearts. Oh, I can't wait to tell them.'

'I think that would be a little premature, my dear Marigold, and the day may come when you are forced to eat your words. So I think silence would be a virtue right now, and perhaps for the next few weeks. I've a feeling Mrs Sinclair is not going to be an easy conquest.'

The next morning Philip was no further advanced with his secretary for her face showed no emotion whatsoever. She most certainly wasn't outgoing, didn't speak unless it was necessary, nor did she smile much. Her greeting to him when he arrived at the office didn't hold much warmth. Still, he told himself, it was early days yet. He would take things slowly, so she wouldn't be put off.

Little did Philip know that every movement and every word was calculated to heighten his interest and admiration. When Evelyn crossed her legs it was done slowly, for effect. She sat upright in the chair, shoulders back to emphasise her breasts in the well-fitted maroon dress. Her eyelashes were used to great effect, and her words spoken softly, in a husky voice. To an onlooker, it would be difficult to say which one was the hunter in this room where there was an unmistakable atmosphere.

'Mr Philip, would you be kind enough to dictate a little faster this morning? Just to see if my speed has improved at all. I did spend an hour on it last night, and feel I have improved a little.' Evelyn's big brown eyes held his as she took a gamble. 'I realise it must be troublesome for you to have been landed with a secretary who isn't up to speed. I would understand if you thought I wasn't up to the job and would perhaps prefer to find someone more suited to your needs?'

'Good gracious, Mrs Sinclair, do you see me as so hard-hearted? I wouldn't dream of replacing you with someone else. I am sure you are more than capable and we will get along very well together.' Then came the grin that usually brought results. 'Besides, where am I likely to find another woman as lovely as yourself? No, from the first time I saw you, I had no doubts that we would suit each other beautifully.'

'You are very kind, Mr Philip.' Evelyn thought it was now time for her to pay compliment. 'There are not many men who would be as patient as you, and I hope you realise I am most appreciative of your understanding. I promise I will repay your kindness, patience, and the faith you have in me. I will not let you down.'

Philip leaned his elbows on the desk. 'Now it is getting interesting. I wonder how you will repay me, Mrs Sinclair? Would it be by returning favour if I were to ask for one?'

Pretending to be shy, Evelyn lowered her head. This was an opening, but she didn't want him thinking she was going to be an easy catch. If she gave in too quickly to a man like Philip, he would soon tire of her. 'Really, you do put me on the spot, Mr Philip. Of course I would be happy to do you a favour, but that would depend upon what it was you were asking of me.'

He chuckled. 'There's no reason to look so serious, Mrs Sinclair. I wouldn't ask you to rob a bank or murder someone. No, it would be a favour we could share and enjoy. Does that not make you curious, not tempt you?'

'It makes me curious, certainly, but how can I be tempted when I know nothing of your intentions?'

Philip decided to take the plunge. 'Would dinner at the State Hotel not be tempting? I can assure you they serve excellent food to a very select clientele.'

Evelyn nodded. 'Ah, yes, the State. It is many years since I was last there, but I do remember they serve excellent food. I also remember the atmosphere there was always pleasant and never noisy.'

'In that case, would you not like to sample the fare there again, Mrs Sinclair? Just for a couple of hours one evening, when you are free.'

'I have plenty of free time, Mr Philip, because I have absolutely no ties whatsoever. It is not lack of time that would stop me, but the fact that you are my boss. It might appear to some that any association between us, outside the office, would be inappropriate. I'm quite certain that tongues would wag.'

'And that would be your only concern, that tongues might wag?'

'Oh, the concern wouldn't be for myself, Mr Philip, for I only have myself to consider, and I never listen to gossip, anyway. It is you for whom I would be concerned.'

As he swung the swivel chair from side to side, Philip laughed heartily. 'My dear Mrs Sinclair, I can assure you that there is, and always has been, lots of gossip about me. Why am I not married, for instance? Thirty years of age and still a bachelor! Oh, I could recount many things I've heard said about myself, mostly behind my back. But I am my own person, it is my life, and I really don't care what opinion people hold of me. I have a lot of true friends, who know the real Philip Astbury, and along with my parents they are the only ones I care about. As for office gossip, well, if anyone dared, I would laugh first, then give them a week's notice.'

Evelyn allowed herself a rare smile. She wasn't to know, but when she allowed that her face was transformed and she looked years younger. 'Oh, that's very drastic, Mr Philip, I really will have to watch myself. I enjoy working here and would not like to be given a week's notice for bad behaviour.'

'Then you had better keep on the right side of me, had you not?' Philip's tone was teasing. 'So, is it to be dinner at the State one night, or do I serve you with a week's notice?'

'I am sure I would find it very pleasant, and also sure you would be an entertaining escort. But I must admit to being afraid of what your Uncle Simon would say if he knew? Would he perhaps think me a gold digger?'

'Good grief, Mrs Sinclair, my uncle is well used to my taking lovely ladies out for meals. So too are my parents. And as I have said, apart from family and close friends, I really don't care what anyone else thinks about me. So forgot all this tosh, and say you will do me the honour of allowing me to take you out for a meal one night? To cement our friendship, shall we say?'

Evelyn pondered as she tapped her pencil on the note-pad on her knee. 'And no one in this office would ever find out about it? As I am a very private person, that is important to me.'

'You have my word.' Philip was so pleased at the way things were going, he would have promised her anything. 'The office staff, my uncle, even my parents, won't be told. Now does that meet all your demands?'

'They are not demands, Mr Philip, I'm merely making sure my private life remains private. Anyway, I'm not sure I have a dress grand enough for the State, I will have to look through my wardrobe tonight. It is sadly depleted, unfortunately. After my husband died, I lost my zest for parties. But I'm fairly sure I can find something that won't embarrass you.'

'And how long am I going to have to wait for this night I am already growing excited about? This week, perhaps?'

Evelyn knew exactly when she would be going out with him, but had to make sure of her clothes first, and also work out what to do about Amelia. 'If not this week, then definitely next. Although I have to say, I am still not sure that this is a good thing. We have only known each other a week, and after two hours in each other's company may end up finding we have absolutely nothing in common. I may even find myself out of a job.'

'I think along different lines, my dear Mrs Sinclair. I believe we are going to get on wonderfully well together.'

Evelyn was in high spirits when she stepped off the tram. Before she'd fallen asleep last night, she had divided her plan into three phases. The first was to captivate Philip Astbury. For once he was hooked, she would never release him. The second phase was to sort herself out with the right clothes. And the third, and perhaps hardest, phase was to find a way of having Amelia minded on the night she wanted to be free. It wouldn't only be for one night either, she had high hopes of returning permanently to the good life. She couldn't abandon her daughter completely for if the neighbours found out the girl was in the house on her own they would create ructions. The only person who might be of help was Miss Maudsley. How fortunate the woman was fond of Amelia. But what excuse could she make? It could be tricky. Her neighbour was uneducated but not stupid by any means.

Evelyn loitered by a block of shops. It was part of the plan for her to be a little late tonight. She wasn't seeing anything in the windows, her mind was too full of all she was greedy for. A good life for herself. It could come about, but she must tread carefully or Philip would find out she was a liar and a fraud. She dawdled for a further five minutes, then turned the corner into her street. Reaching Bessie's yard door via the entry, she paused to force a smile to her face.

'I'm sorry I'm a little late this evening,' she said when Bessie opened the door. 'But I had the most marvellous surprise while I was waiting in Lord Street for my tram home. Standing at the same stop was a girl I went to school with. I haven't seen her for fifteen years.'

'Come in.' Bessie closed the door behind her neighbour and waved her to the living room, where Amelia was playing with a board game. 'Say hello to yer mother, Amelia.'

The girl lifted her head, the dice in her hand ready to throw. 'Hello, Mother.'

Her greeting was answered by a nod as Evelyn sat down and carried on with the lie she had rehearsed. 'Oh, it was truly wonderful! We were both so happy to each other again after all those years. Her name was Elizabeth Donaldson then, but she's married now and Mrs Waterson. She has two children, both at boarding school, and had been shopping in the city. Her husband was picking her up in his car, they'd arranged for her to be at the tram stop. As Elizabeth said, she could have got a taxi home but her husband wouldn't hear of it. So we had much to talk about, too little time.'

Bessie had taken a seat next to Amelia. She leaned her elbows on the table and cupped her chin in her hands. She listened without interrupting, but many thoughts were running through her head. Her usually stuck-up neighbour was being very friendly tonight, too friendly for Bessie's liking. There was something in the wind, but she was in no hurry to find out what, just let her neighbour carry on. They say if you give liars enough rope they will hang themselves, so this should be interesting. Bessie would bet a pound to a pinch of snuff Mrs Sinclair was lying through her teeth at the moment.

Putting Bessie's silence down to the fact that she was interested in her news, Evelyn carried on with her make-believe. 'She asked me to visit her one night so we could talk about our school days and the friends we had. And our teachers, of course, who were very strict and very old-fashioned! But, although I said I would try to visit her, I really don't see how I can. It would mean leaving Amelia in the house on her own . . .'

Bessie wasn't falling for that. And she'd just remembered another saying her mother used to have. It went something like:

liars always get found out in the end 'cos they forget who they've told lies to. Yes, that was it. She could see her mother's face now in her mind, saying, 'Yer need to have a good memory to be a liar.' And Mrs Sinclair was certainly coming out with some whoppers. 'Oh, that's a pity, it would have been nice for yer, talking about yer school days with yer friend.'

Evelyn was growing irritated. She needed to sort something out tonight. Otherwise, if she told Philip tomorrow she hadn't got a definite date in mind, he'd think she was messing him around, or else hiding something from him. As she was. 'I wonder if I could go to visit her next Saturday, since you have kindly offered to have Amelia for tea? Would you mind?'

'It's got nothing to do with me what yer do, ye're old enough to make yer own decisions. I'm having Amelia for tea, so what you do in that time is yer own business.'

'Oh, you are so kind. I will really look forward to catching up with Elizabeth's news as I don't get out very often. And would you mind if I was a little late getting home? I should hate to just rush in and out, we have so much to catch up with.'

Oh, so that's your game, is it? Bessie thought. We're getting to the root of your lies now. Ten to one there's no such person as your old school chum Elizabeth. More likely it's a bloke yer've got a date with. Well, if it is, more fool him. He doesn't know what he's letting himself in for. 'Oh, I can't have Amelia until late, Mrs Sinclair,' Bessie said, enjoying every second of it. 'Yer see, I've invited Rita Wells and Aggie Gordon for eight o'clock, just to have a birthday bottle of milk stout with me. I thought Amelia would probably have gone by then. And I can't put Rita and Aggie off now, they'd be upset 'cos they're me best mates.' Then, because she was so angry at the way this stuck-up bitch treated her daughter, Bessie rubbed salt in the wound.

'If it weren't for that, I'd say Amelia could stay later, even sleep here if it comes to that, 'cos I've got a single bed in the back room. But it's out of the question because I know yer don't like her to mix with the neighbours or any of the kids in the street in case they've got a disease or nits in their head. So I can't help yer out there, I'm afraid. Perhaps yer could visit yer friend another night, when I can keep Amelia for an extra hour or so?'

Evelyn's nostrils flared and she felt like hitting out at this silly old woman who would spoil her chances in life, just for the sake of a bottle of milk stout with her common-as-muck friends. But although she was seething, Evelyn didn't forget the fact that this woman was her only chance, and without her she could say goodbye to all her hopes and dreams. With a huge effort she was able to say, 'I have no objection to Mrs Wells and Mrs Gordon. I'm sure they would behave very properly with Amelia in their company. And I'm sure my daughter would be very happy to stay until I get home. You really are most kind, Miss Maudsley, I am very lucky to have you as a friend and neighbour. So I accept your offer with deep gratitude.'

Although Amelia had her head bent as it studying the board game, Bessie could feel the tension coming from the girl. It was for her sake that Bessie replied, 'Well, in that case, Amelia might as well sleep here. I will send her to bed when I think it's time, or she tells me she is tired.' She put her arm across the girl's shoulders. 'Is that all right with you, sweetheart? Here's me and yer mother making plans without even asking what you want to do.'

The face that turned to her was aglow. Amelia's eyes were full of excitement and a smile creased her whole face. 'Oh, I'd love to sleep here, Miss Bessie.'

'That's settled then.' She got to her feet and gave Evelyn no option but to follow suit. The little woman had had enough of the lying and the high-handedness. 'Yer may as well go and see to yer meal, Mrs Sinclair, while me and Amelia finish our game of Snakes and Ladders. I'll send her as soon as the game is over.'

Evelyn was propelled towards the kitchen door. 'Thank you once again, Miss Maudsley, I will always be indebted to you.'

She was feeling very relieved that the first date with Philip could be set and could see no reason why her neighbour would refuse to help in future. How fortunate it was that she had mentioned the bed in her spare room. 'It is definite for next Saturday then, is it? You see, I must write and tell my friend I shall be coming, and what time.'

Bessie stood as tall as her four foot eleven would allow. 'I do not tell lies, Mrs Sinclair, nor do I disappoint a young girl who is looking forward to her birthday celebration. I'll say goodnight to yer now, and get back to our game of Snakes and Ladders.' She was never rude or impolite unless she was pushed too far, but this was one time Bessie had gone past the stage where she would try to be polite. But for the sake of the girl she wasn't going to start a slanging match. Instead, she closed the door in her neighbour's face.

Chapter Eight

When the knock came on the door of his office, Cyril Lister-Sinclair took off his pince-nez spectacles and laid them on his huge mahogany desk. 'Come in.'

It was his secretary, Miss Williams, and she was carrying a sheaf of letters in her hand. 'I have these ready for signing, will you do them now or shall I leave them on the desk and you can ring for me when you have read and signed them?'

'Yes, leave them on the desk if you will, Miss Williams, and I'll attend to them shortly. I'm afraid this is one of those days when I really don't have the energy or the will, for work.'

When his secretary had closed the door behind her, Cyril let out a deep sigh. It was seven years now since Charles had been killed in action, and those years had not been kind to him. He had aged considerably, both physically and mentally. He had never come to terms with the loss of his son, and not a day went by when he didn't grieve for him. Charles had been the reason Cyril had built up a successful business, and become one of the wealthiest merchants in Liverpool. He loved his son dearly, and wanted to make sure he would never lack for anything in his life. He'd been Cyril's reason for living, and when he was killed there didn't seem any point any more. Why carry on making more money, or take a pride in his business like he used to, when there was no one to leave it to? No one to take up the reins when he retired.

And at home there was no one who understood his grief, and his need to talk about his son. There were photographs of Charles everywhere, but no one mentioned him and that wasn't natural.

It was his wife's doing. She'd wanted all the photographs removed because she'd said it broke her heart to look at them. It was one of the few times in his married life he'd put his foot down. His wife refused to mention her son's name, and said she'd lost the will to live. She was so full of self-pity she didn't notice her husband needed to talk about Charles, wanted to keep the boy's memory alive. Most of all he wanted the arms of a loving wife to comfort him. Even the house didn't seem like a home any more. Once it had been a place where Charles had brought his friends for partying, and the place rang with music, dancing and laughter as they dined on the very best of food and wines. Now the house was silent; even the servants talked in hushed tones. Never any laughter or the hubbub of conversation. Everything changed after Charles was killed.

Cyril's eyes rested on the sheaf of letters, and he was just reaching for them when a knock came on the door that he recognised. 'Come in, my boy, I know your knock by now.'

The face that came around the door had a mop of black hair, flashing brown eyes and a friendly smile. Just the sight of it lifted Cyril's spirits for this was Charles' best friend, Oscar Wentworth. The one person who loved to talk about his son, who had been his school chum at five and was still his best friend when they were twenty-five. He missed him as much as Cyril did. He had been best man when Charles married Evelyn at the registry office on the day he'd left to fight in the war from which he never returned. A year later Oscar had married Gwen, Evelyn's friend and bridesmaid, and they now had two children.

'Sit down, my boy, and I'll ring for a pot of tea.' Just a few seconds after the bell on his desk tinkled, Miss Williams opened the door. She had worked there long enough to be able to say, 'The kettle is on the boil, just give me five minutes.'

'Miss Williams, what would I do without you?'

'Find another secretary who would put her foot down and say,

"Please sign those letters, Mr Lister-Sinclair, so they can catch the lunchtime post".'

Cyril smiled, something he could do when Oscar was there. It brought a blessed release from tension. 'They will be signed by the time the tea arrives, Miss Williams, I don't want to be scolded.'

When they were alone, Oscar said, 'You are lucky with Miss Williams, Cyril, she's perfect. Friendly without overdoing it, and not afraid to smile. My father's secretary is like a little mouse, I've never seen her really smile in all the years she's worked for him. She shuffles along with her head down, and even one of my famous jokes doesn't light up her face. I tried for years, but I've given up now. Father is quite happy with her, her work is faultless. But I would prefer a spelling mistake that came with a smile.'

Cyril signed the correspondence, and pushed it across the desk when the tea was brought in on a silver tray. 'There you are, my dear, signed and sealed.'

'Thank you.' Louise Williams smiled at the boss who was so kind and thoughtful she would go to the ends of the earth to please him. When she caught him looking sad, she was saddened, too. 'I'll be mother and pour. Then I'll leave you in peace and make sure those letters get to the post on time.'

While she was pouring, Cyril looked from her to Oscar, the two people who had helped him keep his sanity. Particularly Oscar who, since the day the telegram had arrived to say Charles had been killed, had seldom missed a day without visiting Cyril either at the office or at home. He was the one who snorted with derision when Cyril said he was thinking of selling off his business interests and retiring, for he had lost the competitive thrust needed to stay ahead of his rivals. But his son's friend wouldn't allow him to. He'd come into the office every day for a year and willed Cyril to reawaken the interest he'd always had. He knew that if his dear friend's father was at home all day, he would slowly fade away through lack of companionship, stimulating conversation and love. There was also the need to talk about Charles. Oscar was fond of Mrs Lister-Sinclair but thought her selfish, a little childish, lacking in humour and with no interest in her husband's businesses or what was going on in the world. And Oscar had been very straight about telling Cyril that if he was at home all day he would go crazy.

The tea poured, Miss Williams made her exit, saying over her shoulder, 'I've left room for a touch of the whisky you have hidden in the side drawer.'

Oscar chuckled. 'She really is a treasure.'

'Clever, too,' Cyril said. 'She knows as much about this business as I do. If I were to absent myself from the office for a month, everything would still run smoothly.'

'If you want to take a holiday, Cyril, I could always come and work with Miss Williams to keep the wheels oiled. You could do with one, you know.'

'Who would I have for a companion? I would be as alone on holiday as I am here.' Cyril opened the side drawer and took out a bottle of whisky. After pouring a small measure into his cup, he handed it to Oscar. 'How is the family, my boy? Mother and father keeping well?'

'Both fine! Dad doesn't seem to grow any older for all he works hard. I'll swear he has more hairs on his head than I have. And Gwen and the children are well, although my wife has her hands full with the two boys. Charles is nearly six, and Richard just a year younger.'

'I was grateful to you and Gwen for calling your first-born Charles, it was very thoughtful of you.'

'Nonsense! Charles was my friend, the best anyone could have, I never considered any other name for my first son. And it was Gwen's wish too, not mine alone.'

Cyril looked down into his empty cup for a while, then asked, 'Gwen was friendly with Evelyn, wasn't she? I believe they were together when Evelyn first met Charles.'

'Yes, I believe they were. I'd known Gwen for a while at that time, but there was nothing between us but friendship. The seeds of romance were sown at the registry office the day Charles and Evelyn were married.'

'Does she still see Evelyn?'

Oscar looked surprised. 'No, I think she only called to see her once after the baby was born. Amelia, I believe the child was called.'

'Yes, I saw the baby, and she was called Amelia, but whether she was ever christened I do not know. Over the years I've many times wondered if I was wrong about Evelyn. You know the story she told me, and I didn't believe her because I didn't think my son capable of treating the woman he wanted for his wife in such a shabby way. The child bore no resemblance to Charles at all. Colouring, features, nothing that would lead me to think she was my son's child. And on top of that there were no tears of sorrow when I told her Charles had been killed, she never went into mourning. In fact, what really sickened me was the way she failed to ask what the telegram said, or where or how Charles died. There was not one tear shed. The only words she uttered, were, "What's going to happen to me?" ' He placed the cup and saucer on the silver tray. 'But always at the back of my mind I'm asking myself, did I do right? I don't worry about Evelyn because I never did like her, she was shallow and selfish. But what if Charles was the father of the baby, and for seven years I've never bothered to find out about the child? I've left it so long now, I wouldn't know where to start. But I'd hate to go to my grave wondering if I had made my son's child an outcast.'

'There must be some way of finding her if that's what you want, Cyril. I'll have a word with Gwen, see if she has any way of finding where Evelyn disappeared to.'

'When I asked her to vacate the house in Princes Avenue, I did suggest she tried the property letting office in Moorfields.

Whether she ever went there I don't know, but it's the last thing I remember saying to her. Oh, and I told her to take whatever items of furniture and bedding she would need. That is all I can tell you.' There was a plea for help and understanding in the eyes searching Oscar's face. 'What are your thoughts, Oscar? Was I wrong in the actions I took? Too quick to judge? Was I perhaps hitting back at her for not being heartbroken, as I was?' Cyril ran a finger across his forehead. 'I know you are the one person I can rely on to tell me exactly what you think. So, in my place, what would you have done, then and now?'

'Acted as you did at the time, Cyril, without any doubt. Evelyn's actions would have hurt and angered me. But they would not have surprised me, I was never an admirer of hers. Never thought she was good enough for Charles, but he was besotted and wouldn't listen. However, since it means such a lot to you, I will be perfectly frank. Over the years, like yourself, I have had doubts niggling at the back of my mind. Was Charles the father of the child? Could he have lost control because he was going away to a foreign country to fight in a bloody war that was claiming the lives of millions of men? If he did act out of character, who are we to blame him? I for one would not think badly of him, for he was a good man and a friend I was proud to have.' Oscar leaned forward to put a hand on the teapot. 'Talking is giving me a thirst, and this tea is still warm enough to be drinkable.'

'I'll ring for a fresh pot,' Cyril said, reaching out to press the bell. 'I feel quite thirsty myself.'

Oscar covered his hand. 'No, don't ring. Why don't I finish what I have to say, then we can adjourn to the club for lunch and a drink? We can spend an hour going over what we've discussed and see where we want to go from there.' He grinned. 'It's nice and quiet there, and although I am partial to a drop of whisky, my favourite tipple is claret.'

'Good thinking, my dear boy. The chairs are more comfortable there, too!'

'I forbid you to fall asleep in them, Cyril. My imagination is fired now, and I want an answer to the question that has plagued both of us for seven years.' Oscar sank back in his chair. 'One thing you should perhaps know is that at the age of one month, all babies look alike. Mine both had blue eyes and mousy hair. At eight months their eyes were brown and their hair dark. Then we could see baby Charles gradually taking on my features, when his nose became the shape of mine. And the same thing happened a year later with Richard. Blue eyes, mousy hair at birth, then six months later the spitting image of me. So you really wouldn't have been able to make any judgement on baby Amelia, she was far too young for anyone to say who she resembled.' He went to push himself out of the chair. 'Shall we make our way to the club now?'

'Can we just go a little further here first, my boy, and then smooth the details out at the club? The main question I want to ask is, do you think it's too late to try and solve the mystery or shall I begin to search for Evelyn and her daughter? I could hire a private investigator, that would speed things up. I wouldn't know where to start myself.'

'I think we both know the answer to that in our hearts, Cyril. If we don't try, we will always wonder what the truth is. I definitely think we should waste no time, enough has been lost already. We may be disillusioned at the end of our search, but at least we will have tried and will not be burdened with guilt for the rest of our lives. But rather than hire a private detective, I would like to start the search myself. I would feel I was helping Charles. I could start at the property letting office in Moorfields. I know that many years have passed, but they must keep records. Have you any recollection of the date Evelyn left Princes Avenue? That would be a help.'

Cyril rubbed his chin, his brow furrowed in concentration.

'I remember the baby was born on the eighteenth of September, the maid brought a note to inform me. That was in seventeen. Evelyn and the baby left the house one month later. That means her daughter will be eight next week.' A catch came to his voice, and an unwelcome tear to his eyes. 'What a stupid, blind fool I've been to have left it so long! If she is Charles' daughter, I have missed seven years of my granddaughter's life.'

'Come now, Cyril, this is no time for self-pity. If we find the girl, and find proof that she is your granddaughter, then think of the happiness it will bring you and your wife. It would change your whole lives, give you something to live for. It will also give you back a part of your son. If we are not successful in finding mother and daughter, then you will have lost nothing. But let's think positive, it's half the battle.'

'Are you sure you want to take such a task on, my dear boy?' Cyril asked. 'I would willingly hire a detective.'

Oscar shook his head. 'I want to do it to put your mind at rest, and my own. But most of all, I want to do it for Charles.'

The following morning Oscar entered the premises of the property letting office in Moorfields. He was well dressed and had an air of authority about him, so one of the two men behind the counter came over to him immediately. 'Can I help you, sir?'

'I hope so, my good man, but my quest is not an easy one. I am trying to trace a woman who may have rented a house from you in October nineteen seventeen. Rather a long shot, I know, but I would be grateful if you could assist me. It's important to a friend that we should trace this woman and her child.'

'We keep records of all our tenants, sir, and they go back some twenty years. If you can give me the family's name, I can certainly look it up for you.'

'The lady in question is a Mrs Lister-Sinclair, and she was a widow with a new baby.'

The man's face showed his surprise, for the Lister-Sinclair name was known by most business people in the city. 'Oh, I don't think I can help you, sir. I've worked here since the office opened, twenty years ago, and know all the names of the people who rent our property. I can safely say I would have remembered if anyone of that name had registered with us, it is a name well known in the city.'

Oscar's heart sank for a second, then he had an idea. 'It is possible the lady married again, so could I crave your indulgence and ask to look in your tenants' book for a name I might recognise? I am prepared to pay you a pound for your time.'

The man's colleague left the person he was talking to and came down the counter. A pound was almost a week's wages, and he wanted his share. Particularly as he was the senior clerk. 'Bring the book out, Watson, and let the gentleman look through himself to see if any of the names rings a bell.' He gave Oscar his best smile. 'We are always willing to help, sir.'

The large, hardbacked book was well thumbed, and as the clerk opened it a sprinkling of dust rose from its spine. Although he was seeing it upside down, Oscar could see the first dates were in January, and said, 'Could you start at the October entries, please? I believe that would be nearer the time she would have applied to you for rented accommodation.'

The clerk turned the book around so Oscar could read the entries. 'If as you say, sir, the lady may have married again, then she would have registered under her new husband's name. But if you wish to check, then you are very welcome.'

Oscar was beginning to think he was on a wild goose chase. He had lost the feeling of optimism he'd had when he'd walked into the shop. It all seemed pretty hopeless if the two clerks didn't remember a name that would stick in most people's minds. Still, the man had been kind enough to take the trouble of rooting the book out, the least he could do was take a look. He went down the list of names, and was about to admit defeat when the name Mrs E. Sinclair seemed to jump off the page. He tried not to let his excitement show, he didn't want to divulge any of Cyril's private business.

'This is a possibility – Mrs E. Sinclair. There was a slight tiff in the family and to alter her name was probably her way of getting her own back. All over a silly quarrel, she was just cutting off her nose to spite her face. Anyhow, it's worth a try, so if you would be good enough to give me her address, I would be most grateful.'

'Oh, I couldn't give you her present address, sir. She is no longer a tenant of ours. She handed in her rent book several years ago. I can remember her vaguely, an attractive woman. A bit standoffish, if my memory serves me right, but a good looker.'

'When she left, did she leave you a forwarding address, or give you any idea where she was moving to?'

The senior clerk had finished with his customer and came down the counter. 'I remember her, too, sir, she rented from us for about four years. When she came in with her money for the week's notice, I did ask why she was leaving and where she was going. But she was reluctant to talk, merely said she had found somewhere more suitable.'

'Would you be allowed to give me her old address, then, and I can try the neighbours there, see if she was more forthcoming with them?'

The older man nodded. 'Get the books out, Watson, and help the gentleman. If I am not mistaken, Mrs Sinclair rented a property in Bedford Road. But if you go through the books, you can give him the correct address. And please be quick about it, Watson, I'm sure the gentleman hasn't got time to waste.'

The clerk disappeared into a back office and was away for ten minutes. When he returned he had a look of triumph on his face and dust all over his jacket. 'I've got it, sir. I'll write the address down for you when I've wiped some of the dust off my hands.' The pound note he'd been promised would now have to be shared with his senior, which he felt was a bit unfair, but still, ten bob was a lot of money and his wife would be over the moon when he handed it over to her. They'd be able to have a roast dinner on Sunday, with a large joint of meat. 'I do hope you are successful, sir,' he said, handing over a piece of paper with an address on. 'Bedford Road is easy to find, it's off Stanley Road and the trams stop on the corner.'

'That is exceedingly kind of you, you have been most helpful. But I know where Bedford Road is, and I have my own transport.' Oscar dipped his hand into his waistcoat pocket and brought out the pound note he'd carefully folded before entering the office. 'Here you are, my good man, this is for your co-operation which I can assure you was most appreciated.'

He placed the note on the counter and out of the corner of his eye could see the senior clerk edging his way towards it. He knew that as soon as the door closed behind him the two men would argue over how the money should be shared.

Once out of the property letting office, Oscar walked the few yards to his car. Sitting behind the wheel, he glanced at the slip of paper, made a mental note of the address, and slipped it into his jacket pocket. Then as he switched on the ignition, he said aloud, 'I can but try. For Cyril's sake, and my own, I pray I have some success.'

It wasn't a great distance from the city centre to Bedford Road, and soon Oscar was sitting outside the house where Evelyn and her daughter had lived. It was a come-down from what she was used to, but nevertheless it was a nice road with plenty of greenery in the gardens, and the houses looked solid and well cared for. He decided not to knock on the door of the address he'd been given but instead to knock at a neighbour's house and ask if the tenant had been living there at the time Evelyn lived next door. It was to be hoped the person wouldn't think he was up to no good and slam the door in his face. But he assured himself that, although he wasn't gifted with film-star looks, he didn't look disreputable enough to be a beggar.

Oscar failed to notice, as he opened the iron gate, that the net curtain in the front window was already twitching. The woman watching him was asking herself who this swank was, coming to her house. He wasn't a canvasser, and certainly not a rag and bone man. His clothes were expensive, and there was the car parked outside her house. She'd never had a toff like him walking up her path before, and she'd never known anyone who had a car. Perhaps she shouldn't open the door to a stranger, 'cos her Ted would go mad if she let herself be talked into anything. Only last week she'd bought some pegs off a gypsy because she believed it was bad luck to refuse, and her husband called her for all the silly buggers going. But she couldn't not open the door to this man 'cos she wouldn't sleep tonight for wondering what he'd wanted. So, when the knock came, Sarah Higgins straightened her pinny and patted her hair before opening the door. She mightn't have much money, but she did have her pride.

'I'm sorry to bother you,' Oscar said, 'but I've come to see if you can help me trace someone for a friend of mine. Her name was Evelyn Sinclair, and I believe she was once a neighbour of yours?'

Sarah nodded. 'She used to live next door, yes.' The thought entered her head that if she did tell this toff what she thought of her former neighbour, then she didn't want the neighbours to know. And remembering she'd given the parlour a good dusting and polishing this morning, she thought she may as well show off. 'Would you like to come in?' she asked in her very poshest voice. 'I'm not one for standing at the door nattering, I think it's common.'

Oscar was amused, but didn't let it show in his smile. 'That is most kind of you, and also very trusting. After all, you don't know me and I could be a bogeyman.'

'I'm a pretty good judge of character,' Sarah said, holding the door open and hoping all the neighbours were watching. 'The parlour is the first door on your left. I'm sorry there isn't a fire going, but my husband and I use the living room in the winter.' She congratulated herself on speaking in her best accent. 'Unless you are cold, of course. If so we can go through to the living room and I can make a pot of tea.'

'That's jolly good of you! Yes, I would like that. A cup of tea is always welcome.'

Ten minutes later he was sitting facing her across a table covered by a maroon chenille cloth, with an aspidistra plant standing square in the centre.

'This is really very kind of you, Mrs, er, Mrs . . .?'

'Mrs Higgins – Sarah Higgins. And can I ask your name, please?'

'Oscar Wentworth, Mrs Higgins, and I have to say I am quite overwhelmed by your hospitality.'

Sarah, who had used her best china cups and saucers, waved the compliment aside. 'I would never keep anyone on the step, especially someone as respectable-looking as yourself. And about Mrs Sinclair – did you say a friend of yours was trying to find her?'

Oscar had no intention of bringing Cyril's name into the conversation, so he chose his words carefully. 'Yes, he is quite elderly, and met her many years ago. He knew she had a daughter and was wondering how they were faring. It's not desperately important that he find her, mind you, but I took it upon myself to try, as a surprise to him. That's if I can trace her, of course.'

'Well, much as I'd like to help you, I'm afraid I can't tell you a lot about her, or where she is now. She wasn't a very friendly person, not the neighbourly type at all. I did offer to help when she was moving in, and so did the neighbour on the other side of her, but she turned us down. Several times in the winter I knocked to say I'd mind the baby while she went to the shops, but no, she refused point blank. If the weather was bad she'd leave the baby in the house alone while she went shopping. And she didn't turn you down in a nice way, she didn't even have the grace to thank you for offering. So after that I didn't bother because she was a cold person and very stuck-up. Thought she was too good for the people round here.' Then Sarah decided she'd better watch her tongue in case she landed herself in trouble. 'The baby was a lovely little thing, though, very quiet and good. I used to feel sorry for her 'cos she seldom went out. And for a child of her age, she was very well spoken. She sounded more like a grown-up than a child, but that's 'cos she never mixed with other children.'

'Did she take after her mother in looks?' Oscar asked casually. 'My friend said Mrs Sinclair was an attractive woman.'

Sarah pursed her lips and frowned as she tried to bring pictures of the couple to mind. 'Mrs Sinclair had dark hair, but the girl's was much darker, almost jet black. And their eyes were different, if my memory serves me right. The mother's were dark brown, but the girl's were more of a greeny-hazel. She had her mother's way of speaking and walked like her, with her back as straight as a rod. I can still hear Mrs Sinclair's voice coming through the wall, saying, "Straighten your back, Amelia, and hold your head high." I often said to myself that she'd make the girl into an old woman before she'd had her childhood.'

Oscar felt his heart pounding as memories of Charles' face flashed into his mind. His friend with his green eyes lit up with humour and a lock of black hair falling on to his forehead. The images seemed so real he felt he could reach out and touch the man who had been his friend for years, and for whom he still grieved. He mentally shook away the memories, for he could see Sarah watching him. 'Was she a good mother to the child?'

'She thought she was, but you wouldn't find any neighbours who would agree with her.' She caught and held Oscar's eyes. 'I don't know you from Adam, and I'm probably talking out of turn, but so help me God, I'm speaking the truth. There was no love in that house while Mrs Sinclair lived there. Far from being a good mother, she didn't seem to have any affection for that poor child. And although it's a few years now since they left, I often think about them. Not the mother, I couldn't care less what happens to her, but I'd like to know if the girl is being well treated. Trying to look on the bright side, I keep telling myself she'll be going to school now, and will probably have made friends of her own age to play with. I certainly hope so, she deserves better than she was getting when she lived here.'

Oscar sighed. 'And Mrs Sinclair gave no hint where she was moving to?'

'Mr Wentworth, she didn't even tell us she *was* leaving. And no one saw her going, so she must have had the removal cart or van here when it was dark and we were all in bed.' The memory was too much for Sarah, who started to feel angry. 'You will have to excuse me, Mr Wentworth. I'm ashamed of what I'm going to say to a gentleman like yourself, but I've got to get it off my chest. Mrs Sinclair left here without so much as a wave, a goodbye or a kiss my backside! She thinks she's the whole cheese, but she is the most ignorant woman I have ever met. And there you have it in a nutshell.'

'She doesn't sound like a pleasant person, I must say.' Oscar was feeling really let down. 'My friend spoke so highly of her, but it seems he is not the judge of character that you are, Mrs Higgins. Oh, dear, I am glad I didn't tell him what I was up to. It would have given him false hope. My best bet is probably to keep quiet and then he won't have lost anything. It does seem strange, though, that a woman and her child can live in a house for four years and not get to make friends with one single human being. One would have thought Mrs Sinclair would have been glad of company and someone to talk to. It must have been a very lonely life for her and the young girl.'

Sarah averted her eyes before saying, 'Oh, she did talk to one person – and that's the man in the pawnbroker's shop. Very often you would see her leaving the house with a wrapped parcel under her arm. I was only one of many who saw her going into the pawn shop with that parcel, and come out five minutes later without it.'

'A pawn shop?' Oscar looked stunned. 'You do surprise me. I thought the lady was comfortably off.'

'I wouldn't lie to you, Mr Wentworth, I'm a regular church-goer and live by the Ten Commandments. The odd swear word slips my lips occasionally, but only very mild ones.'

'You are a good woman, Mrs Higgins, and a kind one. I am very grateful for your help and your friendliness. Now I will leave you, I have taken up far too much of your time. But before I go, I would like to ask one more favour from you. While I am in the area, I think I may as well call in to the pawnbroker's shop to see if he knows the whereabouts of Mrs Sinclair. Could you tell me where I might find it?'

'It's in Stanley Road, Mr Wentworth, not five minutes' walk from here. If you drive back to the junction of Stanley Road and turn left, you'll find it's in the second block of shops. You can't miss it, there are three brass balls hanging outside.'

Oscar pointed to a framed picture standing proudly on the sideboard. 'Are they your grandchildren?'

Sarah was off her chair like a shot to fetch the picture to him. There was real pride in her voice when she said, 'That's Bobby, he's ten in two months, and the girl is Theresa, she's eight. They're bonny kids, and me and my husband love the bones of them.'

'I have two sons, Mrs Higgins, and I love the bones of them!' It was an expression Oscar had never heard before, but he liked it, it sat well on his tongue and in his heart. 'Yes, indeed, I love the bones of them.'

While Sarah was replacing the photograph on the sideboard, and standing back to make sure it was arranged just right, Oscar took a wallet from his inside pocket. He took out two pound notes and returned the wallet quickly before she turned around. He had thought of putting the notes under the plant pot on the table to save any embarrassment, then decided that wasn't quite the thing to do. So when Sarah was showing him to the door, he asked, 'Would you be offended if I gave you a few shillings to buy some sweets for your grandchildren? It would give me great pleasure if you would accept.'

Sarah's brows shot up when she looked down at the notes in his hand. 'I can't take two pound off you, that's a lot of money!'

'Mrs Higgins, you took a total stranger into your home and treated him with warmth and friendliness. The only way I can repay that kindness is through your grandchildren. So please take it, and make me and them happy. What I am giving you doesn't match up to what you have given me.' He placed his black bowler hat on his head, patted the top of it, then smiled. 'Thank you again, Mrs Higgins, and who knows but we may meet again some day?'

Oscar walked down the path leaving Sarah staring down at the two pound notes in her hand. And as he opened the gate, he heard her say, 'Well, did yer ever! Just wait until my Ted comes in, I bet he won't believe the day I've had.'

Chapter Nine

Oscar came out of the pawnbroker's shop feeling despondent. He was no better off now than when he'd walked into the shop. The man behind the counter had been less than forthcoming. Yes, he'd admitted, he remembered Mrs Sinclair, but would give no other details as they were confidential. And no, he hadn't any knowledge of her present whereabouts. He had looked genuinely surprised when Oscar mentioned that she had a daughter, and it was very obvious he was sincere when he said he didn't know there was a child. But as to the transactions between himself and Mrs Sinclair, he was not in a position to divulge the affairs of a customer.

As he sat behind the wheel of his car, Oscar was in a dilemma. Should he tell Cyril what he'd heard from Mrs Higgins, or should he lie and say he was unable to obtain any facts about Evelyn and her daughter? At first he thought that would be the kindest thing to do, and then perhaps Cyril would put the ghost of the past behind him. But, on reflection, Oscar decided he couldn't lie to a man he admired and was very fond of. Besides, he himself didn't want to put the past behind him, he couldn't. Not after he'd been told a child, who might be Charles' flesh and blood, was unloved and being badly treated. Another thing he couldn't ignore: hadn't Mrs Higgins said Amelia didn't take after her mother in looks, and also mentioned jet black hair and green eyes? The woman wouldn't just make that up, there must be some truth in it. And if so, then all the more reason to trace the child who could make a difference to so many lives. It would bring such happiness to Cyril and his wife Matilda. It would give them a new lease of life, something to live for, and hopefully bring them closer together. And as for me, Oscar thought, I would spend the rest of my life happy in the knowledge that if Charles is looking down, he can be at peace, knowing those who have never stopped loving and thinking of him, are there for his daughter.

As he neared the offices of Cyril Lister-Sinclair, Oscar cursed himself for being so sentimental. But he couldn't help being the way he was, nor could he help the tear that rolled down his cheek as he switched the car's engine off. And he knew worse was to come. If he repeated everything he had found out, it was bound to have Cyril in tears.

Without giving himself any more time to think, Oscar locked the car, strode through the double doors and ran lightly up the flight of stairs. He managed a grin at the surprise on Miss Williams' face. 'I know I'm not expected, and if Mr Lister-Sinclair is engaged, I will come back later.'

'He's had a busy morning with meetings, but he's alone now. I've just taken him a cup of tea through. I'll tell him you're here then make a fresh brew.'

'Don't get up, Miss Williams, he knows my knock by now. And I'm going to talk him into coming to the club for an hour so he can see some of his friends. He doesn't get out nearly enough, and needs some male company. If I come out carrying him over my shoulder, don't be alarmed. It just means he's made an excuse not to go out, and I refuse to take it. He needs fresh air and he needs company.'

Miss Williams grinned as she nodded. 'I'm glad you come so often to see him, Mr Wentworth, because you're good for him. His business associates are kind, but they're here to work while you come as a friend. That makes a big difference. Give him a knock, he'll be glad to see you.'

Oscar rapped on the door with a knuckle, waited until he heard his friend's voice, then walked in. 'I've been told by your irreplaceable secretary that you've had a hectic morning, old boy, so I am here to whisk you off to the club for a couple of drinks. And some interesting conversation, of course. There would be no point in leaving here just to sit there looking at each other.'

'I'm afraid I have nothing of interest to talk about,' Cyril said, 'my life is a very dull one and I'm not the most interesting of companions.'

'Have no fear, I shall keep the conversation flowing, my good man, as long as you keep the claret flowing. Am I not noted for being articulate and amusing?'

Cyril chortled as he picked up a stack of papers and put them in one of the deep side drawers. 'How can I resist such an invitation?' But he wasn't fooled by Oscar's jovial manner. He had grown to know the younger man very well over the years, and although he was always happy and talkative, there was something different about him today. It was as though he was bubbling with excitement inside, and trying to contain it. 'You seem in a good mood this afternoon, Oscar, is there a reason for it?'

'All shall be revealed later, when I have a glass of claret in my hand. But don't think I have any earth-shattering news to tell you, I'm afraid that's not the case. Still, there is a topic we can talk about, and that should give us something to mull over while sampling the excellent wines from the club's cellar. So, after giving Miss Williams instructions that if anyone calls you will not be back in the office for the rest of the day, we shall be on our merry way.'

Cyril leaned forward from his deeply sprung leather chair and raised his glass. 'A toast to our friendship, what say you?'

Oscar nodded. 'To our lasting friendship, I say.' He was giving every appearance of being his usual chatty self, without a care in the world. Yet inside he was still full of doubt. He wanted to do what was best for the older man, say what would make him the happiest. But deep down he knew Cyril Lister-Sinclair was a man who would want to know the truth, not a lie that was supposed to make him feel good. 'Now, I don't quite know whether I'm doing the right thing here, Cyril. I have spent an hour going over the pros and cons. However, I have reached the conclusion, rightly or wrongly, that you would prefer the plain unvarnished truth.'

Cyril's hand began to shake around the glass he was holding. 'You have found Evelyn and the girl?'

Oscar shook his head. 'No, I'm afraid this story does not have a happy ending. But one day it will, and that is my promise to you.' He took a deep breath. 'This morning I visited the property letting office in Moorfields.' He held up one hand as Cyril went to speak. 'Don't say anything yet, Cyril, wait until you hear everything I have been able to unearth about Evelyn and Amelia.' He lifted his glass. 'This is to give me courage and to loosen my tongue.' After drinking deeply, he set the glass down and began his tale. He left nothing out, and gave it word for word. He did try to keep it light, though, even repeating Mrs Higgins', remark: 'Mrs Sinclair left here without so much as a wave, a goodbye, or a kiss me backside'.

Nevertheless a sigh came from deep within Cyril. 'That is a heartbreaking story to listen to, my boy, especially as it is possible this child is my granddaughter after all. To think I have left her with a woman who appears to have a heart of stone! This neighbour of hers, Mrs Higgins, appears to be a kind and truthful person. I think we can believe what she says.'

'Oh, without a doubt! I believed her when she said she offered to help with the baby many times, that is the type of person she is. I was a total stranger knocking on her door, yet she took me in and made me feel right at home.'

'We have to find them, Oscar. I couldn't live with myself,

knowing there is the possibility of the girl being Charles' daughter. I will hire the best private investigator there is. If necessary I will bring one from London.'

Oscar gazed down at his shoes for a few seconds, then raised his head. 'Cyril, I'm going to ask you to let me find them. It would be quicker, perhaps, with a detective, but think what sort of private matters he may unearth in the course of his work. There may be skeletons in the cupboard, Cyril, that you wouldn't wish to be come public knowledge. Evelyn used the name Sinclair to both the letting office and to her neighbours, but she could easily revert back to Lister-Sinclair and cause trouble for you.'

Cyril shook his head. 'I never told you because I didn't think it was important at the time. When I believed the child was illegitimate, and because I was so sad at losing Charles and angry at Evelyn for blackening his name, I told her the marriage was to be annulled on the grounds it was never consummated, and if she put Charles' name down on the birth certificate as the father, I would take legal action against her. What a stupid man I was! Why didn't I let more time pass before making a judgement? I pray to God Amelia is my grandchild, but will God think I am worthy of her after the way I treated her mother?'

'Never have any regrets for the way you treated Evelyn, because from what I knew of her, and from what I've heard today from someone who lived next door to her for several years, she is not a nice person. She's selfish, without any capacity to love anyone but herself. I agree we must find her, not for her sake but for the girl's. Now I'm going to ask you again, please let me be the one to seek them out? I need to do it, Cyril, so I can remember my best friend with a clear conscience. It may take me a while, because Liverpool is a big city with many suburbs, but I promise you I will never give up until they are found.'

'You have my blessing, Oscar. All I ask is for you to keep in touch and update me with your findings.'

'I will still call in every day, my dear friend, and keep you informed. I have already begun to make plans in my head. I think a good start would be the schools. I realise there are hundreds of them, if not more. As I said, Liverpool covers a very wide area. But one has to start somewhere, and as Amelia must go to a school, then that is where I shall start.' Oscar lifted his glass. 'A toast to success.'

At the same time the two men were drinking to their hope of finding her, Amelia was running down the street on her way home from school. She was wearing as big a smile today as she wore every day now. Those two hours with Bessie each night had brought about a radical change in the girl. While she was still quiet and polite with her mother, she was vastly different with their neighbour next door. Bessie gave her the hugs and kisses she had never had before. Amelia had come to love the little woman, and in return was loved back. For the first couple of days she had followed her mother's instructions and reached Bessie's house down the back entry, but Bessie put a stop to that. And she did it in a way that had the girl doubled up with laughter.

'Yer'd better start using me front door if yer know what's good for yer, sweetheart, 'cos I got a good telling off over you. "Aren't I good enough for her?" That's what me door said, and it was in a right temper, I can tell yer. In fact, I thought it wasn't going to let me in. "I'm as good as any door in this street, in fact I'm better than some what have got no brass knockers, so you tell her from me I am not a bit happy about her deciding that the dirty old yard door is better than me." '

Amelia had run and put her arms around Bessie's waist then. 'Oh, you *are* funny, Miss Bessie. It was my mother who told me to use the entry, but I think I'd better apologise to the door, don't you? I mean, it might not open and close for me if it doesn't like me.'

'Oh, worse than that, sweetheart, you don't know my door. Because I keep it well washed and polished, and the brass shining enough to blind yer, it thinks it's the pig's ear. And if it thought for one moment that yer didn't think it was the most handsome door in the street, well, it would bang in yer face to let yer know who's boss.'

And so Amelia never used the entry after that. Her mother thought she did, but as she'd never asked, the girl didn't have to lie to her. It was a source of fun to Amelia, and every afternoon she would have something to say before she knocked on the door. Today she said, 'You look very posh today, Mr Door, I think you've been given a good polish. The most handsomest door in the street, I bet.'

Rita Wells had been told the joke about the door, and when she saw Amelia's lips moving gave a satisfied smile. The girl had changed so much in such a short time, Bessie was to be congratulated. As it was the birthday party on Saturday Rita was looking forward to getting to know Amelia better, and wanted her to know that if Bessie was ever late getting in from work, she could always cross the road to the Wellses' house.

Just then the door opposite opened and Bessie appeared with her arms held wide and a smile of welcome on her face. The girl didn't hesitate to walk into them. It was a happy sight, and Rita sniffed up to keep the tears back. She prayed this story would have a happy ending and her best mate's heart wouldn't be broken.

'Hello, sweetheart.' Bessie held Amelia from her for a moment. 'Yer cheeks are as red as the rosy apples on Tommy Flannigan's fruit cart. Have yer been running?'

'I always run home, Miss Bessie, 'cos the sooner I get home, the more time I have to sit with you and listen to you talking to the fireplace.'

Bessie noted the word 'home', and although it gave her a lovely warm glow inside, she was afraid that if Mrs Sinclair heard she might perhaps put a stop to the arrangement, for she looked the type who didn't like to see people happy. 'Oh, I've already had a row with the grate, sweetheart, and believe me it needs taking down a peg or two 'cos it's getting too cocky for my liking. Yer see, when I was walking home from work I thought I felt a nip in the air, and decided to light a fire so we wouldn't be cold. So I laid the paper and wood down, then struck a match to light the paper. I had the shovel of coal all ready, nice-sized cobs what looked as though they'd catch easy. But, blow me, every time I struck a match, a gust of wind came down the chimney and blew it out. And because yer can't see wind to tell it off, or give it a good hiding, I put the blame on the grate and we had a real set-to. And talk about cheek! Well, I've never heard the likes of it. If I'd talked back to my mam like that, God rest her soul, then I'd have had me backside tanned.' They were in the living room by this time, and Bessie nodded towards the fireplace where a small fire was struggling for survival. Shaking her fist, she said, 'If yer don't pull yer socks up, I'll not be cleaning you out in the morning. Yer can wallow in yer dirty ashes till I come home from work.'

As though a magic wand had been waved, a single bright flame shot up, and when it began to flicker it looked as though it was dancing. 'Look, it's dancing, Miss Bessie! I bet it's trying to say it's sorry and it won't be naughty again.'

'Oh, a belly dance won't get it back in my good books, so it needn't bother. When I see flames going up the chimney, then I just might consider forgiving it. Only might, like, that's not for certain.' Bessie put her arm across the girl's shoulder. 'It's only poached egg on toast for tea tonight, sweetheart, 'cos I'm not long in and haven't had time to do potatoes. But I scrounged a few bacon ribs off the butcher, so tomorrow night we'll have potatoes mashed with the top of the milk, and lovely bacon ribs.' She rubbed her tummy. 'Ooh, I can feel me mouth watering at the thought.'

There was a frown on Amelia's pretty face. 'What are bacon ribs, Miss Bessie? I know what ribs are 'cos we've all got them and I can feel mine. But I've never heard of bacon ribs that you can eat.'

Bessie ground her teeth. What on earth had this child and her mother been living on? Never heard of bacon ribs, indeed. 'Then ye're in for a treat, sweetheart, 'cos they are delicious with cabbage and mashed spuds. The best way to eat them is to hold them between yer fingers and bite the meat off the bone. Sweet as honey, it is.'

Amelia's eyes were wide. 'I'm learning a lot from you, Miss Bessie. Things I've never heard of before.' Her green eyes sparkled. 'Like ribs that are as sweet as honey, and you eat them with your fingers. And a talking door and fireplace. I bet none of the girls in my class have doors and fireplaces that talk.'

'Ah, well, they're our secret, sweetheart, and you mustn't tell yer friends or they'll be jealous.' Mentally Bessie added that if anyone knew what they were on about, they'd think her and Amelia were ready for the loony bin.

The girl nodded. 'I won't tell Mother, either, or she'll tell me not to be so silly. But it's not silly, is it, Miss Bessie, not when it's only in fun?'

At that very moment, Evelyn couldn't have cared less what her daughter did. In fact, she very seldom gave a thought to Amelia during the day. Particularly today. She was feeling very pleased with herself. She'd asked Philip if it was possible for her to leave half an hour early as she wanted to pick up an outfit she'd put in to be cleaned and the shop closed at half-past five. As Saturday was drawing near, and he intended to use their date to find out if she was really as cold as she seemed, he agreed to her leaving early so long as she made the excuse of not feeling well to the rest of the staff.

Evelyn hurried down the entry with her head bent. The precious dress and cape were wrapped in tissue paper, and she carried them carefully. She wanted to look stunning on Saturday, and her dress must be free from creases. She had it all planned in her head. On Saturday night she intended to be cool with Philip, but a little coquettish to keep his interest roused. If she played her cards right, she'd have him eating out of her hand before the night was over. The only problem she had was meeting him. He wanted to pick her up in his car, but she'd kept her air of mystery and shaken her head, saying she would take a taxi and meet him inside the State Hotel. The only way she could think of doing this was to leave her best clothes in one of the left luggage boxes in Exchange Station on Friday night, take the tram down on Saturday and change in the ladies' lavatory. Not the best way of doing things, but she couldn't risk letting him see where she lived, nor could she let the neighbours see her walking down the street in her finery.

After opening the entry door, Evelyn crept quietly up the yard. If Miss Maudsley heard her, she'd wonder why she hadn't called for Amelia first. Then she tip-toed upstairs to hang the dress and cape on a hanger. She was delighted it had cleaned up so well and looked almost new. Even the dreaded smell of damp had gone.

In the space of a few minutes she was knocking on her neighbour's door. And because her day had been fruitful, and her future looked bright, tonight she actually smiled at her daughter. 'I hope you've been good for Miss Maudsley? And you do realise how kind she is, looking after you for two hours every night? You and I would be lost without her.'

Just before the knock had come on the kitchen door, Amelia had been shaking with laughter and looking happy and care-free, as any girl her age should. Now she was standing straight-faced, her body as stiff as a board. 'Yes, Mother.'

Bessie had seen the change come over the girl and was boiling inside. 'Your daughter is very well behaved, Mrs Sinclair,' she commented quietly. And because she wanted to get a jab in at her neighbour, she added, 'Her manners are so perfect, they are a gift. She must have been born with them because they come so natural, yer can tell she didn't need teaching.'

Evelyn would have taken issue with her over this slur, but with Saturday looming she was in the hands of this little woman who really wouldn't know what good manners were. Why, if she went into the Adelphi or the State, she wouldn't know where to turn. She wouldn't have the least knowledge of which knife and fork to use, or how to conduct a conversation. But right now she did have her uses, and it would be prudent to keep on the right side of her. 'Yes, I agree, Amelia is very little trouble.'

But Bessie wasn't finished with her yet. 'Oh, by the way, while I think on, has Amelia got a frock she can wear on her birthday? I've only ever seen her in her school clothes, but I'm sure she has a pretty dress at home.'

Evelyn was caught unawares and didn't immediately have a reply. And this was so obvious that Bessie mentally chalked one up for herself. After a moment's thought, Evelyn concocted a lie. 'It was going to be a surprise, but if it puts your mind at rest, Miss Maudsley, I'll have to let the secret out of the bag.' She did this grudgingly for she was stretching every shilling she had so she looked the part for Philip on Saturday. But this stupid little woman had backed her into a corner. 'I am buying Amelia a new dress for her birthday. She will have it on when she comes to you on Saturday.'

Bessie chalked another one up for herself. The lying so-and-so hadn't had any intention of buying anything for her daughter until she'd been shamed into it. Still, never mind if the dress would be begrudged, Amelia would be delighted, and that was what counted. 'Oh, aye, sweetheart, ye're going to be proper posh on yer birthday. I'll have to pull me socks up or yer'll be putting me in the shade.' She thought of something then and began to laugh, for she knew Mrs Sinclair would find it in bad taste. 'Ay, I'll have to tell Aggie to make sure she washes her neck properly. We can't have you and me all dressed up and Aggie with a ruddy big tidemark what yer could sail a ship on.'

Evelyn's lip began to curl in disgust, until she saw Bessie watching her out of the corner of her eye. Then she tried to force a smile to her lips, but it came over more like a snarl and made her look ugly. 'Shall we go now, Amelia? I feel very peckish. Not everyone is as lucky as you, having a meal put down in front of them every night.'

The girl stood on tip-toe to reach her coat which was hanging on one of the hooks near the door. She answered without any trace of animation in her voice. 'Yes, Mother, I know I am very lucky.'

'Then come along, don't dally.'

Bessie looked down at the lino and counted to ten. She and Amelia had been really happy and enjoying each other's company until Misery Guts came on the scene. God certainly slipped up when he'd made this woman a mother, she didn't deserve the child she'd given birth to. And it wasn't only motherly feelings she was lacking, it was all the others too. Selfish to the core, without love or compassion, and a whopping great liar into the bargain was Evelyn Sinclair.

'I'll see you tomorrow, Miss Bessie.' Amelia wanted to kiss her friend goodbye, but knew she'd suffer for it when she got home. 'Sleep well.'

Bessie ruffled the girl's thick mop of black hair. 'You too, sweetheart. And don't forget, it's only two days to our birthday. Yer've got yer nice new dress to look forward to.'

Evelyn was unable to raise a smile as she pushed her daughter towards the back door. She had been forced into saying she would buy Amelia a dress, but where was the money going to come from? She needed every penny to make herself so attractive on Saturday that she would stand out and Philip would be proud of her. Their first night out together. He would either fall head over heels for her and be trapped, or so disillusioned he would step back. 'Goodnight, Miss Maudsley, I'll see you tomorrow,' she said briskly.

Bessie stood on the kitchen step watching mother and daughter walk down her yard and into the entry. All because one stuck-up woman thought she was too good to be seen coming out of her neighbour's front door. 'Silly bugger,' Bessie muttered. 'I feel sorry for her 'cos she doesn't know what it's like to have a good belly laugh with her neighbours. And she needn't think she's pulling the wool over my eyes by saying she's going to see this old school friend of hers on Saturday, the one what turned up out of the blue, 'cos I don't believe it for a minute. Not that I care what she does, as long as the girl doesn't get hurt.' She closed her kitchen door, still talking to herself. 'If I ever hear she's laid a finger on Amelia, she'll rue the day. I'll have her guts for garters.'

Bessie walked through and sat at the table in the living room. Her eyes on the grate, she began talking to it. 'There's some bad 'uns in this world, and our Mrs Sinclair is one of them. May God forgive me if I'm saying things about her what aren't true, but I've always thought there was something fishy about her, even from the first week she moved in, 'cos it isn't natural for a woman to ignore her neighbours and look down on them as though they're muck. Yer never know when yer might need them to help yer. Even dirty Annie, her what lives at the top of the street whose house is filthy and her language enough to make yer hair curl, would knock spots off her next door, 'cos at least she loves her kids.'

Banging her fist on the table, Bessie pushed the chair back and got to her feet. 'I can't spend me night talking to a fireplace what can't talk back to me, so I think I'll nip over to Rita's for half an hour for a natter.' She wagged a stiffened finger. 'Don't you dare go out 'cos I don't want to come back to a cold house.

I don't mind yer dying down a bit if I'm out a long time, but leave a couple of flames to warm the cockles of me heart.' She reached the door, saying over her shoulder, 'And behave yerself. No spitting sparks on to me rug for spite.'

Chapter Ten

'Oh, don't you look pretty!' Bessie smiled down into the laughing face of her neighbour's daughter. 'That's a lovely dress and it really suits yer.' Silently, she was telling herself it was far from being a new dress, you could tell it had seen the dolly tub many times. But who cared if it was second-hand, so long as it made Amelia look like a ray of sunshine? 'Are yer coming in, Mrs Sinclair, or are yer off out now?'

'I may as well be on my way, Miss Maudsley, save being under your feet.' Evelyn was a bundle of nerves, knowing she had so much to do in so little time. And she was painfully aware that at any minute she might be found out. First there was the journey by tram to the railway station, then changing the clothes she had on for the ones she'd yesterday put in a box at the left luggage office. At any time she could be seen by someone who knew her – a person who worked in the office perhaps or a neighbour. Even, heaven forbid, by Philip himself. Still, these were chances she had to take. 'Be good for Miss Maudsley, Amelia, and go to bed when she tells you. I hope you both have a very enjoyable birthday party.'

'Oh, we will!' Bessie held the door wide. 'Come in, sweetheart.' She waited until the girl had passed through to the living room, then said to the woman who wasn't looking at all at ease with herself, 'I hope you have a lovely evening, too, but don't do anything I wouldn't do.' This was a remark anyone would make to another person and it would be taken as a joke. But the telltale blush it brought to her neighbour's cheeks told Bessie she was right in thinking there was more to this night out than visiting an old school friend. 'Give a knock on the wall tomorrow when yer want Amelia to come home.'

'What time would you like me to knock? Are you an early riser?'

Bessie shook her head. 'I sometimes go to church, but I won't be going tomorrow, I'll be having a lie-in. So Amelia can stay as long as yer like. But I'll have to go in now, 'cos I've got to put the custard on the jelly creams before it sets. I'll see yer tomorrow.' She closed the door quickly. She'd only just remembered that before the knock came, she was halfway through putting the custard on top of the jelly she'd set previously in white pleated paper cases. She wasn't changed yet, either, and she wanted to look respectable when Rita and Aggie came over. Not that she'd look like a film star no matter what she wore, but a girl had her pride and should make the most of herself, even if she did have a face that resembled the back of a tram.

Amelia was waiting for Bessie to come back into the living room. 'Do you really like my dress, Miss Bessie? And does it suit me?'

'It looks lovely on yer, sweetheart, and yer look as pretty as a picture.' Bessie grinned. 'Guess what that cheeky front door's just said to me? It said I have a face like the back end of a twenty-two tram.'

Amelia hurried to put her arms around the little woman's waist. 'You've got a lovely face, Miss Bessie, and I've a good mind to give that door a smack.'

'We'll leave it till tomorrow, eh, sweetheart? We don't want to be fighting on our birthday, do we? We're going to have a really good time and enjoy ourselves. But first I've got to see to the cakes and then change meself before me mates come. It won't take me five minutes, then I'll be ready. You sit yerself down so yer don't dirty yer new dress.'

Amelia lowered her head. 'It isn't a new dress, is it, Miss Bessie? You see, I can tell because it doesn't feel new, and there's a little tear at the back, near the hem.'

'Oh, sweetheart, what difference does it make whether it's new or not! It's new to you, and that's the main thing. Perhaps yer mother didn't have enough money for a new one, 'cos times are hard now and lots of people don't even have enough money for food, never mind new clothes. I bet there isn't a girl in this street who wouldn't envy you if they could see how pretty yer look in it. D'yer think they'd worry about whether it was brand-new or not?' Bessie shook her head. 'Not on your life they wouldn't. And, anyway, I haven't got a new dress, and I'll lay odds that neither Mrs Wells nor Mrs Gordon will walk in here dressed up to the nines in brand-new clothes.' She dropped a kiss on Amelia's cheek. 'Ye're a lucky girl, sweetheart, compared to some, believe me.'

'Yes, I know, Miss Bessie, 'cos I've got friends at school who sometimes don't come in because they haven't any shoes to wear. So I know I'm very lucky. But my bestest piece of good luck is having you for a friend.'

'Oh, well, that's a piece of good luck we share, sweetheart, 'cos I look forward to you coming so much my eyes never leave the clock.' Bessie's jaw dropped. 'Oh, my God there's Aggie knocking at Rita's door. They'll be over in a minute and here's me not ready. You let them in, love, while I do a quick change. If yer can think of a joke to keep them amused, they'd be over the moon.'

Amelia was taken aback. 'I don't know any jokes, Miss Bessie.'

Bessie was halfway up the stairs when she shouted down, 'Tell them about the door saying I have a face like the back of a tram.'

When Amelia opened the front door, she stepped aside to let Mrs Wells and Mrs Gordon enter. She was in a predicament. She didn't want to let Miss Bessie down, but she couldn't bring herself to say what she'd been told to say. However, her problem was solved when Mrs Wells told her, 'We heard what Bessie said about that ruddy door of hers, and if I was in her shoes I'd stop polishing its knocker for a while. That would take it down a peg or two.'

Feeling relieved, Amelia told her, 'Me and Miss Bessie are going to leave it until tomorrow, Mrs Wells, because we don't think we should fight on our birthdays.'

'Quite right, too, sunshine, it's a day for yer both to be happy. And seeing as it's a party, don't yer think it sounds unfriendly to call me Mrs Wells? Just for tonight, wouldn't yer like to call me Auntie Rita?'

Amelia frowned, thinking her mother would be angry about that. Then the frown was replaced by a smile when a voice in her head said her mother need never know. 'That would be nice.' Her curls bounced up and down as she nodded. 'Yes, I'd like that, Auntie Rita.'

Aggie Gordon hadn't spoken so far, but she'd been taking all this in with narrowed eyes and decided she wasn't going to be left out. 'If we're going to be pally, queen, yer can call me Auntie Aggie.'

Amelia clapped her hands. She had never had a birthday party before, and she had never had any aunties. She would have to keep them secret, of course, but she was thrilled. 'I've never had an auntie before, now I've got two!'

Bessie almost fell down the stairs in her haste. 'No, yer haven't, sweetheart, yer've got three. Yer wouldn't leave me out, would yer?'

When the girl ran to put her arms around Bessie's waist, and told her she would never leave her out for she was her best friend, Rita and Aggie exchanged glances. Rita wasn't surprised, she'd always felt sorry for Amelia and had a soft spot for her. But Aggie Gordon was having her eyes opened. For the first time she was seeing a young girl who was friendly and affectionate. She certainly didn't take after her stuck-up mother. And Aggie admitted to herself that she'd been wrong, for the child shouldn't be blamed for the faults of the woman who had given birth to her.

'I hope there's going to be food at this here party,' Aggie said, letting her large frame drop on to the couch. There were a few twangs as the springs complained at the sudden weight but Aggie didn't turn a hair. Any chair or couch that couldn't stand her weight was obviously cheap and badly made. After all, she wasn't that heavy. Well, perhaps a bit heavier than most, but not so much you'd notice. She wasn't a flaming giant. 'Did yer hear me, Bessie, 'cos I'm starving. I didn't have no dinner 'cos I thought if I did I wouldn't be hungry, and I'd hate to insult yer by refusing food what yer'd spent hours getting ready for us.'

Bessie and Rita looked at each other and roared with laughter. 'You refuse food, Aggie Gordon? Never in yer life. And I'll bet any money that yer didn't go without yer dinner either, 'cos yer love yer belly too much.'

'I hope yer're not too hungry, Aggie,' Bessie said, ''cos I've only made jelly creams, and they won't fill yer. I didn't bother with sandwiches or anything like that, I was sure yer'd have had yer dinner before yer came.'

Amelia's wide eyes were going from one to the other. She wasn't used to being in a room with more than one person, and had never before heard a conversation going on between three grown women. She'd heard groups of children in the school playground, of course, and she'd always joined in. But she couldn't join in here, for she was at a loss to know why Miss Bessie had said she only had jelly creams when there were sandwiches and a large sponge cake in the larder.

'Some bleeding party this is going to be.' Aggie tossed her head back then turned it sideways so she could wink at Amelia. 'Nowt to eat, and I bet she hasn't even bought a few bottles of milk stout so we can get drunk and forget how hungry we are.'

'Ay, ay,' Bessie said. 'Yer were warned to watch yer language in front of Amelia, 'cos she's not used to women what swear.'

'I'm sorry, queen, and I'll watch me tongue from now on.' Once again she winked at the birthday girl. 'But yer must admit that coming to a party what's got nothing to eat, and not even a bottle of milk stout, well, it's enough to make a saint swear. I'm no saint, mind yer, but I will promise it won't happen again.'

Amelia had never been so close to the big woman before, in fact she was a little afraid of her because she had such a loud voice. But she wouldn't be afraid any more, for she could see laughter lurking in the bright eyes that were almost hidden in the woman's chubby face. 'That's all right, Auntie Aggie, I'll forgive you.'

Aggie was so chuffed she leaned forward, giving the couch false hope that she was about to remove her weight elsewhere. But it wasn't to be, and the largest spring passed the word around to all the smaller ones that it wasn't worth creaking, it would be a waste of energy. 'Ooh, that sounds nice, that does, queen!' Her bosom grew two inches. 'Auntie Aggie!'

Rita tutted. 'D'yer know what would sound nicer? If we wished Amelia a happy birthday and gave her the birthday cards.'

Aggie slapped an open palm to her forehead. 'Oh, stupid Aggie! D'yer know, queen, I'd forget me head if God hadn't had the sense to screw it on. Pass me bag over, Bessie, there's a good girl.'

'Ay, who was yer servant before I came along?'

'I'll get it for her, it'll be quicker.' Rita picked the bag up from the side of the couch and passed it to her neighbour. Then she opened her own bag and took out an envelope. 'Here yer are, sunshine, it's from me and the rest of me family. Have a very happy birthday.'

152

Amelia was beside herself with happiness as she opened up the card to see 'Mr and Mrs Wells' written inside, and underneath the names of the two boys, Billy and Jack. Aggie's card wished her a happy birthday and was signed by her and her husband and the two children, Kitty and Kenny. 'Oh, they are lovely, thank you very much. I've never had a birthday card before – and look at all the names on them. I am a very lucky girl.'

'There's mine to come yet,' Bessie told her. 'It's on the sideboard, sweetheart, you get it while I start to set the table before Aggie dies of hunger.' Once out in the kitchen, she leaned her hands on the draining board, and bit on her bottom lip to keep the tears away. Eight years of age and never had a birthday card. Even the poorest family in the street wouldn't let their child's birthday go without buying them a ha'penny card, even if it meant sitting in the dark with no money for the gas meter. Oh, that girl's mother had a lot to answer for, and if there was any justice in the world, then a day of reckoning would surely come for her.

Evelyn's heart and stomach were all of a flutter as she walked out of Exchange Station under the gaze of people waiting for trains. They must have thought she was mad, parading through the station dressed to kill. She couldn't go through all this rigmarole again, her nerves were shattered. It was a good job it wasn't far to the hotel, she felt so conspicuous. She couldn't tell either if her appearance was perfect. There was only a small mirror in the ladies' cloakroom in the station. She had done the best she could with her hair, but of course, unlike the old days when money was no object, she hadn't been able to visit a hair salon to have it Marcel-waved. But the velvet band around her forehead looked attractive, she hoped.

As she neared the hotel, she stopped for a while to compose herself. The last thing she wanted was to look flustered and unsure of herself. So she took several deep breaths before smiling at the uniformed doorman who held the door open for her. 'Good evening.'

'Good evening, madam, and what a pleasant evening it is.'

Evelyn had barely stepped into the foyer before Philip was standing by her with a smile on his face and a look of admiration in his eyes. 'My dear, you look delightful.' He took her hand and kissed it. 'I think I can safely say you will be the most beautiful woman here this evening, and I'll be the envy of every one of my friends.'

Evelyn allowed him to take her cape which he handed to a nearby page. 'I hope I haven't kept you waiting?'

'If you have, I can assure you it has been worth the wait. I have booked a table for two, my dear, in a quiet alcove where we can talk without interruption.' He had found her attractive from the moment he'd set eyes on her in the office, but tonight she looked more than attractive as she walked with her back straight and her hips swaying gently. She looked positively regal, and Philip was conscious of men turning their heads as they followed the maître d'hôtel past tables catering for larger parties, to the alcove where their table was set with shining silverware, sparkling glasses, a flickering candle, and to add that bit extra to a table set for a lavish meal, a beautiful white and lilac orchid at the side of one of the place settings.

'Oh, how sweet!' Evelyn picked up the delicate flower and held it to her face. Its soft perfume took her back over the years to when one of these expensive flowers was always presented to her by Charles when they were dining out. 'It is really beautiful, Philip, and very thoughtful of you.'

'It matches your beauty, my dear, and my aim in life is to please you.' He waved to the maître d'hôtel who was hovering in the background. 'A bottle of your finest champagne, Alfonso, my companion and I wish to celebrate. We will order our meal later, but first I wish to make a toast.'

Alfonso bowed. 'I will chose the wine myself, Mr Astbury, and it will be the best.'

'What are we toasting, Philip?' Evelyn asked, feeling relaxed now, and very much at home in a room where the women were richly dressed and you could almost smell the wealth. 'Is it your birthday or a special event?'

'A very special event, my dear Evelyn. Our first evening out together socially, which I'm hoping will be the first of many.'

She lowered her eyes and her dark lashes fanned her cheeks. Now was the time to put her plan into action. And because what she was tasting this evening was something she wanted very much for her future life, she had to be word perfect. No more scraping along each week with not enough money to live on, no more living in a poky two-up-two-down house with common people for neighbours. To get what she wanted more than anything in her life, her acting had to be faultless.

'I'm afraid it would have to be the odd occasion for me, Philip, even though I wish it were otherwise. You see, while I am not penniless, I really don't have enough money to buy the sort of clothes I would need for many social outings such as tonight's.' When Philip would have spoken, she silenced him with a raised hand. 'I manage quite well, and am not complaining or looking for sympathy. And I really don't want to have to explain my position, or any part of my past life. That would benefit no one. I would love to see you again, but, as I said, it would only be on the odd occasion, and not often as you suggest. I do not want to lie to you, I prefer to tell you the truth. And the truth is, I have to be very careful with what money I have. I can't afford expensive clothes, nor can I afford taxis every time I go out. My life was very different years ago, but now I must live within my means.'

Much to the irritation of Philip, Alfonso arrived at that moment with a silver bucket half-filled with ice on which rested the bottle of champagne. With an exaggerated flourish, the waiter popped the cork and poured a little into Philip's glass. 'Would you care to taste, Mr Astbury?'

'If it is your choice, Alfonso, then I'm sure it is splendid. Please pour then leave the bottle in the ice. I will attend to it myself and indicate when we are ready to see the menu.'

The only thing that was spoiling the evening for Evelyn was the thought that she might meet up with someone who knew her from the early days, and remembered her connection with the Lister-Sinclair family. 'You appear to be well known here, Philip, is it a favourite haunt of yours?'

'One of them,' he answered briefly, wanting to turn the topic back to Evelyn's situation. 'Let us drink to our friendship, and then I want to know more about you. You see, you intrigue me.'

She sipped the wine, then gave an appreciative nod and giggled as the bubbles tickled her nose. 'I always did like champagne, and I would say this was a very good year.'

'You are a woman of mystery, Evelyn Sinclair,' he said. 'And I very much want to unravel that mystery.'

Again Evelyn's lashes fanned her cheeks. 'There is no mystery, I am what you see.' She raised her eyes to gaze into his. 'My husband idolised me, put me on a pedestal and gave me everything my heart desired. Then came the war, he was killed, and suddenly I found I had to fend for myself. I had little money, and although for the first year after he died I tried to keep in contact with friends, I had to come to my senses eventually, and settle for a comfortable unexciting life.'

Philip reached across the table and covered each of her hands. 'Oh, you poor darling! I can well understand your husband idolising you, it would be very easy to do so. But we can't allow you to hide yourself away, it would be a sin! I want you to let me help you be happy and bring you pleasure. Someone as beautiful as you should not be hidden away.'

Her brain was scheming, but the large brown eyes that stared into his were as innocent as a baby's. 'That is very good of you, Philip. You really are a kind man. And I would like to meet you socially now and again, but that is as far as our relationship can go. I have my pride, and unless I could afford to be fashionably dressed, with my hair waved by a specialist, and able to take a taxi to our meeting place, I would feel most uncomfortable.'

He topped up their glasses. 'Come along, my love, there's nothing quite like champers to cheer one up.' While he drank, his eyes were glued to the face he thought so perfect. Eyes you could swim in, sculpted cheek bones, excellent complexion and a set of perfect white teeth. As well, of course, as a figure any woman would envy. 'I am more than comfortably off, Evelyn, and so are my parents. I don't need to work, I only do so because I would get incredibly bored playing tennis all day and every day like some of my friends. So I am in a position to help you enjoy a pleasurable life.'

Pretending to be naive, she asked, 'What do you mean, Philip? You're not suggesting I should become your mistress, are you?'

He chuckled. 'You say that as though you couldn't bear to be near me! Surely I am not so ugly?'

'You are not a bit ugly, Philip, you are a very attractive man. And I'm sure if I let myself I could fall head over heels for you.'

'After that compliment, my dear, I am determined to help you. And you needn't feel under any obligation to me, as I will explain if you will give me the chance.'

'May we order our meal first? I do feel a little peckish.'

When Evelyn smiled shyly, Philip wasn't to know it was contrived. He felt his heart would surely burst. 'Your wish is my command, my love.' He raised a hand and within a couple of seconds Alfonso arrived with large menu cards. 'Give my companion and me ten minutes to make our choice, my good man, then we will order.'

Evelyn's eyes ran down the menu. She could almost hear her tummy's reaction. It was over eight years since she'd set eyes on such a fine selection of food. But she didn't want to appear too eager as she passed her menu across to Philip. 'I'll have the consommé, and then the fillet of salmon.'

Philip decided he'd have the same, plus another bottle of champagne, and chuckled when Evelyn asked him if he was trying to get her drunk. 'I wouldn't dream of it, my love, but if by some unforeseen circumstance you did become slightly merry, my bachelor flat is just two minutes' walk away.'

'Oh, that's interesting.' Things seemed to be going her way, and Evelyn was prepared to help them along. 'Do you use it often to entertain your lady friends?'

'Not an awful lot, I prefer the comfort of my parents' house. Plus the fact they have a wonderful cook whose pastry melts in the mouth.' Philip sat back in his chair, glass in hand. 'Why do you ask? Do you think that's where I keep my harem?' He was teasing her and also trying to find out more about her. 'Do you object to a man having a mistress?'

'I have never really thought about it,' she told him. 'I imagine there are situations where it would suit a wife for her husband to have a mistress, and in those circumstances I imagine I too would have no objection.'

Philip was digging for her opinion on such subjects, and as he swirled the wine around in his glass, asked, 'What about a young bachelor with no ties? And a young widow who also has no ties? What are your views in these circumstances?

'Really, Philip, I do believe you are teasing me! You are making me blush, and that's something I haven't done publicly for a long time.'

'It suits you, my dear, you look quite enchanting. And it is so refreshing.' Philip saw two waiters approaching with their first course. 'Ah, we will have to continue our very interesting discussion later.'

'Perhaps, when we resume our conversation, we can keep it less personal? Don't you agree, Philip?'

'I disagree, I'm afraid,' he said with a charming smile. 'Things were just getting interesting. I told you I was intrigued by you, and I am determined to get to know the real you, not the small part of yourself you allow strangers to see.'

It was impossible to talk while the waiters were there, dedicated to seeing the thick, white linen napkins were covering their laps at just the right angle before the consommé was served. And having been told by Alfonso that Mr Astbury and his companion must be given the very closest attention, they would have stayed by if Philip hadn't dismissed them, saying he would signal when they were ready for the next course.

'Do they always make such a fuss of you, Philip?' Evelyn had taken a spoonful of the delicious soup and was finding it hard to keep a look of bliss from her face. Oh, what she wouldn't give for a life like this again. 'I think you are spoilt.'

'Alfonso knows he will be handsomely tipped, my dear, and also knows I like the best service in return.' Philip laid down his spoon and patted his lips with the napkin. 'I'll let you into a secret which of course you must not relate to my good friend Alfonso, who would be deeply wounded. I would much prefer being spoilt by you than by him.'

Two glasses of champagne and her plan seemingly on course had the effect of loosening Evelyn's tongue. 'Ah, but I cannot make such delicious consommé, or pastry that melts in the mouth, nor do I have the money to tip you handsomely.'

'All things I could live without, my dear Evelyn.' Philip hadn't failed to notice how relaxed she had become, and wondered if he was making headway. There were so many things he would like to know, but if he rushed her he could scare her off. For instance, she must have parents of her own somewhere, and what about the family of the man she'd married? Why was she so alone in the world? Was there a simple explanation? 'Another glass of bubbly, while we are waiting for the next course?'

Evelyn nodded. Why not make the most of tonight and enjoy herself? 'Thank you, Philip, I think I'm safe with one more glass.'

But an hour later, after the most delicious meal she'd had in years, Evelyn threw caution to the wind when he refilled her glass. 'If I start to giggle or lisp, Philip, then please don't offer me any more drink. I am not used to it these days, and wouldn't like you to see me tipsy and making a fool of myself. Not that I ever have, but I'm relying on you to see I remain sober enough to make my way home.'

'I would not allow you to go home on your own in an inebriated state, my lovely Evelyn, especially in the dark. Have no fear, I will take care of you.'

'I don't want this evening to end, Philip, I'm really enjoying myself. You are very good company. But I want you to promise that you will see me into a taxi when the evening draws to a close?'

'I have another suggestion to make but I don't want to offend you. So listen carefully before you answer. First, would you like to do something to please me?'

Evelyn's brain wasn't too fuddled to know that this could be make or break time. She didn't know what Philip was going to ask, but she had to be prepared. Did she want to stay in her two-up-two-down house for the rest of her days, or would she take whatever terms he offered if it got her out of the rut? 'Why would I not want to please you when you have been so kind to me? Anything within reason, Philip, I will happily agree to.'

'Then let us leave here after our coffee. Come back with me to my bachelor flat. I promise I have no ulterior motive, I will be the perfect gentleman.' He leaned across the table and caught her hand. 'I would like you to see it, and then if you are agreeable, and as eager to see me as I am to see you, we can use it to meet whenever we like. On Monday I take over my uncle's office and you will be my full-time secretary. It will be difficult for us to

160

talk privately there for I would not like there to be a whiff of gossip that would embarrass you. So please come with me now to my flat where we can finish our discussion on how I can help you improve your life. But always remember you are a free agent and can do as you wish. So it's for you to decide, my dear, do you come back to my flat or shall I call you a taxi from here to take you home?'

'I would love to see your flat, Philip. As long as you promise to call a taxi for me when it's time for me to go home.' Evelyn lowered her eyes to hide her look of triumph. 'Even if it's the middle of the night when we finish talking and getting to know each other, you must call a taxi to take me home.'

Philip also felt a sensation of triumph, but warned himself to tread carefully for the time being, he didn't want to frighten her off. 'You have my solemn promise, my dear. I intend to take good care of you.'

Chapter Eleven

'Well, yer did us proud, girl, I'll give yer that.' Aggie Gordon ran the back of one chubby hand over her mouth as she looked across the table to where Bessie sat next to Amelie. 'A feast fit for a king, that was.'

'Aggie's right,' Rita Wells said, her head nodding in agreement. 'And yer made those pies yerself, did yer say?'

'Yeah, I made them last night and put them between plates in the larder,' Bessie said, looking pleased with herself and the world in general. 'I knew it would be too late to make them when I got home from work today, what with shopping and all, so I thought I'd get stuck in last night and get them off me mind.' She chuckled, 'I knew Aggie would have something to say if there wasn't a good spread and she went home hungry, I'd never have heard the last of it.'

Amelia, sitting next to Bessie, couldn't keep still for excitement. This had been the best day of her life and she'd never forget it. 'The pies were lovely, Auntie Bessie, and so were the sandwiches and cakes. I've never had a birthday party before, but I bet this was the bestest anyone ever had.'

'But yer must have been to a party sometime, sunshine, surely a friend's or a relative's?' Rita asked. 'Even if yer've never had one yerself.'

'No, I haven't, Auntie Rita.' It wasn't just the food and the fact it was her birthday that was making Amelia feel so happy. It was being spoken to by adults, and being able to answer them without having to think before speaking. And she had never laughed so much in her life, for Mrs Wells and Mrs Gordon were so funny the way they pretended to be mad with each other and then ended up laughing so much the tears rolled down their cheeks. 'No, I haven't, honest! I haven't got any relatives, you see.' A cheeky grin came to her face as she added, 'Well, I never used to have, but I have now, I've got an Auntie Bessie, Auntie Rita and an Auntie Aggie.' She rocked on her chair with laughter that brought smiles to the faces of the three women. 'There's not many girls get presents like that for their birthday.'

'And the day's not over yet, sweetheart.' Bessie winked knowingly at her two mates who were listening with interest. 'After the table's been cleared and the dishes washed and out of the way, we're going to have a few party games.'

Amelia's eyes nearly popped out of her head and she clapped her hands with glee. 'Ooh, what sort of games, Auntie Bessie?'

'You'll soon find out, sweetheart, after yer've helped me clear the table.'

'I'll help yer with the dishes, Bessie,' Rita said, pushing her chair back. 'Amelia can keep Aggie company.'

It was while the two women were at the sink washing and drying the plates, that they heard Aggie say, 'How come yer always get yer full title, queen?'

Bessie took her hands out of the soapy suds and cocked an ear. 'Oh, God, I hope she doesn't say something she shouldn't. I wouldn't like anything to get back to the queer one in case she stops the girl from coming here.'

'Aggie's not soft, sunshine, she wouldn't do that. Just listen.'

'What do you mean by my full title, Auntie Aggie?'

'Well, queen, I know a lot of women what were christened Amelia, but they always get Milly 'cos it's easier and more friendly. And that's whether they like it or not. It's a case of like it or lump it.'

The girl pulled on a lock of her black hair while giving the matter some thought. 'There's two girls in my class at school called Amelia, and they get Milly. But my mother has told me I must never answer to anything but my proper name, which is Amelia.'

In the kitchen, Bessie tugged on Rita's arm. 'Oh, my God, I hope Aggie doesn't put her foot in it, yer know how outspoken she can be.'

Rita put a finger to her lips. 'Don't look for trouble before it hits yer in the face, sunshine. So far Aggie has been on her best behaviour, only one swear word all afternoon and that's a record for her. But she's taken a fancy to the girl, and I'm positive she'll not say anything that would upset her.'

Bessie's fears were unfounded, for it wasn't Aggie who spoke next but Amelia. 'You know, Auntie Aggie, I would really like to be called Milly, I think it's a nice name. It's just that I don't want to upset Mother, she's very strict. But I could be Milly in Auntie Bessie's house couldn't I, and Amelia everywhere else?'

'That's good thinking, that is, queen, it could be our little secret. And me and me mates wouldn't snitch on yer and get yer into trouble.' Then Aggie said something that sent Bessie and Rita into fits of laughter. 'We'll be the soul of discretion, queen, you'll see.'

Rita poked her head around the door. 'Ye're going up in the world, aren't yer, Aggie? Soul of discretion, where did yer dig that one up from?'

Aggie's laughter was so loud her whole body shook. Her bosom bounced up and down, her tummy pushed the table back, and her chins parted company to go in opposite directions. 'The bloke in the pawnshop said it to me one day when I took Sam's suit in. I was short of a few bob and told him I'd be taking it out again on Saturday before my feller knew it was missing. And 'cos he knows Sam by sight to say hello to, I warned him if he breathed a word to my feller I'd break his bleeding neck. And that's when he said that in his business it paid to be the soul of discretion.' The chair creaked and the table was lifted from the floor as the memory of that day came back to her. 'I've been waiting for an opportunity to use it, and this is the first time it fitted in.' She winked at Amelia. 'I'm sorry about the swear word, queen, but it slipped out, like, before I had a chance to stop it. I don't suppose yer hear swear words in your house, do yer?'

The girl's eyes were alive with devilment. 'No, Auntie Aggie, my mother doesn't swear, she says it's very unladylike. But some of the girls in school do, they get it off their mothers, so I know some bad words.'

The dishes put away now, Bessie and Rita came into the room. 'It doesn't mean because some of yer school friends swear that it's all right, sweetheart,' Bessie said. 'Because while it's bad for older people to use swear words, it's even worse for children. So we'll have to make sure Mrs Gordon doesn't lead yer astray, or yer'll get into trouble with yer mother.'

'I'll not lead her astray, no fear of that!' Aggie was on her high horse now. 'But the girl needs to know a bit more about what life is really like, otherwise when it comes to her leaving school and finding herself a job, she won't have a clue how to mix with other people. And she's bound to hear plenty of very ripe swear words 'cos not everyone she meets will speak as though they've got a ruddy mouthful of plums.'

Amelia's face was glowing and her childish laughter, so seldom heard, was loud. 'Oh, you are funny, Auntie Aggie.'

But Bessie wasn't so sure. 'It's up to her mother to say how she's brought up, not us,' she said, taking a seat on the couch. 'We all have different ideas and think we know what's best for other people, but when it comes down to it, it isn't really any of our business and we have no right to interfere.'

Amelia ran to sit beside Bessie and slipped an arm through hers. 'It doesn't matter how I speak, Auntie Bessie, or what sort of a job I get. Even when I'm grown up, and a young lady, I will always come and see you 'cos you're my very best friend.'

Rita thought it was a sad scene and turned her head away, silently cursing the woman whose child only asked for the one thing that didn't cost anything, and was so easy to give. And that was someone to love her.

'I hope you do, sweetheart.' Bessie squeezed the girl's shoulder. 'I'd be really sad if I ever lost touch with yer. I'm hoping yer live here long enough to grow into a lovely young lady and find the man of your dreams. That would make me very happy.'

Aggie banged a closed fist on the table. 'Before the front of me bleeding dress becomes sodden wet with tears, can we start on these games yer were talking about, queen?'

Bessie shook herself. She knew she shouldn't become too attached to her neighbour's daughter for she could be letting herself in for a lot of hurt and heartache. But she couldn't help herself, no matter what her head told her. For what had started off as liking had turned to fondness and now to love. There wasn't a thing she could do about it. Love wasn't something you could turn off as easily as a tap. 'Right, what about a game of "I spy with my little eye"? Only we'll have to stick to easy words for them what can't spell.'

Aggie took umbrage at that. 'Are you hinsinuating that I can't spell, Bessie Maudsley? I'll have yer know that when I went to school I was always top of the class for spelling.'

Rita chuckled. 'Oh, aye, Aggie, yer've never mentioned that before, yer've been hiding yer light under a bushel. Go on, tell us what the longest word is that yer can spell?'

Without a hesitation, she answered, 'Bleeding,' and she was laughing so much her next words was just about audible. 'And bugger.'

Although Bessie didn't approve, Aggie's laughter was so contagious she couldn't keep a smile at bay. 'Neither of those words will be acceptable in our game, Aggie Gordon, so stick to words with three letters.'

Aggie spread out one of her chubby hands and started ticking the fingers off. 'That's all right then. So I'll be the first one to go, and yer can try and guess my first word which starts with the letter S.'

'It's got to be something in this room, Aggie,' Rita said. 'And it's got to be something we can all see.'

'I know what I'm doing, queen, I'm not thick.' Aggie leaned her chubby elbows on the table. 'Go on, get yer brains working.'

Ten minutes later, and flummoxed, Bessie said, 'We'll have to give in. We've said everything beginning with S in the room, but I'm blowed if there's anything with only three letters in. So shall we give in, Rita and Amelia? Otherwise none of us will get a turn.'

'I give in, Auntie Bessie, 'cos all I can see is the shovel and the sideboard,' Amelia said. 'But they've got more letters in.'

Bessie looked to Rita. 'Do you give in, sweetheart?'

Rita nodded. 'I give in, but there's something fishy here, I can tell by the smirk on Aggie's face. She's having us on, I know.'

'No, I'm not! It's you what's stupid and can't see something what's right in front of yer.'

'Okay, Aggie,' Bessie said, 'we all give in, so what's the word?'

Aggie was gloating. 'S-o-d, sod.'

Rita and Bessie spoke as one. 'Sod! Yer can't use that, it's got to be something in this room!'

Her head wagging nonchalantly from side to side, Aggie asked her next-door neighbour, 'What did yer call me yesterday afternoon, queen, when I spilled a cup of tea on yer?'

Rita looked perplexed for a second, a frown creasing her forehead. Then she slapped a hand on her cheek and said, 'You silly sod!'

Aggie looked as though she'd been cleared of committing a crime. 'That's it, queen, that's what yer called me. A three-letter word, beginning with S, and right in front of yer eyes.'

The first one to laugh was Amelia, and it was as much at the expressions on the faces of Bessie and Rita as the craftiness of Aggie. 'Does that count as a word, Auntie Bessie?'

'No, it flaming well doesn't!' Bessie was red in the face. 'A sod is a piece of earth, it can't be a person or a piece of furniture.'

'Now don't be getting yerself all worked up, queen,' Aggie said, her chins nodding to show they agreed with her, 'or yer'll be having a heart attack. And it would be real thoughtless of yer to have a heart attack and spoil Milly's birthday party.'

While Aggie's two mates roared with laughter, Amelia didn't think it was a bit funny. Her chin jutted out as she said, 'Auntie Bessie isn't going to have a heart attack, so there!'

'No, I'm not, sweetheart, Aggie was only joking. And I think we'll change the game and have another one, so we don't have some silly beggar wasting our time.'

'Oh, no, don't do that, please!' Amelia begged. 'I wanted it to be my turn and I've got a word all ready for you to guess.'

'Of course yer can have a turn, sunshine,' Rita told her, 'after all it is your birthday. Without you we wouldn't be having no party, so go on, what's the first letter? Oh, and before we start, it is something we can see, isn't it?'

Amelia pursed her lips and nodded. 'Yes, and it begins with the letter A.'

Bessie got in first. 'I've got it, it's me aspidistra plant.'

The girl shook her head, looking very serious. 'No, it's not, Auntie Bessie, and you are not even warm.'

Rita's face lit up when she thought she'd guessed the word. 'Armchair! It's the ruddy armchair!'

Again the girl shook her head. 'Wrong, Auntie Rita! And there's not just one of it, either, in case yer say I'm cheating.'

'Got it, got it, got it!' Aggie was over the moon. 'Don't any of yer ever say again that I'm as thick as two short planks. It's the ashes in the grate! I got it as soon as she said there was more than one.'

'Uh-uh,' Amelia said, her face aglow as she swayed back and forth on the couch, her hands clasped between her knees. 'That's not right, either.'

A quarter of an hour later the three women had gone over every item in the room with a fine tooth comb. 'There's nothing else here beginning with A,' Rita said. 'Are yer sure yer've got the spelling right, sunshine?'

'Oh, yes, Auntie Rita, I'm top of the class for English and spelling.'

'What d'yer say then, girls?' Bessie looked from one of her mates to the other. 'Shall we throw in the towel?'

They both nodded. 'May as well,' Aggie said, 'or we'll be here all night.'

'Okay, sweetheart, yer've got us beat, we'll give in.' Bessie raised her brows. 'What's the word that beat us?'

Amelia sat up straight, her hands on her knees. 'It's Aunties! There's more than one of you and you can all be seen. So I haven't cheated, have I?'

Even if she had cheated, there wasn't one woman in the room who was going to tell her and take that radiant smile off her face. 'I think yer've been very clever, sweetheart, I would never have thought of that.'

'Me neither,' Rita told her. 'It took one young girl like yerself to beat three grown-up women. It just goes to show how clever yer are.'

'Aye, and how thick we are.' Aggie was being gracious in defeat. 'D'yer know why I think we didn't get it? Well, it's new to us, isn't it? We're not used to being Aunties. And if anyone in this room contradicts me, I'll clock them one.'

Amelia glanced at the clock on the mantelpiece and saw it was half-past eight. It was past her usual bedtime. But she didn't want the best day of her life to end, not yet. 'Auntie Bessie, I don't have to go to bed yet, do I? I'm not a bit tired, and you said we had another game to play.' Then a picture of her mother flashed through her mind. 'I'll go if you think I should, though, I promised to do as I was told.'

'Of course ye're not going to bed yet, it's yer birthday and that makes it a very special day. A day when ye're allowed a few treats.' Bessie wouldn't have let her go to bed now even if the girl had begged to for there was still a treat in store for her. 'When yer eyes begin to close, then yer can go to bed. But right now we're going to have a game of Pass the Parcel. Which means we'll all have to sit around the table.'

Amelia's hands came together and she held them to her chest. What an exciting day it had been for her. 'How do you play the game, Auntie Bessie?'

'It's easy, sweetheart, yer just pass the parcel on to the one next to yer as quick as yer can, so ye're not caught with it. Anyone caught with it has to pay a forfeit. They either sing or say a piece of poetry.' Bessie pulled a face. 'The only trouble is, there's usually someone who stands with their back to the players and gives a shout when to stop. If one of us does it, there'll only be three playing and it's not worth it.'

'I'll go and get one of the lads if yer like, Bessie?' Rita volunteered. 'They won't be in bed yet, and it'll only be for fifteen minutes at the most.'

So ten-year-old Billy, much to his disgust at having to be at a girl's birthday party, was roped in to stand in front of the window and shout out every few seconds to catch whoever was holding the parcel. There was so much laughing and screaming, he began to enjoy himself, and was surprised to find that the girl who lived opposite with her stuck-up mother wasn't as quiet as he thought, she was really very funny. He for one wouldn't be shouting names after her when she was coming home from school. He couldn't stop himself from cheating by taking sly glances at her when he thought no one was looking, 'cos he wanted each one to have to pay a forfeit.

The first time Billy shouted 'Stop!' Aggie was caught with

the parcel. She tried to shove it towards Rita, but calls of 'Cheat' by the others caused her grudgingly to agree to pay a forfeit. Her choice was the song sung in most of the corner pubs at throwing-out time. It was 'Sweet Nellie Dean', and God help the man who wrote that song for Aggie had a voice like a foghorn and murdered it. But the contortions of her chubby face caused much hilarity and even Billy clapped her at the end. His second victim was Rita, who strongly objected to singing on the grounds that she had a worse voice than Aggie, if that were possible. She opted for the nursery rhyme 'Three Little Pigs'. It didn't go down as well as Aggie's but was worth a round of applause because Rita had at least tried.

Billy timed the third intervention nicely, shouting 'Stop' just as Bessie was handing the parcel to Amelia. The girl was screaming with laughter as she looked down at the parcel in her hand. She had no way of knowing that this was the moment the three women had been waiting for. 'What shall I do, Auntie Bessie? Shall I sing a nursery rhyme?'

'You do what yer want, sweetheart, but remember, the one who is judged to have given the best forfeit gets to keep what's in the bag.'

'Ooh, er, I'm not very good, but I will try.' Amelia took a deep breath and began to sing in a sweet, clear voice.

'Georgie Porgie, pudding and pie, kissed the girls and made them cry,
When the boys came out to play, Georgie Porgie ran away.'

The three women made a lot of noise by banging on the table and shouting 'Hurray'. Even Billy clapped and whistled. 'That's the best so far,' he surprised himself by saying. Usually he gave all girls a wide berth.

Amelia gave him a stern look. 'Auntie Bessie hasn't had her turn yet, and I bet she's the best of the lot.'

'No, I think we'll leave it at that, sweetheart, or me mates will be dying of thirst. I can see by their faces they're ready for their bottle of milk stout. Besides, seeing as it's my house, I can't be the winner or they'll say it was rigged.' Bessie ran her hand over the girl's hair. 'We'll vote now, sweetheart, and if there's a tie Billy can be the judge.'

And of course it was rigged, that was the intention. All hands, even Billy's, shot into the air when Amelia's name came up. 'Go on, queen, open it up,' Aggie said. 'Put us out of our misery. But don't forget, I came a close second.'

'Don't expect too much, sweetheart,' Bessie told her. 'It's only a small token.'

Amelia's hands were shaking with excitement. Never had she dreamed of having a day like today, with so many people being nice to her. Normally her birthday passed without even a mention. 'Can I tear the paper, Auntie Bessie?'

'Of course yer can, sweetheart, but don't be too rough with it in case I want to use it again some time.'

Billy came closer to the table, not wanting to miss anything. And when the paper had been carefully torn and spread open to reveal a doll, instead of jerking his head in disgust as he usually did over girls' sloppy toys, he joined the women in their loud exclamations of surprise. Amelia herself didn't make a sound. She sat wide-eyed, looking down at the first doll she'd ever had in her hands. It was a rag doll, with a pretty china face, long blonde hair tied at the back with a pink ribbon, and dressed in a long dress of pink and white cotton, trimmed at the cuffs and hem with white lace.

Bessie exchanged glances with her two mates before asking, 'Don't yer like it, sweetheart?'

Amelia lifted her head, her eyes wet with tears. 'Is it for me, Auntie Bessie?'

'Of course it is, sweetheart, it's yer birthday present.'

The girl lifted the doll from the paper, stroked its hair, and held it to her chest with one hand while wiping away the tears with the other. Then she pushed her chair back and ran to throw an arm around Bessie's neck. 'She's lovely, Auntie Bessie. She's the first doll I've ever had. You are very kind to me, and I do love you.'

Rita was beginning to understand why Bessie loved this girl so much, no one could help it. Except her mother, of course, who must be heartless. 'You can go now, Billy, we won't be playing any more.'

'Ah, ay, Mam! Can't I stay for a bit, just a few minutes?'

'No, yer can't, sunshine, me and me mates are going to have a drink now.'

'Thanks for helping us out, Billy,' Bessie said over Amelia's head. 'I appreciate it.'

Amelia was feeling happy and sad at the same time, but she didn't forget the manners she'd had drummed into her. 'Yes, thank you, Billy.' Then she had a thought, and giggled. 'It was a good job you stopped at me, otherwise your mother or Auntie Aggie might have ended up winning the doll.'

'Yeah! That would have been funny.' He was chuckling as he stepped into the street. His mother had opened the front door for him, and he grinned up at her. 'She's all right, that girl, not like her stuck-up mother.'

'I don't want to hear yer saying that to anyone else, Billy, d'yer hear? None of us can help the mothers we get, but you just thank yer lucky stars that yer ended up with me.' She watched as he crossed the cobbled street. 'Yer'll be in bed when I get home, so goodnight and God bless, sunshine.'

'Goodnight, Mam.'

Rita closed the door and went back into the living room. Amelia was sitting on the couch next to Bessie, inspecting the doll's clothes. Bessie had bought the doll for sixpence and made the clothes herself on the old Singer hand-machine she kept in her bedroom. She didn't use it much, for she spent her working life behind a sewing machine and never felt like starting again when she got home. 'Ay, sunshine, yer made a good job of that dress, it looks smashing,' Rita said. 'Yer could make a few bob taking sewing in, 'cos that looks really professional.'

Amelia lifted the dress on the doll. 'Look, Auntie Rita, it's got knickers on as well, and they've got lace round the legs.' She held the doll to her chest. 'I do love it, and I'll always love it and always look after it and keep it safe.' She glanced at Bessie. 'Can I keep it in my bedroom here, please, Auntie Bessie? 'Cos my mother thinks dolls are childish and she might not let me play with it.'

'Oh, go 'way,' Aggie said. 'Yer mam won't stop yer playing with the doll, that's what little girls do. Even if it's only for half an hour a night before yer go to bed.'

'Please let me keep it here, Auntie Bessie, please! It can sleep on my bed when I'm not here, and it won't be in your way.'

Bessie could see the girl was agitated and wasn't going to spoil the day for her. 'Of course she can stay here, sweetheart, she'll be company for me as well as keeping the bed warm for you.'

'Aren't yer going to give her a name?' Rita asked softly. 'She'll have to have a name so yer can talk to her.'

Aggie added her twopennyworth. 'And as she's a pretty doll, queen, with a pretty dress and lace on her knickers, yer'll need to give her a nice name.'

The girl looked very undecided, as though she didn't really believe what she'd been told. 'You won't make me take her home, will you, Auntie Bessie, promise?'

'I've said she can stay here, sweetheart, and I never tell fibs or break a promise. So, now can you think of a nice name you would like for her? Or shall we all make suggestions until yer come to one yer fancy the best?'

'I know what name I want to give her, Auntie Bessie. As soon as I opened the paper and saw her lying on my knee, I thought she looked as pretty as a flower and the name Daisy came to me.

I've seen daisies growing in a garden near our school, and they're yellow and bright and look cheerful. So I'd like that to be her name.'

'Then so be it, sweetheart, because she's your doll and it's only right you should call her what you want to. Besides, I think Daisy is a lovely name.' Bessie appealed to her mates, 'Don't yer think so, ladies?'

Rita nodded. 'Whenever I see a daisy, it always reminds me of sunshine. There are usually some growing wild in the park by the swings, and they always cheer me up.'

Aggie was nodding her agreement. 'And what about the song, "Daisy, Daisy, Give Me Your Answer Do"? That's not half a cheerful song, I always have to sing along to it.'

Amelia's face was a picture of happiness as she held the doll to her cheek. It was the first toy she'd ever had to call her own, and her pleasure knew no bounds. 'I'm going to sing her to sleep tonight. And I'll wrap my nightie around her, so she won't be cold.'

'There'll be no need for that, sweetheart,' Bessie said, pushing her chair back and making for a cupboard in the sideboard. 'Daisy's a very posh doll, she's got her own blanket.' She held a square piece of pink blanket aloft. 'I knew yer wouldn't want her to get cold.'

As the three neighbours were to say later, when the girl was in bed and they had their glasses of milk stout in front of them, they couldn't remember seeing anyone so happy. Amelia had wrapped the doll in the blanket, cuddled her to her chest, then rocked her for a while before saying, 'I think me and Daisy would like to go to bed now, Auntie Bessie, because we are both very tired. But we want to thank you for bringing us together, and we both love you very much. And you too, Auntie Rita and Auntie Aggie.'

She'd kissed everyone, told Daisy to be a good girl and kiss her aunties, then she'd made her way up the stairs, cuddling the doll as though it was the most precious thing on earth. And, needless to say, left behind three women whose tears kept their glasses topped up.

Chapter Twelve

Philip had his hand on the small of Evelyn's back as they stepped through the doors of the hotel and into the cool night air. He felt her shiver. 'Oh, you are cold, my dear, let me put my overcoat across your shoulders, I can't have you catching a chill.'

'I'm not really cold, Philip, it was coming out of the warm atmosphere that caused me to shiver. And there is a feel of autumn in the air.'

Philip was being very gentlemanly and draped his fine wool overcoat across her shoulders. Cupping her elbow, he said, 'We'll be at my apartment in a few minutes and you'll soon be warm, I left a fire burning.' Then he asked, 'Did you come to the hotel by taxi?'

'Yes, I could hardly come by tram in this attire, I would look so out of place. And I'm relying on you to arrange a taxi to take me home later, if you will be so kind?'

'Don't let's talk of you going home, my love, I hope you will stay for a while. After all, there is no one at home expecting you, is there?'

Evelyn felt no guilt about continuing the lie, nor did she give any thought to her daughter. That was something she would sort out later, when she knew Philip better and he was well and truly under her spell. She shook her head. 'No, I live alone, as I told you.'

'Then the night is ours, my love. There is so much I want to know about you.' He pulled her to a halt outside a building.' This is where my apartment is.'

Evelyn's surprise could be heard in her voice. 'But I thought all these buildings were business premises!'

Taking a key from his pocket, Philip placed it in the lock of a door set slightly back from the building's frontage. 'The ground floor consists of three offices. My apartment covers the whole of the second floor, and as you can see has a private entrance.' He pushed open the door, waited for her to enter, then followed her, closing the door behind him and switching on an electric light. 'It's just the one flight of stairs, my lovely, and don't look so frightened, there are no bogeymen.'

'I'm not afraid,' Evelyn told him, thinking a few compliments wouldn't go amiss. 'Not when you are here to protect me.'

When they reached the top of the stairs, Philip led her towards one of the four doors she could see leading off the landing. 'In here, my lovely, and I'm happy to say the fire is still glowing.'

It took all of Evelyn's willpower to stop her jaw from dropping at the sight of the luxurious furniture in the huge room. She knew Philip's family must be well-to-do because of his clothes and his air of confidence, but had never expected to see such opulence in the apartment he said he seldom used. 'It seems a large place for one man,' she said. 'Or do you share with another person?'

'Good heavens, no!' he said, taking her cape from her. 'I could never share with anyone, certainly not a man anyway. Besides, I have no need to. My father owns the whole building.'

'You are very lucky, Philip.' Evelyn lowered herself on to the huge brown leather couch. 'I'm surprised you haven't been snaffled up by now, you must have had plenty of chances.'

He chuckled as he walked towards the massive mahogany sideboard where there were four bottles standing on a silver tray. 'Many, many chances, my dear Evelyn, but the right one never came along. Now, what would you like to drink?'

'You choose,' she told him, while crossing her legs and making sure she showed more than a little of her slim ankles.

'But not a full glass, please, Philip. I have to find my way home, remember.'

'Not for several hours, my lovely Evelyn, for I intend to start unravelling the mystery that surrounds you. And I need my senses intact to do that.'

'There is no mystery surrounding me, Philip, I promise you. What you see is what I am.'

He sat down beside her and handed her a glass half filled with deep red wine. 'I like what I see, my lovely, but surely there is more to your life than you admit? Perhaps something too hurtful for you to talk about?'

'I have told you about my husband and how he was killed. What I haven't told you is that although we had courted for a year or two before the war, I only saw him a few times after he joined the Army when he was allowed home on leave. When he learned he was being shipped out, he was given three days' leave and we were married by special dispensation on his last day. I never saw him again after he went back to join his unit.'

Philip placed his glass on a mahogany side table before putting an arm across her shoulders. 'Oh, you poor darling, how very sad. It must have been heartbreaking for you, and I can understand why you have no wish to talk about something that must still cause you great pain and sadness.' He pulled her close. 'And has there been no one else in the years since then? No one to hold you close and soothe your aching heart?'

'I didn't want anyone else. Oh, there were chances, several suitors came along after my hand in marriage, but I could not feel anything for them.' Evelyn was lying so well she actually thought that what she was saying was the truth. So she stretched her made-up story further, for she had an idea Philip was going to delve deeper into her past. 'In fact, because I turned away several men my parents approved of, and they were eager to get me off their hands, it caused a rift between us and I am no longer in touch with them.' Her wide brown eyes stared into Philip's and he could feel his heartbeat quicken. 'How could I marry a man who didn't excite me or make my heart flutter at the sight of him? No, I preferred spinsterhood to marriage to a man I didn't love.'

And Philip believed every word she said. She had solved, for him, the mystery of why she had no family, and he never thought for one second she wasn't telling the truth. 'Oh, my poor darling Evelyn.' He pressed her head to his shoulder and kissed her brow. 'D'you think the time could come when the sight of me might cause your heart to flutter?'

'We hardly know each other, Philip.' She was clear enough in the head to keep to her plan. And that didn't include giving in to him quickly. Anything easily obtained is quickly tired of. 'I am fond of you already, it would be hard not to be, but it would be silly to jump into saying things one might regret within weeks. We will be working together every day from Monday, and that will be the testing time. You may find I am not the sweet woman you obviously think I am. So shall we give it a couple of weeks, Philip, and see what our thoughts are then?'

He raised his eyebrows. 'I am looking forward to seeing you each day, I will walk to the office with a spring in my step. But I want to see you outside work as well. We can work together as diligently and efficiently as ever my Uncle Simon and Miss Saunders did. I have every intention of applying myself to my new job with the same zest and energy I did in my previous firm. But I can't for the life of me see why we shouldn't meet as friends outside the office, can you?'

Evelyn ran a finger down his cheek. 'You are very forceful, my dear, and obviously used to having your own way. But I too am quite stubborn, so our relationship should be a very interesting one. I will give in to you as far as seeing each other outside work, but only for the next two Saturdays. As I have told you, my wardrobe is not what it used to be, and it will take me a while to save for suitable clothes.'

'I have already decided to increase your wages by a pound a week. That should help a little until we come to some other arrangement.'

'I can't take an increase in pay beyond the one I have already received, which is what a qualified secretary is entitled to. Any extra and the other staff would not be happy. Apart from the fact that it would set tongues wagging and they would see me as a painted lady.'

Philip chortled. 'A painted lady! Oh, I do like that description of you. If only it were true we would not be sitting here all sedate and respectable, we would be much more intimate.'

Evelyn slapped his hand playfully. 'I can see I'm going to have trouble keeping you in order, Mr Astbury. Now, you can be a good host and show me around this bachelor flat of yours which I find most interesting.'

He pulled her to her feet. 'Your wish is my command. We shall start off with the kitchen.'

It contained every modern appliance possible, and was an eye-opener to Evelyn after her own tiny kitchen with its huge chipped sink and only one cold water tap. She found the sheer luxury of the bathroom breathtaking. Of course the electric lighting was a novelty to her, for she was only used to gas. 'Very nice,' was her only comment. She was determined not to let him see how surprised she was, and would be bitterly ashamed if he ever saw where she lived.

However, when he threw open the bedroom door she couldn't help but gasp. It was magnificently furnished, and the huge bed with its rich drapes and covers was the largest she had ever seen as well as being the most luxurious. But what struck her most forcibly was the masculine style which had been so noticeable in every room. Not a trace of anything female here. 'You have a very beautiful apartment, Philip, I feel quite jealous,' she said softly.

'My dear, the apartment is at your disposal whenever you feel the need of privacy. When you decide you would like our friendship to progress further, we can spend many a pleasant night in each other's company here.' He squeezed her shoulder and smiled down into her face. 'You have no need to pull away from me, my love, for I spoke in hope, not as a threat.'

'I didn't pull away from you, why should I? I would only pull away from someone I was scared of, and I have no fear of you.'

'Come, let us go back and relax on the couch with our glasses refilled. We can talk until the wee small hours of the morning, then I shall see you safely into a taxi before returning to this room which will hold no pleasure for me without you to grace it.'

Evelyn was feeling the effects of drink by now, and though she was not quite tipsy enough to be careless of what she was saying, she was happy to appreciate the compliments and the nearness of this very handsome man who also happened to be very rich. It was so long since she'd been flattered and pampered, she could feel herself basking in the attention. 'You are spoiling me, Philip, and while I should resist you, and start on my journey home, I feel too snug and warm to move.'

'Why should you move when you have no reason to? No one is watching the clock, waiting for you to come home. No one will be there to welcome you, and no fire to greet you. Make me happy and stay for a while, I want you by my side. Close enough to touch, to smell the sweetness of you.'

A lock of Philip's hair had fallen over his forehead. Evelyn reached up to push it back. 'Oh, you are very tempting, dear, but I'm trying to control myself. This is not the time for flattery. I have had far too much to drink to think clearly.'

He caught her hand and held it to his cheek. 'Are you saying that when Monday comes, and you are stone cold sober, perhaps you will find me unattractive?'

'Good grief, no! I was stone cold sober the first time I saw you in the office; and even at first glance I found you a very attractive man. Never for one second did it enter my head that you were a bachelor, not with your good looks.'

'And not for one second did I think I would ever be sitting in my lounge with the beautiful creature I first saw tapping at a typewriter. Fate has stepped in, my lovely, so let us take advantage of our luck.'

Wrapped in Philip's arms, Evelyn didn't want the evening to end as she revelled in the luxury of her surroundings, and the sweet words being whispered in her ear. They talked and kissed, and never once did Philip overstep the mark. He wanted to – oh, how he wanted to – but he was afraid of frightening her off. After all, hadn't she told him she was only married for one day before her husband was sent overseas? And she'd implied there had been no other men in her life, so she would be a novice when it came to love making. He would have to be patient until the time was right, and she came to him of her own free will. Then he would need to be gentle and tender.

It was the grandfather clock on the wall striking the hour of four that brought Evelyn out of her dreaming. Pushing Philip gently away from her, she said, 'I really must be going, my dear, or like Cinderella my coach will turn back into a pumpkin.' She kissed his lips with the softness of a butterfly. 'Ring for a taxi for me, Philip, please.'

This wasn't to his liking. He was besotted with her and wished she was as free with her favours as some of the other women he knew. But he dismissed that thought before it took root; he didn't want her to be like the other women, he wanted her to be special. 'I will ring now, my love, although it will break my heart. I would like you to stay here with me forever.'

Evelyn was fastening her cape. 'The easiest and quickest way to tire of someone is to be in their company too often. And I don't want you to tire of me, Philip, not when we are just getting to know each other.'

'You promise you will come here again, very soon?'

'I promise. Now ring for a taxi, please.'

'What address will I tell him to take you to?'

She tapped his nose with a forefinger. 'There are some mysteries I would like to retain, my dear. I will give the driver the address when he comes.'

Philip dialled a number, gave his address, then after replacing the receiver, told Evelyn the taxi would be there in ten minutes. He reached for his coat which had been casually thrown over the back of a chair. Taking a wallet from the inside pocket, he slipped his hand inside and brought out a five-pound note. 'This will help towards your taxi fares. I will instruct the driver to make sure you reach home safely.'

'Philip, I can't take money from you!' Even while she was speaking, Evelyn was thinking what she could do with so much money. 'Besides, the driver wouldn't be able to change that, he'd think I was mad. I have a few shillings in my purse, that should be enough to cover the fare.'

Philip folded the five-pound note three times then slipped it down the front of her dress. 'I insist you take it, my darling. I cannot allow you to pay for spending an evening with me, especially when you have delighted and charmed me with your presence. Please take it, my lovely, and put it to whatever use gives you pleasure. If you need anything ... new clothes, jewellery, perfume, or anything else you desire ... you only have to ask.'

Evelyn knew she had him in the palm of her hand now, and felt safe in saying, 'That would make me feel like a kept woman, Philip, and I'm afraid that wouldn't sit well on my shoulders.'

He shook his head. 'Not at all, I would never think that of you. I have had many fleeting romances, none of which were serious, and have always been generous with the women concerned. I can assure you, not one of them has complained about my generosity. I wasn't buying them, I was merely giving them a gift because I like to please the opposite sex. There is nothing sinister in that.'

As though on impulse, Evelyn kissed his cheek. He wasn't to know it, but the kiss was to thank him for enabling her to accept his money. 'How could there be anything sinister in anything you do, my dear? I will keep the money in the spirit it was given. Thank you sincerely, and I apologise if I have displeased you.'

Philip was all smiles again. 'I think we must go downstairs now, the taxi should be waiting for you. I will count the minutes until I see you in the office on Monday, and we can arrange to meet here again next week.'

Evelyn turned to wave to Philip out of the back window then leaned towards the glass partition that separated her from the driver. 'I need to pick up something from Exchange Station, driver, so would you kindly take me there first, please?'

'There'll be no one there this time of the morning,' the driver growled in a husky voice. 'The place will be deserted.'

'I have a key to a left luggage locker so I don't need the services of station staff. You can drive into the station and I'll be less than five minutes.'

'Yer'll have to pay extra for the waiting time.' The driver couldn't stand these poncey people who had more money than they knew what to do with while thousands of families in Liverpool were living below the poverty line. 'It'll cost yer an extra tanner.'

'You will be paid for your time, my good man, have no fear.' Evelyn stepped out of the taxi and shivered. The station was deserted and eerie. She lost no time in opening the locker and taking out the bag with her working clothes in it. She got into the back of the taxi with it, placing it on the seat next to her. When she spoke next it was an order, not a request. 'Take me to Newsham Street, driver, and drop me off halfway down. And please be as quiet as you can, I don't want my neighbours complaining.'

There was a look of disgust on the driver's face as he set the taxi in motion. She must be a good-time girl, this one, been out to make herself a few bob. She was dressed to kill, but her clothes didn't go with the address she'd given him. He knew the area well, and they were two-up-two-down houses. Not that there was anything wrong with living in a two-up-two-down house, for he lived in one himself and his neighbours were the salt of the earth. They never put on airs and graces and pretended to be something they weren't. Not like the one he had in the back of his cab now, giving orders as though she was the Queen of bloody Sheba. She must think he was born yesterday, telling him not to make a noise 'cos she didn't want her neighbours complaining. More likely she didn't want them to see her all dressed up like a scarlet woman.

As the taxi turned into her street, Evelyn asked, 'How much is that, driver?'

'I'll tell yer when I've stopped the cab, and checked the mileage and the waiting time.'

'Stop here, please.'

The tone of her voice rubbed him up the wrong way and he carried on past several more houses. When he heard her knock on the glass, he growled, 'If I'd pulled up sharp, the brakes would have woken the whole bloody street, missus, so yer can't have everything yer own way.' Normally the driver was a pleasant man who would jump out of his taxi to help a passenger. But not this one, talking to him as though he'd crawled out from under a stone. She could get out of the cab under her own steam. 'That'll be three bob, missus.'

That was all the money Evelyn had in her purse, and it would leave her without any change to buy food from the corner shop for her and Amelia. Still, she comforted herself with the thought of the five-pound note nestling between her breasts. The corner shop wouldn't be able to change it, but she could borrow on the strength of it from her neighbour. 'Here you are, and please try not to make a noise as you drive away.'

Evelyn's mistake was in not closing the passenger door behind her. She tutted angrily when she heard the driver slam it shut before driving away. She got herself in so much of a dither, trying to open the front door quickly in case any nosy neighbour had been woken, that her hand was shaking and she had a problem fitting the key into the lock. Once inside, she leaned back against the door and breathed a sigh of relief. She'd got away with it, thank God, but she couldn't go through that again, she'd have to make other plans in future. Far better to stay the night at Philip's and come home at a respectable time when she wouldn't be so noticeable. That could easily be arranged if she was able to leave several changes of clothes at his apartment. The only thing that stood in her way was her daughter. But she'd find a way around that when she'd had a few hours' sleep and her head was clear. At least she hadn't been found out.

However, the banging of the taxi door, and the noise of the engine, had been heard by Evelyn's next door neighbour. Bessie hadn't been able to drop off to sleep, had spent hours tossing and turning. The reason for this unrest was her neighbour, and the manner in which she treated her daughter. Also, Bessie hadn't believed the tale Evelyn had told her about visiting an old friend she hadn't seen since school days. The words didn't ring true. And while Bessie didn't care what her neighbour got up to, she worried it might in some way affect Amelia.

So the slamming of the car door, in the silence of the night, was enough to take Bessie from her bed to the window. The gas lamp in the street didn't throw out much light, but it was enough for Bessie to catch a glimpse of Mrs Sinclair, and that short glimpse was sufficient to make her gasp in surprise and wonder. She thought she was seeing things at first, but the few seconds her neighbour spent fiddling to get her key in were enough to tell her her eyes weren't playing tricks on her. She'd never seen anyone dressed like that before, not in her whole life. The sight certainly confirmed the doubts Bessie had about Evelyn visiting an old school friend. The woman looked as though she'd been to a fancy dress ball, or, more likely, been spending time with a rich fancy man.

Bessie went back to her bed and sat on the side of it. She shook her head, not knowing what to think about the whole set-up. It should be interesting tomorrow when her neighbour came to pick up Amelia. Whatever she said would be a pack of lies, for she was good at that. Still, it would be interesting.

She slipped between the sheets and lay on her back staring up at the ceiling. She wouldn't say anything to Amelia's mother about seeing her coming home at half-past four in the morning in a taxi. No, she'd act daft and ask Evelyn if she'd enjoyed visiting her old school chum. Pretend to be interested, like. The answer she got would be a web of deceit and lies, but it wouldn't be dull and she'd have a good laugh afterwards. And they did say that if you gave a liar enough rope, they would hang themselves. Not that Bessie wished that on the woman. God forbid, she was still Amelia's mother.

Telling herself there was no point lying there wondering what was going on when she would be told tomorrow exactly as much as Evelyn Sinclair wanted her to know, Bessie snuggled down and made a determined effort to go to sleep. Her last conscious thought, as she pulled the blanket up over her shoulders, was that the stuck-up so-and-so wasn't worth losing sleep over. And very soon after that, the room was filled with the sound of her even, gentle snoring.

In the next bedroom Amelia lay dreaming with her rag doll pressed close to her chest, the one thing the child had ever been able to call her very own.

* * *

It was eleven o'clock when Evelyn walked up Bessie's back yard. Amelia, who was sitting on the couch with the doll on her knee, heard the latch clicking back into place, and a look of fear came over her face. 'Don't let Mother see Daisy, Auntie Bessie, or she'll take her off me.'

'Run upstairs, sweetheart, and we'll keep her a secret.' Bessie stood at the bottom of the stairs until she heard the girl reach the landing, then put a smile on her face and went to open the kitchen door. 'Oh, hello, Mrs Sinclair, I wasn't expecting yer until about twelve o'clock, I thought yer'd be enjoying a lie-in.' She stood aside to let Evelyn pass and told herself to be as polished as her neighbour. 'Amelia is upstairs, she won't be a minute. Sit yerself down while ye're waiting and tell me how the visit to yer old school friend went. Did yer enjoy catching up on old times?'

'Oh, yes, it was lovely, talking about all the girls in our class, and wondering what paths their lives have taken. Elizabeth has seen a couple of them over the years, and tells me they married well and have good lives.'

'That's nice for yer, I'm glad yer enjoyed yerself.' Bessie was waiting to see if Amelia's mother would ask how her daughter's party had gone. Surely she wouldn't let it pass without a word? But so far, nothing! 'Would yer like a cup of tea? It won't take me a minute, and Amelia can have one before she leaves.'

'I would love one, thank you so much.' Evelyn laced her fingers together when Bessie went out to the kitchen. How was she going to ask to borrow some money for food? What excuse could she use? Telling her about the five-pound note was out of the question because people in Miss Maudsley's position had probably never set eyes on one in their lives. And Evelyn needed some money, even if it was only a shilling, for there was no food in the house and she was starving. Nor did she have any coal to light a fire, and the house was freezing.

Amelia came down the stairs and stood sedately in front of her mother. 'Hello, Mother, did you have a nice time with your friend?'

'Yes, I did. Have you behaved yourself for Miss Maudsley?'

Waiting in the kitchen for the kettle to boil, Bessie could feel herself getting mad. Couldn't the woman ask her daughter if she'd had a nice party, instead of asking if she'd behaved herself? Was she so selfish she'd never given a thought to whether her daughter enjoyed her birthday? The kettle started to whistle and Bessie poured the boiling water into the dark brown teapot. Then she walked to stand in the kitchen doorway. 'I'll let it brew for a few minutes, I can't stand weak tea.' She watched as Evelyn put a hand in the pocket of her coat, shook her head, then put a hand in her other pocket. 'Have you lost something, Mrs Sinclair?'

Evelyn's acting was perfect. With a look of panic on her face, she tried each of her pockets again. 'Oh, dear, I had two shillings in my pocket when I was on the tram last night, now I don't seem to have them. I must have dropped them getting off and didn't hear them fall.'

Bessie felt like applauding. If she didn't know the woman better, she would have believed what she was being told. Dropped them on the tram indeed? What a ruddy liar! But she'd go along with her neighbour, just for the hell of it. 'Oh, dear, that's a shame. It's a lot of money to lose.'

'It's worse than you think, Miss Maudsley, for I intended to send Amelia to the corner shop for a bag of coal and some food. There's nothing in the house for our dinner.' Evelyn wrung her hands. 'Oh, dear, what am I going to do?'

Bessie was watching Amelia's face and it spoke volumes. She showed no emotion at all. It was as if she wasn't involved and had no worry that there wasn't going to be any dinner. This told Bessie that the child was used to her mother telling lies, and felt no pity for her. And, the little woman asked herself, why should the child pity someone who never touched her, kissed her, or told her she loved her?

It was for Amelia's sake that Bessie said, 'I can lend yer a couple of bob, but I would have to have it back before the rent man comes. I don't miss my rent money for anyone.'

'I will give it back to you tomorrow, definitely.' There was relief in Evelyn's voice, she didn't like having hunger pains. Anyway, her life would be changing for the better very soon and then she wouldn't have to cadge off this insignificant little woman. 'You are very kind and I promise to repay you when I call for Amelia tomorrow night.'

'She can stay here for a few hours, if yer like,' Bessie said, noting the happiness she'd seen in the girl's eyes all morning had now turned to sadness. 'It would give yer a chance to put yer feet up for a while.'

'No, I need her to go to the corner shop for bread and whatever meats they have. And a bag of coal.' And while Evelyn stood waiting for Bessie to get the two silver shillings out of her purse, she silently added, that her daughter could also light the fire and wash any dirty dishes. For in the new life she intended for herself, she couldn't be seen with broken, dirty fingernails. She'd have to be perfectly groomed at all times if she was to regain the luxurious lifestyle she'd once had.

As Evelyn held her hand out for the money Bessie was passing to her, she caught sight of her daughter out of the corner of her eye. And for a second she was brought down to earth. But it was only for a second, because she had no intention of letting Amelia stand in her way. How she was going to get around that she didn't know, but she would do it. For to tell Philip now that she had an eight-year-old daughter would be to say goodbye to all her dreams.

Chapter Thirteen

Evelyn wasn't a bit shy about meeting Philip in the office on Monday morning. Nor was she embarrassed, for she felt there was nothing to be embarrassed about. She wasn't a child, at twenty-nine years of age, and they hadn't done anything improper, though she wasn't stupid enough to think it would always be so. The prospect didn't worry her, she was willing to do anything to get what she wanted. Although she was a little concerned about her inexperience in love making. There was only ever the once with Charles, and that was in the confined space of his car. She couldn't remember much about the actual deed, except the slight discomfort at first. This wasn't the case for Charles, though, for the moans and sighs coming from him had told her he was finding great pleasure in the act. She, on the other hand, was left unmoved.

She was going through the large three-drawer filing cabinet, making sure the correspondence was correctly filed and familiarising herself with the names of clients, when the office door opened and Philip breezed in with a huge smile on his face. 'Good morning,' he said, then closed the office door before adding, 'my lovely.'

'Good morning, Mr Philip.' Evelyn wagged a finger at him. 'Please be careful, anyone could walk in.'

He was grinning as he hung his coat on the ornately carved coat stand. 'There is no one to walk in, my darling. I could hear James dictating to Miss Coombes, and the young lady taken on in your place, Grace Carr, is now making us a pot of tea. And I

192

did tell her that she must never enter either office without knocking.' He walked over to where she stood, kissed her cheek, then sat in his swivel chair. 'Are there any letters awaiting a reply?'

'The post has arrived, but I left it for Miss Carr to sort out. That was one of my duties and I thought it should be left with her. If it pleases you, I will go and collect it from her.'

Philip shook her head. 'It pleases me that you stay here, where I can feast my eyes on you. We can deal with the post later.' He crossed his legs and raised his brows. 'You obviously arrived home safely on Sunday morning, so I won't bore you by asking. What I am interested in is, did you enjoy your time in my company? Did I pass the test?'

Evelyn was leaning her elbows on the cabinet, and smiling up at him. 'Did you really think there was any chance of not passing the test?'

'You are a woman of mystery, my love, so I am not taking anything for granted.'

Evelyn glanced towards the door. 'Please can we keep to "Mrs Sinclair" while we are in the office, Philip? If they knew of our relationship I would feel quite embarrassed and it would sour our friendship.' The words were barely out of her mouth before there came a tapping on the door. 'This will be Miss Carr.'

Philip jumped to his feet to open the door. 'Ah, refreshment. There's nothing better than a cup of tea to charge the brain cells. Leave the tray on my desk, Miss Carr, Mrs Sinclair will bring it out when we're ready.'

As soon as the door closed, Evelyn said, 'That's very high-handed of you, Philip! We only ever have one cup of tea first thing in the morning, not a pot full. If Mr Woodward receives the same treatment, he's in for a shock. He may not like changes being made without his consent.'

'James Woodward is the least of my worries at the moment,' Philip said. 'My main concern is that I am your first priority in this office. Anything that goes amiss outside these four walls, I will deal with. Inside them I want your undivided attention. So now, woman, I want you to pamper me by pouring out the tea.'

Evelyn knew he wasn't being serious, but she intended to show him she wasn't going to be an easy catch. He appeared to get everything he wanted in life very easily, and she decided he would appreciate her more if he had to do some running. 'I'm going to collect the post from Miss Carr, so perhaps *you'll* be good enough to pour the tea while I'm away. There is work to be done, Mr Philip, we need to earn our wages.'

'Have your cup of tea first, the post will wait for ten minutes.'

But Evelyn was already opening the door. 'I can drink it while I'm opening the post, to save time.'

Philip was more subdued for the rest of the morning. As Evelyn opened the letters and passed them across the desk to him, he read each one carefully, making a mental note of its contents before setting it aside ready to dictate a reply. Neither of them spoke again until all the envelopes had been opened and the letters stacked in front of Philip. Then he said. 'You are a slave driver, Mrs Sinclair.'

She shook her head. 'As you know, Mr Philip, I'm not particularly quick at taking dictation, and a couple of those letters are urgent and need to be in the lunchtime post.' She gave him the benefit of her coy smile. 'Besides, I thought if we got through the post quickly, it would give us more time to talk.'

'When you look at me like that, I will forgive you anything. Now, I believe there are four letters that need to be answered right away, so if you will get your pencil and pad, I will start to dictate. And I will speak slowly and clearly, so you can keep up.'

Evelyn left her chair to pick up the tray. 'I'll take this out and ask Miss Carr if she will be kind enough to make us two more cups of tea. Once we're refreshed, we will sail through those four letters – I hope! My typing isn't much better than my shorthand, and it will take me all my time to have the letters ready for the noon post.'

'Don't upset yourself if they are not ready for the lunchtime post, my love. If they're posted by five o'clock they will still arrive by tomorrow's first delivery.'

'Let us stick to the routine of the office, Mr Philip, at least until my speed has improved. I'm afraid that any diversion from that would be put down to my inexperience. The last thing I want is an irate client storming into the office complaining he has not received a reply to his letter. It is I who would have to shoulder the blame, not you. Miss Saunders ran this office like clockwork for your Uncle Simon, I want to do no less for you.'

Philip's cheeky grin reappeared. 'I bet Miss Saunders didn't boss Uncle Simon around, as you seem intent on bossing me.' He held a hand to his heart. 'But I won't complain, for you are much more beautiful than Miss Saunders.'

Like giving a child a sweet to keep them happy, Evelyn blew him a kiss before she opened the door. 'Thank you, my dear. And now I will collect my pencil and pad, and work shall commence in earnest.'

Philip was very fluent in his speech, and spoke clearly and slowly until he found Evelyn was more than keeping up with him. He dictated the last two letters at his normal speed. When he had finished he complimented her. 'Very good, Mrs Sinclair, you can now go to the top of the class.'

'Thank you, kind sir, I am pleased you are happy with me.'

'I am more than happy with you, my dear, and will remain so as long as you remember it is my class you are in, and I am your teacher.'

Evelyn closed her note pad and pushed her chair back. 'Ah, it will be interesting to know which lessons exactly you have in mind.' She was feeling secure in the knowledge that his interest in her hadn't dimmed, but was taking no chances until she had him in the palm of her hand. To do that she had to show she shared his feelings. 'I wonder when I will find out?' Without waiting for a reply, she left the office to type the letters ready for the lunchtime post.

Philip sat for a while staring into space. He couldn't help himself where Evelyn was concerned, he was besotted with her. His only worry was that she didn't feel the same about him. Was she just a tease? he asked himself. Then a voice in his head told him not to be stupid, a woman her age wouldn't be childish enough to tease him. But he wasn't entirely convinced. Only time would tell. So, trying to put her from his mind, he picked up the letters still to be answered, and as he read them composed the answers in his brain, ready to dictate later, probably after lunch. And thinking of lunch, Evelyn was back in his mind. They had an hour, and his apartment was only minutes away . . .

While Philip's mind was on her, Evelyn was intent on typing the letters ready for the early post. While her hopes and the stakes were high, her feet were still on the ground. If an affair with him didn't materialise she would need this job. Especially now when her salary had been increased. So she typed as quickly and as accurately as possible, and as she finished each letter asked Grace Carr to check them for errors. There was only one, and Evelyn was in high spirits to hear it. 'Thank you, Grace, that is very good news. I'm getting back my speed now, thank goodness.'

As Evelyn left her chair, Grace asked, 'How are you getting on with Mr Philip? He's very good-looking, isn't he?' She giggled. 'I know I could fall for him.'

'Mr Philip is a gentleman, and very easy to work with.' Evelyn stiffened. The last thing she wanted was for a young girl to be making cow's eyes at him. 'But I rather think he's out of your league, dear, so I wouldn't waste your time.'

'You never know your luck,' Grace called after her as she

walked towards the office. 'If you don't try, you won't get anywhere.'

Evelyn lifted her hand to show she'd heard before opening the office door to find Philip swivelling in his chair, fingers pressed together to form a steeple shape. She placed the letters before him, saying, 'All ready for your signature, my dear. I have had Miss Carr check each one for spelling errors, so unless you really feel you ought, there is no reason for you to read them.'

'Then I shan't.' He signed each letter with a flourish and handed them back to her. 'Ask Miss Carr to attend to posting them, I want you back in here. There's something I would like to ask you.'

Curious though Evelyn was to know what he had in mind, she didn't want to delay the letters. 'I'll be back before you've had time to miss me.'

True to her word, in less than a minute she was sitting before him. 'Now you can have my undivided attention, sir.'

'Come to the apartment in our lunch hour. If you are afraid of being seen with me, we can make our way there separately. But I want a little time alone with you.'

'Oh, Philip, I'm going shopping in my lunch hour! I'm sorry, but there are some things I need. Also, I have to change the five-pound note you gave me, otherwise I'll have no coppers for the tram fare home tonight.'

'That is a very poor excuse, my love. I can give you small change for your fare, and surely there is nothing so important that you need from the shops it can't wait another day?'

He looked so disappointed, Evelyn found herself feeling guilty. She also realised for the first time that he was getting to her, she was really beginning to like him. 'I was going to use the money you gave me to buy myself something nice to wear when I'm meeting you. Over the years I'm afraid I haven't been able to afford the pretty satin underwear I was used to, nor the fine pure silk stockings and up-to-date shoes. There is little in my wardrobe that is modern and attractive, and I do so want to look my best for you. It will take me a while to get back to where I was a few years ago, but I'm determined to. I want to look my best for you.'

'I wouldn't care if you were dressed in sackcloth, my love, I find you very beautiful. But because spending an hour in your company would make me so happy, perhaps I can come up with a solution. Why don't I give you some small change for your fares and any foodstuffs you may be in need of for the week, and then, if you are agreeable, it would give me great pleasure to buy the satin underwear I'm sure you would look wonderful in. I would delight in choosing it for you, and will have it at the apartment next time you come. Please don't say no, my love, indulge me.'

Evelyn was stunned, her brain trying to take in too many things at once. One part of it was telling her to agree. This way she would be getting the best of both worlds. Money to last her the week, her satin under garments bought for her, and she would still have the five-pound note. On top of that, she knew that anything Philip bought would be far more expensive than the clothes she could afford for herself. But there was a niggle in the back of her mind that stopped her from answering him straight away. If she let him give her so much, what would he want in return? Oh, she knew he would expect sexual favours, she had never thought different and the idea didn't bother her. But would he tire of her sooner if he thought of her as his mistress?

She sighed. 'I don't know, Philip. I feel torn between wanting to please you, and worrying that the time will come when you lose your respect for me because you believe I am only after your money. I would agree to your offer only if it is understood that I keep part of the life I have that makes me feel secure. My own home, although I don't own it, my work here, and to retain what you call my air of mystery. If you agree then I would be happy about the financial arrangement, and would love to spend my lunch hour with you in your apartment.'

A slow grin spread across his handsome face. 'And would you love to spend Saturday evening in my company? We don't need to go out for a meal if you don't wish to, I can arrange for one to be delivered. Whatever you would like to do, I will agree to. You see, my lovely Evelyn, I am completely captivated by you.'

'It is still early days, Philip, let us not rush into anything.' Evelyn could see the time coming when he would ask her to live with him, and she wasn't ready for that yet. There was Amelia to consider, and that would be one piece of news that would put an end to any relationship if he found she'd lied to him. 'We haven't known each other long, let us take things slowly and enjoy getting to know each other. Like a courting couple, except it must be kept a secret during office hours.'

When Evelyn called for Amelia on Monday night, she was filled with the joy of living. And her expression wasn't lost on Bessie. She had never known her neighbour look so happy, or be so pleasant and talkative. More than ever she was convinced there had been a great change in Evelyn's life over the last few weeks, and from the brightness of her eyes, that change wasn't anything to do with her old school chum. More likely it was a man who had brought it about.

'Here's the two shillings I borrowed from you yesterday, Miss Maudsley, and I owe you a debt of thanks, I don't know what we'd have done without your help. You really are most kind. To me and to Amelia, who has grown very fond of you.'

'And she's a treat to have in the house,' Bessie said, smiling at the girl who was looking from one to the other with apprehension. She was still afraid her mother would find out about the doll and forbid her to have it. 'She's company for me,' Bessie went on, 'someone to talk to instead of the four walls.' Then she set a trap, wondering if her stuck-up neighbour would walk into it. 'Yer can leave her any time, if yer want to go somewhere. To visit yer old school friend, like.'

Evelyn was hoping for this and gushed, 'Oh, that *is* thoughtful of you. I'm sure Amelia would like that, I can tell she's happy here. But I can't allow you to feed her six days a week for a shilling, that would be most unfair. I'm expecting another raise in my salary soon. The man to whom I am private secretary is so pleased with my work he has intimated I will be receiving an increase in the next week or so. I am able, therefore, to give you two shillings a week, which should help you out.'

'I like having the child here, I don't do it for money. But an extra shilling would come in handy with the winter coming on and me needing extra coal. As I say, though, I would mind Amelia for nothing, she's a mate to me.' Bessie tilted her head. Her neighbour had walked into one trap, for there was no boss living that would give a worker a raise in pay twice within three weeks. Still, it was no skin off her nose if the woman lived in a fantasy world and was a compulsive liar. But would she walk into another? 'She can stay here any time yer like, Mrs Sinclair. Perhaps when yer visit yer old school mate yer could sleep there overnight, save coming home in the dark?'

These words were music to Evelyn's ears. 'Well, if you wouldn't think I was taking advantage of your good nature, it would be lovely to stay overnight at Elizabeth's. I will write to her tonight, she'll be really pleased.'

Amelia knew better than to show she was delighted. Her voice was soft when she asked, 'Does that mean I'll be sleeping here on Saturday night, Mother?'

'Yes, it does. And I hope you realise what a lucky girl you are.' Evelyn pushed herself off the couch feeling everything was going her way. The future looked very bright, except for the problem of her daughter, but she'd worry about that when the time came. Until then she intended to live the good life and take everything that Philip offered. 'Come along, Amelia, I'm really quite hungry tonight. I have brought something in for our tea.'

Bessie opened her mouth to say the girl had enjoyed a meal only an hour ago, but closed it before the words came out. The most she'd be offered by her mother would be a sandwich, and she could manage that. It was funny that Bessie had never thought about it until the last few weeks, but never once had she smelled cooking coming from the house next door. It was no wonder the girl cleared her plate every night. When she'd finished her meal it was always as clean as a whistle.

Half an hour after Evelyn left with her daughter, Rita was knocking on Bessie's front door.' I haven't got me bed with me, so yer don't need to worry about me taking root in yer house. But you are the only bit of social life I get, sunshine. If it weren't for our little chats I'd go round the bend with boredom.'

'Sit yerself down, girl, yer know ye're always welcome. And although I haven't got any earth-shattering news for yer, I do have a tit-bit that might give yer something to think about. I'll put the kettle on for a cuppa first, though, 'cos I always seem to find more to talk about when me whistle is whet.' Bessie turned when she reached the kitchen door. 'D'yer know, Rita, at one time I couldn't stand women who had nothing better to do than jangle. Now I'm getting to be as bad as them. Not that I stand in the street gossiping, I don't have time for that with going to work, but yer'll see what I mean when I've made the tea and we can talk in peace.'

'How is Amelia?' Rita asked as she took the cup and saucer Bessie was holding out to her. 'Still thrilled with the doll, is she?'

Bessie held the saucer steady while she lowered herself on to a chair. 'If I'd spent a pound on a present for her, she couldn't have thought more of it than she does that doll. She talks to it all the time, and sings to it when she pretends to be getting it to sleep. And when I'm in the kitchen, and she thinks I can't hear her, she talks to it like her mother must talk to her. I can hear her saying, "Now, Daisy, what have I told you about keeping your dress clean? Just look at that mark, made with a dirty hand. I haven't got money to buy you new clothes, so do as I say and make sure you wash your hands before touching anything. Don't make me have to tell you again or I shall have to punish you. And remember, cleanliness is next to Godliness." '

Rita shook her head and tutted. 'She's got the poor kid like an old woman, so serious and old-fashioned. The only time I've ever heard the girl laugh was here on Saturday for her birthday. And she looks so pretty when she's acting her age, any mother would be proud to have her for a daughter. I know I would.'

'Oh, she knows how to laugh, don't worry. She has me in stitches sometimes when she's taking off one of the girls in her class. We get on like a house on fire, me and her.' Bessie tapped a finger against the side of her forehead. 'She's all there, Rita, believe me, and the more I see of her, the more I realise the poor kid learned from a very early age that the way to stay out of trouble is to do everything she's told. She never answers her mother back, just keeps quiet and does as she says. But she's a clever kid and must know that she doesn't get the love and attention most children get from their mother. I've never seen the queer one give her a smile, never mind a kiss. Yer want to be here at night when it gets near the time for her mother to come and pick her up. She changes from a happy, laughing child to one who is a bag of nerves, terrified in case she says the wrong thing. It's a crying shame, for she's a girl crying out for love and attention.'

'Mrs Sinclair doesn't deserve her.' Rita stretched forward to put her cup on the table. 'But yer want to watch yer don't get too fond of the girl, Bessie, 'cos if yer do, yer'd only be heading for a load of heartache. I can't see them staying in this street for much longer, it's not posh enough for Her Ladyship.'

'Ah, well, now, I think there's something in the wind.' Bessie lifted the corner of her pinny and wiped it across her mouth. 'Nothing's been said, but I think our posh neighbour is up to no good, and I'd lay odds there's a man involved.'

Rita sat forward, her eyes wide with interest. 'A man! Oh, go 'way, what makes yer think that, sunshine?'

'Intuition, girl, that's all. I might be miles out, but I'm not very often wrong. I know it's going to make me sound like a nosy so-and-so, but I set two little traps for her tonight and she walked into them. Not that it proved anything beyond doubt, and I really don't care what she gets up to as long as Amelia doesn't get hurt in the process, but I'll be interested to see how things go in the next few weeks.'

'If yer think yer can get so far with yer story and then not tell me the rest, yer've got another think coming, Bessie Maudsley!' Rita sat back. 'I'm not moving from this chair until I've heard the lot. And another thing, didn't we agree that in this house we'd call the girl Milly and not Amelia? She's only a kid and she's got such a lovely, cheeky smile, she'd suit being called Milly.'

'Yeah, I do call her Milly when we're on our own. But when it comes to six o'clock she's Amelia. Anyway, back to what I was telling yer. I don't know anything for sure, so it might only be me imagination. But whichever way, I don't want yer to pass anything I say on to Aggie. If the queer one got to know I'd been telling tales about her, she'd have me ruddy guts for garters and I'd never be allowed to have Milly again.'

'If yer don't get on with it, sunshine, it'll be midnight and my feller will be out looking for me. Or he might even decide to teach me a lesson and lock the front door and go to bed!'

Bessie pictured Rita's placid husband and chuckled. 'That'll be the day, when Reg Wells puts his foot down with you! He started off the wrong way when yer got married, by being too soft with yer. It's too late for him to change now. Anyway, yer don't know when ye're well off, having such a good husband.'

Rita nodded her head vigorously. 'Yes, I've got a husband in a million and I love the bones of him. He's got one fault, though, and that is he's dull! He never comes home from work with any juicy bits of gossip for his wife who has had a bloody miserable, boring day. And that is why I rely on you, and why I'm sitting here waiting for you to put some interest back into my life. But trying to get it out of you is like getting blood out of a stone. So instead *I'll* give *you* a piece of gossip that will have yer falling off yer chair.'

It was Bessie's turn to sit forward in anticipation. 'Go 'way! What have I missed?'

Rita puckered her lips and slowly nodded her head. 'Keep tight hold of the arms of the chair, sunshine, 'cos ye're in for a shock. D'yer know Doreen Brown, her from number sixteen at the top of the street?'

'Yer mean, the nice-looking blonde woman?'

'Yeah, that's her. Blonde hair and a smashing slim figure. Well, didn't she go and run off with the milkman this afternoon! The whole street saw them. Running like hell they were.'

'Ooh, I can't believe it! She seemed such a nice girl. And she's got two young children and a very handsome husband, too!' Bessie looked genuinely shocked. 'He's the man who delivers our milk in the mornings, isn't he?'

Rita let a smile appear. 'That's right, but yer don't need to worry, yer'll get yer milk in the morning as usual. Him and Doreen were only running for the twenty-two tram to take them to the Atlas.'

'Well, I'll be blowed!' Bessie said, chortling. 'I must be getting slow on the uptake, 'cos I fell for that hook, line and sinker.'

'Ye're not only getting slower on the uptake, sunshine, ye're getting a damn' sight slower on the out-take! I've been here half an hour and still haven't heard enough to whet me appetite for a bit of excitement. So come on, Bessie, tell me why yer think there's dirty works at the crossroads regarding yer neighbour?'

'Okay, sweetheart, but don't blame me if nothing is going on. It might just be me bad mind. Anyway, here goes.' Bessie crossed her thin legs, making sure to pull her pinny down over her knees. And she told an enthralled Rita all that had been said in conversation with the woman next door. How she'd casually offered to mind Milly if Evelyn wanted to visit her so-called old school chum on Saturday. And if she wanted to stay overnight, well then, Milly was welcome to sleep in Bessie's spare room.

'And did she accept yer offer?' Rita asked, sitting so near the edge of the couch she was in danger of falling off. 'Is she staying out on Saturday night?'

'Oh, she accepted all right, it was what she'd been angling for. Nice as pie she was, I've never seen her smile so much. And I'll tell yer another thing, she's a bloody good liar. She told me about two weeks ago that she'd been offered this job as a private secretary, and because it meant a rise she would pay me a shilling a week to look after Milly for the two hours each night. Well, now she says her boss is so pleased with her work he's going to increase her wages again, so she's going to give me *two* shillings a week to look after Milly.' Bessie shook her head. 'And the woman thinks I'm stupid enough to believe every word she says!'

'But what makes yer think there's a man involved, sunshine, has she ever mentioned having a man friend?'

'No, she's always been very brief with her words until a week ago. Never said anything except "hello" and "goodbye". And she was always so dead bloody miserable, with a face like a wet week, she used to give me the willies. But these days she's all sweetness and light. She even looks happy, in her own way, contented like, and that's what makes me think there's now a man in her life.' Bessie pulled a face and held her hand up. 'But don't take that as gospel, I could be wrong.'

'Yer mean, there's no old school friend?' Rita asked. 'That's a lie as well?'

'We'll just have to wait and see what develops over the next few weeks. If she has got a man, and he makes her happy, then good luck to her. As long as she doesn't stop Milly from coming here.'

But Rita still wasn't satisfied. 'Surely if she had a man friend she would have brought him to the house by now, to meet her daughter?'

'Unless he's rich, and she'd be ashamed to bring him here.' Bessie got up to poke the fire and put some life back into it. 'It might be me being bad-minded, Rita, and in that case I should apologise to the woman if I'm wrong. But it'll all come out in the wash, and then we'll see if I'm right or a foolish, bad-minded spinster. Only time will tell.'

Rita glanced at the clock and jumped to her feet. 'I'd better go, I haven't done my feller's carry-out yet. But I'll be looking forward to the next instalment, sunshine, so keep me informed.'

Bessie saw her to the door. 'I'll let yer know if anything exciting happens, girl, but keep it under yer hat in case I'm making a fool of meself.'

Rita turned as she stepped off the pavement. 'My money's on you, sunshine! And if yer turn out to be right, well, that'll be enough excitement to keep me going for a couple of weeks.' She waved her hand as she crossed to the opposite pavement. 'Goodnight and God bless, sunshine, see yer tomorrow.'

'Goodnight and God bless!' Bessie waited until her mate was safely in her own house before closing the front door. And once in the living room, she told the grate, 'She's a good mate, is Rita. And so is Aggie, except she doesn't think before she opens her mouth. No secret is safe with her, especially when she's had a couple of milk stouts.' Grinning to herself, Bessie put the fireguard in front of the fire. 'This is in case you heard everything I told me mate tonight, and yer decide to spill the beans to the wallpaper. Ye're as bad as Aggie, yer can't be trusted.'

Chapter Fourteen

Evelyn could hear Bessie's footsteps climbing the stairs and wondered what she would do without her neighbour. She was a blessing, and it would be wise to keep her sweet. Future prospects looked very rosy, and the time might come when Miss Maudsley would be asked for more help than she was giving now. She would be paid well, of course, for Evelyn would have plenty of money to spare. And the little woman next door wasn't the kind to ask awkward questions, she was too naive. So far she'd believed everything she'd been told.

Turning on her side, Evelyn drew her knees up and wrapped her arms around them. She couldn't sleep, but then she didn't want to. She wanted to relive over and over in her head the hour she'd spent in Philip's apartment. In all the time she'd gone out with Charles, and he'd kissed and cuddled her, he had never sent a thrill down her spine the way Philip did when he held her. The first time she felt it, it was so strong it took her breath away. He only had to stroke her face, or kiss her, and her whole body tingled. He was very experienced where women were concerned, that was obvious, but Evelyn didn't care. She'd never had these feelings before, and even now, lying in bed in the cold room, the very thought of them sent a warmth through her whole body. They hadn't made love, although Philip had begged her. But as she explained, if their first act of love making had to be rushed, over in fifteen minutes so they could go back to work, then it wasn't for her. She would feel no better than a woman kept solely to service his sexual needs, and she had more pride than to sell herself like that.

Evelyn smiled and clasped her knees tighter. Philip had been full of apologies. He hadn't meant it to seem like that, but told her he couldn't control his feelings when she was close to him. And to please her, he said he was taking a long lunch hour tomorrow when he'd go shopping to buy the clothes he'd promised. And when she asked how he would know her size, he tapped his nose and said to leave it to him, she wouldn't be disappointed. They were going to the apartment again on Wednesday lunchtime, so Evelyn could see what he had bought for her, but then she insisted they shouldn't meet outside the office until Saturday, when she would be spending the night with him. And when Philip had held her tight, nibbling her ear, his whispered words left her in no doubt that on Saturday she would be taught her first lesson in how to satisfy his sexual needs. And she wasn't afraid, she was looking forward to it. Even the memory of his hand running down her back brought a thrill which caused her to shiver. When she finally closed her eyes in sleep, there was a smile on her face.

Evelyn reached the apartment a few minutes after Philip on the Wednesday and found he had left the door open for her. She could hear him in the kitchen. When she called his name, he called back, 'Go straight to the bedroom, my darling, and you will find some presents on the bed.'

He was right behind her, and in time to see the pleasure on her face as she looked down at the array of cream-coloured satin underwear. There was everything she would need from brassieres to cami-knickers, short underskirts, long underskirts with matching lace insets, and several pairs of pure silk stockings. Next to them, laid out on the huge bed, were two nightdresses, one pale blue, the other a deep red. And beside them were matching satin dressing gowns.

'Oh, Philip, they're beautiful. But you shouldn't have bought so much, I feel quite embarrassed now.'

He slipped his arms around her and pulled her tight. 'There's no need to feel embarrassed, my darling, it gave me a lot of pleasure choosing things for you. And I can't wait to see you wearing them.'

Evelyn was more excited than she would let him see. She didn't want him to think she'd never known what it was like to be rich and wear such fine clothes. 'You are very clever, Philip, they're all my size! How did you guess?'

He knew that the truth, that this wasn't the first time he'd been in the lingerie department of George Henry Lee, wouldn't find favour, so said what he thought she would be happy with. 'I chose an assistant I thought was your size, and she was very helpful.'

Evelyn stroked the fine satin of the red dressing gown, then turned her head to ask, teasingly, 'I believe the women in houses of ill repute wear this colour?'

Philip's head tipped back and he roared with laughter. 'In that case, my lovely, when you wear it I shall pretend I am in a house of ill repute. I have it on good authority that the women there are very knowledgeable when it comes to making men happy.'

'Then I feel sorry for you, because I am only a novice and will need lessons.' The lovely lingerie had put Evelyn in high spirits, and she found herself being more outspoken than she'd ever been before. 'Would you like me to visit a brothel to learn the tricks of the trade?'

Philip pulled her even closer. 'I'll let you into a secret, my darling. I have never wanted anything in my life as much as I want to make love to you. I want to pleasure you as much as I am certain you will pleasure me. And now, my love, if we don't make a move, we will be late back at the office. Difficult as it will be, I shall have to keep my feelings in check until Saturday.'

* * *

Evelyn was still in very high spirits when she called for Amelia, and her good mood wasn't lost on Bessie. 'Ye're looking very well lately, Mrs Sinclair. Happy, like, as though yer've had good news or something nice has happened to yer.'

'I must say, I am feeling very well, Miss Maudsley. It must be the satisfaction of my new job, that's all I can put it down to. I have a very good boss, and he's really pleased with my work. Oh, I shall be getting my raise in pay from this week, so I'll be in a position to give you the extra shilling from this Saturday.'

Bessie nodded and smiled in a friendly way. 'It's nice when yer get on with the people yer work for. Makes going to work each day a bit easier, doesn't it? You seem to have a very good boss, is he elderly or young?'

Evelyn dampened her enthusiasm. 'Mmm, I really wouldn't know. If you were to ask me to guess, I would say somewhere in the region of fifty-five or thereabouts. He has children in their twenties, so that might give you an idea.'

How well you lie, the voice in Bessie's head was saying. It would take more than a fifty-five-year-old married man to put that sparkle in your eyes. But it hasn't anything to do with me, so good luck to you. 'So I'll know about food for the weekend, is Amelia still sleeping over on Saturday night? And d'yer want me to give her a dinner on Sunday? It would be no trouble, just a few extra roast potatoes.'

Evelyn averted her eyes as her brain ticked over. Oh, how tempting the offer sounded. It would mean she could lounge around that luxurious apartment with Philip until the afternoon. Then she sensed her daughter standing nearby, waiting for her reply, and didn't want her neighbour to think she was neglecting the girl. 'Oh, it's kind of you, Miss Maudsley, but I don't think I should leave Amelia so often. You'll be thinking you have no mother, won't you, dear?'

As usual the girl kept her face straight and her voice flat. 'I don't mind, Mother, if you want to stay at your friend's house.

Miss Bessie looks after me very well. She plays cards with me, and Snakes and Ladders.'

'So you would prefer to stay with Miss Maudsley, would you?' Evelyn managed to keep the eagerness from her voice, but her fingers were crossed. 'I told you she'd taken a fancy to you, Miss Maudsley, but you mustn't let her put on you, it wouldn't be fair. I am quite prepared to come home on Sunday morning and cook a meal for us both.'

Bessie shook her head. 'No, we'll leave it that she has dinner with me. I enjoy her company. So you come home when yer like. Yer may as well enjoy yerself while yer can.'

'I must admit I am enjoying the first bit of freedom I've had in eight years,' Evelyn said. 'And it's thanks to you.' She stood up, and for the first time in Bessie's presence, reached for her daughter's hand. 'Come along, Amelia, I'm sure Miss Maudsley is sick of the sight of us. Let's leave her in peace.'

When mother and daughter were going out of the kitchen door, Amelia turned to say, 'Thank you, Miss Bessie, I'll see you tomorrow.' And gave a wave with her free hand.

Bessie watched through the kitchen window as they walked down the yard. She was glad she was going to have the girl overnight on Saturday, and probably until Sunday afternoon. She was really good company for a woman who had lived a lonely life for so many years. Rita was only being sensible when she'd told her not to get too fond of Milly, and Bessie appreciated her mate's concern. But how could she not be drawn to a child who hugged her tight while gazing up with wide green eyes that were crying out for affection? Oh, she might be storing up heartache for herself, as Rita said, if Mrs Sinclair ever decided to move away from the street. Bessie had warned herself about this on several occasions, and each time, a little voice in her head had told her that at least the girl would leave knowing what love and affection were. And another thing, she would be old enough by then to come and visit. As Amelia grew older, she would have a mind of her own and Bessie had a feeling they would always be in touch with each other.

Reg Wells lowered the evening paper to watch his wife hopping from one foot to the other as she kept watch through the window. 'In the name of God, woman, what's the matter with yer? Anyone would think it was a matter of life or death, instead of you just being nosy.'

Rita grinned at him. 'It *is* a matter of life or death, sunshine, but I don't expect you to understand, 'cos ye're too busy reading the ruddy paper to notice that yer poor wife is bored rigid. It's the same every night! Yer come in from work, have yer dinner, then all I see of yer for the next few hours is the top of yer flaming head. Yer never think of asking yer dear wife what sort of a day she's had. Oh, no, the *Echo* comes first. Then, when yer've finished, if it's not bedtime, yer might condescend to notice I'm still here.'

He grinned back. 'If yer feel that way inclined, love, I can always fold the paper, put it under the cushion, and we can have an early night. D'yer think that would bring a bit of excitement into yer life? Make yer more content, like?'

Still keeping an eye on the house opposite, Rita told him, 'I'm waiting to nip over to Bessie's, sunshine, and if she hasn't anything of interest to tell me then I'll come back and take yer up on the offer. That's if yer've had a shave. Otherwise ye're not on 'cos that stubble of yours isn't half rough on my delicate skin.'

Reg rubbed a hand across his chin. 'I'd have a shave if I was sure I was on a real promise, otherwise I'll leave it till in the morning.'

Rita, who loved her husband dearly, pretended to be giving it some thought. 'Ooh, er, decisions, decisions. Ooh, heck, it's a hard one. I'll tell yer what, sunshine, you have yer shave and work yerself up into a state of excitement while I ask Bessie if she's got any news. And if she has, I'll tell her to speak quickly 'cos my feller is on a promise and the waiting won't be doing him no good.'

Reg chortled. 'Bessie's a spinster, yer shouldn't be putting those sort of thoughts in her head. She probably doesn't know what it means to be on a promise.'

The clock told Rita it was ten minutes now since Bessie's visitors had left, and as she reached for the coat hanging on a hook behind the door, she said, 'Yer think Bessie's education's been lacking, do yer, Reg? Shall I ask her if she'd like yer to tell her about the birds and the bees? Ye're very good at explaining things, you are.'

He knew his wife was quite capable of repeating what he'd said for a joke, and shook his fist at her. 'You do that, Rita Wells, and I'll never be able to look the woman in the face again. Now get over there and don't spend too much time jangling. Just remember, I'll be having a shave for your benefit, and one good turn deserves another. I'm on a promise, and if ye're not back by the time the kids are in bed, I'll come over and carry yer home. This is one promise I won't let yer break.'

Rita bent to cup his face in her hands. 'Ooh, I do like masterful men, yer've got me heart all of a quiver. The strong silent type . . . yer remind me of Rudolph Valentino. Remember that picture we saw him in, where he picked his women up and laid them down on satin sheets in the big tent in the desert? Ooh, it wasn't half romantic.'

Reg's rich chuckle filled the room. 'While you had yer eyes fixed on the screen, with yer mouth wide open, thinking how wonderful he was, I was busy trying to figure out how he never used to get sand in his eyes. And where the hell he could get satin sheets from in the middle of the ruddy desert! Not a shop for hundreds of miles, but he had everything to hand.' Again he chuckled. 'You women are daft enough to fall for anything.'

Rita pulled a face. 'Yeah, I know, we'd fall for the ruddy cat. We tell lies, too, which yer forgot to mention. Tell lies and break promises, that's us women.'

He was off the chair like a shot. 'Give me yer hand, love.'

'What d'yer want me hand for?'

He made a grab and caught her wrist. 'Come on, I'm taking yer across to Bessie's.'

'Don't be daft, I can take meself across there.' Rita was still protesting when her husband opened the front door and pulled her down the steps. Her two sons were playing with their mates, and they all stood like statues as Reg dragged Rita across the cobbles and knocked on Bessie's door.

There was a look of surprise on the little woman's face when she saw Reg with Rita in tow. She'd been washing some clothes in the sink, and wiped her wet hands down the side of her pinny. 'Well, this is a surprise. When I heard the knock I thought it would be Rita, but I never expected you, Reg.' She stood back. 'Come on in.'

'No, I won't come in, Bessie love, but thanks for asking. I've just brought the wife over, and in half an hour I want yer to remind her not to forget the promise she made. She's got a head like a sieve, and she'll forget all about it if someone doesn't remind her.'

Now Bessie might be a spinster, but that didn't mean she was totally out of touch with married life. Although she kept her face straight, she was shaking with laughter inside. 'Oh, I won't forget to remind her. On a promise are yer, Reg?'

The man didn't know where to put himself. The only face-saving thing he could think of was that the boys were on the other side of the street with their noisy mates, and wouldn't have heard. His face the colour of beetroot, he dropped Rita's hand and hurried back across the cobbles with his wife's laughter ringing in his ears. But as he was stepping on to the top step, he heard her call, 'Half an hour, sunshine, I promise.'

It was then he forgot his red face and embarrassment for he had more pressing things on his mind. First he would bring the boys in and make them a hot drink before seeing they gave themselves a good wash. Left to their own devices they'd be going to school tomorrow with a huge tidemark round their necks and dirt behind their ears. Then, when they were settled in bed, he would set about giving himself a very close shave. He would hate to be rough on his wife's delicate skin.

Bessie closed the door, tittering to herself. 'Your feller will kill yer when yer go home. His face was like thunder. And me putting me foot in it didn't help. I should have had more sense.'

Rita knew her husband too well to be afraid. He'd never really lost his temper with her in all the years they'd been married. And she had to admit there were many times she'd given him cause to. 'It was a bit thoughtless of yer, sunshine, especially as I'd asked him if he'd explain to yer about the birds and the bees, and he didn't refuse. So, yer see what yer've missed, eh? I'd have sat in on that conversation meself, 'cos I'd love to hear Reg trying to explain how babies are made. It would have been hilarious.'

'Oh, aye, and I'd have been expected to sit here with me eyes open in amazement and acting the picture of innocence! Oh, yeah, that and cut me throat would be the last thing I'd be doing.' Bessie pointed to the couch. 'Sit yerself down, sweetheart, but don't expect me to make a cup of tea, not while your feller is pacing the floor waiting for yer.'

'Nah, he's just called the boys in, and it'll take him half an hour to get them ready for bed. But I won't have a drink, anyway, 'cos it wouldn't leave us much time to talk.'

'Sorry to let yer down, Rita, but there's not a lot to tell yer. Except Mrs Sinclair is going to her old school friend's again on Saturday and sleeping over. And I've told her she needn't rush home on Sunday, I'll give Milly her dinner.'

'Ooh, er, Bessie, yer might not have much to tell me, but think how much we can read into those few sentences. I mean, d'yer still think she's telling fibs about the old school friend? If she is, then where is she going to spend Saturday night, and who with?'

'I have no way of finding that out,' Bessie told her. 'She's more open than she used to be, more pleasant, like, but she still doesn't give anything away. If yer were to ask me to guess, I'd say she has a man friend, and he's a wealthy one. I am to get an extra shilling a week from this Saturday for having Milly more often, and she must be getting the extra money from somewhere to pay me so much.'

'It's a good help that, two bob a week. But it's not the money ye're doing it for, sunshine, is it? I bet yer'd mind Milly even if yer didn't get paid for it.'

'Of course it's not the money I do it for, I can live very comfortably on me wages. I've always paid me way and never owed anyone. But I'm not going to refuse the two bob a week, that's for sure. I'd be daft to when she's out enjoying herself. Anyway, I can spend it on Milly. I don't think she's ever been into town, so I might take her down on the tram on Saturday to look around the shops. It'll be an outing for me as well.'

Rita tilted her head. 'Would yer like another companion? It's years since I've been into the city, I've never had the money. Yer don't mind me asking, do yer, don't think I'm being pushy?'

'Of course I don't, yer daft ha'porth, I'd be glad of yer company. And Milly will be over the moon, walking between the two of us.'

'Ooh, that hasn't half cheered me up, it's something to look forward to. And tonight is a very good time to scrounge the two pence tram fare off my feller. If I get him at the right time he'll promise me anything.'

'That sounds like blackmail to me,' Bessie said, with a shake of her head. 'A married man is entitled to his rights, yer know, he shouldn't have to pay for them.'

'Bessie, I feel in such a good, generous mood now, thanks to you, my feller will think he's got a strange woman in his bed. By the time I've finished with him, he'll be thinking two pence is a small price to pay.' Rita pushed herself to her feet. 'In fact, when it's over and he's got his breath back, he'll probably ask when we're going into Liverpool again.'

'Have you no shame in you, woman?' Bessie followed her mate to the door. 'I feel really sorry for Reg.'

Rita stepped down on to the pavement. 'No need to, sunshine, 'cos in half an hour's' time my feller will be the happiest man in this street. And that is my solemn promise.'

'Oh, I believe yer, sweetheart,' Bessie said. 'Just remember, though, he has to go to work tomorrow.'

It was only after Rita had left that Bessie realised it might not be possible to take Milly in to town on Saturday afternoon after all, for she didn't know what time Mrs Sinclair would be going out. If she was meeting a man, it would probably be in the early evening, and that would dash any hope of Bessie and Rita taking Milly into town. Bessie felt really disappointed because she'd been looking forward to giving Milly a surprise, and Rita would feel let down, too! But there was no point in waiting and wondering what Saturday was going to bring, she may as well come right out and ask her neighbour. She could always tell a little white lie and say she was thinking of taking Milly to the park. Yes, that's what she'd do, she'd ask her neighbour tomorrow night and get it over with. After all, the woman couldn't expect an eight-year-old girl to spend all her time in the house, it wasn't healthy.

Bessie was late getting in from work the following night, and found Milly sitting on the kitchen step waiting for her. 'I'm sorry I'm late, sweetheart, we had an order to get out in a hurry and there was nothing I could do about it. Come on in, yer must be freezing. I'll put the kettle on and put a light to the fire. It won't be long, I'll soon have you warmed through.'

'I'm not cold, Auntie Bessie, I folded my arms across my chest and put my hands under my armpits, and they're nice and warm.'

Bessie smiled down at her with affection in her eyes. This girl was one in a million, never gave any cheek, kept herself clean and tidy and was always well mannered. Her mother didn't appreciate how lucky she was. 'I've brought some sausages in, we'll have them with an egg. How does that sound to you?'

Milly giggled. 'My tummy says it sounds very good, Auntie Bessie, and when it arrives it will be made really welcome.'

Bessie threw her coat on a chair and knelt in front of the fire which she'd set ready for lighting this morning before she went to work. After striking a match, she held it to the balls of newspaper laid out under the firewood. 'I'll give it a minute to catch, then I'll pull the damper out and we'll have a roaring fire in no time.' She felt the girl's arms coming round her neck and then soft lips kissing her cheek. 'Oh, that's nice, sweetheart, but what have I done to deserve it?'

'That's 'cos I love you, Auntie Bessie, you're my very bestest friend.'

'Well, I think you must be a mind reader, sweetheart, because I was just thinking the same thing. That you are my very bestest friend. And you know they say great minds think alike, so you and me must be very clever.' Bessie disentangled herself from Milly's arms and used her closed fists to push herself off her knees. 'Now, while I'm frying the sausages and eggs, you can help me by setting the table. Like your tummy, I'm famished.'

When Milly had set the table, she went into the kitchen to where Bessie was standing by the stove, leaning as far back as she could to escape the spitting fat. 'Why are the sausages spitting, Auntie Bessie? Is it because they are angry?'

Bessie chuckled. 'No, they're not angry, sweetheart. It's not the sausages that are spitting, it's the fat. So don't come too close, 'cos yer might get burnt, and then what would I say to yer mother when she comes?'

'She wouldn't know, Auntie Bessie, 'cos I wouldn't tell her. But she wouldn't shout at you, she would scold me for being careless.'

Not wanting to criticise her mother, Bessie changed the subject. 'Dinner is ready now, so go and sit at the table, sweetheart. I'll cut us a round of bread each, to dip in the egg yolk.'

The fire was established now, and the bright, dancing flames gave the room a nice warm glow. And with Milly relating a funny incident in the school playground, and her infectious laughter ringing out, Bessie was feeling really contented. She'd taken on a new lease of life since the girl had been coming into her home, and not for the first time she was questioning the decision she'd made all those years ago when she'd told the boy she was courting that she couldn't leave her ailing parents to marry him. She'd said it was her duty to care for them, and when in anger he'd asked if she didn't have a duty to him after courting him for several years, her heart had been torn in two. She was an only child, born when her mother was forty years of age. By the time Bessie was courting, both her parents were old and frail. She chose them over the boy who'd wanted to marry her. Now, looking at Milly's happy face, she wished she could have married her boyfriend *and* cared for her parents. Perhaps if she had she would have had a family of her own now.

'That was lovely, Auntie Bessie, and my tummy said to thank you very much.'

Bessie shook her head to empty her mind of thoughts of what might have been. 'I'm glad you and your tummy enjoyed it, sweetheart.' She patted her own. 'And I have to admit I've had an elegant sufficiency.'

'Ooh, those are big words, Auntie Bessie!'

Bessie chuckled. 'Yes, I know, I frightened meself 'cos I don't know where they came from. I'll have to try them on yer

Auntie Aggie some time, I'd love to see the expression on her face.'

Milly's laughter rang out. 'I bet she'd use some words back at you.' Her deep green eyes rolled. 'And I bet they'd be naughty ones, too!'

'Aggie means no harm, sweetheart, she's got a heart of gold. But I admit she uses some words she shouldn't. Not in front of children anyway.' Bessie reached for the girl's empty plate and put it on top of her own. 'I'll wash and you can dry. Then when the place is tidy, you can play with Daisy for half an hour before your mother comes.'

The girl scrambled from her chair. 'I'm going to tell her about the three bears tonight.'

Bessie grinned. 'And I bet she'll enjoy it. In fact, I might just listen in meself and yer'll have an audience.'

When Evelyn called for her daughter later, Daisy was tucked up in bed in the spare room and Milly's face had lost its sparkle.

'The weather has turned very cold,' Evelyn said, shivering. 'I won't sit down, Miss Maudsley, thank you, I want to get in and light the fire. Get your coat, Amelia, and don't dawdle.'

Bessie decided to strike while the iron was hot. 'Before you go, Mrs Sinclair, there's something I'd like to ask yer. Do you know what time yer'll be going out on Saturday? Yer see, I thought it would be nice if I took Amelia to the park for a walk. I don't like her to be indoors for so long, I think we both need a little fresh air. But it depends on what time you will be going out. If it's late afternoon, then it will be too late and we'll leave it for another time.'

Evelyn stared at her. This woman is either a mind reader or my guardian angel, she thought. Only this morning Philip had asked her why she couldn't come early on Saturday morning, so they could spend the day together? He would take her for a run to Southport in the afternoon, and they could stroll along famous Lord Street with its many exclusive fashionable shops. He would buy her anything that took her eye, he said. And what she did want was another day coat, so she could have one at home and one in the apartment. She had promised to think about it without knowing how she could wangle it. She'd never dreamed this opportunity was going to fall in her lap. But although she was cheering inside, she didn't want to appear too eager. She gave a deep sigh and closed her eyes as though deep in contemplation.

'You have been so kind to Amelia and me, I really can't let you down. So what I'll do is write to Elizabeth tonight, and tell her I find myself with Saturday free and could she possibly put up with me for a few extra hours. I'm quite sure she'll be agreeable.'

Bessie didn't know how she kept her head from shaking and her tongue from clicking. This woman was the best liar she'd ever known. There was always an answer to everything, and it appeared she made a career out of telling the most exaggerated fibs Bessie had ever heard.

'Oh, no, don't do that!' she said, to put the wind up Evelyn. She knew there was now no doubt that Milly would be going into town on Saturday with her and Rita, but she could play games as well as Mrs Sinclair with her posh voice. 'I wouldn't dream of putting you or yer friend to any trouble. We'll leave it until another time.'

Amelia had been standing quietly by, taking it all in. Her face had lit up when she'd first heard about the walk in the park, then when her mother hadn't seemed too keen her spirits had dropped. They'd been lifted again for a short while. Now, listening to her Auntie Bessie, she looked really crestfallen. This gave Evelyn the way out she'd been looking for.

'Don't look so sad, Amelia, I won't do anything to upset Miss Maudsley's plans. I insist on making myself invisible on Saturday, come what may. And I hope you appreciate what a lucky girl you are, having Miss Maudsley for a friend. I too am lucky in that respect.'

Wearing the look of someone who has generously put herself out for the sake of others, Evelyn gave a slow, sideways nod of the head to Bessie. The little woman didn't know whether to laugh in her face or curtsey. But she was prepared to put up with her neighbour's shenanigans for Milly's sake. She gave a wide smile while inwardly calling her all the polished buggers under the sun. 'Oh, that is kind of yer, Mrs Sinclair. You enjoy yerself on Saturday now, and don't worry about Amelia 'cos I won't keep her out too long.'

The wink Milly gave her as she followed Evelyn out of the house told of her pleasure. And Bessie also wondered if it was a wink of victory. If it was, then good for her.

Chapter Fifteen

Bessie had told Rita not to call for her until two o'clock on Saturday, in case her neighbour had had a change of plan and was at home. Milly still hadn't been told they were going into Liverpool, she was excited enough at the prospect of going to the park. 'Will I be allowed to go on the swings, Auntie Bessie?'

'Of course yer will, sweetheart, there's no charge, the swings and see-saw are free.'

Bessie looked into the girl's shining eyes and thought it was time to tell her the truth. There'd been no sight or sound of Evelyn, so it was safe to presume she had kept to her word. 'Me and Auntie Rita have got a surprise for yer, sweetheart, but I won't tell yer what until she comes.' She heard a door bang and, looking through the window, saw her mate crossing the cobbles. 'Here she is, and I think yer'll like our surprise.'

Milly couldn't think of anything more exciting than going to the park and having a turn on the swings. 'I would like to go to the park, Auntie Bessie, you don't need to do anything special just for me.'

'We'll see, sweetheart, you might have a choice of two options. But open the door for Auntie Rita, there's a good girl.'

Rita came in bright and breezy. It was a rare treat to be going into the city on the tram, for she had to stretch her housekeeping like a piece of elastic to make it last the week. But her feller had come up trumps with sixpence for her to pay her fares and buy a cup of tea in a cafe. She patted Milly's cheek. 'Hello, sunshine, all ready with yer coat on, eh? Looking forward to seeing the sights with yer aunties, are yer?'

Milly's brow creased as she wondered what sights they'd see in the park, and Bessie was quick to notice. 'I haven't said anything to her yet, Rita, except that we had a surprise for her. But I said she had two options, and we'd let her choose where we go.'

Rita's heart sank. Surely she hadn't gone through all that with Reg just to go to the swings?

Milly also looked downcast. 'I thought we were going to the park, Auntie Bessie, that's what you said?'

'Yes, I know that, sweetheart, and that's what I told your mother. But since then, me and Rita have had a little talk and we thought perhaps yer might rather go into town than go to the park? We could get the tram from the top of the street to take us into the city centre, and spend some time there looking in the shops. But it is entirely up to you. Me and Rita will fit in with whatever yer want to do.'

Milly's mouth was wide open and her eyebrows nearly touched her hair-line as she gazed from one to the other of them. It was a few seconds before her voice came out in a squeak. 'Go into town on the tram?' She knew Liverpool was a big city, but she'd never been there. 'Are you pulling my leg, Auntie Bessie?'

'Am I heckerslike! I don't get all dolled up to pull no one's leg. This is your day, and me and Rita want you to choose where we go. But if you don't decide soon, all the shops will be closed before we get there.'

Rita put her hands behind her back and crossed her fingers. Please don't say you want to go on the swings, sunshine, please!

'I'd like to go into town on the tram, please. I've never been there, but some of the girls in my class have, and they've told me about the shops that are as big as the Queen's palace.'

'Well, not as big as Buckingham Palace, sweetheart, but ten times bigger than the shops around here. I think your friends were bragging a bit. But yer can put them straight when yer go to school on Monday.'

Milly's chest seemed to swell with pride as she held out a hand to each of her adopted aunties. 'You are very kind to me, and I do love you.'

Over her head the eyes of the two women met, and it wouldn't have taken much more for the tears to appear. 'Come on, let's be on our way and make the most of the time we have,' Bessie said gruffly.

They walked down the street with Milly between them, each holding one of her hands, and she smiled at the other children who stopped in their play to watch the girl they knew by sight but had never spoken to or played with. Rita's youngest son, Jack, skipped alongside them, his socks crumpled around his ankles and patches of dirt on his face.

'Why can't I come with yer, Mam?' Jack was skipping backwards now, so he could see their faces. 'Go on, I'll behave meself.'

'Some other time, son, not today.' When Rita saw the disappointment in his eyes, she felt so guilty. Her boys, like all the other kids in the street, didn't get much out of life because of the shortage of money. But, like Jack now, they didn't whinge when they were told they couldn't have everything they asked for. Nevertheless, he must be feeling a bit jealous, and she couldn't blame him. 'Yer can't come now, sunshine, just look at the state of yer. Yer knees and face are as black as the hobs of hell. But next time I have the chance to go into town, I'll make sure I take you and Billy with me.'

They'd reached the top of the street by now and Jack grinned. 'I don't mind, Mam, 'cos yer'd only make me wash me neck. I'll go back to me mates and me game of marbles.'

Milly's heart went out to the boy, for she knew what it was like to be left behind. She still remembered hearing the key turn in the lock of the room she was confined to while her mother went out shopping. Still remembered the feeling of fear at being left alone in the house. 'I'll tell you about it when we come home, Jack, and if Auntie Bessie ever takes me out again, I'll ask her to let you come. I know she will, she's very kind.'

Jack grinned, then turned to run hell for leather back to his mates with his mother's voice following him. 'Pull yer socks up, for heaven's sake, yer make a holy show of me!'

'Leave him be, Rita,' Bessie said. 'He's only a lad, yer can't expect him to be spotlessly clean all the time.'

'Bessie, I'd settle for him being clean for half an hour. Sometimes he's got that much grime on his face, I don't recognise him! A while back I passed him in the entry and wouldn't have known it was him if he hadn't said, "Hello, Mam".'

Milly thought that was really funny and she was still giggling when the tram came trundling along. She begged to be allowed to go up to the top deck, and when Bessie nodded ran up the stairs with the speed of a whippet while the two women pulled themselves up by the rail, fighting to keep their footing while the tram rattled from side to side. When they finally reached the top it was to see Milly sitting in a seat by the window, her smile bright enough to bring out the sun in a sky that was overcast with dark clouds.

'Can I sit by the window, please, Auntie Bessie, so I can see all the people rushing in and out of the shops? They look really small when you look down on them, like little diddy people. They look cold, too, but I don't feel cold at all.' Milly fingered the beige scarf Bessie had wrapped around her neck. 'This is keeping me nice and warm.'

Bessie sat beside her, while Rita sat in the seat in front. 'It is cold out today, sweetheart, it seems winter is coming early.' She heard the conductor coming, clicking the handle of his ticket machine and calling, 'Fares, please. And try to have the right money ready if yer can.'

Rita was opening her bag to get her purse out, when Bessie tapped her shoulder. 'I've got the fare ready, girl, so put yer purse away.' She took sixpence from her pocket which she handed to the conductor. 'Two twoppenny returns to Church Street, and one child's fare.'

Milly was intrigued to see the conductor turn the little handle at the side of the machine which hung down from a wide leather strap over his shoulder. And when three tickets came out from a slot in front, she thought it was magic. 'Ooh, isn't that clever, Auntie Bessie? I'd like to be a conductor when I grow up, and have one of those to give people their tickets.'

The conductor passed the tickets to Bessie before smiling at the young girl. 'You wouldn't like it, love, not when the novelty wore off. In the winter months yer've got to fight against the wind to get up the stairs, and yer hands get so cold yer expect yer fingers to fall off.' He leaned towards her and lowered his voice. 'And yer get some ruddy awkward passengers, as well. I had one this morning. Some bloke fell asleep and missed his stop. He blamed me, said I should have woke him up, and now he was late for work he'd have his pay docked. Anyone could see why he'd missed his stop, he'd been out boozing last night and was bleary-eyed. He was so bad-tempered and shouting the odds, everyone on the tram could hear him. But we all had a laugh when he went to punch me 'cos he wasn't quite sober. He could see three of me and missed by a mile.' The conductor was chuckling at the memory. 'To top it off, I went to help him off the tram 'cos he wasn't capable of walking straight, but he pushed me away and fell down the ruddy step! It had passed the time away for other passengers, and they all jeered and clapped. I don't know where the bloke worked, but this is one day his boss won't be getting his money's worth. It brightened my day, though, it's not often I get a drunk taking a punch at me.'

Bessie and Rita were shaking with laughter. The man was a good storyteller; doing all the actions as he told the tale. Milly had a hand over her mouth while her eyes glistened with happiness. Oh, this was going to be the most exciting day of her life!

While her daughter was sitting on a rickety tram, swaying with each movement and shudder, Evelyn was sitting back in Philip's luxurious car with a travelling rug covering her knees. She was revelling in the smell of its leather seats and the comfort all around her. It was over eight years since she'd been in a car, and without warning she remembered the last time. It was in Charles' car that she'd become pregnant with Amelia. She shivered at the memory, and Philip was quick to lean sideways to tuck the rug closer, thinking she was cold. 'Tuck it in the other side, my lovely, I can't have you catching a chill.'

'I'm not cold, my dear, it's very warm and comfortable in here. It was just someone walking over my grave, as the saying goes. I've no doubt it has happened to you at some time. No one seems to know the reason for it.'

They were driving down country lanes, and some of the properties they passed were lovely, beautiful big houses with large, well-kept gardens. 'How peaceful it is here compared to the city,' Evelyn said. 'The only problem would be shopping. We haven't passed any shops to speak of.'

'My darling Evelyn, everything in the way of foodstuffs and coal is delivered. The only shopping local residents do is for clothes, and then they drive to the city, either by car or horse-drawn carriage.' Philip turned his head briefly. 'I remember my father having a horse and carriage when I was younger, before automobiles became fashionable. I actually prefer to ride in a carriage because I love horses and am glad there are still so many of them on the streets of Liverpool. They're loyal, trustworthy and hard-working, and it would be a sad day indeed if man ever forgot their strength, loyalty and courage.'

Evelyn patted his arm. 'I can't see horses disappearing, dear.

Without them there would be no milk or coal deliveries, and of course no furniture removals. That's apart from the haulage companies down at the docks, who wouldn't survive without horses and carts.'

Houses were becoming more frequent now as they drove through the lush areas leading into Southport. There were no streets of two-up-two-down houses here; only people with money could afford to live in this affluent area. Every property was large, and built to accommodate maids, housekeepers, gardeners, and cars or carriages. Although she couldn't see them, Evelyn was sure there would be stables at the back of the houses.

'I'll drive into Lord Street and park the car in front of the hotel,' Philip said. 'Then we'll have some refreshment, I feel quite peckish.'

'Yes, I would appreciate a drink myself, I'm thirsty.' Evelyn was never free from the fear of bumping into someone from her past, if not Cyril or Matilda Lister-Sinclair themselves then one of their acquaintances who would be only too eager to spread the news that she had surfaced and been seen on the arm of a man. Worse still, they could accost Evelyn while she was with Philip, then the truth would come out and he would be so horrified he would walk away. She had altered her hairstyle in an attempt to make herself less obvious, but there was little else she could do except pray.

Philip parked the car in the forecourt of the Prince of Wales Hotel, the grandest in Southport. He opened the passenger door and helped Evelyn from the car. 'We'll have something light here, my love, to ease the pangs of hunger. But we won't dine here. I have ordered a very lavish meal to be delivered to the apartment at eight o'clock. It will be piping hot, served by waiters from the hotel.' He tucked her arm under his as they walked together into the foyer of the large hotel, and while his eyes searched for the most discreet table he whispered in her ear, 'I am secretly wishing the time away, my lovely Evelyn. I can't wait until the afternoon is over, and we have dined in the apartment on a delicious meal accompanied by excellent wine to give you that lovely warm glow. The waiters will be encouraged to clear away quickly then and leave us alone. And I can take you in my arms and show you how much I need you, and what you have been missing by keeping me at arm's length for so long.'

Evelyn could feel herself colour as she looked around her to see if anyone was close enough to have heard. 'Really, Philip, see how you have made me blush?'

He chuckled as he led her to a table in an alcove. 'That is what I love about you, my very dear darling. You are so innocent. And while I hope you do not remain so for ever, I would be very sorry to see you change too swiftly.' He held her hand as she lowered herself into a chair. 'Besides, if you look around, people are far more concerned with their own affairs than they are with listening in to ours.' He sat facing her, ran two fingers down the perfect crease in his trousers, then leaned forward. 'But none of them have as much to look forward to as I have, especially with such a beautiful woman.'

Evelyn was secretly lapping up the compliments she'd been starved of for so long. To be treated like someone special was boosting her confidence. 'Really, Philip, I think such talk should be reserved for when we have complete privacy.'

He had never met a woman so retiring before, and found it refreshing. And she didn't use a lot of make-up on her face either, didn't need it with her colouring and complexion. Some young women looked like painted dolls, but not Evelyn. Tonight he was hoping to find that she had not been with any man since her husband was killed. He caught the eye of a waiter and beckoned him over. 'A pot of Earl Grey tea, my good man, and a selection of sandwiches and cakes.'

When the waiter retreated, Philip asked, 'Tell me, my love, have you ever smoked?'

Evelyn looked surprised. 'What a curious question, Philip! Yes, I smoked when I was younger, in my late-teens, but it is many years since I've held a cigarette. It was quite the rage at one time. I remember one was thought to be quite a frump if one didn't walk around at parties with an ebony or silver cigarette holder.'

'I'm glad you don't, my love. There is nothing so off-putting as kissing a woman who smells of smoke.'

'You sound as though you are very experienced in the ways of women,' Evelyn said, crossing her shapely legs to remind him she could compete with the best. 'I am not a jealous person, or at least I hope not, but I'm wondering whether I should be a tiny bit jealous of you or not? Do I have reason to be?'

'Good heavens, my love, no! No woman has ever come near to having the qualities you possess. I consider myself very lucky to have found you.'

Conversation ceased then as two waiters appeared bearing trays of tea, a variety of thinly cut sandwiches and cakes. Evelyn sighed, 'They look delicious.'

While Philip and Evelyn relaxed in the comfort and luxury of the Prince of Wales Hotel, the child he didn't know existed was sitting in a cafe in a little side street with her two new aunties. There were no tablecloths on the wooden tables, and a cup of tea and scone cost only threepence. The customers were all working-class, not used to luxury but quite content with their lot. Milly was more than content. All this was new to her and she was finding pleasure in everything. Her green eyes were wide as she gazed at the people around her, and listened to them talking loudly and cracking jokes. Some of them wore black knitted shawls over their shoulders and their hair was plaited into buns, either at the nape of their neck or one by each ear. They were a few of the well-known Mary Ellens who brought colour to the Liverpool scene as they went about the business of selling their wares. Having sold out of flowers early today, they had nipped into the cafe for a cuppa before making their way back home with their empty baskets balanced on their heads. Milly was intrigued by them. Two had gold teeth, and when they smiled the metal flashed, causing the young girl to stare, mesmerised.

Rita leaned sideways to whisper in Bessie's ear, 'It's to be hoped a certain person doesn't tell another certain person about what she's seen today. That would really let the cat out of the bag, and it would be goodbye to future outings.'

'If you knew a certain young person as well as I do, you would give her credit for having more brains than that. I've told yer before, sweetheart, Milly has more sense than any of us. And though I shouldn't say it, she's got more on top than her own mother gives her credit for. She knows what's at stake. I am so sure of her, I'm not even going to mention that she should keep today's outing a secret.'

'I'm surprised she's never been into town before, aren't you? To hear her mother talk yer'd think they were used to living like rich people.' Rita tutted. 'I can't stand people who think they're better than anyone else, sunshine, they get on me nerves. God made us all equal, and money doesn't make one person better than the rest.'

Bessie nodded in agreement. 'Ye're right, Rita, definitely. Yer hit the nail right on the head. But Milly is going to have the last laugh, for she will have known both worlds by the time she's older. She'll never be a snob like her mother.'

Rita sighed. 'Let's hope not. Anyway, let's settle up before we leave here so I know I'm out of debt. How much have yer paid out altogether, sunshine?'

Bessie made sure Milly was still listening to the conversations going on around her before answering. 'This is my treat, Rita, so don't be making a fuss. If the truth were known, it's really Mrs Sinclair's treat 'cos it's her two bob I'm using. So she's come in handy and done us a good turn, after all the times we've called her fit to burn.'

'Yer don't get the two bob for nothing, Bessie, yer earn it. So don't forget that, and let me pay me way or I won't come out with yer again.'

'I was living all right before Tilly Mint started paying me, and for what it costs to give Milly some tea each day, well, it's not worth talking about. So I'm really two bob a week better off than I was. And in bed last night, I dreamt up an idea of how you can give me a hand, and in return we'll make sure all the kids have a Christmas party this year and get a present off Father Christmas.'

Rita folded her arms and leaned her elbows on the wooden table. 'That sounds just up my street, sunshine, but where do I come into it?'

'You and Aggie, sunshine, 'cos we can't leave her out. I felt mean not asking her to come with us today, but I'll make it up to her. And what I thought up in bed last night was a way to help us all to a better Christmas than we've had for the last few years, with so many men out of work. But I can't tell yer more now, for it's a well-known saying that little pigs have big ears.'

Milly happened to turn towards them just in time to hear the last few words. 'Who has big ears, Auntie Bessie?'

Bessie gave her mate a kick under the table. 'You wouldn't know her, sweetheart, she's a woman lives in the next street. But don't think I was saying anything bad about her, 'cos I wasn't. And her ears haven't anything to do with it anyway, that was just a chance remark I made.' She felt like cupping the lovely little face and kissing it. But she had to refrain from getting too close to the child, or letting the child get too close to her. It could end in heartbreak for both of them. 'Well, have yer enjoyed yer afternoon in the big city?'

Swinging her legs under the table, Milly gave a big sigh. 'I have had a wonderful time, Auntie Bessie. All those big buildings, and big shops it would take a week to walk around. And

I've never been in a cafe before, so I feel like the girl in *Cinderella*. Except she had two ugly sisters, while I have two lovely kind aunties.'

'Well, all good things come to an end, sweetheart, and we've got to be making tracks for home. If we leave it any longer, we'll have a devil of a job getting on a tram 'cos the queues will be miles long with women wanting to get home to make tea for their families.'

'That goes for me too, sunshine,' Rita said. 'If my feller doesn't get his tea by six o'clock, the people down at the Pier Head will hear his tummy rumbling. It's been known for people in the street to think it was thunder. And one old lady, terrified that thunder doesn't come without lightning, didn't she take a chair and sit under the stairs for an hour until her son convinced her it wasn't thunder at all, only Mr Wells letting his wife know he was hungry.'

Milly had learned many things since spending time with her Auntie Bessie, and one of those things was that it wasn't bad manners to laugh out loud, like her mother had always told her. When you laughed, you made other people feel happy. So now she let her head drop back and her childish giggles filled the air, causing people to turn and smile indulgently. 'Oh, you are funny, Auntie Rita, you do make me laugh. I wish I could think of funny things like you do, things that would make people happy.'

'Oh, you do, sweetheart! You make me very happy indeed!' There was affection in Bessie's eyes. 'I lived all alone until you came along, and even though my friends the front door and the grate were company for me, they're not the same as having someone real who can answer me back. I'm really glad your mother lets yer come to me, yer've cheered my life up no end.'

'Are yer going to tell yer mates in school about coming to town today, sunshine?' Rita asked. 'I wonder if any of them have been in this cafe?'

'I will ask them, Auntie Rita, but the first one I'm going to tell is Daisy. I'm going to sit her on my knee and tell her every little thing that's happened.' Milly giggled. 'I bet she'll laugh when I tell her about the conductor on the tram, he was very funny.'

'Yeah, he was a corker, he was,' Bessie agreed. 'It's no joke running up and down those stairs in bad weather, 'cos they're open to all the elements. It's certainly not a job I'd thank yer for, not when it's blowing a gale or snowing.'

'It's not the best of jobs,' Rita agreed, 'but there's thousands of men in Liverpool who'd be glad of it. They'd put up with the bad weather and the drunks, just to bring a wage packet home to their wives every Saturday. I feel sorry for the poor buggers who go out every morning and traipse around begging for a few hours' work.'

Milly's eyes rolled. 'You said a bad word, Auntie Rita.'

Rita looked surprised. 'Did I?' Then she remembered. 'Oh, yeah, I did, it must have slipped out.' Her eyes narrowed. 'How d'yer know it's a swear word? Yer mother doesn't swear, I'm sure, and neither does Bessie. So how come yer know a swear word from any other word?'

'Because one of the girls in my class got three strokes of the cane for using it in the playground. Teacher sent her to the headmistress, and as well as getting the cane, she had to write out fifty times, "Nice girls do not swear".'

Bessie bit on the inside of her bottom lip to stop herself from chuckling. This young girl knew far more than she was letting on. And what a shock it would be to her mother if she ever found out! 'The headmistress was right, sweetheart, 'cos nice girls shouldn't swear. It's bad enough for a grown-up to use bad language, but it's ten times worse coming from the lips of a child. So don't you forget that, young lady.' Bessie picked her bag up off the floor at the side of the table. 'Come on, let's make our way to the tram stop in Lime Street. And stay downstairs this time, Milly, 'cos it's murder climbing those stairs with this wind blowing.'

As Rita slipped her arms into her coat, she said, 'I might nip over tonight, Bessie, about eight, after the meal's over. I can't wait to find out what thoughts yer came up with when yer were in bed.'

Milly took hold of Bessie's hand as they left the table. 'Auntie Bessie talks to the wallpaper in her bedroom, Auntie Rita. I know, 'cos I've heard her.'

And the three of them walked through the cafe door roaring with laughter.

Chapter Sixteen

Milly was sitting on the couch with Daisy propped up on her knee, telling the doll once again about the wonderful time she'd had in the city and the sights she'd seen. It was half-past eight, way past the girl's bedtime, but she was still so excited Bessie didn't have the heart to insist she went to bed.

When Rita arrived, she raised her brows in surprise. 'I thought yer'd have been in bed ages ago, sunshine, tired out with all the walking yer did?'

Milly smiled at her. 'I'm telling Daisy about the shops, and the cafe, and she really is interested. She said she wants to come with me next time.' She looked across at Bessie. 'Do you have to pay to take a doll on the tram, Auntie Bessie?'

'No, sweetheart, they don't charge for a doll.' Bessie saw the query in her mate's eyes and shrugged her shoulders. 'There's no sign of sleep, she's wide awake.' But knowing Rita had come for a purpose, Bessie decided firmness was the order of the day. 'I think yer should go to bed now, though, Milly. You can talk to Daisy while ye're laying down, nice and warm, and me and Rita won't be interrupting yer story.'

The girl didn't argue, for she saw the sense of talking to her doll in bed. 'All right, Auntie Bessie, I am beginning to feel a bit tired.' She held the doll close to her face. 'I've still got a lot to tell you, though, before we go to sleep.'

'Don't forget to tell her about the conductor on the tram,' Rita reminded her. 'I know she'll enjoy that. I told my family and they were in stitches.'

Milly's childish giggles rang out again. 'I was saving that until the last, Auntie Rita, so me and Daisy could go to sleep with a smile on our faces. She does know what I'm saying, you know, I can tell by the way she looks at me.' She kissed the two woman, but Bessie was also given a special hug and a whispered, 'I love you, Auntie Bessie.'

'And I love you, sweetheart. But poppy off now so me and Rita can talk about the day, too! Ye're not the only one who enjoyed themself, yer know. It was a treat for me and me mate, for we don't often get the chance to go into the city.'

The two women listened as Milly scrambled up the stairs, and when they thought she was out of earshot, Rita said, 'I'd give anything for a daughter like her, she's a little gem.'

'Same here, girl.' Bessie heaved a deep sigh. 'She's a beautiful child to look at, and her beauty doesn't stop at looks, she's got a beautiful nature too. I'd be the happiest woman alive if she was mine.' She gave a few shakes of her head to clear away such longings. 'What's the good of wishes and dreams? We should be thankful we're alive and have got our health. There's many a one would swap places with us.'

'Ye're right there, sunshine, that goes for half the people in this street. All they've got to look forward to, week after week, is scrounging enough money to keep body and soul together. We've nowt to complain about.' Rita slipped her shoes off and swung herself round so she could stretch her legs out on the couch. 'Anyway, don't let's start feeling sorry for ourselves, not after having such a nice afternoon. Tell me about the idea that came to yer in bed last night? If it's any good, I'll tell yer what came to me in bed last night. The trouble with that, though, is yer might be too embarrassed to look Reg in the face again.'

'Rita Wells, I'll have yer know I have no interest in what happens in your bedroom.' Bessie feigned disgust, but she was chuckling inside. 'I wish yer'd remember I am a spinster, as innocent and as pure as the driven snow.'

'We've only got your word for that, sunshine, but once again we're getting away from the matter in hand. What is this idea yer've come up with? If it means a better Christmas for the kids, then I'm all for it.'

Bessie leaned back in the fireside chair, her fingers gently tapping on the wooden arms. 'Well, yer know I changed me working hours when I started minding Milly? I go in at seven now so I can finish at four, whereas I used to go in from eight till five. They're always asking me to work longer hours, 'cos although I say it as shouldn't, I've been doing the job so long I get through twice as much work as the younger ones. I used to work all the hours they wanted me to until Milly came on the scene. But what I was thinking, which will help out with the money, is that if you and Aggie have Milly for an hour each night, so I can work until five, it would give yer a few extra coppers every week. It would only be a tanner a week each, but if you and Aggie did help me out, I could put that shilling a week to the two bob I get off Mrs Sinclair, and that would be three bob a week I'd put away until Christmas. I'd still give Milly her tea every night, so it wouldn't cost you or Aggie any money, and we're just into October now which means we've at least twelve weeks to Christmas. That would be enough for a party for the kids and a present each. There might even be enough over for a few drinks for us grown-ups.' Bessie took a deep breath and blew out slowly. 'Well, sweetheart, what d'yer think?'

Rita swung her legs around and put her feet on the floor. 'And what do you get out of this, sunshine? Sweet bugger all from what I can see. Yer've got no kids, while me and Aggie have four between us, and yer've got no family! No, I wouldn't be happy with that, it wouldn't be fair. It would be you doing all the giving, and us doing all the taking. No thanks, Bessie, I couldn't go along with that. I'll mind Milly for an hour every night for yer, but I don't want paying for it. I'd be tickled pink to have her, I've always wanted a girl in the house.'

Bessie tutted. 'Don't be so ruddy quick off the mark, Rita Wells, just wait until yer hear the whole story. I went a lot further in me plans last night before I went to sleep. I'd never drop off unless I had it all sorted. So listen to what I think, and hope, might happen. And I've a feeling it's more likely to happen than not.'

'Ye're getting me all mixed up with yer mights and might nots, sunshine, so give it to me in plain English.'

'Well, I think it's quite likely that I'll have Milly over Christmas. I'll lay odds Mrs Sinclair has got herself a man, and I'll also lay odds she hasn't told him she's got a daughter. If she had, it would be only natural he'd want to see the girl. Even this imaginary school friend of hers, Elizabeth, wouldn't she wonder why Milly never came with her mother on a visit? No, the whole situation is cock-eyed, and the queer one is lying through her hat and taking me for a sucker. At least, she thinks I'm a sucker, and I'm happy for her to go on thinking so for as long as it suits my purpose. When it gets nearer the time, I can actually see her, in me mind of course, sitting in that chair trying to find the right excuse so as I'll have Milly and she can spend Christmas with her man friend. And I'll admit to yer, Rita, that if she gets all flustered and finds it hard to make an excuse that sounds plausible, I'll help her out! I'll be as nice as pie and encourage her to go out and enjoy herself. She's selfish enough to take me up on it.'

Bessie grinned ruefully. 'I don't usually think badly of people, Rita, and it's got nothing to do with me what Mrs Sinclair gets up to. She can walk Lime Street picking men up for money for all I care. It's what happens to Milly I'm concerned about. What sort of a Christmas would she have if there was nowhere for her to go except be with her mother? Whether it was to the boyfriend's, or the old school chum's, she'd have a miserable time because she wouldn't be wanted. And they wouldn't be having the same sort of Christmas we have because snobs don't know how to let their hair down like we do. I can't stand the thought of Milly sitting in someone's house, watched over by her mother in case she spoke out of turn or put a foot wrong, and being unhappy. I'd crawl to the stuck-up snob next door rather than have that happen.' The look in Bessie's eyes begged for her mate's understanding. 'So, yer see, Rita, I might have a child over Christmas after all. I'm going to say so many prayers, God will give in just to shut me up.'

'It would be wonderful if it turns out that way, sunshine. Milly would have a lot of fun with my two and Aggie's. But don't pin yer hopes on it, Bessie, 'cos I'd hate to see yer let down. And it wouldn't only be you disappointed, it would be Milly, too. I know she'd rather be with you than with her mother.'

'I'm not even going to consider her not being here, Rita, I'm going to be positive and work on the assumption she's going to spend Christmas with me. And that's not because I'm selfish in wanting to keep her away from her mother, it's because I know she gets more love while she's in this house than she does anywhere else. So, are yer prepared to help me out if I take an extra hour's work on? If yer are, yer can mention it to Aggie if yer would, see if she's agreeable to what I've suggested. If it turns out I can't have Milly, it won't make no difference to you or Aggie, the kids will still have their party and presents, I'll make sure of that.'

Rita clicked her tongue on the roof of her mouth. 'Yer should have had half a dozen kids of yer own, Bessie, 'cos yer'd have made a marvellous mother. And I hope to God things work out as yer want them to. But, that aside, you go ahead and work the extra hour, me and Aggie will look after Milly. It'll do the girl good to mix with other kids.' She suddenly took a fit of laughing. 'But I have to say, neither me nor Aggie will take any responsibility if the girl's mastery of the English language suffers a severe setback. It's too late in life for either of us to go back to school to learn how to speak properly. I will ask Aggie to try and control some of the more colourful words she comes out with, but I can't guarantee success.'

Bessie chortled. 'I'd be more afraid of Milly teaching Aggie some new words. The girls in her class must hear their parents cursing to high heaven.'

'My kids don't hear me swearing often, I try to control meself in front of them. Yer can't expect children not to repeat things they hear in their own homes, they're not to know some of them are bad.' Rita slipped her feet into her shoes. 'I'll have a word with Aggie in the morning, sunshine, and tell her what yer've got in mind. She'll be more than agreeable to helping, she'll be over the moon. If it means a halfway decent Christmas for the family, she'd walk to Timbuctoo and back. But, so she doesn't think we're making plans behind her back, I'll come over with her tomorrow night, after Milly's gone to bed. Aggie will feel better if she's involved, and it'll give her something to look forward to. Like meself, she doesn't get any social life because of lack of money, and this scheme of yours will be just the job to keep the pair of us going. And if it turns out as you think it might, then it will take a lot of the worry of Christmas off our minds and we'll be yer friends for life.' She patted Bessie's arm. 'We'll be that anyway, sunshine, 'cos we couldn't have asked for a better mate over the years. Yer've always been there when we were in trouble, and yer know that even if we've never told yer, we've always appreciated yer kindness.'

Bessie nodded and followed her friend to the door. 'Make it half-past eight, then Milly will be in bed. I'll make us a pot of tea, which is more than yer got tonight. I've been that busy talking I forgot me manners. It won't happen again, sweetheart, I promise.'

Rita waved when she reached the opposite pavement. 'Good-night and God bless, sunshine, and go straight to sleep, no more laying awake, d'yer hear? Yer've given me enough to think about, but it won't stop me from getting me beauty sleep.'

'Goodnight and God bless.' Bessie blew a kiss before closing the door.

As Bessie was closing her front door, Philip was holding his apartment door open for the two waiters to pass through. They were carrying boxes filled with crockery, glassware and cutlery used in the meal they had served earlier. The food had been delicious, and the serving of it faultless. This was much appreciated by Philip who, as they passed him at the door, gave them a pound note each to show his gratitude. Then with the door closed behind them, he rubbed his hands in satisfaction. Now he and Evelyn were alone, and from their conversation over dinner he was sure she was aware he was no longer going to be satisfied with kissing and petting. He wanted to possess her, and teach her the ways in which she could please and satisfy him. That wouldn't happen in one night, and he wasn't a cad who would force her into doing things she objected to. But his passion needed satisfying tonight, he could wait no longer.

Evelyn turned her eyes to meet his when Philip entered the room. 'I must say, dear, that the meal was absolutely perfect in every way. I thoroughly enjoyed it.'

'I agree, my lovely, it was far better to dine in comfort here than going out to a restaurant. I feel quite full, though, and think we should change into something not quite so restricting. Do you wish to use the bathroom first, or shall I?'

'You go first, my dear, I'll relax here until you return.' Evelyn wasn't afraid of what she knew was going to happen, it was inevitable if she was to keep him. But she wasn't quite sure what was expected of her now. What did he mean by changing into something not quite so restricting? She wasn't about to show her ignorance, nor make a fool of herself by asking, so she'd wait and see what Philip was wearing when he came back. 'Hurry, my dear, I shall be lonely without you by my side.'

Her words were like music to his ears. 'I shall be ten minutes at the most, my dearest Evelyn, I am loath to leave you for even such a short time.' With that he turned on his heels and left the room, humming softly to himself.

Evelyn sat back in the comfortable couch feeling happy and contented. It had been a lovely day and Philip the perfect escort. He had walked with her down Lord Street, stopping when she spied anything in a window that caught her eye. She could have had anything her heart desired, but she refused all the evening and party dresses, saying what she really needed was a coat to wear for work. She only possessed the one, and it needed to be cleaned. So without further ado, and giving her no chance to object, Philip cupped her elbow and marched her into one of the elegant shops. To the assistant who hurried forward to help, he said, 'My fiancée would like to see a winter coat. Would you bring several out for her inspection while we take a seat?'

Against Philip's wishes, Evelyn chose one of the least costly coats, and nothing he said would make her change her mind. She would have loved several of them, but she couldn't walk down her street in a coat that was obviously expensive nor would she feel comfortable wearing it to the office. So she chose one in a deep plum colour, in pure wool, that came with a matching scarf. She was delighted with it, could never have afforded one so fine with the money she had left from the five-pound note. And when she told the assistant she would like to leave the shop in her new coat, Philip was so delighted that she liked it so much she wanted to keep it on, he instructed the assistant to see his fiancée's wishes were carried out. So they had left the shop with her old coat in a very exclusive shopping bag, and in her purse she still had money left from the five pounds he'd given her.

The opening of the door brought Evelyn's thoughts back to the present. Although she was surprised to see Philip walking towards her in a deep maroon, heavy satin dressing gown, she didn't let her feelings show. 'You have been quick, my dear, and I really have to say you look extremely handsome.'

He bent to kiss her, then took her hand and pulled her to her feet. 'Thank you, my darling, for the compliment. And I am sure that when you return from doing what women do, you will look very beautiful. Now, make haste, my love. I am eager to hold you in my arms.'

Evelyn took off her dress and hung it in the wardrobe, then stood for a while, not knowing quite what to do. She hadn't seen any sign of pyjamas under the dressing gown Philip was wearing so presumed he was naked. This brought a blush to her face, and set her heart beating faster. What would he be expecting her to wear? Perhaps she should take herself to the bathroom to wash herself thoroughly with his beautiful perfumed soap, and brush her hair until it shone. She really did want to look her best to please him. Perhaps the red satin nightdress would be the most suitable item of clothing to wear. Or, like Philip, should she just wear the dressing gown to cover her nakedness? She shook her head. No, it would have to be the nightdress to spare her blushes. After all, it would be the first time any man had seen her naked, for her husband never had.

Having decided, she moved a little faster. She knew Philip would be impatient and she didn't want him to come looking for her. She wanted to go to him, not the other way round.

Fifteen minutes later, a faint smell of the perfumed soap pervading the air, her face glowing and hair shining, she stood framed in the doorway of the lounge. She had no idea how appealing she looked. The satin and lace nightdress did little to hide her firm breasts, slim waist and curved hips. Philip sat drinking in every inch of her, until she became uncomfortable under his gaze. Her voice timid, she asked, 'Do I pass inspection, then?'

He jumped up from the couch and crossed the room in a few strides. 'My dearest darling, I have never wanted anyone so much in my life as I want you.' He bent down, lifted her off her feet and carried her through to the bedroom where he laid her down gently on top of the bed. There was a look of trepidation on her face and her body was tense, which he didn't fail to notice. 'It's all right, my darling, there is nothing to fear. If you don't want it to happen, then it won't. Please relax, we'll lie together under the bedcovers.'

Her eyes averted, Evelyn felt him move his naked body closer. 'Would you allow me to remove your nightdress, my darling?' he asked. 'Or would you rather not?'

She nodded, curious now that they'd gone so far to know what it was that Philip so desperately craved. 'Yes, please.' She raised herself from the bed to assist in the removal of the nightdress, and as it slipped over her head could feel her bare flesh next to Philip's. A tingle ran down her spine. Then he lowered her gently before covering her body with his, whispering huskily, 'Don't be afraid, my darling, I want to teach you the pleasure that comes from love making.'

Evelyn could feel her body being caressed, and gradually it awoke in her a passion she had never experienced before. She gave low cries of pleasure as her body arched to meet Philip's. And when he asked softly, 'Am I pleasing you, my darling?' she sighed and murmured, 'Oh, yes, my love.'

Then she felt the weight of his body leave hers as he rolled away and lay next to her, his breathing heavy. 'What is it, my love?' Evelyn thought she had disappointed him in some way. 'Am I not satisfying you?'

'I don't want what we have now to be over too soon, so let me rest a while. But you are the most lovable, adorable creature imaginable, and you possess a passion I was not prepared for. I want this feeling of ecstasy to last, my darling, therefore I must let my passion subside for a short while.'

Evelyn was too inexperienced fully to understand the meaning of Philip's words, and in her naivety turned on her side and put an arm across his waist. As she was kissing his shoulder, she let her hand stroke his chest and heard him sigh. 'Please take it easy, my love, I can only stand so much.'

'Shall I bring us a drink in?' Evelyn asked. 'We left a bottle on the table and our glasses, I'll go for them while you get your breath back.' She was reaching for her nightdress when Philip stayed her hand. 'No, go as you are, my lovely Evelyn. Seeing you naked is like seeing a dream walking.'

She knelt on the bed and kissed him, showing no sign of embarrassment or shyness at seeing him naked. 'Yes, my master, I shall do your bidding.'

Philip watched her walking towards the door, delighting in the sway of her hips and long shapely legs. She really was a beauty, and he would hazard a guess no other man had touched her. For although she had lost her shyness and aloofness, and was perfectly at ease with him, she couldn't understand why he had suddenly halted the love making. Any woman experienced in the ways of men would have known without having to be told. For him this added to the attraction she had for him. He had never felt like this about any other woman, and there had been plenty. Evelyn satisfied him in every way, and tonight he'd proved to himself, beyond a doubt, that he had fallen in love with her. But he wasn't going to tell her so, she might not have the same feelings for him although he didn't think it was just in his imagination that she was drawing closer to him. She'd amazed and delighted him tonight when she hadn't tried to hide the pleasure she'd experienced as he'd fondled her. What was happening was something new to her, and he couldn't even imagine the heights they could reach when she'd learned all he had to teach her.

Evelyn came through the door with a bottle of wine in one hand and two glasses in the other. The fact that she was naked seemed not to affect her at all. 'Here you are, my love, your favourite wine. Sit up and I'll hand you a glass. I'll have mine sitting on the side of the bed. We can chat, and say nice things to each other.'

Philip sat up and plumped the pillows at his back before taking the glass of red wine from her. He watched as Evelyn poured her drink before sitting on the side of the bed and lifting her glass. 'A toast, my dear, to a lasting friendship.'

As he sipped the wine, Philip couldn't tear his eyes away from her breasts. So full and ripe, and so near he couldn't resist the temptation to fondle them. As he did so, he felt a stirring in his loins and groaned. He couldn't hold out much longer. 'Put the glass down, my lovely, and get back into bed. My need is desperate and I can no longer ignore it. I'm sorry, it's out of my control. I will do my best to be gentle, but tell me if I hurt you.'

The pain Evelyn experienced was sharp, but it lasted only seconds, and soon she was lost in a world she had never known, writhing in ecstasy with Philip panting above her. Wave after wave of the most thrilling pleasure she had ever known overtook her. She cried out while her hands clasped his shoulders. It was a wonderland for her of sheer sensuous pleasure. When Philip stopped, wanting to see on her face the pleasure he was able to bring about with his love making, she begged, 'Don't stop, my darling, please!'

He rolled away from her. 'I am sorry, but to lose my head and carry on would be foolish. That is how babies are made. But I can satisfy your needs in other ways.' He threw all the bedclothes on to the floor, then his hands began to stroke and explore her body as Evelyn, with her eyes closed, reacted to his touch by stretching, and arching as her passion reached peaks of pleasure she had never thought possible. In the end, she could take no more and begged, 'Please, my darling, no more for now.'

He took her in his arms. 'Am I right in saying you have never been made love to before? Never known what a wonderful thing passion is?'

'You are right, my darling, I have never been made love to before. My husband was a good man who I had been courting for a while, but I never lay in bed beside him for he went away to war the day we were married.' This was the first time she had talked of her husband to anyone since her parents and the Lister-Sinclairs had refused to believe that Charles was the father of the baby she was carrying, and had disowned her. She was left with nothing, except a baby who wasn't born out of love, and a heart full of bitterness.

'I don't want to rake up the past, it achieves nothing. You know now as much as you need to know, and as much as I am prepared to tell you, for talking of it is painful. Let us leave the past in the past, and talk of more pleasant things.' She stroked his cheek. 'Thank you for being so gentle and understanding, and for showing me what I have been missing all these years. And most of all, thank you for making me into a woman who is complete. The last hour or so has been absolute bliss, unbelievably thrilling and very fulfilling.'

'It is I who should be thanking you, my darling Evelyn. Last week in the office I said you were a slave driver. Well, you may be a slave driver in the office, but you are an angel in bed, and I adore you. Did I really please you?'

'Oh, how can you ask that, my dear, when it must have been very obvious I was lost in a passion I didn't even know I was capable of? If you had told me a few weeks ago that one day I would be walking around your apartment naked, or lying next to you in bed, I would have said you had lost the run of your senses. If you had tried to explain passion, and the delights it can bring, I would not have believed you. Oh, there is so much I have to thank you for, Philip, I really don't know where to begin. You have taught me so much.'

'Not everything, my darling, there is more for you to learn. And that is the way in which you can please me, and take me to the heights you have just come down from. Give me your hand, my love, and I will show you.'

Chapter Seventeen

Philip walked across the bedroom floor carrying a tray set with a pot of tea, a plate of pale golden toast, pot of marmalade, and the appropriate crockery and cutlery. He stood by the bed, gazing down at the sleeping form of Evelyn, and felt a quiver of excitement run down his spine at the memory of the joy she'd given him last night. He placed the tray on a small table near the bed, then gently shook her shoulder. 'Evelyn, my lovely one, I have brought you some tea.'

She stirred, turned on her side, then after a few seconds opened her eyes. 'Oh, Philip, for a while I couldn't make out where I was.' Her eyes caught sight of the tray, and she was pushing herself into a sitting position when she realised she was naked. She made a grab for a sheet to cover herself, but Philip anticipated her move and took hold of her hand. 'Would you spoil a day which I am sure is going to be such a happy one for both of us?'

It was then she noticed that once again he was wearing no clothes beneath the dressing gown. 'Pass the tray, my dear, then get into bed and we will enjoy breakfast in each other's company.' She was wide awake now, and felt a tingle as the memories came flooding back. 'How thoughtful of you to bring me breakfast in bed. I will have to watch you don't spoil me. I do believe it should have been me waiting on you.'

He placed the tray carefully on her lap, then slid into bed. 'I want to spoil you, and go on spoiling you. What man in his right senses would not spoil a woman who is so beautiful and passionate?'

Evelyn was pouring the tea into small china cups. 'Please be still, my love, otherwise the tray and everything on it will spill over. I think we should drink a cup of tea first, put the empty cups on the table, and have our toast. We can always have another cup of tea later.'

'Oh, there won't be time for a second cup of tea, darling,' Philip said, a twinkle in his eye.

There was surprise on Evelyn's face, and a look of disappointment. 'But I thought I wasn't going home until this afternoon? That is what we arranged.'

'If I can bear to part with you, then yes, it will be this afternoon when you go home. But, my wonderful lover, I am hoping for several repeat performances of last night before then. That is if you are agreeable?'

The anticipation started with butterflies in her tummy and accelerated with her racing heartbeat. She held on tight to the tray while she closed her eyes. At twenty-nine years of age, she was just finding out the real meaning of happiness and pleasure, and she wasn't going to throw them away. 'I find I am not so hungry after all, so shall we just have one cup of tea and one slice of toast?'

Philip nearly sent the tray flying when he put his arms around her and kissed her cheek. 'You, my very darling Evelyn, are the most adorable woman I have ever met. And one slice of toast will be ample. I have an appetite, but it is not for food.'

Evelyn searched his face. 'Talking of food, how is it you always have a well-stocked kitchen? Does your mother shop for you?'

'Good grief, no! The person who does my shopping for me is the same person who keeps the apartment clean and attends to my washing and ironing.'

There was a look of horror on Evelyn's face. 'Then she must wonder who owns the ladies' clothes in the wardrobe, and satin underwear in the drawers. Does she know you have a lady friend, or does she think you have a mistress?'

'Keep calm, my love, keep calm.' Philip began to chuckle. 'I don't know, though, they say anger is excellent for enthusiastic love making.'

'Philip, please be serious. I do not want anyone thinking I am your mistress or that I am a paid paramour. It would spoil our relationship for ever.'

'My maid of all work is a woman in her fifties, with a husband and four children. She is an excellent worker, doesn't ask questions, just gets on with what needs doing. I stole her from my mother who has never forgiven me. Annie had worked for her for ten years. Now, does that explanation satisfy you?'

Evelyn raised her brows. 'And she will never be here when I am due?'

'Certainly not!' Philip was enjoying this. 'I could never attend to two women at the same time, I haven't the stamina for it.'

This brought a smile to Evelyn's face, another indication of how she had changed. 'Oh, from what little I have seen of you, my dear, I would say you are perfectly capable of attending to two women at the same time. But I would not advise it, as I have a very jealous streak.'

'You would be prepared to fight for me, then, my darling? What a very lucky man I am. Now shall we partake of a little sustenance to give us the strength for the very pleasant task ahead of us? I should hate to fall by the wayside before lunch.'

Their love making became more playful, each teasing the other and both filling the room with laughter. It was perfect heaven for Evelyn who had never known what it was to be so happy. She felt contented, taking the love Philip was giving her and giving it back in return. She was shocked to realise she had never before known what true love was. For her parents weren't loving or even affectionate towards her. She couldn't remember ever once being kissed or hugged, and never a word of endearment.

Evelyn gave a start as Philip cupped her chin and turned her face towards him. 'You look so serious, my darling, what thoughts were in your head to bring a frown to that beautiful face?'

'They weren't pleasant thoughts, my dear, but they have helped me understand why I have never known any real happiness until the last few weeks when you came into my life. Oh, I thought I loved my husband, and if he hadn't been killed perhaps our love would have blossomed. But it was not him I was thinking of, it was my parents and the miserable existence they lived.' Evelyn felt Philip pull her close to comfort her, and opened a little of her heart to him. 'My parents were never loving towards me. All they cared about was money, it was their only topic of conversation. They were very frugal, almost miserly, and I was never given pocket money or allowed to bring my school friends home. There was never any laughter in the house, it was frowned upon. On my nineteenth birthday I was allowed to go to my first dance with a girl I knew from school. And because my mother bought my clothes, ones in the style she liked, I was the frumpiest girl at the dance.'

Philip was shaking his head in disbelief. 'How could they treat you like that? They should have been so proud of you!'

'I could have understood if money had been scarce, but it wasn't! Father had a decent position and earned a good salary, but he and Mother hated parting with a penny.' Evelyn felt she had said enough now about her past, but hoped what she had told Philip would help him understand why she might have appeared aloof and secretive. He had been drawn to her by her air of mystery, and it was vital she should keep back the most important part of that mystery, her daughter Amelia. If he became aware of her existence, it would surely have him walking away . . . their association at an end. She realised now that would break her heart, for she had fallen in love with him.

'In a few short weeks, you have brought me out of my shell and shown me how loving a person can bring happiness,' she told him. 'Especially last night. You were so understanding, so gentle and loving. I will always love you for that.'

'My poor darling.' Philip pressed her head to his shoulder and stroked her hair. 'Never again will you be without laughter or love, I shall make sure of that. From now on, my main priority in life will be to protect you, take care of you, and love you. In fact, my darling, I think it would be a good idea if you were to move in here permanently and then I can take care of you, properly. If you would agree, my life would be complete.'

A cold hand clutched Evelyn's heart. There was nothing in the world she would like more than to be with Philip every day, but she knew that could never happen. At least not for the forseeable future. 'No, Philip, much as I would love to live with you, I think we should have more time to get to know each other. It's barely a month since we met for the first time.'

'I know all I want to know about you, my love.' He looked disappointed. 'I know every part of your body, as you know mine. And, little by little, I am finding out what you have done so far in your life. I really see no reason to wait.'

'But what about me, Philip? I would have to get used to being a kept woman, and even though I do love you, that wouldn't sit easy on my shoulders. I do not want to give up my job, I enjoy it and it makes me independent. The staff at the office would soon notice the difference in our relationship, too, and I'd feel they were talking about me behind my back.'

'Hang the office staff! Who cares what they think? I wouldn't want you to live here as my mistress but as my wife! And under no circumstances would I permit a wife of mine to go out to work.'

Evelyn was stunned. For a brief moment she listened to the voice in her head which was saying, If only your life wasn't such a mess . . . But it *was* a mess, and although she would like nothing better than to be his wife, that could never be. 'Philip, I feel very honoured, and I know your intentions are good. But I don't think you have had time to consider what you are saying, or what the consequences would be if I were to encourage you into asking me to be your wife. For your sake I suggest we carry on as we are for a few more months, to give us both time to find out if getting married is what we both want.'

'I don't need time to consider.' Philip's expression mirrored his stubborn streak. 'I know without any doubt that I want you to be my wife. We may only have known each other a short time, as you point out, but I think I knew from the second I set eyes on you that I wanted you. I admit that in the beginning, when you were so cool and off-hand with me the attraction was more of a challenge.' He managed a grin. 'I was going to stalk you, like a tiger stalks its prey, until I got what I wanted. But as each new day came, and you walked into the office, I could feel a pounding in my heart which went beyond lust.' He gazed at her naked body, the firm breasts jutting out so proudly, and stroked a finger over a taut nipple. 'I have opened my heart to you, my lovely, now it is your turn to tell me your thoughts.'

'Let us snuggle down under the clothes,' Evelyn said, 'and we can hold each other close. I want to feel you near me.'

With a soft feather eiderdown over them, they snuggled up close. 'The way I feel about you now, Philip, I would marry you tomorrow. I have truly fallen head over heels in love with you. But in my life so far I have been dealt some hard blows and have learned to be cautious. That is why I am going to ask you to wait a few months, until we know each other inside out. Our good points, and our bad. I am considering your welfare, not just my own. It's Christmas soon. Why don't we carry on as we are until the festive season is over, see how we feel then? It is not an eternity, my love, just a matter of weeks.'

'And we'll see each other as often as possible in those weeks, won't we?' Philip pushed a lock of dark hair back from her forehead. 'I won't agree to your terms unless we continue to meet as often as possible.'

'Yes, I promise.' Evelyn had something on her mind that was troubling her. 'What about your mother? Does she know about me, and my visits to your apartment?'

'No, she doesn't. Until last night your visits have been on a friendly basis, remember. But I am going home today. When you are ready to leave, I shall leave with you. Mother rang this morning while you were still asleep, to ask if I had forgotten where I live. So I'll have my evening meal and sleep there for the next two or three nights. That will keep my parents happy. Which means, apart from Annie coming in to clean, the apartment won't be used until we meet for our tryst at lunchtime on Wednesday. I shall leave a note asking her to have a light lunch set out for us.'

'I'm going to request, Philip, that my name is not mentioned while you are at home. Promise you won't tell your parents about me? If your mother knew I visited you here, unaccompanied, she would be entitled to think I am not the sort of woman she would welcome as a wife for her son. So you would do our relationship no favour by discussing our friendship.'

A sheepish grin crossed Philip's face. 'You are far more practical than I am, my love. I want to tell the world about our romance. But that would be foolhardy of me. My parents are quite strait-laced and I haven't always lived up to their standards. But being free from any tie, old enough to know what I'm doing, attending parties several times a week where the girls were practically throwing themselves at eligible males . . . well, my parents must have known I wasn't living the life of a saint! And I have never pretended to you that I was inexperienced, have I? I have had several affairs. None of them has lasted longer than a week or two. I find myself getting short-tempered with females who cannot conduct an intelligent conversation, whose only interest in life is having the most fashionable clothes and being invited to the best parties. They make very dull companions.'

'But not too dull to go to bed with?'

Philip wasn't in the least embarrassed by the question, and didn't see why he shouldn't be truthful. 'With the light out, my lovely, they all look the same. Those were not acts of love on my part, but acts of necessity. I can honestly say that last night was the first time I made love to someone I was in love with. The other women served their purpose, over in a short time and forgotten immediately I was outside the bedroom door. Last night was a miracle for me. You transported me to a place I had never been before, and I shall never make love to anyone but you for the rest of my life.'

Evelyn had felt her jealousy rising as he spoke about the other women he had bedded, but quickly pushed the thoughts out of her mind. They were in the past, and best forgotten.

'Considering you are my first lover and I am twenty-nine years of age, I didn't do too badly, did I?'

Philip frowned. 'I only have a vague recollection of the night's events, my love, so could you please give me a repeat performance?'

Evelyn was learning fast, and surprised herself by asking, 'You mean, on my own?'

He chortled. 'Oh, I think I will join in somewhere along the way. In fact, even talking about it has my heart pounding, so I think I will start off the proceedings and you can just lie still and enjoy yourself.'

Evelyn walked down the entry with her head bowed, deep in thought. On the journey home, as the tram rattled and lurched, she had taken stock of her life and been surprised and shocked by some of the things that occurred to her. She had told Philip how her parents had never shown her any affection, no hugs, kisses or endearments. And suddenly it had come to her that she had treated her own daughter in the same way. She had never kissed Amelia, even when she was a baby. The wet nurse and the maid had taken care of the child's needs. And when the wet nurse had left, Amelia was put on a bottle. So did Amelia hate her, as Evelyn had hated her own parents? She really hadn't been fair to the child, blaming her for everything that had gone wrong in her life. Still, she couldn't honestly say she loved her daughter, for she didn't. She felt sorry now for the way she'd treated her, and wouldn't hurt her or wish her harm, but she couldn't conjure up these maternal instincts she'd heard people refer to. And it was going to be difficult putting Philip off after Christmas, he wasn't stupid enough to keep on believing her lies and excuses.

What a mess my life has become, she thought. And all because no one would believe that Charles could be such a cad as to get me in the family way before we were married. Even Gwen, her best friend, hadn't believed her. And because they wouldn't believe the truth, she'd been left without family or friends. But she'd put all that behind her if she could marry Philip. She was besotted with him. And Amelia was the only obstacle in the way.

Evelyn sighed as she stopped outside Bessie's entry door. She knew it would be on the latch, they would be expecting her, so pressed it down and entered the yard. As she walked over the uneven, broken tiles, she decided fate had a lot to answer for. Miss Maudsley loved Amelia and would make a wonderful mother, naturally kind and loving as she was. And the girl certainly loved the little woman, you could see it in her eyes. That look was never there when she was talking to her mother.

Bessie had the kitchen door open before the knock came. 'Come on in, Mrs Sinclair, and get a warm by the fire.' She steered her neighbour into the living room. 'Say hello to yer mother, Amelia.'

'Hello, Mother, have you had a nice weekend?'

'Yes, dear, really nice. It's been a real treat for me over the last few weeks, quite a change from just bed and work.'

'D'yer fancy a cup of tea, Mrs Sinclair?' Bessie asked. 'It'll warm the cockles of yer heart. And I made a batch of fairy cakes, which are nice and light. I'll put one on a plate for yer.'

'Thank you, Miss Maudsley, it's very good of you. A cup of tea and one of your fairy cakes will be much appreciated.' Evelyn was seeing her neighbour in a new light now. Instead of looking down on her for her lack of education, her Liverpool accent and lack of social skills, she now saw her as a woman to be envied. She had so much Evelyn herself was lacking in. A warm and happy nature, a ready smile and sense of humour, and real friends. And, judging from the way her daughter was looking at their neighbour, she also had Amelia's love. 'I'm afraid I'm hopeless at baking, my cakes always turn out like rocks,' Evelyn said.

'I'll put the kettle on. And I would much prefer you to call me Bessie, that's what my friends call me.' She ruffled Milly's hair as she passed, and was on the threshold of the kitchen when she heard her neighbour reply.

'You're right, it is more friendly. But if I'm to call you Bessie then I must insist you call me Evelyn.' Remembering how badly she had treated this little woman, who had only ever been good to her, Evelyn sounded humble. 'That's if you don't mind?'

Bessie turned and grinned. 'That's fine by me, sweetheart, I can't be bothered with people what stand on ceremony. Now, Amelia, you can help get the cups and saucers ready before yer mother dies of thirst.'

It was while they were having their tea and Bessie's light-as-a-feather fairy cakes, that she asked, 'Was yer friend all right, Evelyn?'

'Yes, she was as bright as ever.' Evelyn lowered her eyes. She no longer found it easy to lie to this woman, but there was little else she could do if she wanted the freedom to meet Philip. 'She has a lovely house, a husband who spoils her, and well-mannered children.'

Milly was sitting quietly taking it all in. She could sense the change in her mother, and was pleased she was being so friendly towards Auntie Bessie. But the child had lived long enough with her mother to know she wasn't always truthful, and that her mood could change quickly, for no reason at all. Still, Auntie Bessie wasn't soft, she wouldn't be taken in by lies. And Milly didn't really care what her mother did, as long as she never put a stop to her coming here every night. She couldn't bear it if that happened. She looked forward to coming home from school each day now, knowing she would have a couple of hours where she could say what she liked, laugh when something funny happened, play with her doll, and hug and kiss Auntie Bessie. And she had Auntie Rita and Auntie Aggie now, too, and Jack. She thought he was lovely, even though he always had dirty knees and socks round his ankles.

Milly's lips clamped together as these thoughts ran through her head, and felt a rebellious mood coming on. If her mother ever said she was moving to another house, far away from this street, then she wouldn't go. She'd run away and hide somewhere until her mother had left, then come back and live with Auntie Bessie. Such were the thoughts running through the head of the eight-year-old-girl who in the last few months had found a love and happiness she'd never known. The prospect of living with her mother, away from the new friends she'd made, filled her with dread.

Evelyn touched her daughter's knee. 'Amelia, I want you to stay here for a while until I get a fire going next door. The house will be very cold, so be a good girl and stay with your Auntie Bessie until I knock on the wall.'

'Yes, Mother.'

'You are sure you don't mind, Bessie?' Evelyn asked. 'I always seem to be asking favours of you. But just for half an hour, while I get a fire going.'

'Poppy off, sweetheart, Amelia is all right here for as long as it takes. It'll be flipping perishing in your house with not having a fire lit for two days.'

When her mother had left, Milly ran upstairs for her precious doll. Clutching it tight, she sat on the couch. 'It was cold upstairs for her, Auntie Bessie, so when Mother knocks for me, will you let Daisy stay down here with you so she's warm?'

'Of course she can stay down here, sweetheart, she'll be company for me. And when I go to bed, I'll wrap her in her blanket and she can sleep on the couch. It stays warm in this room with having had the fire burning all day.'

'I wish I could stay here with her,' Milly said, wistfully. 'We could keep each other warm. She told me this morning that she misses me when I'm not here.'

'Well, that's only natural, isn't it? I mean, you're her mother and you look after her. I bet she loves the bones of yer.'

The girl smiled. 'I know she loves me, she tells me every day. She's never said she loves the bones of me, but if she loves me, then she must love all of me, mustn't she?'

Bessie nodded. 'That means yer bones, yer arms and legs, pretty face and yer lovely smile. There's lots more, of course, but I'm hopeless about the names of some parts of me body. I couldn't pronounce half of them, let alone spell them. Still it wouldn't do me any good if I did know them, would it? Imagine Rita if I asked her where her hepaglotis is, she'd think I'd gone barmy.'

'Where is her hepagots, Auntie Bessie?' Milly looked suitably impressed. 'You must be very clever, 'cos I've never heard of it.'

'Neither have I, sweetheart, but don't tell my mate if she says anything to yer. Let her carry on thinking I'm a genius.' Bessie chuckled. 'I'll get it into the conversation tomorrow, and I can't wait to see her face.'

'Ooh, I'm hope I'm here, Auntie Bessie. But I'll have to be very careful not to let her see me smiling or it'll give the game away.'

Bessie bent down to take the poker from the brass companion set, and then rattled it between the bars on the grate. There was a sudden flare, with flames dancing, and she nodded as she put the poker back in its place. 'There, that's better. Yer can't beat a good fire on a cold night.'

Milly waited until Bessie was seated, then said, 'My mother looked very different tonight, didn't she? She must have really enjoyed being with her friend. It must be a long time since she'd seen her, 'cos I've never heard of her before.'

It ran through Bessie's mind that although this girl was only eight, she didn't miss anything. Then again, there would have had to be something wrong with her eyesight if she hadn't noticed the change in her own mother. 'Well, they lost touch with each other when they left school, Milly, and only met by accident a few weeks ago. But it's nice for yer mother to have a friend, 'cos we all need one. I'm very glad about it because it means I get to see more of you.'

Milly seemed satisfied. 'I'll never stop coming here, I know I won't. So you and me will both be very happy, Auntie Bessie.'

'We sure will, sweetheart, we sure will.'

Chapter Eighteen

It was half-past three on the Monday afternoon when a flustered Rita knocked on her neighbour's door. 'Ay, Aggie, I'm in a bit of a dilemma. Milly is supposed to be coming straight to me today, but I don't think Bessie realised that when she gets home from work there'll be no fire lit. And it's too cold for her to take Milly over to a house what's freezing. But Bessie left me her key in case Milly wanted to go in there for her doll, or to go to the lavvy, and with her doing the extra hour in work to help us all out for Christmas, I was wondering if I should go in and put a light to her fire.'

Aggie's head and chins agreed. 'Oh, that would be nice of yer, queen, I'm sure she'd be grateful to yer. And when it's my turn tomorrow to have Milly, I'll do the same. Be nice for Bessie to walk in to a roaring fire.'

'That's what I had in mind,' Rita said. 'But I'm worried she might think I'm only being nosy, and going in there to snoop.'

Aggie pooh-poohed the idea. 'Away with yer, Bessie's not bad-minded. Anyway, she's only got the bleeding same as we've got in our houses, so why should she mind?' Aggie's laugh was more of a hoarse cackle. 'Mind you, hers is a damn' sight cleaner than mine. Yer can see yer face in her sideboard, it's that highly polished, where mine is full of finger marks. Still, I'm not a proud woman.'

Rita mentally compared her house, and Aggie's, to Bessie's, and shook her head. 'You and me aren't in the same league as her, sunshine, she's got her house like a new pin. Mine looks passable until the boys come in from school, then it looks as though it's been hit by a bomb.'

'My old ma, God rest her soul, had the same problem. I remember her saying, time and again, that if it wasn't for me and me brother, her house would be a little palace, and she wouldn't be afraid to invite the Queen for tea.'

'Well, that's settled then,' Rita said, with a determined nod of her head. 'I'll walk up to the top of the street to meet Milly coming home from school. I'll take her in to Bessie's while I light the fire, then bring her to mine for a hot drink. I'll nip back home now and put me coat on, it's too cold to be hanging around.'

When Milly saw Rita waiting for her at the top of the street, her face lit up. And not for the first time, Rita thought what a beautiful child she was: a heart-shaped face with high cheek bones, green eyes that changed colour by the second, and a smile to melt the hardest heart.

'Are you waiting for me, Auntie Rita?'

'Yes, sunshine, I'm minding yer for an hour, like yer Auntie Bessie told yer. But 'cos she's left me her key in case of emergency, I thought you and me could light the fire for her and give her a nice surprise.'

Milly reached for her hand. 'That really would be nice for her, Auntie Rita, you are kind. Are we walking down the entry?'

Rita reached a quick decision. Sneaking down the back entry like a couple of thieves – blow that for a joke. The sooner this girl got used to mixing with her neighbours the better. 'No, me and you are going to walk down the street with our heads held high and our backs straight. We'll pretend I'm a queen and you are a princess.'

Milly put a hand over her mouth while her eyes brimmed with laughter. 'Oh, you do say some funny things, Auntie Rita. I'll like pretending I'm a princess, yes, I will. I'll put my nose in the air and wave to everyone.'

'Oh, I wouldn't go that far, sunshine, or they'll send for an ambulance to take us away to an asylum.'

They began to walk down the street, Milly's hand clasped in Rita's. 'What is an asylum, Auntie Rita? Is it somewhere not nice?'

All her life, Rita had objected to people making fun of people who were mentally ill. When she was a young girl, there had been a woman living in their street who'd acted strangely and everyone used to make fun of her. Except Rita's mother, who had once clipped her around the ear for saying the woman was doolally. And her words had stayed with her daughter all her life. 'Never mock people who can't help themselves, queen,' she'd said. 'Remember, there but for the grace of God go I.' Rita was too young at the time to understand what her mother had meant, but she had never forgotten her words.

'An asylum is for people who are sick. Some people who are physically sick go into hospital to be made better, but those who are sick in their head, they go in to an asylum until they are better.' While she was talking, Rita could see the looks directed their way. It was very unusual for Milly to walk down the street, never mind walking down it clasping Rita's hand. But it would only be curiosity on the part of the neighbours, there would be no ill-feeling against the child. They weren't keen on her mother, who they saw as being a snob who believed she was too good even to pass them the time of day, but none of that animosity would be aimed at the young girl.

When they reached Bessie's house, Rita slid the key into the lock. 'Come in with me until I've got the fire going, sunshine, then it's across to mine for a nice warm cup of tea.'

'Can I go upstairs for Daisy?' Milly asked. 'She would like to come with me.'

Rita pursed her lips and blew out. 'Well, it's like this, sunshine, I've got two boys in my house, and I think they'd pull yer leg soft if they saw yer nursing a doll. They're not like girls, they like games where they play with balls, or marbles, and get their knees dirty. It's up to you, though, sunshine, as long as yer don't mind getting laughed at.'

'In that case, boys aren't fair, are they?' Milly's chin jutted out determinedly. 'Girls don't laugh at them for playing football or marbles and getting themselves very dirty, so why should they laugh at the games girls play? At least we don't get filthy.'

Rita struck a match and held it to the newspaper balls Bessie had set under the sticks of firewood. 'I wish I was as organised as Bessie is. She left the house at half-past six this morning to go to work, but the fire's set and everywhere neat and tidy.' She grinned at Milly, who was kneeling down beside her. 'Yer won't find my house as tidy as this, sunshine, and I've been at home all day! Lazy beggar, that's what I am.'

Milly wasn't going to agree with that. After a lifetime of living with just her mother, and never even having one visitor crossing their front doorstep, she wasn't going to hear a word against her newfound aunties. 'You are not a lazy beggar, Auntie Rita, you must work very hard with a husband and two children to look after. Especially when both of them are boys, and play marbles in the gutter.'

Rita saw the firewood was now alight, and took the tongs from the companion set to pick out some small cobs of coal from the scuttle at the side of the hearth. 'Oh, my two are no different from any of the other children. They're only kids once, so let them enjoy themselves while they can.' She turned her head to study the girl's face. 'I bet you get dirty sometimes, as well?'

'Oh, no, Mother wouldn't allow it, she would get very angry. She won't let me sit at the table if my hands are the least bit grubby. And if we have no soap, then I have to wash them in cold water and use the scrubbing brush. I don't like having to do that, it hurts, but Mother stands over me and makes sure I do it properly.'

Rita lowered her eyes to hide her anger and shock. There was no self-pity in the girl's voice, no whingeing, so it was obvious she believed all children were treated the same way by their mothers. It wasn't Rita's place to tell her different. She wasn't going to set daughter against mother. But, oh, dear, wouldn't she like to give Mrs Sinclair a piece of her mind? A lovely daughter like this, and to treat her so badly, it just wasn't right.

The flames were licking the coals now, it wouldn't be long before there was a fire roaring up the chimney. 'I'll put the fireguard in front of it now the coals have caught, just in case any sparks fly.' Rita used her curled fists to push herself up. 'I want Bessie to come home to a nice, warm welcoming fire in her grate, but not her house on fire. D'yer know where she keeps the fireguard, sunshine?'

Milly nodded and made for the kitchen. 'I'll get it, Auntie Rita, it's in the larder.'

The guard safe in front of the fire, Rita looked around to make sure everything was as they'd found it, then held out her hand. 'Come on, sunshine, I'm dying for a cuppa, me mouth feels as though it's full of feathers.'

Aggie was standing at her door when the two crossed the cobbles. She smiled at Milly. 'Are yer all right, queen?'

The world was opening up for Milly who had never known such happiness. 'I'm fine, thank you, Auntie Aggie. We've lit the fire for Auntie Bessie, so won't she have a lovely surprise when she gets home?'

'She will that, queen, she will that. And tomorrow it will be my turn to light it, so will yer give me a hand? Help me out, like?'

'Oh, I'd like that, Auntie Aggie! I'll get the fireguard for you, just in case some sparks fly out and set fire to the place. Auntie Bessie wouldn't be a bit happy if she came up the street and found her house on fire.'

Aggie kept her face straight and told her chins to stay put. 'Oh, yer think she'd be upset, do yer, queen?'

'Oh, yes, Auntie Aggie, she would be very upset. In fact I believe she would be so upset she would cry.' Then the girl had a horrible thought. 'Oh, and Daisy would get caught in the fire! She's upstairs and there would be no one rescue her.'

Rita gave her neighbour a look that said she should knock it off, she was frightening the girl. 'There won't be no fire, sunshine, we've put the fireguard in front to keep it safe. So Daisy won't come to any harm, today or tomorrow.' She glared at her neighbour, daring her to say different. 'Isn't that right, Aggie?'

If Aggie hadn't nodded of her own free will, her chins would have done it for her. They didn't want to see a young girl frightened. But Aggie came up trumps. 'I'll tell yer something, queen, I've lived in this street for nigh on eighteen years, and there's never, ever been a fire in any of the houses. Not in any of the streets around either, so yer've no need to worry, the odds are stacked against it.'

Milly looked confused and turned to Rita. 'What does Auntie Aggie mean, about the odds being stacked against it? I don't understand.'

Rita put an arm across her shoulders. 'That's nothing, sunshine, 'cos I've lived next to Aggie for eighteen years and I still don't understand her. But I'll have a guess at this one. I think that, roughly translated, she was telling yer there isn't a snowball's chance in hell of there being a fire in Miss Maudsley's house, or any other in the street. Am I right, Aggie?'

'As near as damn it, queen, as near as damn it.' Aggie folded her arms and hitched her mountainous bosom. 'Now go and make the girl a cup of tea before I come out with another of my gems that yer'd have to explain.' She gave a broad wink to Milly. 'I'll see yer tomorrow afternoon, queen.'

Milly nodded and took Rita's hand, just as her two sons put in an appearance. The eldest, ten-year-old Billy, jerked his head and let out a sigh when he saw Milly. Why did his mam have to mind her for an hour every night? Girls were nothing but trouble, always crying before they were hurt. They talked too much, and most of the time it was a load of rubbish. 'Did I hear yer were making a cup of tea, Mam? I'll have one with yer before Tommo calls for me. We're having a competition tonight, to see who's the best at playing marbles.'

Milly shook her head and tutted, just like she'd seen Bessie doing a few times. 'That means you're going to get your knees all dirty, and your socks. Why don't you play a game where you don't have to kneel in the gutter?'

Billy glared. 'And why don't you mind yer own business? I can get dirty if I want to, it's got nowt to do with you.'

'That's enough now, in the house all of yer.' Rita thought it time to intervene. 'And while Milly is with us, we'll have none of yer cheek or sarcasm. Get inside and wash yer hands if yer want a cup of tea.'

Nine-year-old Jack was looking on with a grin on his face. He waited until his brother went into the house then winked at Milly. 'Take no notice of our kid, he's like that with all girls. If yer ignore him, he'll soon get fed up of being sarky.'

Milly followed him up the steps. 'Why doesn't he like girls? And how can he be sure whether he likes them or not if he doesn't know any?' They were in the living room when she said, 'I know why your brother doesn't like girls, it's because we are more clever than boys.'

Billy was at the kitchen sink, about to put his hands under the running tap when he heard Milly's words and flew into the living room. Once again he glared at her. 'What makes yer think ye're more cleverer than boys? The only thing girls are good at is whingeing. They run crying to their mother at the least thing. And if the boys won't let them play footie with them, they tell fibs and say we hit them.'

Rita was standing in the kitchen waiting for the kettle to boil, and wondered whether she should put a stop to her son's protests. Then she decided to wait and see whether Milly was capable of sticking up for herself. When the girl started to speak, Rita moved to peep through the gap at the side of the door. The sight she saw had her clamping her lips together to keep the laughter back.

Milly's head was jutting forward and there were sparks coming from her green eyes. 'That shows how wrong you are, Billy Wells. I do not tell fibs, and I don't go running to my mother every time I don't get my own way. And I'm certainly not stupid enough to kneel in the gutter and play with little glass balls.'

Billy was so taken aback he just stared. He'd never for one moment thought this girl, who lived opposite and never came out to play, would answer him back. He was so dumbstruck, he was lost for words. All he could think of, which even to his own ears sounded daft, was, 'I've left the tap running, ye're not worth bothering about.'

Rita would have loved to take the mickey out of her son. He was rude to all the girls in the street, and it was about time he got his comeuppance. But if she said too much, it would be like pouring oil on troubled waters. And she thought Milly had done a good job of cutting him down to size. Still she couldn't resist a little taunt when she looked at him with raised brows. 'I think yer've just met yer match, sunshine. But do us a favour and don't keep picking on her while she's here. She's a nice kid if yer'd give yerself time to get to know her.'

'She's still a girl, isn't she?' he grunted as he turned the tap on. 'But if she doesn't come out with any more of her wisecracks, I'll keep out of her way.'

Rita ruffled his hair. 'That's my lad! It shows ye're growing up.' These few words worked wonders, and while he sat across the table from Milly as they drank their tea, he didn't speak to her. But he couldn't help noticing those green eyes. He'd never seen eyes that colour before. And her jet black hair, heart-shaped face and winning smile brought him to the conclusion she was all right as far as girls went. Then he became disgusted with himself for finding things to like about her, and starting looking for faults. He found one. It wasn't really true, but it was the only one he could think of. She was not as pretty as Doreen, who lived at the top of the street. He'd bet she wouldn't like it if he told her that! But he wasn't going to say anything to her, and when she came over every night, he'd keep out of her way so his mam wouldn't be at him all the time. Oh, and so she wouldn't have anything to criticise him for, he'd wash his hands as soon as he came home from school.

Billy looked across the table to where Jack was sitting next to Milly, laughing and joking with her. He was even laughing at things that weren't funny. Billy was disgusted. He'd have a word with his brother later and tell him he'd looked a right cissy. When they were in bed tonight, he would tell him not to be making such a fuss of the girl 'cos it looked daft. If she was made so welcome, she'd never be away from their house. And *that* would mean them getting washed so often they'd have no skin left.

When Bessie got in from work her face lit up when she saw the fire roaring up the chimney, a pot of tea made and Milly sitting on the couch playing with her doll. 'Oh, I wasn't expecting yer to do this, Rita, it wasn't part of the deal. But, by golly, I'm glad yer did. I'm perished right through to me marrow, and me fingers are like ice.'

Milly rushed over to put her arms around her waist. 'Why didn't you put gloves on, Auntie Bessie, then your fingers wouldn't be cold? And your face must be cold too, it's bright red.'

'Let me take me coat off, sweetheart, so I can feel the heat from the fire.' Bessie slipped her arms out of her coat and handed it Milly. 'Hang it up for me, there's a good girl.'

Rita came through from the kitchen. 'Sit down, sunshine, and I'll hand yer this cup of tea. We'll have yer as warm as toast in no time.'

'Ooh, it's not often I get spoilt, so I'm going to make the most of it.' Bessie took a sip of the hot tea and could feel it going right through her body. 'The best cup I ever tasted, Rita, ye're an angel. It's murder working in that factory in winter. The sewing room is freezing. The only heating we've got is a small black stove in the middle of the huge room, with a pipe going up through the ceiling to let the smoke out. And the boss is so tight with his flaming money, he goes mad if one of the women puts more than a small shovel of coal in every few hours. He watches from his office window, and I'll swear he counts the pieces of coal that go in. The miserable bugger doesn't even buy the decent sort, there's more slate in the bags than there is coal.' Bessie was warming up now, and stretched her legs towards the fire. 'He's not so mean with himself though, he's got an electric fire in his office.'

Milly was kneeling down at the side of her chair, Daisy tucked under one of her arms. 'He's a very naughty man, Auntie Bessie, sitting in a nice warm office while the workers are freezing cold. Why don't you ask him to let you put more coal on?'

Bessie chuckled at the child's innocence. 'Anyone who was brave enough to do that, sweetheart, would find themselves without a job. Yer see, a lot of the women there are sole bread-winners with their husbands out of work. Their wages just barely keep the wolf from the door. Same with me, I couldn't do without me wages coming in, I'd really be in Queer Street then.' She pulled herself to her feet. 'I'll see to our meal, it won't take long 'cos I peeled the spuds last night. And you, Rita, you poppy off home and see to the family's dinner. And thanks a million for lighting me fire and looking after Milly, I really appreciate it.'

Rita reached for her coat off the hook behind the door. 'It's Aggie's turn tomorrow. She'll have the fire lit for yer, and she'll see Milly has a warm drink when she comes home from school. So, yer see, sunshine, we've got yer whole life planned out for yer.'

Bessie walked to the door with her. 'I'm lucky to have friends like you and Aggie, I'd be in a right fix without yer. Not a soul to call me own.' She pretended to be playing on a violin. 'Is this music sad enough for the occasion, d'yer think?'

Rita grinned as she stepped down on to the pavement. 'Oh, yeah, sunshine, it certainly adds to the melodrama.' She hurried across the cobbles. 'See yer tomorrow some time, but until then, don't do anything I wouldn't do.'

'I'll try, sweetheart,' Bessie chortled, 'but it's going to be hard with all the men beating their way to me front door.'

'Split them into groups, sunshine, and divide them between yerself, me and Aggie. I think the three of us could manage them between us.' Rita was shouting by now from the opposite side of the street. 'Mind you, they'd probably take one look at our faces and run like hell for cover.'

'You speak for yerself, Rita Wells, there's a bloke at work thinks I'm a cracker. He said he would ask me to marry him but his wife might object.' Bessie gave a last wave before closing the door. 'Now I'll get cracking with something to eat, sweetheart, or yer mother will be here before we've had our meal.'

Milly followed her in to the kitchen. 'Why are these men beating a way to your front door, Auntie Bessie? And why does the man in work say he'll marry you, when he knows he's already got a wife?'

Bessie put a light under the pan of potatoes, then blew out the match before grinning at Milly. 'Not a word of truth in any of it, sweetheart, it's all wishful thinking on my part.' She could see the puzzlement on the girl's face and cupped it between her hands. 'What I mean is, it was all said in fun. Grown-up fun, what young girls wouldn't understand.'

Milly hugged her tight. 'I'm going to have a word with the front door, just to be on the safe side. I'll tell it that if any men come along and start hitting it with sticks, it must tell them to go away, you don't want to see them. And if I'm here when they come, I'll chase them with the yard brush.'

Bessie pictured it in her mind. 'The stiff brush or the soft one, sweetheart?'

Milly pursed her lips and drew her brows down in thought. Now that was a poser, she didn't know there were two brushes. 'Which one do you think, Auntie Bessie?'

'Oh, the stiff brush would cause more damage, sweetheart, without a doubt. And now you go and play with Daisy while I get a move on.'

Bessie had just finished washing up when Evelyn passed the kitchen window. She hadn't been told about the new arrangement with Rita and Aggie because Bessie was of the opinion she would definitely disapprove. Although she hadn't told Milly not to mention it to her mother, she was confident the child would know without being told. So, no one was actually telling lies, and what the eye didn't see, the heart didn't grieve over.

'Come in, Evelyn, I'm just drying me hands.'

She came in, shivering and bringing the cold air with her. 'If today is anything to go by, we're in for a long, hard winter. I'm sure it couldn't be colder living in Iceland than it is sitting on our trams with the wind blowing right through.'

Bessie steered her to the living room. 'It's not too bad if yer get one of the new trams where they've filled in the staircase, but with the old ones, open to all the elements, yer get blown off yer feet.'

'Oh, what a lovely fire! I feel warmer just looking at it.' Evelyn held her hands out to the flames. 'If I had three wishes right now, one of them would be that when Amelia and I open the living-room door, there would be a fire like that in our grate. And the second wish would be to find a tray with a pot of hot tea on it, and several rounds of toast.'

Bessie waited for a few seconds than asked, 'And the third wish?'

'Oh, I'd have to think carefully about the third and last wish. I wouldn't want to waste it on something so trivial as a fire and a pot of tea. It would have to be something important, something that would change my life so I could live happily ever after.'

'That's a miracle ye're looking for, Evelyn, and miracles don't happen in Walton. At least not to my knowledge they don't.' Bessie held out a hand. 'Give me yer coat and sit near the fire. I'll make a fresh pot of tea, then yer'll be warm enough to face the icebox next door.' On her way to hang the coat up, she tilted her head at Milly. 'Have yer said hello to yer mother, Amelia?'

'Not yet, Auntie Bessie, I was waiting for her to be settled.' The girl walked to the side of the couch. 'Hello, Mother.'

And to the surprise of Bessie and her daughter, Evelyn patted the seat beside her. 'Sit here and tell me what you've done in school today.'

There was suspicion on the girl's face, and it was obvious to Bessie that her mother being so friendly was something new to Milly. It was a while before she answered. 'I've got my exercise book, Mother, you can look in that and see how I'm getting on in class.'

'The kettle's boiling now,' Bessie said, in a bid to avert embarrassment, 'so let yer mother have a hot cup of tea and she can look through the book later, when ye're in the comfort of yer own home. After the fire's lit, of course, 'cos there won't be much comfort while ye're sitting there like blocks of ice.'

She poured a cup of tea out and carried it through to Evelyn. 'I got a nice surprise when I got home from work today, I was over the moon. Rita had been in and lit the fire for me so the room was lovely and warm to walk into. *And* a pot of tea into the bargain. I was so pleased, I felt like kissing her. She's always had a key to the door, ever since I moved in and we became friends. It's so she can let the coalman into the yard, otherwise there's many a time I'd be without coal. I thanked my lucky stars for her today, there's nothing worse than working all day then coming home to a cold, cheerless house.'

There was a little bit of snobbery back in Evelyn's voice when she asked, 'Do you not mind letting strangers loose in your house?'

Her tone got Bessie's back up, but she did her best not to ruffle any feathers. 'Good grief, no! I've known Rita for fifteen years, she's as honest as the day is long. Besides, what harm could she do?' Bessie shook her head vigorously. 'I would trust Rita Wells with me life, and Aggie Gordon, too! Like meself, they're ordinary working-class people, struggling to make ends meet. There's no shame in that.'

'Of course not!' Evelyn's brain had been at work when she'd heard Rita had lit the fire for Bessie. Now she was worried she may have spoiled her own chances. 'What I said was out of curiosity, not a reflection on the honesty of your friends, Bessie, please believe me. You are indeed very lucky to have such thoughtful neighbours. I only wish I was so lucky. It must have been a wonderful surprise, and relief, to come home to such a warm welcome.'

Bessie's brain was also at work. She's a devious one all right, this one is, and she's angling for something. Well, I too can be devious, especially when it comes to my two mates. 'Oh, I wouldn't let her do it every night, not without some reward. So I'm going to give her a shilling a week for lighting the fire every night. Until the weather improves, that is.'

'Do you think she would like another shilling a week to light my fire for me? I can afford it now I'm better off, and it would be such a relief to come home to a warm house, both for Amelia and myself.'

Bessie could hear applause in her head for her own ingenuity, but kept her face straight. 'I couldn't possibly answer that, Evelyn, I'd have to ask Rita first. But if you want me to, I'll put your request to her tomorrow and see what she says. That's all I can do, I'm afraid, I can't speak for her.'

'If you would put in a good word for me, I'd be really grateful, Bessie. It would make my life so much easier.'

And a shilling a week would make life a lot easier for Rita, Bessie thought. She'd share with Aggie, doing a night each, which would mean an extra tanner every week. They could spend it if they were stuck, or add it to the money she was putting by each week so the three families would have a really happy Christmas. 'I'll have an answer for yer when you call tomorrow night. But it would mean yer leaving yer key with them. Would that suit yer?'

'I'll leave the key here, so Amelia can let Mrs Wells in. I would have no objection to that. Please do your best for me, it would help enormously.'

Bessie nodded, and followed mother and daughter to the door. Once it was closed on them, she hurried back to the living room, pulled her chair nearer the fire, and let her chuckles out. Ah, well, she thought, rubbing her hands in glee, life is full of surprises. Wait until her two mates heard they were in for a tanner each, every week. Well, it would be enough to send Aggie running to the corner pub for a bottle of milk stout to celebrate.

Chapter Nineteen

Oscar Wentworth looked across the breakfast table at his wife Gwen, and sighed. 'I have visited twelve schools in the area around Aigburth and the Dingle, all to no avail. To cover the whole of the Liverpool, into Lancashire, will take me almost a year. I'm becoming quite despondent, losing faith in ever finding Evelyn or her daughter. She just seems to have vanished off the face of the earth. I mean, neither we nor any of our acquaintances have set eyes on her. Never bumped into her in the city, never even heard her name mentioned.'

Gwen indicated to the maid that she could leave the room and they would serve themselves. She disliked holding a personal conversation in front of staff. 'Evelyn could have married again, have you thought of that? Which means the child's name will no longer be Sinclair.'

Oscar nodded. 'I have thought of that, of course I have, but I can't let such a possibility stop me from doing what is important to me, and more so to Cyril. He is blaming himself for not giving Evelyn the benefit of the doubt, at least until the child was old enough to show a likeness. And I don't come out of it very well. As Charles' friend, I should have thought things out more clearly, instead of jumping to conclusions.'

'I am to blame for that, my love, I was the first to call her a liar. And don't think I haven't asked myself a thousand times why I didn't believe her. We'd been friends since school, and I was almost certain she had never been out with any other man but Charles. Yet I could have been wrong about that. Maybe she wasn't the innocent little goody-two-shoes I thought she was. We are still not certain Charles is the father, but like you and Cyril, I believe if we don't try and solve the puzzle, it will haunt us for the rest of our lives.'

'If I am to be honest, darling, it is not Evelyn I am interested in. I would feel guilty if it turns out she was telling the truth, but I will never really forgive her for her lack of emotion when told of Charles' death. She was cool and remote, as though he'd meant nothing to her. She never even visited his parents to offer condolences or comfort and help them in their hour of need.'

'I'm afraid Evelyn was always lacking in emotion, even when she was young. But that was due to her parents. They were dreadful people who never should have had a child. She didn't know what it was to get a goodnight kiss, or be tucked up in bed and have a story read to her. I was her only real friend, but I was never allowed to visit her. When I called for her to go to school, I was never invited in. That says a lot about her parents.'

Oscar sighed. 'From what little I've heard, she is treating her daughter as she was treated. That's why I must try and find her. Charles would expect no less from me.' He wiped his mouth on a damask napkin then laid it on his plate. 'I'll call and see Cyril, then try the next three schools on my list. I keep telling myself that one day I'll walk into the office of a headmistress and be told that, yes, they do have an Amelia Sinclair attending their school.' He walked to the other end of the long dining table and kissed his wife's brow. 'How lucky I am to have you, my darling. A wonderful wife and mother.'

'I wish you well today, love, and please don't give up hope. Patience and endurance will pay off in the end. And give my love to Cyril.'

Cyril Lister-Sinclair was lost in reverie when the knock came on his office door. He quickly gathered himself together and called, 'Come in.' He smiled when he saw Oscar, and waved his friend to a seat facing his across the desk. 'I was lost in thought when you knocked. It happens very often these days.'

'You should get out more, old man, you're too young to live the life of a hermit. Why don't you and Matilda come to us for dinner one night, we would be delighted to have you.'

Cyril tapped his fingers on the desk. 'It is very kind of you, my boy, but I wouldn't be very good company, I'm afraid. And, as you know, my wife goes out very little. If she needs a new dress or whatever, she gets a taxi to her favourite shop, has the driver wait for her, and when she's bought what she wants, it's straight back home again. Actually she spends most of the day on the chaise-longue, fast asleep. Nothing seems to interest her any more, and I'm at a loss to know how to change her for she refuses to hold a sensible conversation. Her maid is the only one who can get through to her. I don't know what I'd do if it weren't for her.'

'If Matilda refuses to visit friends, it shouldn't stop you. It's not as though she needs you, there are enough staff to attend to her.'

Cyril shook his head. 'No, I would never go out socially without her. I come down to the office each week day because I need to keep an eye on my business affairs so she is without my company on those days. I know Matilda is not the easiest woman to get along with, has no interest in business or politics and subsequently no real conversation. Also, she can be quite childish and demanding. But I fell in love with her the moment I set eyes on her at a mutual friend's house, and I still love her.'

There was affection in Oscar's eyes as he gazed at the man who had always made him welcome whenever he'd called for Charles. Cyril was like a second father to him, and Oscar loved him dearly. 'I'm afraid I've had no success with the schools so far, Cyril, but I've got another three to visit today so I'm keeping my fingers crossed. If I'm not successful I shall just carry on until I've covered every school across the city. It is possible, however, as Gwen pointed out his morning, that Evelyn may have remarried, and then the child will no longer have the name Sinclair.'

'I've been considering all the possibilities too,' Cyril told him. 'In fact, the matter is seldom far from my thoughts. The easiest and most sure way of finding them is to go to the police or put a notice in the local evening paper so that, if she didn't see it herself, it would at least be seen by a neighbour. But either way could have its drawbacks. The notice might send Evelyn into hiding and then we would never find her or the girl. Although I toyed with the idea of a private detective at one time, I agree with you now that it is not the right way.' He sighed and swivelled his chair. 'If we make a song and dance about it, the whole thing would become public knowledge and perhaps alienate Evelyn completely. If she was telling the truth, she has just cause to hate us. Or, I should say, hate me, it is I who turned her out of the house. She would have no cause to hate you or Gwen.'

'If she is a fair-minded person then she will understand the reasons why you acted as you did. Any father who had just lost a son would have found it very difficult to believe her story.' Oscar was saying this after years of heart-searching. 'At the time, I would have found it hard to believe it of Charles. But on reflection, he knew he was shortly to be shipped abroad and perhaps lost his head for a while. Who are we to say we would have acted differently? None of us is a saint.'

'That is very true, war changes people. So the sooner we find Evelyn and the girl, the sooner my heart will be at rest and we can put the whole sordid affair behind us. I wish you well today, Oscar, but if it isn't to be the day we must continue to be patient.'

'I second that.' Oscar got to his feet and stretched his tall frame. 'I won't share a pot of tea with you this morning, Cyril. I want to visit two of the schools on my list before lunch. Then I'll call to see my father and spend some time in the office with him so I can keep abreast of business affairs. Later, I will visit the third school on my list.'

'You shouldn't let my problems interfere with your work or home life, Oscar,' Cyril told him. 'I don't want to poach you from your family business.'

'Not at all! My father has an excellent staff, plus my brother, and his office runs like clockwork.' Oscar looked at his friend. 'It must be a while since you and Father met. Why don't I pick you up in the morning and take you to see him? I know he would be delighted, he never fails to ask about you. And the two of you could talk shop for an hour, after which I'd be free to run us down to the club for some lunch.' He could see Cyril was uncertain, and waved a hand. 'No excuses, old man, I'm sure your excellent secretary can rearrange your diary to enable you absent for a few hours. In fact, I will have a word with the very efficient Miss Williams on my way out, and tell her you are not to be allowed to change your mind under any circumstances. I shall also ask her to have a pot of tea sent in now. After all, what is the point in being your own boss if you can't do as you wish?' He leaned across the desk and shook the older man's hand. 'I will see you at eleven-forty-five tomorrow.'

The following day was Wednesday. As Oscar and his father Richard, with Cyril walking between them, strolled down Castle Street towards their club, little did they know that about thirty yards from them, Evelyn was letting herself into Philip's apartment. Had they seen her, they would have hurried towards her, filled with relief. Had she seen them, she would have fled in the opposite direction, afraid of the consequences. But they didn't see each other, and a golden opportunity was lost.

Evelyn went straight to the kitchen to make a pot of tea to go with the delicious sandwiches and cakes Annie would have left ready for them. She had never met the cleaner, deliberately keeping away when the woman would be at the apartment. The fewer people who knew of her business the better. Evelyn lived in fear of being caught out, and losing the man she had fallen deeply in love with. He was the only person who could bring her to life, appreciate all the emotions that come with being in love. The very thought of him sent a shiver down her spine as she carried a tray through to the lounge. Hearing his key in the door, she put down the tray and ran to meet him in the hall. They had spent the morning together in the office, but even though their relationship had moved on away from work, Evelyn still insisted they remain businesslike in front of their colleagues. Not that Philip was as strict about it as she was, for if he couldn't resist a kiss then she was well and truly kissed. He derived great pleasure from seeing her blush with embarrassment in case anyone walked into the office. He would be quite happy for everyone to know of their relationship, for he was deeply in love with her and very proud. He couldn't understand why she wanted to keep it secret for the time being, but went along with it. After all, she'd said that after Christmas she would discuss the subject of marriage, and he could wait that long.

Philip cupped her face. 'Now, when we are married, that is the sort of welcome I'll expect every night when I come home from the office.' And to bring a blush to her cheeks, he added, 'I would expect you to be wearing less than you are now, though.'

'You are incorrigible, Philip, I really don't know what I'm going to do with you. And I am a fool for allowing you to make me blush.'

'Do I have a power over you, my lovely Evelyn? Do I really?'

'Of course you do, my love, and well you know it.'

'Oh, I am not so sure, my darling.' They were still standing in the hall, their arms around each other. 'I would like to test this power you say I have over you. Would you permit me to try?'

Evelyn tutted. 'You are like a child who is over-indulged by his parents. But if it makes you happy, then you may.'

'Good!' Philip moved out of her arms and cupped one of her elbows. He proceeded to walk her towards the bedroom. 'Well, so far my magic seems to be working.'

Inside the bedroom, Evelyn stared at him in bewilderment. 'What are you up to, Philip? Remember, we don't have much time.'

'Sshh! Don't break the spell! Just slip your coat off, my lovely, and lie on the bed like the Sleeping Beauty. I will waken you with a kiss.'

'Philip! I have made a pot of tea and our lunch is set out on the tray . . .'

He put a hand over her mouth. 'I am using my magic powers on you now, my beauty. The tea can wait, my desire cannot. It is two whole days since I held you in my arms and made love to you. Two whole days and nights of longing for you. Even my parents noticed I was preoccupied and asked if I was sickening for a cold. Having you so close to me in the office, and be unable to touch you, it is agony.' While he was talking, Philip slipped the coat off her shoulders, then scooped her up in his arms and laid her gently on the bed. 'I will disrobe in the bathroom, my darling, please be ready for me when I return.'

Even if she'd had the willpower to resist him, Evelyn didn't want to. Her own body was crying out. She undressed quickly and slid between the sheets. She was eager to have him hold her and thrill her with his love making, but remained clear enough in the head to remember she had to be back in the office for two o'clock. Philip wouldn't remember because he didn't care. If they were late, they were late, that was all there was to it. After all, there was no one above him to tick him off. But Evelyn wanted to keep her job as a safety net, and couldn't afford to ruffle feathers or cause gossip.

Philip lifted the sheet and gazed lovingly at her naked body. 'You are so beautiful, my darling Evelyn, I could spend my life making love to you.' He ran a hand over her breasts, tummy and thighs, and smiled with pleasure when he heard her gasp. Then he climbed into bed and lay on top of her. 'This, my darling, is as close to heaven as it gets. I want to marry you, to have you all to myself forever, please don't keep me waiting long.'

She put a finger to his lips. 'Make love to me, my darling.'

On Tuesday it had been Rita's first night to have Milly for an hour, and also light Bessie's and Mrs Sinclair's fires. Everything had gone to plan. When Bessie's fire had caught, Milly had taken Rita next door and let her in with the key. She'd stayed with Rita until the fire was well and truly lit. She hadn't told anyone that the night before her mother had sat her down and given her a good talking to. She'd been given strict instructions that under no circumstances was Mrs Wells to be left on her own in the house. Amelia must stay with her the whole time, and when they left she must make sure the door was locked and that she kept hold of the key. And Milly had done as she was told, although she couldn't understand why it was necessary, not when she could be playing catch with Jack. Anyway, Tuesday went off without a hitch, and Bessie and Mrs Sinclair were delighted to walk into rooms that were warm and welcoming.

Wednesday started off all right, with Aggie having a cup of tea ready for her two children, Kitty and Kenny, and Milly. She didn't usually make tea for her children, but as this was her first night with Milly, she wanted to make a good impression. But it aroused suspicion in her two children.

'What's this in aid of, Mam?' Kitty asked. 'Are yer sickening for something?'

'She must be,' Kenny said. 'Either that or she wants us to go on a message for her. I bet she wants us to go to the corner shop for a loaf or summat on tick. Well, I'm not going for nowt on tick, I feel a right lemon with the shop packed and me trying to whisper.'

Aggie gave him a light slap across the face. 'I don't want yer to go on no message, so there, clever clogs. And will yer remember we've got a visitor, and behave yerselves?'

It was then Kitty saw the light. She looked across the table at Milly, who was sitting very quietly taking it all in. 'So, this is in your honour, eh? In that case ye're very welcome 'cos a hot drink is just the job when it's so cold. What do we call yer anyway, yer must have a name?'

Milly began to swing her legs under the table. 'My name's Amelia, but you can call me Milly as long as my mother doesn't hear. She doesn't like me being called that.'

Kenny huffed. 'Pity about her, isn't it? My proper name is Kenneth, but I don't mind being called Kenny. That's 'cos I'm not a snob.'

That remark would usually have earned him a thick ear, but before Aggie could reach him, Milly spoke. 'Are you saying me and my mother are snobs? Well, perhaps you can explain to me what a snob is, 'cos I don't know?'

Kitty gave her brother a sly kick on his shin. 'Yer asked for that, our kid. Now explain to her what a snob is.'

Kenny gave her daggers. 'Everyone knows what a snob is, soft girl. It's someone what walks round with their nose stuck in the air, and talks funny.'

Milly's green eyes were flashing. 'Oh, you think I talk funny do you? That means you can't understand me. So I won't talk to you any more because I'd only be wasting my time. I'll talk to your sister instead.'

Kenny wasn't going to be beaten by a girl, especially one younger than him. He had his pride. 'I never said I couldn't understand yer, I said yer talk funny, an' yer do, so there!'

Aggie thought they'd carry on for ages if they were let, so she said, 'Drink yer tea up, Milly, then yer can come to Bessie's with me while I light her fire.'

Rita was standing at her front door to make sure Aggie did

her fair share. And it was Rita, watching her neighbour and Milly crossing the cobbles, who saw Aggie's fleecy-lined bloomers showing below her skirt. 'Ay, sunshine, I see yer've got yer blue fleecy-lined ones on today, eh? Giving the neighbours an eyeful, are yer?'

Aggie stopped when she reached the opposite pavement and looked down. She shook her head and tutted. 'Bloody things, I'll pull them up when I get in Bessie's.' But she was only on the second step when she nearly tripped over. The elastic had snapped on the waist of her bloomers, and the whole lot was around her ankles. 'Oh, bloody hell! The elastic's gone, I'll have to take them off.'

Rita gasped. 'Not in the street, Aggie! Wait until yer get in Bessie's!'

'I can't walk in the bleeding things, d'yer want me to break me bleeding neck?'

'No, I don't want yer to break yer neck, Aggie,' Rita said, dying to laugh. 'And I don't want yer to make a spectacle of yerself either. Ye're letting the tone of the street down.'

'Sod the tone of the street, that's what I say!' Aggie bent down and lifted one foot after the other to climb out of the offending bloomers. Holding them aloft, she shouted, 'I've only got the same as every other woman in the street, so to hell with modesty.'

Milly's face was a picture no artist could paint. She had never seen anything like it in her life, and although she knew her mother would be disgusted, she herself thought it was very funny. When she saw Rita doubled up, it was a signal for her own infectious giggle to make itself heard. And Aggie's son and daughter, not surprised or ashamed of anything their mother did, were in stitches. 'Oh, Mam,' Kitty croaked, the tears running down her face, 'wait until we tell our dad, he'll laugh himself sick.'

'If either of yer say one word to yer dad,' Aggie warned, pointing the hand holding the bloomers at them, 'then I'll separate yer head from yer body.'

Rubbing the tears from her eyes, Rita ran across the cobbles. 'I'll light Bessie's fire, sunshine, you go and put another pair of bloomers on.'

'No can do, queen, 'cos I haven't got another pair to put on,' Aggie said, stuffing the bloomers into her pocket. 'I'll go without, no one will be any the wiser.'

Rita managed to look horrified. 'Yer can't walk around with no bloomers on! How would yer feel if yer got run over and yer were laying on the ground, a crowd of people around yer, and you with no knickers on? I'd have to pretend I didn't know yer, I'd be that mortified.'

Cool as a cucumber, Aggie asked, 'Oh, aye, queen, how long have the trams been running down this street then?'

'Well, it wouldn't have to be a tram or a car, sunshine, it could be the coal cart or the rag and bone man. It could even be the milkman with his pony and trap.'

'Ooh, ay, queen, yer've given me a belting idea.' Aggie thought if she was giving all her neighbours a laugh, she may as well have one herself. 'If the rag and bone man does happen to come down the street while I'm in Bessie's, will yer ask him to hang on a minute while yer give me a knock? I could give him the pair of bloomers in exchange for a goldfish. Then that would be my feller's dinner sorted out, 'cos he's partial to a bit of fish is Sam.'

'And yer don't think he'd notice it was a goldfish on his plate?' Rita asked, while telling herself Aggie had more to do than stand and talk, there were two fires to be lit. 'I don't think there's anything wrong with Sam's eyesight.'

'Nah! I'll smother the plate with chips and he'll tuck in without a word. It'll be a nice surprise for him when he gets a taste of fish.'

'Ye're past the post, you are, Aggie.' Rita held out her hand to Milly. 'Give us the key, sunshine, and I'll light Bessie's fire while my mate runs home to make herself presentable.'

But Aggie was quick to intervene. 'Not on yer bleeding life, Rita Wells, I'll light the ruddy fire if it kills me. And I'll do it without bloomers on.' Her chins anticipated movement and nodded in unison with her head. 'And I bet the grate won't notice nothing. If it does, think of the treat it'll get.' She nodded to Milly. 'Go on, girl, open the door and let's get on with it.'

'Yer better had get on with it, Aggie Gordon,' Rita told her retreating back. 'Bessie will be in soon and yer haven't even made a start. And yer've got Mrs Sinclair's to do as well.'

Aggie's laugh reached the few neighbours who were watching through their windows. 'I was going to say don't get yer knickers in a twist, queen, but as bloomers and knickers are a delicate subject right now, I'll say don't be getting yerself all het up, it's not worth it. Life's too short to spend it worrying.' She grinned into her mate's face, then said to Milly, 'Come on, queen, let's get this here fire lit.'

As Milly sat on the couch watching Aggie light Bessie's fire, she was thinking how lucky she was now, with all these friends. They were always so cheerful, and they were really funny, especially Aggie, who always seemed happy even though she only had one pair of bloomers. Mind you, she was right when she said no one would know the difference. As she knelt in front of the grate, you could see the top of her stockings, but that was all.

'There yer are, queen, that should be roaring up the chimney by the time Bessie gets home.' Aggie didn't find it easy to get to her feet because of her size, so she shuffled her bottom along the floor until she was by the couch, then pulled herself up. 'Straight to your house now, queen, and get the fire lit for yer mam. She doesn't come in until after six, so the place should be warmed through by then. I'll have it done in no time, you'll see.'

Unfortunately for Aggie, she couldn't have been more wrong. She was expecting the grate to be cleaned and the fire laid out ready for lighting, like it was in Bessie's. So she got an unpleasant shock when Milly let her into the living room and she found the grate with the remains of the night before's fire. It was full of ashes and they'd spilled over on to the hearth. The bars were grey with it as well. Aggie was taken aback. 'Ay, queen, doesn't yer mam clean the grate out before she goes to work?'

Milly shook her head. 'No, Auntie Aggie, she cleans it out when she gets home, then sets it for a new fire.'

Aggie got very uppity, and so did her bosom, tummy and chins which all quivered in unison. 'Well,' she bridled, 'no one told me I'd have to clean the ruddy grate out. Wait until I get me hands on that Rita Wells, I'll marmalise her for lumbering me with this.'

'But Auntie Rita had to clean it yesterday,' Milly said. 'I know 'cos I was here with her. She got a surprise, like you, but she soon raked the ashes out and wiped the hearth down. It didn't take her long.'

'Well, she might have said something to me. I mean, I don't know where the ashes go, or where there's a floor cloth.'

'Shall I do it, Auntie Aggie? I know what to do 'cos I've done it for my mother.'

But Aggie wasn't going to let a young girl show her up. 'No, queen, I'll do it. I see there's a poker on the companion set, I'll rake the ashes down into the ashcan, then carry it to the midden.'

The first mishap occurred when Aggie was being too rough with the poker and brought down a fall of soot. It went on her hair and face, and her hands and arms were black. When she tried to wipe it away, she only made matters ten times worse. As she turned her head, an open-mouthed Milly could only see the whites of her eyes. 'Don't worry, queen, I'll get a good wash down when I get home. Everything is under control. I'll take these ashes out, then set the fire ready for lighting,' Aggie told her.

Trying to be helpful, Milly pointed to what looked like a

small poker. 'If you put that in the handle of the ashcan, Auntie Aggie, it will be easier to carry out to the yard.'

'Yes, queen, we've got one of them and they're very handy.' With all the ashes now in the ashcan, Aggie got to her feet with the help of the coal scuttle at the side of the hearth. And all would have gone well if she hadn't tripped over the fireside rug, fallen flat on the floor and sent the ashes flying everywhere.

Milly put a hand over her mouth, closed her eyes and pictured her mother's face if she could see what was happening in her living room. There was soot and ashes on the sideboard, the mantelpiece, the couch, the table the chairs. Not to mention the whole floor and in the air of the room. 'I'll try and help you up, shall I, Auntie Aggie?'

'Yer'll never make it, queen, and I'll never be able to get meself up. So will yer take the ashcan out to the yard, and then run for Rita? She's very good in a crisis, is Rita, never gets flustered or nothing like that. And hurry, queen, 'cos we don't want yer mam coming in to this.'

Milly's feet didn't touch the ground. Fear of her mother coming home to the house in such a mess lent her wings. She was out of breath when she knocked on Rita's door. 'Come quick, Auntie Rita, 'cos there's been an accident.'

'Oh, my God, what sort of an accident, sunshine?'

'Auntie Aggie is lying on the floor, and the room is full of ashes and soot.'

Rita didn't even bother to close her door, she was over the road like a shot, followed by Milly. She stood in the doorway of Evelyn's living room and didn't know whether to laugh or cry. I'll do neither, she thought quickly, there's no time. Crying won't help, and I'll leave the laughter until tea time, then all the family can join in. 'What the hell d'yer think ye're doing, Aggie, lying on the floor instead of getting some of this dirt washed off? Mrs Sinclair will have a fit if she comes in to this.'

'Oh, I'm having a little nap, queen, what d'yer think I'm doing?' Aggie's mountainous bossom was beneath her, and it wasn't very comfortable. 'Don't just bleeding well stand there, give us a hand up! And none of this would have happened if Mrs High and Mighty had cleaned her bloody grate out before she went to work, instead of leaving the dirty work to some other poor sucker.'

Rita stood astride her. 'Let's talk later, eh, when ye're standing upright. Now if yer can press the palms of yer hands into the floor and raise yerself a little, I'll try and get me arms around yer tummy. While you're pushing, I'll be lifting.'

She'll never do it, Milly said silently as she looked on. She'll never lift Auntie Aggie, not in a million years. But much to the girl's surprise and admiration, after one big heave Rita had pulled her mate to her knees. 'I'll give yer a hand to get to yer feet, Aggie, but yer'll have to help yerself as well, 'cos I'm not Man Mountain. But for heaven's sake, don't put yer hands on anything, the room's bad enough without you making it worse.'

After a struggle, Aggie was standing upright, her eyes blazing out of a black face. 'If yer so much as grin, Rita Wells, so help me I'll strangle yer.'

'Oh, I've no intention of laughing now, sunshine, there's too much to do. I'll do me laughing with Reg and the kids while we're having our meal. They'll think I'm exaggerating 'cos this is like a slapstick Laurel and Hardy film, but they'll get a good laugh.' Rita surveyed the room. 'I think the best thing is for you to go home and clean yerself up, Aggie, 'cos ye're covered in soot and yer'll only make things worse here. I'll put the kettle on for hot water, and while I'm waiting for it to boil, I'll get Milly to show me where the brush is, to clear the worst of the top dirt off. Then I'll mop out.'

'I'm not leaving yer with this lot,' Aggie said. 'I'll nip over and give me face and arms a good swill, then I'll be back. But I'll tell yer something for nothing, queen, I ain't clearing this grate out again. If she wants her fire lighting, then she'd better set it before she goes out.'

'Get moving, Aggie, we'll talk it over after. In fact, I'll have a word with Bessie, and if this fire isn't set for lighting each day, then I'll do here and you can do Bessie's. Yer can't get up to any mischief in Bessie's, all yer need to do is strike a match.'

While Aggie was at her sink trying to get the worst of the soot off, Bessie was walking up the street on her way home from work. She was looking forward to a warm house and to seeing Milly. She was surprised when Kitty Gordon came running over to her. 'Me mam fell over in Mrs Sinclair's house, Auntie Bessie, and she's come home black with soot.'

Bessie's heart sank. Just when things were going to well, something was bound to come along and spoil it. Giving a deep sigh, she passed her own house and entered the open door of her next door neighbour's. The room was a hive of activity, with Rita on her hands and knees washing the hearth down, and Milly brushing the floor as best she could. 'Oh, dear, what's happened, Rita?'

The story didn't take long, and the way Rita told it, it sounded so funny Bessie was laughing as she took her coat off. 'Another pair of hands won't go amiss, sweetheart, I'll get the mop and bucket ready. We've got three-quarters of an hour at least, so we should make it. We'll leave the front and back doors open so the lino will dry before Mrs Sinclair arrives.'

When Aggie came back over, most of the work had been done. There was still a smell of soot in the air, but with back and front doors wide open, that should disperse pretty soon. 'I'm sorry I had to leave yer to it, but I couldn't get the bleeding soot off meself. Me hair is still thick with the ruddy stuff, but I'll give it a good wash tonight. And I had to take me dress off and put it to soak in the sink.' She pulled at the skirt of the dress she was wearing. 'This was the only one to hand.' Her eyes were taking in all the work that had been done since she'd gone home. 'I feel bad leaving yer to do the dirty work, Rita. And you, Bessie, yer've put in a full day at work, as well.'

Bessie tried to keep a straight face. 'Well, Aggie, yer did very well for yer first day, I must say. There's not many could bring about a fall of soot, then trip up and spread the ashes over everything in the room. I wonder what trick yer've got in store for us tomorrow?'

'Now, now, queen, there's no need to get sarky with me, anyone can trip over a ruddy rug what's curled up at the corners. And the fall of soot must have been an act of God, 'cos I didn't do nothing to cause it. Milly is my witness, she'll tell yer I didn't do nothing.' Then she saw the unfairness of it, and got her dander up. 'Anyway, I'm giving me notice in, I'm not having anything to do with lighting that fire no more.'

Rita chuckled. 'That's good, sunshine, it saves us giving yer the sack.'

'Giving me the sack! Well, the bloody cheek of you! You ain't giving me the sack 'cos I won't let her!'

'Yeah, we agreed to sack yer,' Bessie told a disbelieving Aggie. 'But the minute we gave yer the sack, we had another job lined up for yer. Same pay, less work.'

Aggie looked suspicious. 'Oh, aye, pull the other one, it's got bells on.'

'Leave it if she's not interested, Bessie,' Rita said. 'I'll do both jobs.'

'Sod off, Rita Wells, and mind yer own business. Now, Bessie, what did yer have in mind for me?'

'You light my fire, and Rita lights this one. How does that suit yer?'

'Suits me fine, Bessie.' Aggie was grinning from ear to ear. 'I'll take the job.'

Chapter Twenty

Each Wednesday before their tryst in Philip's apartment, to allay suspicion Evelyn would leave the office at one o'clock and Philip would follow a little later. Then she would be back at her desk dead on two o'clock, while he strolled in ten or fifteen minutes later. After all, he could please himself what he did, there was no one to question his movements or time-keeping. He would have been quite happy for them to leave and return together, and to hell with what the rest of the staff thought, but Evelyn wasn't prepared to have her name bandied about. So far no one had made any comment on the regular pattern set for each Wednesday lunchtime.

But the regularity of their timing hadn't gone unnoticed by one member of staff, and that was Mr Woodward's secretary. Janet Coombes had watched the comings and going of the pair, and was convinced they were having an affair. Secretly she was consumed with jealousy. She had made several advances towards Philip, to whom she was very attracted, waylaying him whenever the opportunity arose. But although he was very polite, he made it perfectly clear he wasn't interested. The attention he paid to Mrs Sinclair was like a slap in the face for Janet, who was much younger than Evelyn, and considered herself much prettier and more modern in her dress. And she had never been married, so wasn't second-hand goods.

Her jealousy was like a festering sore that wouldn't go away. She strongly suspected that although they left the office separately each Wednesday, they met up somewhere and spent the lunchtime together. But where? Consumed with jealousy and bitterness, she determined to find out.

When Evelyn left the office on this particular Wednesday, she made her way to the apartment feeling happy and looking forward to having Philip to herself for an hour. Little did she know she was being followed.

Janet kept back at a safe distance, with an excuse ready if Evelyn should turn her head and see her. She stopped when Evelyn stopped, and watched with mounting interest as her target let herself into a door between two office blocks. There's something underhand going on here, she told herself, but is Philip Astbury involved? The only way to find out was to wait in a doorway opposite for ten minutes to see if he turned up. If he didn't, then what was the snobby Mrs Sinclair up to? Perhaps she had another fancy man, Janet wouldn't put it past her. She'd wheedled her way into Mr Philip's heart. How many others had she done the same to? It would be worth watching that door, even if it took up the whole of her lunch hour.

So Janet crossed the busy road and stood in the entrance of another office building. She was careful to stand back in the shadow so she wouldn't be seen. Her feet were cold from standing still, and she did some on the spot walking to warm them up. She popped her head out to see if there was any sign of anyone she knew, and when she saw the familiar figure of Philip striding down the pavement quickly drew back into the shadows. From where she was standing she had a really good view. She saw him stop outside the door opposite, feel in his pocket for a key, insert it in the lock, open the door and disappear, all in the space of one minute. It left Janet blazing and bitter. Just showed she'd been right all along. They were definitely having an affair, and were very keen to keep it quiet from the sly way they were going about it. Apparently, while she wasn't good enough for Philip Astbury, Evelyn Sinclair was. She was probably giving him what he wanted, which was why he was interested in her. It certainly couldn't be for any other reason because there was nothing so special about his private secretary. She wasn't bad-looking and had a decent figure, but she was nothing out of the ordinary. And with his looks and money, Philip would only have to snap his fingers and dozens of women would be falling at his feet.

Janet's imagination was running wild. Evelyn Sinclair could be doling out her favours to several men, in return for gifts or even money. And to look at her, you'd think butter wouldn't melt in her mouth! But all this didn't explain what went on behind the door opposite. Was it an office, and Philip and his secretary had legitimate business there? Or was a room in the office block hired out for clandestine meetings? Oh, how she would love to know. She would like nothing better than to expose Mrs Sinclair in front of the rest of the staff.

Time was ticking by, and Janet realised if she waited to see Evelyn or Philip come out, her whole lunch hour would be gone. She couldn't go all day without a bite to eat. Best to nip to the little cafe in Dale Street for a sandwich and pot of tea. While she was sitting, she would put together a plan on what to do about the secret she'd found out today. For she fully intended to bring the high and mighty Evelyn Sinclair down off her pedestal. And it would have to be done in such a way it wouldn't cost Janet her job.

She ordered a toasted teacake and a cup of tea, and while she was waiting glanced at the people seated nearby. She was the only person sitting on her own, the other tables were occupied by two or three people, mostly men, all of them deep in conversation. She could hear snatches of what they were saying, and it was obvious they were work colleagues. This gave her food for thought. Perhaps she could suggest to Evelyn that they should have lunch together one day. But as quickly as the idea entered her head, she dismissed it. That would surely make the woman suspicious.

The waitress came with her order, and for a short time Janet was busy pouring herself a much-needed cup of hot tea. The teacake, oozing with butter, looked so appetising she couldn't resist folding it in two and sinking her teeth into it. It wasn't until the cup and plate were empty that her thoughts returned to the subject that plagued her: Philip Astbury and Evelyn Sinclair. Not that she had bad thoughts about Philip, she didn't. She wanted him for herself and was sure she could prove to him that she was more his sort than Mrs Sinclair, if only he would let her. In fact, if Evelyn was out of the picture, Janet was convinced he would take more notice of her.

The clock on the wall of the cafe said it was a quarter to two, and Janet told herself if she hurried she might catch Evelyn coming out of that door in Castle Street. She could hang back until the door opened, then catch up with her prey and pretend she was surprised to see her. Yes, that was a good idea. So she picked up the bill the waitress had left and counted out the right money from her purse. Then, hoping that being generous would bring her good luck, she left a penny tip on the table for the waitress.

Standing outside the cafe, Janet could feel the cold wind coming off the River Mersey, and shivered as she pulled on her gloves. She'd walk slowly up Castle Street, and if she was lucky and Evelyn came out of the door on cue, that would be marvellous. But if it wasn't to be, she wasn't going to hang around, it was too cold.

Evelyn pulled the door closed behind her, then tucked her handbag under her arm while she put on the warm, fur-lined soft leather gloves which Philip had surprised her with this morning. He'd said her old ones had well served their purpose and she should put them in the bin. This was one time she'd thrown caution to the wind and kissed him for being so thoughtful. Winter had certainly come with a vengeance, and people were saying it was the worst for many years. So as she stepped into the street, she was thanking him mentally for the warmth of the expensive kid gloves. He really was an angel, and she was falling more in love with him every day.

She had only covered a few yards when she heard running footsteps and her name being called. She turned her head and felt her heart miss a beat when she saw Janet Coombes. Had she been spotted coming out of the apartment? She hoped not, for Janet was the one person in the office she couldn't take a liking to.

'I thought I recognised you.' Janet was smiling in a friendly manner when she caught up. 'You've just come out of one of those offices, haven't you?'

Evelyn quickly pulled herself together and decided to brazen it out. She ignored the question. 'You gave me quite a scare, calling my name so loudly. I thought something dreadful had happened.' Without giving Janet time to answer, she went on, 'Have you been out for lunch? You need to get something warm inside you this cold weather.'

Janet nodded. 'Yes, I've been to that nice little cafe in Dale Street. They do wonderful toasted teacakes.' She couldn't let this opportunity pass, she may never get another one. 'I did see you coming out of one of the offices, didn't I? Have you a friend in there?'

As calm as could be, Evelyn, who was several inches taller than Janet, looked down with her eyebrows raised in surprise. 'I haven't just come out of an office, you must be mistaken.' Then she added, 'Oh, I understand now, how silly of me. I had stepped into a doorway out of the wind while I fixed my scarf. It had worked itself loose and my neck was freezing.'

Janet was lost for words. At least there were plenty of words wanting to tumble out of her mouth, but they weren't the right ones. If she came right out and called Evelyn a liar, she knew she would bring down on herself Philip's wrath. She was also sure she would lose her job. So she bit her tongue. There were many ways of skinning a cat, and Evelyn wouldn't be allowed to get away with making a fool of her.

'It's a lovely warm scarf.' Janet had to force herself to speak in her normal tone of voice as she kept in step with the woman she disliked intensely. 'And I do love your gloves, they look like real kid.'

They were nearing the office when Evelyn answered, 'Yes, they are. They were a gift from a very good friend.'

Janet couldn't keep the sarcasm out of her voice when she said, 'Lucky you to have such a generous friend. He must be a man of means.'

They walked up the three steps to the office door, and with her hand out ready to push it open, Evelyn drawled, 'And what, pray, makes you think they were a present from a man? You should never pass a remark like that unless you have your facts right.' She pushed the door open. 'And now it's back to work, and reality.'

'Yes,' Janet said between gritted teeth. 'I wish I could meet a really rich man who would take me away from all this.'

'They are few and far between, Miss Coombes, but I wouldn't stop wishing if I were you. You might just be one of the lucky ones.'

Being addressed so formally enraged Janet. She felt like a child being put in its place. 'Is that what you're wishing for, Mrs Sinclair? To be one of the lucky ones?'

'Good heavens, no!' Evelyn slipped her arms out of her coat. 'I am more than content with my lot in life, there's nothing more I could wish for.'

Evelyn was sorting the second delivery of mail with Grace when Philip strolled into the office. 'Any post for us, Mrs Sinclair?'

'Half a dozen letters so far, Mr Philip. When Grace and I are finished sorting them properly, I'll open those which are addressed to you and file them in order of importance. Give me half an hour and I'll bring them to you.' Evelyn averted her eyes, afraid Grace would see the special look she reserved for him. 'There are two letters on your desk needing your signature. If you could attend to them, Grace will put them with Mr Woodward's letters to be posted later.'

When Evelyn carried the post through to Philip's office later, he jumped to his feet as always. 'Sit down, my love, I've missed you.'

She sat facing him. 'It's been about half an hour, Philip, if that! But it pleases me to hear you say you've missed me, for I've missed you.' She crossed her legs and pulled her skirt down. 'I missed something else as well.'

'Oh, and what was that, my lovely?'

'I just missed getting caught coming out of the apartment. In fact, I was caught, but I think I got out of it by telling lies.'

'Why was it necessary to lie? You were coming out of my apartment as you have every right to if you wish. Surely there was no reason to pretend?' He leaned his elbows on the desk and leaned towards her. 'Who was it you found it necessary to lie to?'

'Janet. I believe she's noticed the regularity of our Wednesday meetings, and today set out to find if we meet up outside the office. Whether she followed me and saw me going in the building, I don't know, but she pounced when I left.'

'Surely you don't care what Janet thinks, do you? She is insignificant, of no consequence. Did she dare to question you?'

'No, of course not.' Evelyn wasn't about to tell him more or he would surely bound out of his office and into James Woodward's to confront Janet. 'I told her I was standing out of the wind while I fastened my scarf. It was a lie, of course, and I really do not like to be in a position where I have to lie to the likes of Janet Coombes. So all I'm asking is that we are more careful in future.'

Philip was angry. 'How stupid all this secrecy is! I love you and want to marry you. And I am of the opinion that you love me. Why should we hide it?'

'For my sake, my darling. Look at it from my point of view. We haven't known each other very long, I know that matters little when we adore each other, but think what a field day the rest of the staff would have. Me, a widow, throwing myself at you. That is what they will think, and what they will say behind my back. I am not so thick-skinned it wouldn't hurt me.'

Philip was becoming impatient. He could not understand why Evelyn was so insecure she allowed his partner's secretary to have this effect on her. The girl was an employee, nothing more. And if Evelyn was to become his wife in the very near future, there was no reason on earth for her to fear anyone. 'I'm going to ask you a question, my darling, and I want you to answer truthfully. Do you really love me?'

'Philip, I love and adore you! And that is the truth.'

'Then I will bear with you, as promised, until all the Christmas and New Year festivities are over. After that I will accept no delay or argument about our future. This is what I have planned.' Philip wished they were in the privacy of the apartment so he could hold her in his arms, for she was looking at him now with apprehension in her eyes. 'You will give in your week's notice here on the day we return to work after the New Year break, and when you have served your notice you will move into the apartment until we are married. I will tell my parents tonight that I have met you, fallen in love, and that you are the girl of my dreams. I will add that in the near future I will be asking you to be my wife. I will take you to meet them when you are no longer an employee of this firm, and will also take you to meet my best friend who, with his wife, already knows about you. When that is done, we shall set a date for the wedding. That is how it will be, my darling, for I love you too much to listen to any further excuses for delay.'

'You will have to be a little more understanding, Philip, and try to see things from my point of view. Your life is easy, always has been, but I haven't been so lucky. There are many things I'm afraid of that you appear not to have given any thought to. First, I am a widow of twenty-nine. I have no money or assets to bring with me, and how are your parents going to react when you tell them that? Or your friends?'

'They will love you as I do, and they'll be very happy that at last I have found someone I truly feel for. Of this I am certain, I know my family and friends. But if I am wrong, and my parents object to our marriage, it will not alter my feelings for you, or stop me from marrying you. I would be sad, but it is my life and I have at last found someone I want more than anything in the world. Nothing, and no one, can change my mind.'

Philip smiled as he leaned across the desk and took her hand. 'Don't look so afraid, my lovely, I won't let anything happen to you. And now that we have a timetable set for the events that will lead to the happiest day of my life, and yours, I hope, then let us put it from our minds for now. We will continue to meet as often as possible, I have become addicted to you. And you must bear in mind that I expect you to spend time with me in the apartment over Christmas. In fact, I not only expect you to, I demand it. I couldn't live a whole week without seeing you.'

Evelyn's mind was in a turmoil. She would give anything to be able to round the desk, hold him in her arms, kiss him soundly, tell him she idolised him and agree with everything he'd said. For what he was offering her was nothing short of life in paradise. But it would not be right to agree to it for what he was asking was also impossible. She was living a lie, and he would hate her when she was forced to tell him the truth. But for now she would enjoy what little time they had left. She would take and return his love, and when it was over, as it surely would be over when he knew she'd been lying, she would at least have the memory of that love to cherish forever.

'As always, your wish is my command, Philip. We will continue to meet, as often as it pleases you, and to hell with what people think. And with regard to Christmas, I will try to fit in with your plans.'

Her words pleased Philip. His mischievous grin appeared. 'You will be my Christmas present. And if you would give me an inkling what you would like, it would be of enormous help. I want to buy something that would please you. Will it be French underwear, my darling, or jewellery perhaps? A hint would be very useful.'

'As I can't buy you an expensive gift in return, I would prefer an inexpensive present. I am not complaining, but the facts are that I am on a very tight budget. I have a couple of people I need to buy presents for, neighbours who have been good to me, and I have to be careful. So please don't embarrass me by giving me a present that costs the earth.'

This was the first time Evelyn had mentioned anyone else in her life, and Philip was interested. 'You have good neighbours then?'

'Yes, they are very kind. One lady in the street does little jobs for me, which I pay her for. When I get home every night there's a fire lit and it makes the house seem more lived in.'

'Then I have an idea,' he said. 'Let me pay for the presents you want for your neighbours. If they are good to you, then they are good to me. Let me reward them, please, it would make me happy.'

'Oh, I shall only be buying them some small items, just to show my appreciation. Something for their children, perhaps, because they are quite poor and will have little money to spare for Christmas presents.'

'Then let me be their Father Christmas.' Philip had taken to the idea. He would enjoy helping poor families, and could certainly afford to. 'Yes, I would like that. But as I don't know the age or sex of these children, I will have to leave the buying of the presents to you.'

'I can manage to buy their presents, Philip, I'm not exactly a pauper.'

'But I would like to! Many of my friends give to organisations who help the needy at Christmas but I've never even given the matter any thought, been too busy enjoying myself. So you see how you are changing me, my lovely Evelyn, by reminding me there are people who are not as fortunate as myself.'

'If it will make you happy, my love, then so be it. I know the ages of five children, three boys and two girls. Although I am reluctant to take money from you, in this instance it will be in a good cause.'

'I don't have much ready cash on me today, but tomorrow I will give you an envelope with money in. And nearer Christmas, I will give you an afternoon off work to do your shopping. I will mention it to James, and if he is agreeable, we will give each member of staff an afternoon off to do their shopping too.'

'You are kind, thoughtful, and I love you very much. How lucky I am that you love me in return. My life is so much happier since you became part of it.' There was a shaky smile on Evelyn's face, but tears in her heart. How was she ever going to be brave enough to walk away from this man?

'Yer look a bit off colour tonight, Evelyn,' Bessie said when her neighbour called to pick her daughter up. 'I hope ye're not sickening for a cold, there's a lot of them around. Sit yerself down and I'll pour yer a cup of tea. It is fresh, I've only just made it.'

Bessie's kindly face, and honest concern, had an effect on Evelyn. How she had lied and used this little woman for her own ends, when all Bessie had done was offer the hand of friendship! Right now Evelyn needed a shoulder to cry on. 'I will have a cup of tea, Bessie, thank you. And if you're not too busy, I would like to talk to you in private. Can you spare the time?'

'Of course I can.' Bessie saw Milly sitting at the table, her coat on ready to go home, and wondered if by saying she wanted to talk in private her neighbour meant that what she wanted to say was not for her daughter's ears. Well, if she was going to tell a secret, then Bessie would get hers in first. 'Oh, Evelyn, before I pour yer tea out, I've been meaning to tell yer for a week or two, but I keep forgetting. I bought Amelia a doll the other week, then wondered if I should have asked you first. But yer don't mind, do yer? After all, there's no harm in a young girl having a doll. I had one when I was young, I still remember it.'

'I have no objection to Amelia having a doll.' A few weeks ago this would not have been true, but Evelyn's head and heart were going through major changes. 'Where is it?'

'It's upstairs on the bed I sleep in on a Saturday night, Mother.' Milly couldn't believe her luck. As Auntie Bessie had said, perhaps her mother wasn't feeling very well. 'And her name is Daisy.'

Bessie jerked her head towards the stairs. 'Go and get it, sweetheart, and perhaps yer mother will let yer take it home to play with while me and her have a little talk.'

When Milly had gone, clasping the doll to her chest and looking so happy to be taking Daisy home, Bessie pulled her chair nearer the fire. 'I could tell there was something bothering yer as soon as yer walked through the door, Evelyn, so whatever it is, get it off yer chest. It'll do yer no good to bottle it all up. And anything yer say will go no further than these four walls.'

Evelyn dropped her head. 'I'm afraid you're not going to like me by the time I've said what I feel I must. You have never been anything but kindness itself to me and Amelia, and yet I've lied to you since the day I first became your neighbour. In fact, I have lied to everyone I've come into contact with for the last eight years. But someone has come into my life who has made such a difference, made me see myself for what I am – and that is not a very nice person.' She raised her eyes to Bessie's. 'I know I don't deserve your friendship, not after the way I've treated you, but I need to talk to someone who will not judge me too harshly, and you are the only one I can turn to. So I'm going to ask you to listen while I take you back more than eight years, to what my life was like then and how I have lived since.'

'Look, I can see ye're distressed. Why go over old ground and make yerself worse?' Bessie asked. 'Just tell me what ye're upset about now, and yer might feel better once yer've got it off yer chest.'

'No, I have to tell you all I've gone through for you to understand. I need to go back to the year I was nineteen years of age and still living at home with my parents.' Evelyn dropped her head as she gathered her thoughts together, then began by describing her parents and how, for her nineteenth birthday, she was allowed to go out with a girl friend for the first time. Then the meeting with Charles, the whirl of social activity that lasted for a year, how he gave her everything she wanted. Then the day he told her he had joined the Army. She said he came from a very wealthy family, but gave no name. She raced through the episode before they were married, when they'd sat in the car and she had allowed him to take liberties with her because he was going away and she felt sorry for him.

Evelyn stopped then to try and clear her throat of the lump caused by unshed tears. And Bessie, who had been enthralled by what she was hearing, didn't know whether to offer words of comfort, or leave her neighbour to get what was troubling her out of her system.

'I'm sorry, I needed to breathe for a while,' Evelyn said, her face pale and drawn. 'I don't want to upset you with my troubles, but I'll go mad if I don't tell someone so please bear with me, I won't keep you much longer.' Then she took up the story again.

When she reached the part where Charles' family wouldn't believe it was his baby, and she was disowned by her own family and friends for having an illegitimate child, she was shaking and sobbing so much she couldn't continue.

Bessie crossed the room to sit beside her, and put an arm around her shoulders. She couldn't see anyone in such distress without trying to comfort them. 'I think yer should leave it for now, Evelyn, if it's going to affect yer so much. You can tell me the rest when ye're feeling up to it.'

Evelyn became more agitated. 'No! I have to tell you everything! I've lived with this for so long because I've never had anyone to confide in. If you won't listen, I have no one to turn to. Please hear me out, then with you seeing things from a distance, you may understand them more clearly and tell me what you think I should do.'

Bessie patted her shoulder then stood up. 'Okay. I'll go and sit in me own chair, and as yer say, I'll hear yer out. But as for telling yer what I think yer should do, well, I don't feel as though I'm in a position to do that. But anyway, go ahead, sweetheart, it's better out than keeping it in and making yerself ill.'

Evelyn took a deep breath and let it out before taking up her story. 'When my father-in-law came to tell me Charles had been killed in action, he said I was no longer their responsibility and that I must be out of the house in two weeks. I moved from a beautiful, grand home to a six-roomed house. Then I slid further down the scale and could only afford a house in this street.'

Bessie couldn't keep quiet. 'May God forgive them, the miserable rotters! Fancy throwing you and the baby out!'

'Don't think too badly of them, Bessie, I don't. I did at first because I was selfish and wanted to keep the life I had become used to. But I wasn't a very nice person then. I didn't even mourn my own husband, so I could never really have loved him. I refused to wear black, as I should have being a new widow, and did nothing but complain and whine to his father. Never once did I think how he and his wife must have suffered, losing the son they adored. I was too busy feeling sorry for myself. And I was childish enough to put the blame on Amelia, always thinking if it wasn't for her, I'd still be living a life of luxury. I have made that child suffer for my own mistakes. It is only since a certain man has come into my life that I can see what a dreadful mother I've been. He has helped me realise that the problems I've had and dreadful life I've led for eight years, were all due to my feeling sorry for myself. Now I see myself as others see me, and I don't like what I see.'

'Oh, I'm glad yer've met someone, sweetheart, that will make up for all the bad years. Are yer serious about each other?'

'He loves me very much, and I can honestly say he is the only person I have ever loved in my whole life. He makes me feel special, and I'm a different person altogether from the one I was a few months ago.'

'Is he coming to your house to meet Amelia? She'd be over the moon to have a dad.'

Evelyn closed her eyes. This was the part that would take the concern from Bessie's face and replace it with dislike. 'I haven't told him I have a daughter. He is my boss at the office, and at first there was no reason to tell him any of my business. He knows nothing of my past, nothing at all. Then there was a spark between us, we both felt it. I should have told him about Amelia then, but I was afraid of losing him. Now it's too late. He wants to marry me, and he will think I've lied to him if I tell him now. He'll walk out of my life, and I couldn't bear that.'

'So what are yer going to do? Yer wouldn't put him before Amelia, would yer?'

'Bessie, I'm out of my mind with worry. I haven't been a good mother to Amelia, I know that, I don't have any maternal feelings towards her. It's something I can't help. Maybe I'm not normal or maybe it's because of the way I was treated.'

'Is Amelia illegitimate?' Bessie couldn't help but ask.

Evelyn shook her head. 'No, Charles was her father. Anyone who knew him would recognise that straight away, the resemblance is remarkable.'

Bessie felt a little of her anger drain away. Thank God for that. 'Then why don't you go to see your late husband's parents? They have a right to know, and would probably be over the moon to see her now. She is part of their son after all.'

'I have thought about that, Bessie, but after the way they treated me, I don't think I would be very welcome.'

'You might not be, but their granddaughter would, I'll bet! As I said, sweetheart, there were wrongs on both sides, but that should not be allowed to keep Amelia from a family she doesn't know she has.'

Evelyn glanced at the clock and jumped to her feet. 'I forgot she'd been left in the house on her own, I'll have to fly. But can I talk to you again, Bessie? I do feel a lot better for having got so much off my chest.'

'You're welcome any time, Evelyn. And we'll let Amelia go and play with Rita's kids next time, save her being in the house on her own.'

'Yes, we'll do that, as long as Mrs Wells doesn't mind.' Evelyn reached the door, then put her hand on Bessie's arm. 'Thank you for being a friend in need. I don't deserve your friendship after the way I've treated you in the past. I have been short with many of the neighbours, and I'm really sorry about that. I'll be a better person from now on, I've had my eyes opened.'

Evelyn was turning the key in the door when Bessie remembered Aggie's disastrous trip over the rug. The place had been cleaned and all traces of ashes and soot been removed. But when Bessie was in there, there was still a smell of soot. 'Oh, before I forget, sweetheart, yer need yer chimney sweeping. There was a fall of soot when the fire was being lit, but it's all been cleaned up. I thought I'd better tell yer in case yer can still smell it. Yer know how the smell stays in the air for a while.'

'Do I need to get the sweep in, then?'

'Nah, I think it'll be all right until after Christmas. Yer've got enough on yer plate.' She waited until she saw her neighbour open the door. 'Goodnight and God bless. Get a good night's sleep, it'll do yer the world of good.'

Chapter Twenty-One

Bessie lay awake till the early hours of the morning, going over in her mind all that Evelyn had told her. What a story it was, almost like sitting in the pictures watching a drama unfold. She was at a loss what to make of her neighbour now. There were times in the story-telling when she'd felt sorry for her, then others where she would like to have given her a good shaking. But when it came down to it, it wasn't Evelyn she worried about. The woman was old enough to take care of herself, and make up her own mind what she wanted to do with her life. But Milly couldn't, and this was what Bessie was fretting over. She was eight years of age, a little angel, but she hadn't had much pleasure or love in her life, and God knows what was going to happen to her in the future. She had grandparents she didn't even know about, and who would probably love her to death given the chance. Perhaps they had been hard on her mother, but as Evelyn had admitted herself, she'd deserved it, after behaving badly. Whichever way it was there was no reason why the child should suffer for it, and next time her neighbour came for a heart to heart, Bessie would tell her so in no uncertain terms.

It was with this determination to protect Milly's interests that Bessie turned on her side and counted sheep until she fell into a deep sleep.

Meanwhile, next door, Evelyn was tossing and turning. She was glad she'd unburdened herself to Bessie, although she still hadn't told her that Philip was expecting her to spend time with him at Christmas or that he wanted her to give her job up and live in the apartment until they'd fixed a date for their wedding. And she hadn't the strength of character to tell the truth: that she would like nothing better than to walk away from everything in her life now, and go to the man she loved. But there wasn't much point in talking about something that wasn't possible.

Evelyn sighed deeply and turned on her side, wiping a tear away. How was she to face Philip and see the hurt on his face when she shattered his dreams? Her own dreams, too, but she had known all along their love was doomed, and he'd hate her for leading him on. The only other option, which Bessie had brought up, was to go and see Mr Lister-Sinclair. But what if he still wouldn't believe her, even though Amelia was the spitting image of his son? She would be totally humiliated then and made to feel worthless. No, she didn't think she could face that. Then she asked herself if it wouldn't be worth a try? Anything that would lead to her being free to marry Philip would be worth it. But she began finding obstacles to put in the way. What if she told Mr Lister-Sinclair who had asked her to marry him, and it came about that Philip's family were well known to them? This was very likely, for the wealthy people of the city usually mingled in the same circles, frequenting the same parties and social events.

Once again Evelyn turned over in bed, this time telling herself there was no way out. The best thing she could do would be to make the most of the next couple of weeks with Philip, and then either pluck up courage to tell him the truth or just disappear out of his life.

When Evelyn called in the following night she didn't accept Bessie's invitation to sit, saying she was hungry and urging Amelia not to dawdle and put on her coat. She felt she couldn't sit and go over her troubles again, last night had left her drained. 'Come along, Amelia, I'm really starving.' She thought Bessie would take the hint, but her neighbour had other ideas.

'Rita was asking me if yer were satisfied with her work. Was the room left clean and tidy enough for yer?'

'Oh, yes, I am well satisfied. Please tell her so.'

'I can see ye're eager to be away so I won't keep yer long,' Bessie said. 'But I was wondering about Saturday. Will yer be going to yer friend's and staying overnight? It doesn't matter to me, yer can please yerself, Evelyn, but I need to know if Amelia will be staying over so I'll know what bread and milk to get in?'

Evelyn's eyes darted towards her daughter, putting her coat on. She hadn't expected this, not after telling Bessie about Philip. But from the sound of things her neighbour hadn't taken it for granted that she was sleeping with him. 'I thought perhaps you wouldn't want me to stay at my friend's, not after our heart-to-heart last night. I was under the impression it may have changed your opinion of me?'

'Not at all!' Bessie said. 'It's not for me to judge, or tell yer how to run yer life. If yer want to go to yer friend's, I'll be more than happy to have Amelia.' She smiled when she saw the girl's eyes light up. 'We get on like a house on fire, don't we, sweetheart?'

'In that case, I'll be delighted to go to Elizabeth's.' Evelyn nodded to her daughter. 'You have the key, Amelia, you run and open the door while I have a quick word with Bessie.'

'If yer starving, Evelyn, why don't yer go home and have something to eat? Amelia's had a meal, so yer've no need to worry about her. But I bet you haven't had much since yer left the house this morning.'

'Only a sandwich, and that wasn't very filling.' Evelyn laid a hand on Bessie's arm. 'Thank you, you are a friend indeed. I'll go and make myself something warm, then I'll come back, for I have something to tell you that I hope will please you.'

When Evelyn knocked an hour later, she had Milly with her. 'Bessie, Amelia asked if she could go over to Mrs Wells, to have a game of cards with one of the boys.'

'The boy's name is Jack, Mother, and he's very good to me. We play together.'

'Will Mrs Wells mind?' Evelyn looked up at her neighbour, who was standing on the top step. 'Shall I go and ask?'

'There's no need,' Bessie assured her. 'Like me, Rita doesn't stand on ceremony.'

Milly didn't wait to hear any more, she was across the road like a flash and knocking on the Wellses' door. It was opened by Jack, whose dirty face beamed when he saw her. 'Hi, Milly, come on in.' His greeting was missed by her mother, who had deliberately been ushered quickly into Bessie's living room out of earshot. She and Evelyn had come a long way in the last few days, but giving her daughter a change of name might not go down too well. 'Yer've no need to worry about Amelia, she's in good hands over there.' And for good measure, with a silent chuckle, she added, 'Two well-behaved boys they are, and yer'll not hear bad language in there either.'

Evelyn sat down without waiting for Bessie to ask her to. She was feeling a little happier now she knew she had the weekend free, and wanted to give a little happiness in return. 'I won't bore you with my tales of woe, Bessie, at least not tonight. But I have some good news for you, and hope you will take it as such.'

Bessie was thinking Evelyn must have had a good education, her English was perfect. Still, the little woman thought, it's too late in life for me to remember to sound me Gs and me Hs.

'I could do with a bit of good news to cheer me up, Evelyn, we don't get much chance in work for telling jokes. If our machines stop for a minute, the boss is down on us like a ton of bricks. The only time we get a smile out of him is when he's got a rush job on and he's coaxing us to work either later or faster. And then he's a smarmy toad.'

Evelyn smiled, hoping the news she'd come with would indeed cheer Bessie up. 'I want you to believe me when I tell you that every word out of my mouth tonight will be true. I have lied before, not only to you but to everyone around here and I am not proud of myself. Tonight is different, I come with the blessing of another person's generosity. So please hear me out before judging me. And please don't take this as an insult, or think it's given out of pity, it is far from that.'

'For God's sake, Evelyn, will yer get on with it! Yer've got me on pins now, so get a move on before I throw a wobbly.'

'Well, you know about my relationship with Philip, and this is his doing. We were talking about Christmas presents, and I said how some people couldn't afford to buy their children presents because there were so many men out of work, and even those who worked were on very low wages. He asked me how I knew, and although he doesn't know where I live, I did say I had seen for myself that some boys and girls were running around barefoot.' Evelyn was watching Bessie's face for any sign of indignation, but her neighbour's face remained expressionless. 'He said many of his rich friends give to charities at Christmas, but he never has because he'd never really given it thought. Then he insisted I take some money from him to help anyone I thought was in need. So will you help me, Bessie, and tell me who is most in need in this street? I don't want anyone to know where it comes from or think it's been given out of pity. That would rob them of their pride. I've seen boys at the top of this street running around without shoes on, and I would like to help them.' She was worried that her neighbour hadn't yet said a word. 'You're not happy about it, are you, Bessie?'

'Not happy! I'd be over the bloody moon if I could help some of the families hereabouts afford a proper dinner over Christmas, *and* get shoes for the kids. They needn't be new shoes, they could be good secondhand ones from the market. I could easy do it without them knowing it was charity. I could always say the shoes came from the Wells boys, and they'd grown out of them. And Kenny Gordon, he's always growing out of shoes according to Aggie. Her and Rita could take the shoes up and the women wouldn't think anything about it, they'd be that glad to see their kids shod. It breaks a woman's heart if she can't afford to feed and clothe her children, but there's nothing they can do if their husbands are out of work.'

Evelyn bent down to pick up her handbag from the floor at the side of her chair. 'I have the money in an envelope. I would like to buy presents for Mrs Wells and Mrs Gordon, and also for their children so they can open them on Christmas morning. And it would be nice if you could buy books and games for Amelia, you will know what she likes better than I do.' She handed over the large envelope. 'I will be buying her a nice dress and a new coat, so she will have a lot to make her happy over Christmas. And if you won't be insulted, I would like to buy you something for your kindness, if you would give me an idea of what you would like?'

Bessie looked down at the envelope which was sealed. 'Don't worry about me, Evelyn, I'll be all right for the holidays, I've got clubs in most of the shops. I put a few coppers in each week and it soon mounts up. I'm lucky I can do that, with me working and only meself to worry about.' She waved the envelope. 'Would yer mind if I opened this in front of yer? I'd feel better if yer would watch me and we agree what's inside.'

'By all means, go ahead, Bessie. But it isn't necessary, I would trust you with anything. You are the only one I have spoken to about the last eight years of my life. I wouldn't have done so if I didn't trust you implicitly. However, I understand why you would want me to see you open the envelope. So please do.'

Bessie ran her thumb along the inside of the flap and took out the contents. Her mouth gaped and she looked as though she couldn't believe what she was seeing. She thought the white paper was wrapped around the money Evelyn had mentioned, but it was a five-pound note! She'd never had one in her hand before. And when she opened it up, she found it had been wrapped around a further three. 'Oh, my God, Evelyn, there's twenty pounds here! I've never had so much money in me hand at one time in me whole life! I can't keep this, it's a fortune!'

'It's not my money, Bessie, it was Philip who gave it to me. And believe me, he can well afford it. He is so happy knowing he is helping children who are not as privileged as he has been. He didn't do it to look good, he will never meet those he's helped and is not a snob. He would treat anyone the same, be it a king or a tramp.'

Bessie couldn't keep her eyes off the notes in her hand. She'd never thought the day would come when she'd have one of those white ones, never mind four! She was shaking her head in disbelief when she gazed across at Evelyn. 'Are you sure about this? Do yer not want to keep some to buy Amelia's coat and dress? And something for yerself to wear over Christmas?'

Her neighbour shook her head. 'I have enough for Amelia's clothes, and I'll only be wanting an inexpensive dress myself. Please help as many of the poorer people as you can, Bessie, and you mustn't say where the money came from. Not a word, please, even to Mrs Wells and Mrs Gordon. Oh, you can tell them I paid for their children's presents as a thank you for lighting my fire every night and leaving the house neat and tidy, but nothing else.'

'I feel as though it's Christmas Eve, and Father Christmas has just come down the chimney.' Bessie grinned. 'I'll really get a kick out of buying shoes for those children at the top end, because when I was going to school I remember a lad in our school coming barefoot, and the other kids didn't half make fun of him. I can still remember the look of shame on his face. But he had someone come along like your Philip has, only his benefactor was one of the teachers. And she didn't make a show of him by giving them to him in front of the class, she took them to his home. I can still see that lad's face when he came to school the next day, he didn't half swank. He walked across that playground as though he was ten foot tall.'

'You're a good woman, Bessie, and it's a pity I didn't have the sense to see that years ago. We could have been friends. I'm sorry I won't be able to help you with buying the presents, but I will help you wrap them up when Amelia's not around. And tomorrow I will tell Philip how his money is to be spent. He will be really pleased, he's quite tender-hearted.'

Bessie was beginning to grow excited. 'He has been very good, and yer can thank him from me. With this money, I can help so many people in the street who are on their uppers. I'll make a list of names and presents. He has a right to know where his much-appreciated money has gone. There's not many people give this much away, I'll bet. He must be a very special man.'

'Oh, he is, Bessie, a very special man indeed.' Evelyn pushed herself to her feet. She didn't want to talk about Philip for she was in danger of crying. 'I'll knock for Amelia, and then go home and sit on the couch with my feet up in front of the nice warm fire. I'll see you tomorrow night and you can tell me what thoughts you've had on how to make best use of the money. Perhaps you could write a list of those most in need? But of course you don't need me to tell you what to do, you are a very sensible lady.' She shivered as she opened the front door. 'Tell Mrs Wells I bless her every night when I open the door and see the flames flickering in the hearth. It makes that house feel like home, which it never has before.'

As soon as she'd closed the door on her neighbour, Bessie was so eager to start making a list she moved too fast and banged her shin on the sharp corner of the sideboard. 'You bloody nuisance,' she said, rubbing her shin, 'why don't yer get out of the way!' Then as she opened one of the drawers she burst out laughing. 'I'm talking to the ruddy sideboard now. It's the sight of so much money what's gone to me head.' She took a notebook from the drawer, then rummaged through the bits and bobs in there until she found a pencil. 'One of these days I'll get down to cleaning the drawers out, I should be ashamed of meself.'

The fireside chair was pulled closer to the hearth and Betty sank back, telling herself she felt like the Man Who Broke The Bank At Monte Carlo. Then she hugged herself before licking the pencil, hand poised ready to start writing. 'Now, let me see,' she said aloud, 'I can think of four families at the top who badly need help. Mrs Roseby . . . her husband's been out of work for ages, and the whole family look half-starved. So it'll be shoes for the two boys, and if I can wangle it somehow and she won't wonder where it's coming from, I'll make them a box of food up for Christmas. And the same goes for the Summerhill family, father out of work and a boy and a girl needing shoes. Then the Andersons and the McCarthys, all in the same boat. Shoes for the kids, and a box of food for Christmas. I'll think of some way to give it to them without it looking suspicious.'

Bessie licked the end of the pencil again and began to write. The names of the families went in a column at one side of the page, and she jotted down all that they needed beside these entries. That was the worst off accounted for. There were others who could do with help, but she wanted to do the job properly, and take her time. She looked up at the ceiling, hoping for help from above. 'I could sit here all night staring at this ruddy book, but that wouldn't get me anywhere. So here goes, I'll try and price them. Secondhand shoes from the market, in good nick, would cost between a shilling and two bob a pair, and there are eight kids so that could come to sixteen shillings at the most. I could make up a good food hamper for seven and six which would see them a few days over Christmas. So for those four families, it would come to, let me get me thinking cap on, two pounds, two shillings. That's not bad, and the families would be made up. It would make all the difference to them. I'd still have nearly eighteen pounds left . . . that's a lot of money.'

The notebook open on her lap, Bessie stared into the fire. She'd promised Evelyn not to tell anyone where the money came from, but couldn't get away with buying things for everyone without them wondering what she'd been up to. What was she supposed to say to her best mates? Rita and Aggie weren't soft, they wouldn't fall for any cock and bull story she came up with. Anyway, how could she carry boxes of food to the women at the top of the street without being seen? No, she couldn't do it on her own, she'd have to tell too many lies, and Him up there wouldn't take kindly to her telling fibs on His birthday. He'd know it was in a good cause because He knew everything, but still she wouldn't feel right about it. 'No, I'm going to have to let me mates in on it,' she told the poker in the companion set. 'I'll tell Evelyn tomorrow night, then have Rita and Aggie over on Saturday afternoon and explain everything to them.' She nodded to the hearth. 'They'll get the shock of their flaming lives. I can't wait to see the look on their faces. I bet Aggie will say they're fake notes, but seeing as she's never seen a five-pound note in her life, like meself, she wouldn't know the difference.'

Bessie put a hand in the pocket of her pinny and brought out the envelope. She fingered the notes. To look at, you wouldn't think just one of them was more than five men earned for a week of hard work. And the rent would have to come out of that, plus food and clothing, coal and gas. There wouldn't be any luxuries, not even enough to go to the pictures one night or a bag of sweets for the kids. But that was the way of the world. The rich got richer and the poor got poorer. But even though Evelyn's man friend was one of the rich ones, Bessie still thought he was a good man to want to help others. She wouldn't let him down. She'd use the money wisely, and make it stretch to help as many poor folk as she could. With Evelyn's blessing, she'd have her two mates to help her.

She was getting a headache now with the excitement and the calculations, so Bessie left her chair to put the money away. 'I'll have to find a safe place to hide it,' she told the sideboard, 'where can I put it?' As though she'd been given an answer, she nodded. 'Yeah, I'll do that, it's a good idea.' So she pulled a drawer out of the sideboard, pushed the envelope to the very back, then fitted the drawer back in. Then she rubbed her hands together as though dusting them, and went back to her chair with a smile of satisfaction on her face. All in all it had been, as Evelyn would say, a remarkably good day.

On the Friday evening, Milly walked over with Rita when she went to light the fire. This was their routine now, as she had the front-door key. She would sit on the couch and watch as the fire was lit, then wait with her Auntie Rita until the fire was burning brightly. But Milly was fidgety that Friday night, and her eyes kept going to the stairs. She'd always known about the trunk in her mother's bedroom, but had never been close to it for she was afraid her mother would catch her and give her a telling off. But she had always been curious about what would be inside, and had made up her mind that tonight she would try and sneak a peep in it.

'I'm just going upstairs to my bedroom for a few minutes, Auntie Rita, is that all right?'

'Of course it is, sunshine!' Rita was kneeling in front of the hearth placing the sticks of wood carefully in a criss-cross pattern on top of the screwed-up pieces of newspaper. 'It's your home, yer can do as yer like.'

'I won't be long, call me if you need anything.' Milly took the stairs two at a time, but hesitated outside her mother's room. It had always been out of bounds to her although she could never understand why. There was nothing in there she could break; besides she was always very careful and never broke anything. And she was only going to look anyway!

She tip-toed across the room and stood in front of the trunk. It looks very old, she thought, I bet it's a hundred years old. It looked as though it was locked, for there was a big rusty bar coming down from the lid, and it had a slit in it which fitted over a rusty ring in the front of the trunk. Milly wasn't expecting to be able to open it, but when she played with the bar, it came out of the ring and dangled between her fingers. Afraid she'd done something wrong, and her mother would know she'd been in her bedroom, she let the bar fall. But it didn't fall back into the ring, it rested on top. And this was too much of a temptation for the young girl. She gently lifted the lid.

There wasn't much light in the bedroom for it started to get dark early these nights, and Milly couldn't hold the heavy lid up and at the same time have a proper look at what was inside. With her free hand, she touched something, and after feeling it carefully, knew it was a big hat. Then her hand fumbled around and she could feel feathers. Not just one or two feathers, but a long string of them. They felt lovely. She wanted to pull it out and see what it was, but was afraid her mother would know if anything had moved. And then the matter was decided for her.

'Are yer coming down now, Milly?' Rita shouted from the bottom of the staircase. 'The fire is lit and the guard in front. Let's go to mine and have a hot cup of tea.'

Milly closed the lid very softly, put the bar back in the ring, then tip-toed on to the landing. 'Coming, Auntie Rita! I'll bring Daisy over with me.'

'On yer own head be it, sunshine, 'cos yer know what our Billy's like for pulling yer leg.'

'I'm not coming to play with him, I'm coming to play with Jack. So your Billy can take a running jump. Anyway, I haven't got dirty knees like him, and I'll tell him so.'

Rita grinned. She was becoming very fond of this girl, and was surprised at her spirit. She always appeared to be shy, and quiet, but she could certainly hold her own if anyone rubbed her up the wrong way. And that someone was usually Billy, who thought girls were nothing but a ruddy nuisance. There was a young girl lived a few doors away, Polly, who dogged his footsteps everywhere he went. No matter how much he shouted at her, and told her to vamoose, she was never far behind him. When Rita pulled his leg about it, he swore he'd never have a girl friend, and he'd never get married. He was going to stay at home with his mam, 'cos she was the only one who didn't talk the ear off you. Poor Polly. According to Billy she was as thick as two short planks. When she told him, truthfully, that she'd come second in class, he'd snorted and told her not to tell so many lies.

Rita let Milly pull the front door behind her, for she knew it made the girl feel important. Also because she guessed Evelyn had given strict instructions that she must never let anyone be alone in the house, but must stay with them.

Sure enough, there was Billy kneeling in the gutter with his mate Tommo. The concentration on both faces was enough to bring a smile to Rita's face. Anyone would think there was a lot of money riding on who won this game of marbles for neither boy lifted his head, afraid the other would cheat.

'I'm making a pot of tea, son,' Rita said, 'are yer coming in for one?'

His eyes fixed on a blue and white glass marble, Billy said, 'I'll come in when this games's over, Mam, I'm winning right now.'

'You flippin' fibber!' Tommo actually took his eyes off the prized marble, he was so angry. His mate was showing off because he didn't like Milly, but Tommo had a mind of his own and thought she was nice. 'I'm a game ahead of him, Mrs Wells, he's only saying that to show off. If I win this shot, that marble will be going in my pocket and coming home with me.'

'Take no notice of him, Mam, it's him what's showing off 'cos yer've got a girl with yer. The daft beggar always does the same thing.'

'I'll thump yer if yer say that again,' said a very vexed Tommo. 'The trouble with you is ye're not a good sport. Yer can't stand losing, and ye're like a big soft baby.'

Milly thought that was a very good description, she couldn't have done better herself. Her infectious laughter filled the air. It also fuelled Billy's embarrassment. 'Take her in the house, Mam,' he growled, 'she's spoiling our game. And I won't bother with a cup of tea, I'll wait until the nuisance has gone over to Auntie Bessie's. If I lose this game, it'll be her fault for putting me off.'

Milly tugged on Rita's arm. 'Come on, Auntie Rita, let's leave the baby alone before he starts crying. He'll blame us if he loses. Not like your Jack, he's a good sport. I bet we won't hear him moaning when I win the game of Snakes and Ladders we're going to have.'

Rita chuckled as she followed Milly up the steps. This was one little lady who wouldn't be pushed around. Perhaps her mother's strictness with her would pay dividends in the end. Or was the change due to someone else? The girl had certainly come out of her shell since she'd been coming to Bessie's. That's what a little warmth and love did for you, it gave you confidence.

Chapter Twenty-Two

Bessie came home from work on the Saturday at one o'clock, and spent the next hour and a half drumming it in to herself that she had to put her foot down and be firm. Never mind what reasons Evelyn came up with, they had to be brushed aside. But being firm in your head, and full of good intentions was a different kettle of fish to being as firm when the time came to face your problem. When a knock heralded the arrival of her neighbour and her daughter, Bessie's heart did a double somersault as she went to open the door.

However, part of her problem was solved by young Jack Wells, who was standing outside his house, opposite, learning against the wall. He waved to Milly, and called, 'Can yer come over for a game of Snakes and Ladders, Mill— er, Amelia?'

Evelyn shook her head and was about to push Milly up the step when Bessie barred her path. 'Let her go over to Mrs Wells' for half an hour. I want to have a few words with you and I'm sure Amelia would be bored stiff.' The look in her eyes told her neighbour it was a matter of importance.

'You may go over, Amelia,' Evelyn told her daughter. 'But you must come back here when Miss Maudsley tells you to. And mind you don't lose the key or I shall be very annoyed.'

Milly was off like a shot. Last night, for the first time, Jack had beaten her at the game, and she intended to get her own back. 'Yes, Mother,' she called over her shoulder, 'I won't forget to do as I'm told.'

Bessie waved to the couch. 'I won't keep you long, I know

yer'll be eager to be off to yer friend's, but I've been thinking things over very carefully, and although I'm more than delighted with the money given so generously by your man friend, I don't feel easy in my mind that you and me are the only ones who know about it. No matter which way I look at it, I can't give food and clothes out like Lady Bountiful without it looking suspicious. Mrs Wells and Mrs Gordon aren't stupid, they'll know I'm not paying for everything out of me own pocket. And being me mates, they're bound to ask where the money is coming from. If it was only a few bob then it would be fine, but it's twenty pounds and that's a fortune to anyone living in this street.'

'But I was under the impression you were really pleased, and knew who you could best help with the money,' Evelyn said. 'Why have you changed your mind?'

'Oh, I haven't changed me mind, Evelyn, or me gratitude, but to do it alone would be impossible. I've made a list of all those I would love to help, and I can show it to yer if yer like. The kids going round barefoot would get shoes, and the poor families would get boxes of food to see them over Christmas. I know you and your generous friend would be more than satisfied that the money was being used to help those most in need. But I can't go round giving boxes of food out without someone asking where the hell I got the money from. Besides all that, it would be physically impossible for me to do it all on me own. So I'm going to ask yer to let Mrs Wells and Mrs Gordon in on the secret. I promise that they will not be told any more than they need to know, and I swear on my life that yer can trust them. Like meself, they may be rough and ready, but they're as honest as the day is long. With their help, it would be so much easier. Any shoes and clothes we get from the market, we can say their children have grown out of or we got them off a relative. And boxes of food I can explain away by saying I'd heard a Good Samaritan was helping the poor, and I'd been to see him. People will be so happy to have food for the table over Christmas, they're not going to ask too many questions. Not when there'll be three of us giving the hampers out.'

Evelyn heard her out, then nodded. 'Of course it would be too much for you to do on your own, I should have realised that. Please ask your friends for help, but I beg you to protect my privacy.'

Bessie nodded her head vigorously. 'I would never discuss your affairs, you need have no fear of that.' She put her hand under the cushion of her chair and brought out the notebook. 'I know you are eager to be on yer way, but just cast yer eyes over the list and yer'll see how many I have down as being in desperate straits. Every family on that list is worthy of help, but a few more so than others. There are women in this street walking round with hardly any flesh on their bones, 'cos whatever money they get they spend on food for their kids. I promise you they will be blessing you and your friend when they sit down to a proper meal on Christmas Day.'

Evelyn studied the list. She'd been shaken by Bessie's words, and would repeat them to Philip. There were no addresses in the notebook, so she wouldn't be giving herself away by showing him the list. 'Would you let me take this to show to my friend? I'm sure he would be very touched by what you intend doing with the money.'

'Ah, not today, Evelyn, it took me ages to go through this street from top to bottom, both sides, and write the names down. I could write it out again tonight, and give it to yer tomorrow, would that do?'

'Yes, it would.' Evelyn got to her feet. 'Thank you for showing it to me, Bessie, I'm sure you and your friends will do a good job. I would give you a donation myself if I was able, but unfortunately I am not in a position to do so.'

Bessie went to the door with her. 'Yer've done enough, Evelyn! If it weren't for you, we wouldn't have this money. It's me what should be thanking you, not the other way round.'

She watched her neighbour walk up the street, her back ramrod straight. What a difference there was in her over the last month or so. Just went to show what love can do.

Bessie shivered with the cold, rubbed her arms briskly, then went inside and closed the front door. When she'd had a warm through, she'd nip over and ask Rita to come over for an hour tonight, and bring Aggie with her. Oh, and because little pigs have big ears, it would have to be an early night in bed for Milly. Not that the girl would mind, she was quite happy to go to bed at half-eight as long as Daisy went with her.

Milly had something on her mind and lost the game because she wasn't concentrating. This made Jack whoop for joy. 'That's two games I'm up on yer. D'yer want another game, yer might get lucky next time?'

'No, I'd better go over to Auntie Bessie's, she'll be lonely without me.' Milly pushed the chair back under the table then went out to the kitchen where Rita was rinsing some clothes through. 'I'm going in my house for a minute, Auntie Rita, before I go to Auntie Bessie's. Is that all right?'

'Of course, sunshine, yer don't have to ask me. Yer mam's let yer have a key, so she must think ye're old enough to look after yerself.'

'I only want to fetch something, then I'll go to Auntie Bessie's.'

'I'll come with yer, if yer like?' Jack offered. 'In case yer might get frightened being in the house on yer own.'

Rita walked through from the kitchen, wiping her hands on a small piece of towelling. 'No, yer can't go with her! Anyway, why should she be frightened in her own house? Let Milly do what she wants, and you go and play with the lads.'

As Milly skipped across the cobbles, in her mind's eye she could see the trunk. She couldn't wait to have a proper look inside. It wasn't dark yet so she would be able to see instead of feeling. Once inside the house, she made sure the door was firmly closed before tripping up the stairs and turning into her mother's room.

Minutes ticked by as Milly gazed at the trunk, willing herself to open it. But she was nervous after letting her imagination run away with itself. It was very old, perhaps a hundred years or more, and there might be nasty things inside, like mice or creepy-crawlies. Then she began to tell herself off for being stupid. Of course there wouldn't be nasty things inside, her mother wouldn't allow that. And besides, the hat and the feathers she'd felt the other day were real enough, and it was the feathers in particular she wanted to see. So with her lips clamped together and a look of determination on her pretty young face, she lifted the lid before she lost her nerve. She let it fall back against the wall, and this gave her the freedom to use both hands in her search for the feathers. She found the hat which was right on top. Looking mischievous she placed it on her head. It was a very grand hat, in dark blue, with a wide brim trimmed with a lighter shade of blue lace. But as it was too large for her, it came down over her forehead and her eyes rolled upwards, filled with laughter. Afraid to make a sound in case Auntie Bessie would hear her, she covered her mouth with one hand. She'd bet her auntie would love to see her, but best not to let her in case it got back to her mother.

The next item Milly picked out was the feather boa, and she was filled with delight when she put it around her neck and felt the soft feathers next to her skin. The girl began to think how lovely her mother must have looked in this finery. Milly had only come to the house with the intention of looking for the feathers, wanting to know what they were. Now the temptation to look further was so great she couldn't ignore it. So with the hat falling over her eyes, and the feather boa hanging over her thin shoulders, she began to explore the contents of the trunk. But she was very careful to remember exactly where each item was when she'd first opened it. A satin dress caught her eye and she took it out for a better look. She knew it wasn't an everyday dress, for it was in blue satin, had no sleeves and was cut very low at the back and front. Milly rubbed the satin against her cheek and thought how lovely it would be to wear a dress like this one. With the feather boa and the hat, of course. And the shoes she'd seen pushed down the side of the clothes. They were in silver, with narrow straps and heels higher than she'd ever seen before.

More curious than ever now, Milly hung the dress over the side of the trunk and delved down the side of the clothes to find the shoes she'd spotted. When I'm older, I'll wear shoes like this, she told herself. And satin dresses, hats like this one, and a scarf made of feathers. Then a mischievous little voice in her head asked why she didn't try them on? No one would see her, and she could put everything back the way it was. So she quickly took all her school clothes off except her vest, it was too cold to take that off. Five minutes later, with the dress trailing on the floor, the feathers on the boa tickling her nose, and wobbling on the high heels, she stumbled her way over to look in the wardrobe mirror, and smiled at what she saw. Why had her mother never shown her the contents of this trunk, and why had she never worn them? To a child's mind, it seemed a shame to have such beautiful clothes and never put them on. She wasn't to know there were many reasons why the clothes had been locked away for the last eight years.

'I'll go and show Auntie Bessie before I take them off,' Milly told her reflection in the mirror. 'I bet she'll get a surprise. It's only next door and no one will see me.' Then she remembered something else she'd seen in the trunk, next to the shoes. It was a silver evening bag, although the girl wasn't to know that. To her it was just a pretty handbag which matched the shoes.

Lifting the dress, Milly turned away from the mirror, forgetting the shoes were miles too big for her. As she turned, the high heels gave way and she would have fallen if the bed hadn't been there. 'Oh, dear,' she said aloud, 'I'll never get down the stairs in them, I'll fall and break my neck. I'll carry them until I get to the front door, then I'll put them on.' She was carrying the shoes by the straps, with the silver handle of the bag over her wrist and her other hand holding the dress off the floor. She got on to the landing when she suddenly remembered the front door key. She thanked her lucky stars for if she locked herself out she wouldn't be able to get back in until her mother came home, and then there'd be ructions.

Jack had been waiting for Milly to come out. When he saw her hanging on to the door for support, with this large hat on her head, a dress that was now trailing on the ground and a feather thing around her neck, his jaw dropped open while his eyes couldn't believe what he was seeing. 'Eh, Billy, look at the state of Milly.'

Billy and his mate thought they were seeing things. Then when they realised there was nothing wrong with their eyes, they started to point at the girl and laugh. This upset Jack who gave his brother a shove. 'Don't you be laughing at Milly, she looks lovely.'

'Ay, who d'yer think ye're pushing!' Billy gave his brother such a push, Jack ended up on his backside. He scrambled to his feet, with fists flying, and landed a couple of blows on his brother's back before Billy knew what hit him. Then a couple of boys from up the street came to see what was going on, and those who laughed and poked fun at Milly were set upon by a very irate Jack. Now Billy didn't like being hit by his brother, but he wasn't going to stand by and watch Jack being thumped by two bigger boys. So he gave his mate Tommo the eye, and they both got stuck in.

While all this was going on, Milly was standing with her eyes popping at the scene before her. Boys fighting, and girls laughing and making fun of her. But not all the girls were laughing. A couple came over to her and stood admiring the dress, the feather boa, the shoes and handbag. 'Are these yer mam's clothes?' One girl was fingering the satin. Neither she nor any of her friends had ever seen such a dress, although it was miles too big for Milly and they didn't think you were supposed to wear a vest with it. Still, it must have cost a lot of money. And the feather boa was given the thumbs up by all the girls. They swore they'd have one when they grew up and started work. Milly was wishing they would go away, in case they left fingermarks on the dress. But this was the first time any of them had spoken to her and she wanted to be friends with them. Her biggest worry was the boys fighting, though. She knew it was all her fault, but couldn't really understand why. She hadn't done anything wrong, hadn't said anything to start a fight. She hoped Auntie Bessie wouldn't be upset by it all.

Rita was in the kitchen and could hear a racket going on in the street, but Reg was sitting in the living room and she was sure he'd have said if anything untoward was going on. After a few minutes, she put the potato knife down and walked through. She had to make sure her two boys were all right. 'Are yer deaf?' she asked her husband, half-asleep in the chair by the fire. 'Can't yer hear the rumpus?' She didn't wait for an answer, it would be a waste of time. Reg had been working all morning and had probably dropped off in the warmth from the fire. Men didn't half have an easy life.

When Rita opened the front door the first thing she saw was a gang of lads beating hell out of each other. And two of them were her sons! 'Ay, come on, break it up now.' She collared Billy, who was the nearest. 'What started this off, yer stupid nit? Yer should have more sense at your age.'

Rubbing his chin, he growled, 'It all started because of the soft girl across the street. Just look at the state of her, she's barmy!'

Rita glanced across to the group of girls on the opposite

pavement. One of them moved, and she saw Milly in all her glory. 'Oh, dear God in heaven, what does she think she's doing!' The girls heard Rita and scarpered quick, in case they got the blame for the boys fighting. By the time she'd crossed the cobbles, they were hot-footing it home. 'Milly, sunshine, where did yer get those clothes?'

'None of this is my fault, Auntie Rita, I didn't say anything. In fact, I never opened my mouth to anyone. The first I saw was Jack and Billy fighting. That wouldn't be Jack's fault, it would have been Billy that started it. And it wasn't anything I said, for I haven't said a word to either of them. I was just going to Auntie Bessie's to let her see me dressed up, and then some boys and girls were laughing at me, and the fighting started.'

'I thought yer were in Bessie's,' Rita said. 'Have you been in yer own house since yer left ours?'

Milly was feeling guilty now. But she wasn't going to lie, her teacher was always telling the class that it was a sin to tell lies. 'Yes, I have, Auntie Rita. I didn't mean to stay so long, but I was looking at some of my mother's clothes and thought I would put some of them on and show Auntie Bessie how I looked. I thought she would enjoy seeing me all dressed up. But I didn't get the chance to get as far as her house before the boys started fighting. I don't mind being laughed at because I know I look funny in my mother's clothes, but why the boys started to fight, I don't know. Boys are silly, aren't they?'

Rita felt like hugging her. In fact she wished they owned one of those camera things what took photographs. It would be lovely to have a photograph of Milly as she was now, with a satin dress trailing the ground, heels so high she was swaying to balance herself, a hat that must have been bought for a wedding, and a feather boa. She looked funny, but at the same time vulnerable and lovable. 'I'm surprised Bessie hasn't been out, unless she's in the kitchen and didn't hear the commotion. But I'll tell yer what we'll do, if yer want to surprise her. You stand behind me while I knock on the door, and when she opens it, I'll step aside. Just imagine the surprise on her face. Would you like that, sunshine?'

'She won't be upset with me, will she?'

'Bessie Maudsley be up upset with you? Never in a million years, sunshine, 'cos she loves the bones of yer.'

'Will you let me link you, Auntie Rita, because I can't walk in these shoes. I'll topple over if I try.'

Rita held out her arm. 'Stick yer arm in, sunshine, and I'll help yer on yer way.'

Bessie smiled when she saw Rita. 'Ooh, yer've saved me a journey, I was coming over to your house later.'

Rita stepped aside. 'I've brought someone to see yer.'

Thinking it was all a joke that Rita was part of, and that she would be expected to show surprise, Bessie lifted her hands and cried, 'Oh, my, who is this little lady?'

Milly's green eyes shone. 'It's me, Auntie Bessie, can't you tell?'

Bessie pretended to fall back in astonishment. 'Well, I never! I'd have passed yer in the street and not known it was my little sweetheart.' She looked over the girl's head to Rita. 'Where did yer get the clothes from?'

'Ah, well, I think Milly will have to explain that. And I'll come in with her 'cos we'll both catch pneumonia if we stand out in this cold much longer.' Rita winked. 'Will yer give Milly a hand, 'cos she's not very safe on her feet?'

As soon as she was in the living room, Milly kicked the shoes off and made straight for the warmth of the fire. She wasn't looking forward to telling her Auntie Bessie what she'd been up to. It wouldn't have been so bad if the boys hadn't seen her and started fighting, then nobody would have known. She could have had a laugh with the woman she had grown to love, then put the clothes back and no one would have been any the wiser.

Rita had been replying to Bessie's silent questions by pulling faces and rolling her eyes. She wasn't sure herself how Milly had got hold of the clothes, so couldn't have told her mate anything even if she'd wanted to. Then, knowing the girl was playing for time by standing warming her hands by the fire, she mouthed, 'Ask her!'

Bessie nodded before saying, 'Sit down, Rita, and take the weight off yer feet. I'm sure Milly will solve the mystery of the clothes when she's ready.'

'Oh, there's no mystery, Auntie Bessie.' Milly turned to face the two women. 'They belong to my mother. I've been naughty, though, because I didn't ask her if I could wear them.' She lowered her head so she didn't have to face them. 'I've been naughty two times over, because the clothes were in a big trunk in Mother's bedroom, and I only knew they were there, yesterday. I knew the trunk was there, 'cos you can't help but see it, but I never knew what was in it, and I didn't like asking my mother. As far as I know, she never opens it.'

'Oh, it was very naughty of yer to look in the trunk without asking your mother. There may be things in there that are important to her, like memories from the past.'

'I only wanted to put these things on to show you.' Milly fingered the dress and the feather boa. 'I was going to be very careful with them, and put them back exactly as I found them.' She was close to tears now, couldn't bear to think her actions had upset her Auntie Bessie. 'If the boys hadn't started making fun of me, and then fighting, I would have got here without causing any trouble. I'm sorry I've been naughty, Auntie Bessie, I won't ever do anything like this again.' Then, her lips quivering and eyes wet with tears, she asked, 'You won't stop me from coming here, will you?'

That did it for Bessie. She pushed herself off the couch and put her arms around the trembling girl. 'Of course not, sweet-heart, why would I do that? I know yer didn't mean any harm, even though, as I've said, yer shouldn't have touched anything in the trunk without asking yer mother first. But everyone does things they shouldn't when they're young. I was no angel meself at your age.'

'Me neither!' Rita didn't like seeing the girl so upset. What she did was nothing compared with what her two sons got up to. 'And our Billy and Jack get in more trouble in one day than you will in a lifetime, sunshine. They'll both get a thick ear when I get home, fighting in the street like hooligans.'

Milly was biting on her bottom lip, for laughter was fighting with the tears, and she didn't know whether this would be the proper time to laugh. But it came out regardless. Peals of infectious laughter filled the room. 'It was funny, wasn't it? I was standing there, holding the wall so I wouldn't fall over in those shoes and at the same time trying to hold the dress up off the ground, when the next thing I know there's about six boys pushing and punching each other.' But the girl never forgot where her loyalty lay. 'It wasn't Jack that started it, though, Auntie Rita, I'm sure it wasn't.'

Rita chortled. 'Yer've got a soft spot for our Jack, haven't yer, sunshine? And he's got one for you, 'cos *that's* how the ruddy fight started. From what little I've heard, our Billy was laughing at yer, with Tommo, and Jack thumped him one. It started off with just the two of them, then before they knew it, a gang had joined in. But I'll get it all out of them later and let yer know the ins and outs. Anyway, right now, don't yer think yer should take those clothes off before yer do any harm? If yer rip that dress then yer mother will be very annoyed.'

A smile was lurking behind Milly's eyes when she said, 'I can't take them off because I've left my clothes on top of my mother's bed. I thought I would only be away for about five minutes, and then I was going to sneak back home, change into my own clothes and put Mother's things away neatly, so she wouldn't know I've been naughty.'

337

Bessie held out her hand. 'Let me have the key, sweetheart, and I'll go and pick up your clothes. Then, when yer're dressed, and yer look like my little sweetheart once again, I'll help yer with those very posh clothes ye're wearing. Yer could pass for a proper princess in them, and we'd all have to curtsey to yer.'

In her auntie's good books once again, Milly regained her sense of fun. She had a very vivid imagination and it was up and running now. With green eyes shining with devilment, and her cheeky grin, she held up the back of her hand to Bessie. 'You needn't curtsey, Auntie Bessie, because you are my friend. You may kiss my hand instead.'

'Oh, aye, Miss High and Mighty.' Rita pretended to get on her high horse. 'If Bessie is yer friend, what does that make me? An enemy?'

'Oh, no, Auntie Rita, you're not an enemy.' Her childish laughter ricocheted off the walls and brought a smile to the faces of the two women. 'You may kiss my other hand.'

'While you two are deciding how to address each other, I'll nip next door and get yer clothes, sweetheart, so hand the key over.' Bessie lifted her coat down from a hook. 'It'll be freezing in there with no fire lit, and I don't want to come down with a cold. Keep Milly company till I get back, Rita, there's a pal.'

'Don't be long, Bessie, 'cos my feller will be wondering where I've got to. Unless he's still asleep, of course, and that wouldn't surprised me. Stick him in front of a fire and he's away in no time. The only thing that would wake him would be his tummy, and I imagine it'll be starting to rumble any minute now. So get yer skates on, kiddo.'

Bessie was in and out of her neighbour's house in less than a minute. She grabbed Milly's school clothes off the bed, ran down the stairs and out of the front door. She didn't give a second glance to anything in the bedroom or living room, feeling as though she was trespassing. She wouldn't like a stranger wandering around her house, and was sure Evelyn wouldn't either.

'Blinking heck, that was fast!' Rita said. 'I asked yer to be quick, but I didn't tell yer to fly.' She stood up from the couch. 'I'll get over to my feller. Probably see yer tomorrow, Bessie.'

Her mate tried to send a message with her eyes. 'Oh, I was going to ask you and Aggie to come over tonight, I've something to tell yer.'

'Ooh,' said Rita, who had received the message, 'what time would yer like us?'

Bessie rolled her eyes towards Milly. 'Not until about half-eight, if yer get me meaning.'

'I'll be glad to get out of the house for an hour,' Rita said. 'Me and Aggie will be over around eight-thirty then, sunshine. Ta-ra for now. Ta-ra, Milly.'

Chapter Twenty-Three

'I think it's time yer were in bed, sweetheart,' Bessie said, 'it's half-past eight and yer know I'm expecting me friends.'

'Ah, can't I wait up and see them?' Milly asked, running a comb through the doll's hair. 'I promise to go to bed when I've had a goodnight kiss from them.'

'That won't be long, 'cos they're on their way.' Bessie said, making for the door. 'I can hear Aggie's voice. It's like a foghorn, I bet the whole street can hear her.'

'I heard that!' Aggie said when Bessie opened the door. 'If I was the kind what got upset easy, I'd take the huff over that. A foghorn indeed, I'm surprised at yer. I'll have yer know I can beat a foghorn any day. If I put me mind to it, or someone says something what they shouldn't, then I bet they can hear me down at the docks, never mind just in this street.'

Rita let her neighbour go up the steps first, then jerked her head at Bessie. 'Fancy bragging about having a voice like a foghorn. Honest to God, she's as common as muck and yer can't take her anywhere for fear she makes a show of yer.'

Aggie took her coat off, threw it over the back of a chair, then winked at Milly. 'Hark at her, queen, yer'd think she was born with a silver spoon in her gob to hear her talking. But it's all put on, 'cos she forgets I live next door and can hear everything what goes on in her house. And although she's me mate, and I shouldn't be snitching on her, I'll let yer into a secret 'cos I know yer'll keep it to yerself. Sometimes her language is so bad I have to cover me ears. And because I haven't got no cotton wool, I make the kids put their fingers in their ears until the worst of it is over. Anyone who didn't know her would think she was as innocent as a new-born babe, but yer have to live next to her to know what she's really like.'

'Just listen to her,' Rita said, handing her coat to Bessie, 'talk about the kettle calling the pot black isn't in it. Everyone knows she invented most of the swear words, half of which I don't even know the meaning of. When she takes off in one of her tempers, I go down the yard and sit on the lavvy until I think she's finished, 'cos I don't know where to put me face with my feller sitting there listening.'

'She's got no flaming manners, either,' Bessie said, her hands on her hips and her jaw set. 'Just look at the way she's flung her coat down. Ye're not at home now, Aggie Gordon, so yer can just hang that coat up in a proper manner.'

Aggie gave Milly a very exaggerated wink as she picked up the offending coat. 'Miserable buggers, if they smiled their faces would crack. But I'd better hang me ruddy coat up or I'll be the talk of every wash-house from here to the Pier Head.'

Milly was rocking with laughter as Aggie ambled out to the narrow hall where the hooks were. She had never known anyone like these three women in all her life. She knew her mother would disapprove of their bad language, but coming from them it was funny and you couldn't help but laugh at the expressions on their faces. Her life had changed so much since the day her mother had asked Miss Maudsley if she would mind her. It was the luckiest day of Milly's life, for she had made new friends that day and found love and happiness with the woman who was now no longer Miss Maudsley but her Auntie Bessie.

When her two mates were settled, Bessie looked at Milly meaningfully. 'Get yer kisses, sweetheart, and then up the wooden stairs to dreamland. Me and me mates want to sit and have a good old chinwag.'

Milly pouted. 'Can't I stay up for a while? Not even if I promise not to listen?'

'God bless yer cotton socks, sweetheart, but it would be really hard not to listen with us three women talking fifteen to the dozen.' Bessie held her arms wide and the girl ran into them. She hugged her tight, then said, 'The reason I want yer to go to bed is that me and me mates are going to be talking about the Christmas party we're hoping to have. We don't want any of the children to know what's happening, we want it to be a surprise. And it wouldn't be fair to the other kids if you knew and they didn't. You can understand that, can't yer, sweetheart?'

Milly moved away a little so she could look up into Bessie's face. 'Will I be coming to your party, Auntie Bessie?'

I don't want her to go to bed feeling sad, Bessie thought, so I'll tell a little lie, it won't do no harm. 'I'm not sure yet, me and yer mother haven't discussed Christmas. But I think I can safely say I'll be able to get around her. Perhaps her friend is having a party, most people do, so when I ask if yer can stay here, I'm pretty sure she'll be agreeable.'

She was rewarded by a big hug, and a muffled voice saying, 'I love you, Auntie Bessie, more than anything in the whole world.'

'After yer mother, sweetheart, for she must always come first.'

Green eyes gazed up at her. 'I do love my mother, Auntie Bessie, but I love you too.'

'And I love you,' Bessie told her as she gently pushed her away. 'Now give my guests a big kiss, and then take Daisy to bed with you, there's a good girl.'

Kisses and hugs exchanged, and then Milly climbed the stairs with her beloved doll. It was only when they were sure she was in her bedroom, out of earshot, that Rita said, 'It's to be hoped that kid's mother doesn't take her away to live somewhere else 'cos she wouldn't half fret. It would break her heart if she lost you.'

'D'yer think I don't worry meself sick about that? Every night when I go to bed it plays on me mind so much I lie awake for hours. But last night I made an early New Year's resolution, and that was not to worry about something I can't change. So I'm going to enjoy Milly for as long as I can, and pray to God she is never taken far from me.' Bessie bustled towards the kitchen. 'I'll make us a pot of tea, and yer'll be glad to know I've mugged you and meself to a cream slice. I didn't leave Milly out, she had hers with her tea.'

'What's the celebration,' Rita called, 'it's not yer birthday, is it?'

'I'm not telling yer what the celebration is until the tea's made and we can sit round the table while I tell yer me news. And yer'll be bowled over when I tell yer, but that's all ye're getting until we're all sitting comfortably.'

'In the name of God, Bessie, this is bleeding torture, this is.' Aggie plonked her cup down so hard on the saucer she even frightened herself in case she'd cracked it. Bessie was fussy about her crockery, didn't like cracks or chips in anything. And she never gave yer a drink in a cup with no handle. 'It's all right, queen, I haven't put no crack in it. But if yer don't tell us quick what yer news is, I might just break this over yer bleeding head.'

'I'm with Aggie on this,' Rita told her. 'I don't know what ye're keeping us in suspense for, 'cos if yer don't tell us soon we'll both have heart attacks.'

Bessie leaned forward and put both elbows on the table. Oh, how she was going to enjoy seeing their faces. This sort of luck didn't come their way very often. 'Well, how would yer like to be Father Christmas's helpers for two days before Christmas?' She laughed when she saw their blank expressions. 'I'm not pulling yer legs, I wouldn't do that to yer, not over something that will make a lot of poor people happy.'

'Yer'll have to tell us more than that, sunshine. Explain to us in simple terms – what and where, when and how?'

'Now I know we've all called Mrs Sinclair fit to burn over the years, but for the last few months she's been different, changed like. She's friendly with me and doesn't talk down to me like she used to. And although it's not her herself who's being generous over Christmas, 'cos she's not well off, it's through her in a roundabout way.' Bessie pushed her chair back. 'Hang on until I get me notebook out, and I'll show yer how I want us, me and you two, to give certain things to certain people through the goodwill of someone that Mrs Sinclair knows. He's very rich apparently, and wants to help some poor people who are in dire straits. When Evelyn heard this, she remembered the kids in the street who have no shoes, and those families where the father is out of work. She told this person she knew of people in need, and that's how come we are going to be Father Christmas's little helpers.'

Bessie took the notebook out of the sideboard drawer and threw it on the table. Then she took the whole drawer out and stretched her arm to reach the envelope at the back. She threw this on the table, too, so she could manoeuvre the drawer back in place. Then she sat down with the notebook and envelope in front of her. 'I've made a list of the families I think are worst off, so will you and Aggie look at it and see if I've left anyone off?'

Rita pulled her chair nearer to Aggie's, their faces expressing their doubt that Bessie could possibly have enough money to do all the things she said she would. It would cost a fortune, and no one in their right mind gave a fortune to strangers. After a quick glance down the list, Aggie growled, 'I see yer haven't put me or Rita on the list. Is that because yer think we're rolling in money?'

'Don't start crying before ye're hurt, Aggie, just hold yer horses until we sort that list out. Can yer think of anyone I haven't got down, Rita?'

'Yeah, old Mrs Ponsonby, she's probably worse off than anyone in the street. She's still scrubbing steps, at her age, just to earn enough to pay the rent and keep the wolf from the door. She's had that coat she wears for at least ten years to my knowledge, and it's practically in tatters.' Rita ran her eyes down the page again. 'The money yer've got by each name will come to quite a sum. With the best will in the world, sunshine, yer'd never be able to cope with all this.' She waved the book before handing it back to Bessie. 'I bet if yer add it up, it would come to about six or seven pound, and no one is that generous with money.'

Bessie pushed the envelope over to her. 'I don't know the gentleman's name, so I can't tell yer, but take the money out of the envelope and yer'll see for yerself how generous he's been.'

Intrigued, Rita took the contents out of the envelope, Aggie's head on her shoulder. 'If yer got any closer, sunshine, yer'd be sitting on me ruddy knee! Move back a bit, will yer, and stop breathing down me ear.'

'I'm just as keen to see how much there is as you are, so don't be getting narky with me, queen, 'cos ye're not the only pebble on the beach.'

'It's a five-pound note.' Rita turned her head quickly and found herself rubbing noses with her mate. 'It's one of those five-pound notes what only the rich can afford. Ay, I've never had one of these in me hand before.'

'Let's have a feel.' Aggie went to snatch the note, so she could brag to her husband about it, and anyone else who would listen. Mind you, when Aggie spoke everyone listened, they were afraid not to. But Rita pulled her hand away quick. 'If ye're not careful, yer'll tear it, and then they won't take it off yer in the shops.'

'Open it up, Rita,' Bessie said, waiting with mounting excitement to see the look on their faces. 'Go on, it won't bite yer.'

Rita was very careful unfolding the thin white piece of paper which was more than her husband earned in a month. It had been folded four times to fit the envelope, and when she opened it up and saw there were four notes in all, the colour drained from her face. 'In the name of God, Bessie, I've never seen so much money in me life. There's twenty pound there!'

Aggie's mountainous bosom was hitched up, and her mouth was working but no sound was coming from her lips. She was dumbfounded. It was so unusual for Aggie to be lost for words, Bessie thought the shock might have been too much for her. 'Are yer all right, Aggie? Don't let it upset yer, it's only money.'

'Only money!' She croaked. 'Bleeding hell, queen, that's not only money, it's a ruddy fortune!'

'She's right, sunshine, it is a fortune. D'yer think it's true what Mrs Sinclair told yer, that it was given by a rich person to help the poor? There's nothing dodgy about it, is there?'

'Don't be daft, Rita,' Bessie tutted. 'How would she, or anyone else, get hold of dodgy money? No, it's all above board, I can assure yer, 'cos there's no way I'd get involved in anything that wasn't honest. There's twenty pound there, and your two names are not on the list because Mrs Sinclair told me she would like you two to have something for being so kind to her, and I've reckoned on five bob each for yer.'

Aggie's bust went back on the table and her voice was restored to normal. 'She didn't say that, did she? Ooh, er, after me calling her for all the stuck-up cows going. It just goes to show yer should never pull anyone to pieces 'cos yer might be wrong about them. D'yer hear that, Rita, we're not going to call Mrs Sinclair bad names in future.'

Rita looked at her mate in horror. 'Why, you cheeky monkey! It's you what's been calling her fit to burn since the day she moved into the street! I've told yer off about it time and time again, but yer wouldn't have it. May God forgive yer, that's all I can say.'

'Oh, He will, sunshine, 'cos He knows I've done nothing to

hurt her. I mean, a few words, even swear words, won't do her no harm, especially as she didn't hear them.'

'I don't know how yer can be so polished, Aggie Gordon,' Rita told her. 'And I don't know how yer keep expecting God to forgive yer for everything. Yer tell yer husband lies, and some of the swear words yer come out with would shame the devil. So if ye're expecting to go to heaven when yer die, yer can forget it 'cos yer stand no chance.'

Aggie began to laugh, and as her tummy lifted the table up, her bosom pressed it down again. 'He will if you and Bessie give me a good reference. Seeing as the pair of yer live like saints, I'm sure ye're very well thought of in heaven. So on your recommendation, St Peter will let me go through the pearly gates with yer.'

Bessie chuckled, 'I don't think much of the odds on that, sweetheart. Are yer expecting us all to die on the same day?'

'For heaven's sake, can't we talk about something more pleasant?' Rita gave her mate daggers. 'Here's us, sitting at the table with more money in front of us than we've ever seen in our lives before, and all you two can talk about is what's going to happen when we die! I think we should look after ourselves in that department, as long as we keep in mind that wicked people don't go to heaven no matter how holy their friends are.'

'Ooh, er.' Aggie's brows almost touched her hair-line. 'She's only had that money in her hand for five minutes, and already she's talking so bleeding far back yer can hardly hear her.'

'Stop larking about and let's get down to business,' Bessie said. 'How many names are on that list, Rita?'

'D'yer want me to count Aggie and meself, in, sunshine?'

Bessie nodded, 'Yes, go on.'

Rita's finger went down the names. 'There's fourteen here, and yer mustn't leave Mrs Ponsonby out because if this was my list she'd be on top of it.'

'Right, now I'll tell yer what I've got in mind. I'd like to have a party and invite all the kids in the street who won't be getting much in the way of presents at Christmas. Which means all the kids who are on that list. We'll never have this much money again, so let's give the kids the best Christmas they've ever had. What d'yer think?'

'I think the idea is wonderful, sunshine, and it would be marvellous. But where would yer have the party? Ye're talking about eighteen kids, and these houses weren't built to cater for that sort of number.'

'We can try, Rita,' Bessie said softly. 'Where there's a will, there a way. And I've set me heart on it now. I could move as much out of this room as possible, with the help of your men, and I'd have to borrow one of yer tables. It would be a squash, I know, but d'yer think the kids would worry? I bet most of them have never been to a party. They wouldn't care if they were standing on each other's heads.'

'Ye're dead right there, queen.' Aggie's chins were having a field day as she nodded her head. 'And I think the man who gave that money would feel the same. Some of the kids in this street have never had a cake, never mind been to a party. The poor buggers don't know what it is to have a farthing for sweets. So yer can count me in, queen, I'm all for it. And my feller will help with the table, and anything else yer want doing.'

'Yeah, the more I think about it, the more I agree,' Rita said. 'The five bob yer said I was going to get, well, I'd rather it went towards the party. I'd be in me element to see the kids with smiles on their faces. It's a very good idea, sunshine, and only you would have thought about helping others and leaving yerself out.'

'Oh, I'm not leaving meself out, sweetheart, how could yer think that? Won't I have all the kids here, and won't I be over the moon to see their faces when they see this room done up with paper decorations and balloons? That will be all the thanks I need. And when the party is over, and the kids have gone home, we can have a party for us grown-ups.' Bessie pulled the notebook towards her. 'I reckoned on twelve bob for the boys' shoes, and say seven and six for each hamper. So how much does that come to. Let's see, there's four five shillings in a pound, so say fifteen seven and sixes, how much does that come to?'

Aggie didn't even bother trying to figure that out. She could add two and two together, and that was her limit. So she sat and watched her mates counting on their fingers. 'As near as I can get without writing it down,' Rita said, 'is about six pound three shilling. But I must be wrong, it's bound to be more than that.'

'I get it near enough the same, Rita, so I'd better write it down and make sure.' Bessie licked the end of the stub of pencil and put a line under the fourth name. 'I'll split the list into fours, it'll be easier. Otherwise I might end up spending more than we've got, and then I'd feel a right nit.' So while her mates looked on, Bessie went over the sums four times to make sure. 'It's just over six pound, so we've got enough to give every name I've got down here an extra couple of bob so they can get coal in to last them over the holiday. Are yer both in agreement with that?'

'It's you what managed to get the money, queen, so it's up to you,' Aggie said. 'But I'll go along with yer, 'cos I'm over the bleeding moon. Just to see those poor lads having shoes on their feet, and the mothers having food for the table at Christmas, well, if I knew the man what gave the money, I'd shake the hand off him.'

'Then can I ask a big favour of you both?' Bessie waited until her mates gave her the nod, then said, 'Could yer find out what size shoes the lads take? Yer could knock tomorrow and pretend your lads have outgrown theirs and so have the lads of yer mates. And don't forget to say yer hope they won't be offended, because there's nothing worse than them thinking yer feel sorry for them. Just be casual and say the shoes don't fit any more, and they're too good to throw out.'

'Yeah, we'll do that, won't we, sunshine?' Rita grinned at Aggie. 'And we'll be very diplomatic, as well. No swearing or nothing, just friendly.'

'I'm going to be hard-faced, girls, and ask yer if yer'd take the tram down to Great Homer Street market, if yer've got time, and buy the shoes? With the weather what it is, the boys may as well be wearing them now as wait until Christmas. I'll give yer the money for the shoes and the tram fare.'

'Not one of those five-pound notes, Bessie.' Rita was shaking her head. 'I don't want the responsibility of carrying one of those around. Besides, the stallholder will think I've nicked it.'

'I wouldn't expect yer to take one of those, sweetheart, I'll give yer the money out of me own purse and get it back later.' Bessie smiled and gave a sigh of contentment. 'It will do me heart good to see those poor lads with shoes on their feet. And it'll be only the first of our good deeds. I won't be able to do all the shopping with me only having Saturday afternoon off, so I'm hoping you two will get most of it in. I'll write out a list of what is going in each food hamper, like dry goods, vegetables and a large chicken.' She looked from one to the other. 'Yer don't mind, do yer? The dry goods we can get any day now, but the veg and chickens will have to be ordered for Christmas Eve.' She pushed her chair back and went to the sideboard where her purse was in the large glass fruit bowl. 'I've only got about twelve bob now, but I think that'll be enough for the shoes, won't it?'

'More than enough, sunshine, yer'll have change out of that.'

'I'll take one of the fivers to work with me,' Bessie said. 'Ask the boss to change it for me. I'll tell him how I came to have it, and that I've got more I'd like him to change. He'll believe me, he's known me long enough to know I'm honest and don't tell lies.'

'Give us the money then, sunshine, and we'll be on our way. My feller likes a cup of tea before he goes to bed, and he'll have a cob on if I leave him to make it himself.'

Aggie used the table for leverage to get to her feet. 'We'll have good news for yer tomorrow night, queen, and there'll be a few lads blessing yer for being a guardian angel.' She grinned when she saw Bessie's mouth open. 'Don't worry, I know when to keep me mouth shut. As far as anyone will know, the shoes will have come from us or one of our friends.'

Bessie stood at the door until her mates reached their own houses, then they all wished each other a goodnight and three happy women closed their doors.

A few miles away, Evelyn and Philip sat on the couch in a room which was warmed by radiators. It was a luxury for Evelyn not having to put pieces of coal on a fire to keep warm. With Philip's arm across her shoulders, she was happy and contented. Every now and again he would put a finger under her chin and turn her face towards him for a kiss. He was eager to go to bed, so he could hold her in his arms and make love to her, but Evelyn told him to be patient as she had something to show him. She left the shelter of his arms to fetch her handbag and from it took the list Bessie had given her. She had thought long and hard about showing it to him, but there were no addresses on it, only names, so the street could be anywhere in Liverpool.

'I've brought you a list of deserving people who will be the recipients of your very generous gift of money. There are a lot more people in need in Liverpool, of course, because there is so much unemployment as you well know, but one can only do so much. There are more names to go on the list, but my friend has put beside each name what the family is most in need of.' Evelyn pointed out the names where the word 'shoes' was written at the side. 'These are the children who are going around barefoot in this freezing weather. They will be getting shoes, and their parents a food hamper so they won't starve over the Christmas period. My friend is being meticulous about where the money goes, and said to tell you that you have been the means of many people having the best Christmas they've ever had. There'll be almost twenty families helped, so I'm sure that must give you great satisfaction, my darling.'

Philip looked at her with eyes wide with disbelief. 'All those people! But I only gave you twenty pounds, surely that's a mere drop in the ocean? How can she possibly buy shoes and food for so many people on so little money?'

'My darling, when you have absolutely nothing then sixpence is a lot of money. I've learned a lot in the last few years, which you have yet to learn. My friend will make that twenty pounds go a long way. She will make sure the barefoot children are shod, and that every family has enough food for a Christmas dinner. The shoes won't be new, of course, but she assures me they will be good secondhand ones. And the food hampers will contain everything from a chicken to potatoes and vegetables, tea, sugar, milk and biscuits, plus a bag of coal delivered to each house so they will be warm over the holidays.'

'Who is this friend of yours? I would very much like to meet her.'

Evelyn folded the piece of paper over and reached down for her handbag. It was all to buy her a few seconds in which to compose herself. This afternoon, after she'd dropped Amelia off at Bessie's, while sitting on the tram into the city she had reached a decision. She could no longer put Philip off with lies, and wouldn't give him up without a fight. So she had made up her mind to seek out Cyril Lister-Sinclair and throw herself on his mercy. And she would take Amelia, she'd decided, for when he saw her, he would know she was his son's daughter. That was the only way she could see of standing a chance of keeping the man she adored.

'You will meet her one day, my love, but it won't be until after the holiday, she works every day. She has to earn a living, she's not a wealthy woman.' Evelyn stroked his cheek and smiled. 'She is a spinster of fifty who has lived alone since her parents died many years ago. And she is not your type, otherwise I wouldn't let her within a mile of you.'

'She must be a very caring person to go to all this trouble to help people less fortunate than herself. It reflects badly on me to say this, being too lazy to follow her example, but it's a good job there are people like her. If you think I can help ease her load with another donation, I will gladly give it. I have far more money than I need.'

Evelyn nodded. 'You are quite right, she is a very caring person. Someone who would give you her last penny. But I don't think you should offer more money, I'm sure she will manage very well on what she already has.'

Philip's eyes were twinkling. 'And what about your Christmas present? Have you given it any thought?'

She shook her head. 'I would rather you gave me a surprise. Not an expensive one, though, or you will embarrass me. Perhaps perfume. That is a present I would appreciate for it is a long time since I had a bottle of French perfume on my dressing table.'

He pulled her closer. 'You need have no worry about what to buy me, my adorable Evelyn, you have it already.'

She raised her brows. 'But I haven't bought any presents yet!'

'You are my present, and there is nothing in the whole world that I would rather have. Two whole days alone with you will be like heaven. To wake up with you lying beside me, to make love to you before breakfast, before dinner, whenever we feel the need. For I believe your need is as great as mine.'

'It is, my darling, it is.' Evelyn was fervently hoping Bessie would come to her aid and have Amelia for the two days. She thought this very possible as her neighbour adored her daughter. 'More so now than ever.'

'Then why are we sitting here when there is a very comfortable bed awaiting us in the next room? I'll set a tray with bottle and glasses while you retire to the bedroom. But don't bother putting a nightdress on, my lovely, allow me to see what a beautiful body awaits me. And hurry, please. I'm eager to hold you and caress every inch of you. I love you so much, my lovely Evelyn, it hurts.'

As she undressed, she asked herself how she could possibly leave this man and never see him again? No, she couldn't, it would break her heart. There must be a way she could keep him, and she intended to find that way.

Chapter Twenty-Four

Bessie sat on one side of her table, her two mates opposite. 'I've made two lists out, one for each of yer, for groceries that will keep, like tea, sugar and tins of condensed milk. Oh, and I've put down a red jelly on each, and a packet of custard powder. We can get round Molly in the corner shop for some biscuits. She'll throw in a few broken ones if I ask her nicely, and I'm sure whoever gets the hampers will be too happy to worry about a few broken biscuits. Anything is better than nothing when ye're hungry.'

Aggie's chins and hitched-up bosom agreed. 'Ye're not kiddin', queen. There's many a time broken biscuits have been a luxury in our house while Sam was out of work. And the same goes for Rita, doesn't it, queen?'

She nodded. 'I can remember us having half a biscuit each and thinking ourselves lucky to get that! No biscuit ever tasted so good.' She grinned at Bessie. 'Are yer going to tell the families who are on the list what they're getting? It would take a load off their minds and stop them from worrying about not having anything for Christmas.'

It was Bessie's turn to nod. 'I've been in two minds what to do about that, but in bed last night I decided it would be best to tell them so they're not worried sick. I'll wait until yer've been to the market for the shoes, then I'll tell them.'

'We're going for the shoes tomorrow, aren't we, queen?' Aggie felt really important. 'We've found out the sizes we need, and the mothers almost kissed us to death they were so happy. We

355

told them our lads had outgrown theirs, and one of Rita's sisters has a lad who can't get his feet into his any more. So that part of it is over and, please God, the kids will soon be able to go to school swanking with a pair of shoes on their feet.'

'I've changed one of the fivers so I can give yer enough money to cover the food on the lists and the shoes. How much d'yer reckon yer'll need?' Bessie took her purse from the pocket in the wrap-around apron which would have wrapped around her twice, it was so big. 'Add a bit on to what yer think, just to be on the safe side.'

'Yer haven't put how much tea or sugar,' Rita said, fingering the list. 'Is it two ounces of tea and half a pound of sugar?'

'No, the money will run further than that, sweetheart, so make it a packet of tea and a pound of sugar. Two ounces of tea in a sweet bag looks paltry, we may as well go the whole hog and give them a real treat. God knows, they deserve it. Most of the women on that list look twenty years older than they are because of the worry. Their faces are haggard and careworn, and there isn't an ounce of flesh on them. So while we've got the chance, let's do what we can for them.'

'I couldn't agree with yer more, sunshine, it breaks my heart just looking at them. It takes me and Aggie all our time to keep our families going, but we're not as badly off as some poor buggers. You, Mrs Sinclair, and the man who generously gave the money, are going to make a lot of people happy. I take me hat off to all of yer.'

Aggie nudged her friend. 'I didn't know yer had no hat, queen! I haven't never seen yer in one in all the years I've known yer.'

'No, yer wouldn't, sunshine, 'cos I haven't got no ruddy hat. But if yer want me to be precise, I'll say that if I did have a hat I'd take it off to them. Now then, does that make yer feel better?'

Aggie put on a sad face and even made her lips quiver. 'No, it doesn't make me feel better, queen, it makes me feel sad. Fancy, a mate of mine with no hat. Well, that's really touched my heart. If I wasn't so bleeding skint, I'd fork out and buy yer one.'

'Oh, that is kind of yer, sunshine, but yer needn't worry about little old me. If the occasion arises, like say if our Jack ever decides to get married, I can always borrow yours.'

Aggie grinned. 'Yer'd have a ruddy job, queen, 'cos I haven't got no hat. But I have got a mobcap, and if yer stuck a feather in the side of that, it would go down a treat.'

Bessie banged her fist on the table. 'Ladies, can we get our business sorted out, please? If there's any money over, I'll buy yer both a ruddy hat!'

Rita giggled as in her mind's eye she could see herself and Aggie walking down the street in posh hats with huge ostrich feathers sticking up at the side. Oh, what a field day the neighbours would have! Her hat and feather were in two shades of blue, Aggie's was bright red. 'Aggie,' she said now, 'don't ever wear red, sunshine, 'cos it doesn't suit yer.'

Aggie frowned at Bessie. 'What's wrong with this one? She's not having a funny turn, is she, not in the middle of a business meeting.'

'If you two don't stop acting the goat,' Bessie told her, 'this business meeting will never get off the ground. Now tell me how much yer think the shopping will come to, and I'll give yer the money?'

'Lend us yer pencil, then.' Rita totted the money up in her head. 'I can't tell yer to the penny, sunshine, but I would hazard it's at least a pound. And I'm going to be very cheeky now, Bessie, and ask, if I see a cheap coat in the market, would yer let me get it for Mrs Ponsonby? I worry meself to death about that woman. She always looks starved of food and heating. Yer never see a coalman there, so she must never have a fire lit. And at her age, God knows, she deserves some comfort. She's out cleaning and scrubbing steps for people in all weathers, it's a wonder she doesn't catch pneumonia.'

Bessie nodded. 'You get her a coat if yer can, sweetheart, and a pair of gloves and a scarf. We've got twenty pound to play with, and she's as deserving as the rest. I'll put her down for the coalman to drop her a bag in before Christmas, and yer can tell her the same tale as we're going to tell all the others. That a very kind gentleman gave us some money to help people out, but wouldn't give his name. We'll all tell the same tale and then we won't get ourselves mixed up.'

'That's a good idea, queen,' Aggie said. 'Yer know what my mouth is like for running away with itself. But what yer've just said is easy to remember, so I won't get meself in a muddle.'

Bessie opened the back compartment of her purse and took out some pound notes she'd folded over. 'There's two pounds to pay for what's on the list, the coat for Mrs Ponsonby, and the shoes.' She passed the notes to Rita. 'Seeing as ye're going to the market, would yer like some of the money I've been saving for you? Yer might see something yer like for yerselves, or something for the kids.'

'That would be marvellous, sunshine, 'cos both my boys could do with another pair of kecks. And I bet Aggie would be pleased, wouldn't yer, sunshine?'

Aggie's nod sent her chins swaying, her folded arms raised her bosom, and her tummy lifted the table off the floor. 'Ooh, I'll say I would! Our Kenny's got no backside in his kecks. He was moaning last night because the wind was getting inside the patch I put on a couple of weeks ago, and is only hanging on by a thread.'

'Well, I'll give yer what I've saved for yer. And d'yer want the five shillings Mrs Sinclair told me to give yer? Yer can have it now if yer want to buy things for the kids for Christmas.'

Rita shook her head. 'No! We want yer to keep that towards the party yer said we're having. You hang on to it, Bessie, there's a good girl.'

'Ahem!' Aggie put a hand to her mouth as she'd seen posh people do when they cough. 'Don't I get a say in this? You speak for yourself, Rita Wells, and let me do me own talking.' She smiled sweetly at Bessie. 'This is me what's telling yer to keep the money for the party. I haven't been to a real knees-up, jars-out party since me wedding, and I'm really looking forward to it.'

'You'll have the party even if yer take the money what I've got saved up for yer,' Bessie said. 'I've been doing a lot of working out in me head, and this money I've got will cover all I'm expecting it to, and a damn sight more. Yer have my word on that.' She pushed another pound note over the table. 'Take this, Rita, and if you and Aggie see something yer'd like for yerselves to wear at Christmas, then buy it. Yer might see some nice, decent, secondhand dresses, and yer can titivate yerselves up for the party. So spoil yerselves for once. It's not often yer get the chance.'

'And what about you, sunshine, what are you getting yerself for the party?'

'I'm making a dress for meself, when I get the time to nip into town for material. I won't leave meself out, don't worry. And I'm making a dress for Milly, as a Christmas present.'

'Will yer be having her over Christmas?' Rita asked. 'Or don't yer know yet?'

'It hasn't been mentioned, but I'm keeping me fingers crossed. Milly keeps asking me, but I haven't the nerve to bring the subject up with Evelyn. Not after she's turned out to be a much nicer person than we thought. I'll have to see how the land lies over the next few days. If she seems in a good mood when she calls one night, I might mention it to her.' Bessie hadn't told her mates anything about Evelyn's private life, and had no intention of doing so. She was told in confidence, and that's the way it would stay as far as she was concerned. As for having Milly for Christmas, her hopes were quite high for she thought Evelyn would want to spend time with her man friend. But it wouldn't do to take anything for granted. To do that could mean heartache and disappointment, not only for herself but for Milly too. So best keep things close to her chest for the time being until she picked up the courage to ask Evelyn.

'Look, we know ye're rushed off yer feet, we can see that for ourselves,' Aggie told the very flushed and irate stallholder. 'Me and me mate aren't blind, and we're not bleeding well daft, either.' She nodded her head vigorously to add weight to her words. 'Of course yer think we are, otherwise yer wouldn't be trying to tell us those shoes are worth two bob! No one will give yer that much for shoes what are well worn.'

The stallholder thought it best to do business with the one who hadn't opened her mouth yet, for he knew he'd never win with the big woman. She was some size, and he wouldn't stand an earthly if she clocked him one. 'The shoes are not very well worn, missus,' he said to Rita, 'yer can see for yerself there's still plenty of wear in them. I'm not trying to diddle yer into paying more than what they're worth.'

'Oh, I'm going to let me mate deal with yer, 'cos the shoes have nothing to do with me.' Rita thought she'd go for the sympathy touch. 'Yer see, she's got a big family, her husband earns buttons, and she's only got so much to spend. After all, she wants eight pair of shoes, and her money will only stretch to eighteen pence a pair at the very most. But if yer can't do a deal with her, don't worry, we'll try another stall.'

Aggie's mouth opened wide in surprise. What did her mate think she was doing? But a kick in the shin warned her to be quiet. It was a painful warning, and if anyone else had done it they'd have been flat out by now. But Rita had a way with people so Aggie told herself to go along with her. That was why, when the man turned to her, he thought he was looking at a different woman. There was no sign of the battleaxe of a few minutes ago.

'Is it right that yer've got a big family, missus, and yer want eight pair of shoes?'

'That's right, lad, but I don't want to plead poverty. It's my feller's fault we've got so many kids, but he doesn't have the flaming worry of trying to feed and clothe them.' When Aggie sighed her bosom almost touched her chin. 'Still, that's not your worry, lad, so we'll try another stall. There's one not far from here.'

'Hang on a minute, don't let's be too hasty.' The man was thinking if she bought eight pairs of shoes he'd still make a good profit even if he let them go for eighteen pence a pair. 'Perhaps we can reach a mutual agreement. If yer buy eight pair of shoes, then I'll let yer have them for the one and six a pair. Now I can't be fairer than that, can I? I'm robbing meself at that price, but I'm all heart when it comes to children, I've got four meself.'

Aggie could afford to grin now. 'Not as active as my feller, then? Mind you, ye're on yer feet all day, while my feller thinks the only reason we were born with backsides was to sit on them.'

The stallholder managed a smile. If he'd been a brave man, he'd have said she probably thought we were born with mouths so we could talk all bleeding day. But he wasn't a brave man, so he said, 'Have a look around and see if yer can find what yer want, but they must be children's shoes, not adults'.'

'God bless yer, lad, there'll be a place in heaven for you, that's for sure.'

Rita smiled at the man while pulling her mate away from the stall. If she hadn't, she'd have burst out laughing. When they were out of the man's hearing, she chuckled, 'What a two-faced cow I've got for a mate! Yer were on the point of clocking him one five minutes ago, now yer've promised him a place in heaven.' She doubled up with laughter. 'What a pity you won't be there to see him.'

'Ay, I wouldn't be too sure about that if I were you, queen, 'cos I think I'll have the last laugh when the time comes. God has a sense of humour, yer know, and He might think I'll brighten the place up.' Aggie had just had a thought that pleased her. 'Anyway, ye're always saying I tell lies. Well, what about yerself? It was you what told that man I had eight kids, queen, not me.'

Rita had a joker up her sleeve, which she now brought into play. 'I bet your feller will get a laugh when he hears that yer told the stallholder he was very active in bed.'

'Oh, I won't tell him that, queen, I'm not daft. He'd do his nut if he thought I'd been speaking to a man about . . . er . . . about . . . well, you know, personal things.'

'You might not tell him, but that doesn't mean no one else will.' Rita saw a mound of shoes on one of the trestle tables, and was making her way towards it when she was pulled up sharp. She'd been expecting it, and quickly dropped the smile from her face. 'What was that for, sunshine? Yer frightened the life out of me.'

'A fine mate you'd be if yer snitched to my feller! Yer know he's got no sense of humour, particularly when if comes to what happens behind bedroom doors.'

'I was pulling yer leg, sunshine, I'd never tell Sam anything like that! And if anyone else told him in front of me, I wouldn't know where to put me face, I'd be wishing the floor would open and swallow me up.'

Aggie's smile was wide. 'Ye're not the only one who can pull legs, yer know, queen, so don't be getting those fleecy bloomers in a twist.' Her eyes lighted on the piled-up shoes. 'Ooh, eh, queen, let's get stuck into that lot. I've got a feeling we're going to have a lucky day today.'

Rita agreed. 'I was just thinking the same thing. If we get the eight pair of shoes, which I'm sure we will out of that lot, then fate is on our side and we'll find what we want for our kids, and ourselves. I'd like to get meself a nice dress to wear on Christmas Day, just to remind Reg what I used to look like when we were courting. It's years since I've had anything nice to wear.'

'Oh, yer'll have no trouble finding a dress to suit you. You're so lucky, if yer fell down the lavvy yer'd come up smelling of roses.' Aggie had a pair of boy's shoes in her hand, joined together by one of the laces. 'Whereas I'm so bleeding fat I need a tent to fit me. And there's not much chance of finding a tent with sleeves in.' Then she saw the funny side, and grinned. 'Not in a colour that would suit me, anyway.'

Rita didn't like to hear her mate making fun of herself, for she knew that deep down Aggie would give anything to be thinner. 'We'll find you a dress, don't worry. There's lots of big-made women around, ye're not on yer own.' She changed the subject, but made up her mind that they would look for a dress for her mate first, then she'd try for one for herself. 'Let's get the shoes, and that'll be one job off our mind.'

Rita had brought a big, well-worn canvas bag with her, thinking it would be large enough to hold everything they'd be buying in the market. It took the shoes with room to spare. The two friends left the stall in a happy frame of mind. They'd got what they wanted at the price they wanted. The next priority was trousers for the boys. They were in luck at that stall as well, for they walked away with three pair of decent trousers for the grand sum of two shillings and threepence. The trousers were all in good nick and had plenty of wear left in them. A good pressing with a hot iron and a wet cloth, and they'd come up like new. The boys would consider themselves very lucky.

'I was going to say there's only our dresses to get now, but I've remembered we said we'd get a coat for Mrs Ponsonby.' Rita changed the heavy bag over to her other hand. 'She's about my size, near enough, so what fits me should fit her.'

'We've passed a few stalls with coats on so yer should find something suitable.' Aggie put her hand on the handle of the bag. 'Give it to me, it's heavy and we'll take turns carrying it.'

Rita was glad to pass it over for the canvas handles were digging into the flesh of her palms. 'Anything would be better than the coat she's wearing now. It's nearly falling to pieces, and it's always so crumpled I'm sure she sleeps in it.' She sighed. 'We're not exactly well off ourselves, but yer can always find someone worse off than yerself.'

They reached a stall with coats spread out on top of each other, and Aggie stood the bag between her legs. 'You have a root, queen, and I'll keep me eye on the bag, If yer see anything exciting, give us a shout.'

It took Rita five minutes to find a really nice coat for Mrs Ponsonby. It was a heavy tweed with a trim fur collar, and although the cuffs were slightly frayed, they could easily be turned up a little. She tried it on to show Aggie, and they both agreed it was a bargain at two shillings. But it wasn't the only coat Rita spotted. There was a navy blue heavy winter coat which seemed in good condition from what she could see of it. So she handed the first coat to Aggie, and pulled the navy blue one from under the pile to hold up against her.

'That's no good, queen,' Aggie shouted, 'yer'd get two of Mrs Ponsonby in that, it's miles too big.'

'The coat yer've got over yer arm is for Mrs Ponsonby, sunshine, I was thinking this one would fit you.'

Aggie pulled a face. 'Nah, it wouldn't.' She was so used to not being able to buy anything to fit her, she shook her head. 'Yer need glasses, queen, if yer think that'll go anywhere near me.'

'There's nothing wrong with my eyesight, Aggie Gordon, and I'll bet yer a penny that this coat will go on yer.'

'Away with yer, and don't be acting the goat.'

Rita huffed and she puffed. Grabbing the tweed coat off her mate's arm, she pushed the navy blue one at her. 'I'm not asking yer to try it on, sunshine, I'm telling yer to. Now do as ye're told and don't be so ruddy stubborn.'

And didn't the coat fit Aggie like a glove, and didn't the smile on her face show how pleased and proud she was? 'Ay, queen, it feels as though it's been made for me. Do I look posh in it?'

'Only like a million dollars, sunshine, or else Mae West.'

'Ooh, I wonder how much it is?' Aggie asked the question, but in her mind was already telling herself that no one was going to separate her from that coat. She loved the colour, it was a thick, warm material, and she felt at home in it. 'You go and ask how much it is, queen, 'cos yer seem to have more luck than me.'

The stallholder was an elderly woman with white hair plaited into a bun at the nape of her neck. A thick black knitted shawl covered her shoulders, and her heavy black skirt reached down to her sturdy buttoned boots. She had been watching the two women, and when Rita approached, said, 'That coat fits yer friend like a glove. Good quality, too, and never been worn much.'

Oh, dear, thought Rita, it sounds as though she's after a good price for it. It was probably worth it, too, but could Aggie afford it? 'She loves it, and with her being so big it's unusual for her to get anything that fits her. She's conscious of her size, too, so I had to talk her into trying it on.' There was no way Rita could tell even little white lies to this stallholder who was no doubt having to work hard to keep body and soul together. 'It depends how much yer want for the coat, 'cos my mate doesn't have much money.'

Faded blue eyes moved from Rita to where Aggie was standing. 'I couldn't let it go for less than three shillings. It's worth a lot more than that, it hasn't been worn much. Came from a house where the people can afford to throw clothes out after wearing them only a few times. My son goes out with his cart to the rich areas in the city, and sometimes gets a real bargain like the coat yer friend has taken a fancy to. I hope she can manage the three bob. She looks good in it, and looking at her I'd say she was a warm-hearted woman.'

Rita couldn't believe her luck. She wanted to run to Aggie, but made herself walk as she normally did. But with her back to the stallholder now, she was able to let her wide smile show. 'Three bob, sunshine, and a real bargain if ever I saw one. But don't look too pleased or the price might be put up. In all honesty, though, Aggie, it's the bargain of a lifetime, and yer'd be crazy not to jump at it.'

'And I would bleeding well jump if I didn't have this ruddy bag between me legs.' She thrust Mrs Ponsonby's coat at Rita and waved like mad to where the stallholder was standing. 'Go and pay her for me, queen, and tell her I'm really happy. Go on, I'll settle up with yer when we get home and are sitting down with a nice hot cuppa.' She grabbed Rita's arm as her friend went to walk away. 'I'll tell yer what, queen, you are definitely my lucky mascot, and I ain't going nowhere without yer in future.'

The stallholder took the three silver shillings. 'Is yer friend keeping the coat on?'

Rita grinned. 'It would take a very strong, brave person to separate my mate from that coat. Tomorrow she'll be walking up and down our street, swaggering like Mae West, until she's sure every neighbour has seen it. She'll be like a child with a new toy. But I'm made up for her, it's not often nice things happen to people like us. So thank you, and we both hope yer have a very happy Christmas.'

The little woman smiled. 'And the same to you, girl, the same to you.'

'I'm not going home without something for meself,' Rita said, a determined expression on her face. 'How soft you are! Yer get the bargain of a lifetime, now yer want to go home! It's a case of I'm all right, so sod you! Well, we're not leaving this market until I get meself a dress to wear on Christmas Day. And seeing as I'm the one with the purse what has the money in for the tram fare home, then it's just too bad on you, isn't it? Unless yer feel in the mood to walk home, like.'

'There's no need to be sarky, queen, I only said me feet were killing me and me corns were giving me gyp. That's all I said, and yer jump down me throat.' And Aggie was only telling the truth, for her feet had a very heavy weight to carry around. 'I'll stay with yer till the bitter end, queen, so march on and I'll follow.'

Rita felt sorry for her, but didn't fancy going home with everything they had on their list except something for herself. 'There's only one more stall what sells decent dresses, so can yer hang on for a bit longer?'

Aggie knew how to bring a smile to her mate's face. 'When yer've got yer dress, will yer give me a piggyback to the tram stop?'

Rita grinned. 'Oh, yeah, 'course I will! And all the shopping as well!' She spotted a trestle table with dresses, blouses and jumpers all jumbled up together. 'Ay, keep yer fingers crossed, sunshine, there's a good girl. And while ye're standing there like a miserable wet week, say a little prayer I'll find something for meself.'

Aggie rolled her eyes towards the dull sky. 'Of course I'll say a prayer for yer, it'll pass the time away. Now get a ruddy move on before my feet take off on their own.'

Fifteen minutes later Aggie saw Rita walking towards her with a smile on her face and a scruffy paper bag in her hand. 'Got one then, did yer, queen?'

Rita nodded. 'Yeah, I got what I wanted, and the woman even put it in a bag for me. So we've had a very successful day all round, sunshine, don't yer think?'

'Well, let's see the ruddy dress, queen, unless ye're keeping it a secret?'

'No, there's nothing hush-hush about a sixpenny dress. I'm pleased with it though, and that's the main thing. I'll show it to yer when we get home, and you've got yer feet up on the couch.' Rita lifted the heavy bag from between her friend's feet. 'I'll carry this, sunshine, and those two coats, it'll take the weight off yer. If we're lucky with catching a tram, we'll be home in twenty minutes.'

Aggie held her arm out so Rita could take the coats. 'Did yer hear that, queen?'

'Hear what, sunshine?'

'Yer must be going deaf, queen, if yer didn't hear nothing. When yer said we'd be home in twenty minutes, me corns said, "Thank God," and me feet said, "It's the last time we come to this bleeding market with yer." '

'Oh, I see, yer've got yer feet swearing now,' Rita said. 'It's a good job ye're the only one what can hear them.'

Their luck stayed with them, for a tram came along just as they got to the stop. And the conductor was standing on the platform, which was a godsend. 'Will yer be a pal and take this bag off me, please?' Rita asked, holding out the heavy canvas bag containing all their shopping except the two coats. 'Then I can give me mate a hand getting on.'

The conductor put the bag down in the well under the stairs, then looked from Rita to a very downcast Aggie. My God, he thought, she's carrying some weight. 'Hang on a tick. If you get on first, missus, I'll get off and give yer mate a hand from the back.'

Despite feeling miserable, Aggie couldn't help but laugh. 'Yer'll need both hands, lad, one for each cheek.'

Rita turned towards the aisle down the centre of the tram when she heard the driver and the conductor laughing. That was all Aggie needed. A bit of encouragement, and she'd be in her element telling the kind of jokes Rita would find embarrassing in front of strange men. So best find herself a seat and keep out of it, even though she could see smiles on the faces of passengers in front. But before she reached her seat, Rita heard gales of laughter and was too curious not to turn. And what she saw was one of the funniest sights she, or the passengers on that tram had ever seen. The conductor was on the pavement trying to get his shoulder under Aggie's bottom, and the driver had hold of each of her hands, trying to pull her on board. But she was laughing so much, really enjoying herself, they couldn't manage to get her eighteen stone off the ground.

In the end Rita walked back and stood behind the driver. 'If yer don't want to be here all day, let go of her and I'll show yer how it's done.'

Aggie was still grinning. 'Ye're a spoilsport, you are, a real misery guts!'

'Put one hand on that rail, sunshine, and the other on that one. Like we always do. And if yer don't behave yerself, so help me, I'm going to tell Sam yer've made lewd suggestions to two men today, and we'll see what he's got to say to that.

Once on the platform, Aggie grinned down at her. 'Ooh, I wouldn't if I were you, queen, 'cos my feller is dead ignorant. He'd ask yer to explain what lewd means, and then where would yer be, eh?' She frowned. 'By the way, what does it mean?'

Chapter Twenty-Five

Aggie flopped on to the couch without even taking her coat off. One shoe after the other flew across the room. 'Thank God for that, me bloody feet are dropping off. That walk from the tram stop was murder.'

Rita put the shopping down on the floor. 'You sit there, sunshine, and I'll make us a nice cup of tea. And I'll put some warm water in the bucket, if yer like, and yer can put yer feet in to steep for half an hour. It'll do yer world of good.' She grinned. 'And I'm sure yer feet would be grateful.'

'Ooh, ay, queen, that would be just what the doctor ordered. Me feet have bucked themselves up no end, and me corns are throbbing for joy. They can't wait to soak in some nice warm water.' Aggie jerked her head. 'Well, don't just stand there, droopy drawers, get cracking.' Rita had reached the kitchen door when Aggie called, 'While ye're waiting for the kettle to boil, yer can show me yer dress.'

Rita popped her head around the door. 'Stop giving yer orders, Mrs Woman, just one thing at a time if yer don't mind. When yer've got yer feet in water, and a cup of tea in yer hand, then I'll show yer the dress. So have a little patience.'

After filling the kettle and putting a light to the stove, Rita stood the bucket in the sink and ran some cold water into it. She'd add hot water when the kettle boiled. While she was waiting, she leaned against the wall near the living room. 'Don't forget, we've got to give those shoes out this afternoon, and go to the Maypole for the groceries on the list Bessie gave us.'

Aggie groaned. 'Ay, queen, there's no way I could walk to the Maypole and back, me feet really are in a terrible state. Couldn't we leave it until tomorrow, when I'll feel more up to it? Besides, one day isn't going to make any difference.'

'It is if ye're running round in bare feet in this weather. And we promised Bessie we'd let the lads have them today. But there's no need for you to bother, I can take the shoes up meself, it won't take ten minutes. All I need do is hand them in to their mothers, 'cos the lads will be at school. And once I've had a cup of tea and a little sit down, I'll be refreshed and ready for the walk to the Maypole. I know that could wait till tomorrow, but I want to try and have a word with the manager. We'll need some cardboard boxes to make up the hampers, and if I can get him in a good mood I'll ask him to start saving some for us. And I'll ask the corner shop, as well, 'cos all those boxes are not going to be easy to come by.'

The kettle began to whistle and Rita made haste to switch the gas off. She poured half the boiling water into the brown teapot, the other half into the bucket. 'Take yer stockings off, sunshine, I'm bringing it through.' She lifted the bucket out of the sink by the handle, and after testing the water wasn't too hot or too cold, was carrying it through to the living room when the sight she met brought her to an abrupt halt. 'In the name of God, Aggie, have yer no shame? I can see everything yer've got!' Rita was shaking her head, wondering whether she dare laugh, for her friend was trying to cock one leg over the other, hoping by doing so she could reach down to pull her stocking off. But her knee kept slipping off, and her bosom and tummy were no help, they flatly refused to move out of the way.

Bright red in the face, and huffing and puffing, Aggie glared at her. 'I've got nothing you haven't got, queen, so don't be going all bleeding shy on me.' Her eyes narrowed. 'If yer so much as crack yer face, so help me I'll pour that bucket of water over yer.'

'I really don't think ye're in a position to make threats, sunshine, do you? Besides, I'm much faster on me feet than you are, yer'd never catch me.' Rita put the bucket down and doubled over with laughter. 'I'm sorry, Aggie, but if yer could see yerself, yer'd see the funny side of it.' She moved forward. 'Here, let me take yer stockings off for yer, then yer can have a nice cup of tea while yer feet are soaking.'

After a few seconds, when Rita was having no success, Aggie said, 'It would help if yer took me garters off first, queen, 'cos they're what's keeping me stockings up.'

'Yer can just sod off, Aggie Gordon, I'm not putting me hand up yer clothes. Yer can take yer own garters off, I'll see to the tea.'

Aggie grabbed Rita's arm before she could move away and with her free hand lifted the skirt of her dress to reveal a garter. It was a piece of well-worm elastic, tied in a knot, holding up her stocking. Only to the knee, though, for the top of the stocking was hanging loose.

'In the name of God,' Rita said, 'don't ever get run over when ye're out with me, sunshine, 'cos I'd either die of shame, or say I wasn't with yer.'

'Listen to me, queen. Let me tell yer that for me to get a garter on at all is no less than a ruddy miracle. If I sit down, I can't reach me bleeding feet, me chest and me tummy are in the way. And if I stand up, I can't even see me feet or me legs. I do what I can, but I'm not a ruddy contortionist. So think on that when I'm lying in the gutter and you're telling everyone that yer've never seen me in yer life before.'

'Oh, stop feeling sorry for yerself, Aggie Gordon, and let me get those stockings off yer. If yer carry on much longer, the water in the bucket will be cold and so will the teapot.' The stockings were removed in a flash and put on Aggie's knee. 'And if yer behave yerself, I might just have a nice surprise for yer.' Rita brought the bucket nearer to the couch. 'But one moan out of yer, sunshine, and I'll give it to the woman next door.'

'Ah, yer wouldn't do that, not to yer mate.' Aggie frowned. 'And what are yer playing at? You *are* the woman next door!'

Rita grinned. 'I know that, sunshine, and aren't you the lucky one, having me for a neighbour? Yer should be counting yer blessings, not moaning.'

It was three o'clock when Rita got back to Aggie's, but she was feeling very pleased with herself and wearing a wide smile. 'Oh, Aggie, yer missed a treat. Yer should have seen the faces on the women when I gave them the shoes. They were absolutely over the moon. They couldn't thank us enough. They'll tell yer themselves when they see yer. I said yer would have been with me but yer feet were tired. So stick to that story, sunshine, and don't forget the shoes were from us and a friend of ours.'

'How did yer get on at the Maypole? Did yer manage to have a word with the manager?'

Rita nodded. 'When I told him Bessie had been lucky to get a sum of money from a man who wanted to help some poor people, he was really pleased. And of course it helped when I said she would be buying the groceries from his shop. So, to make sure I got some boxes off him, I gave him the order and said we'd pick it up tomorrow. And he said he may have a few more boxes by the weekend.' Rita gave a sigh of contentment. 'So, sunshine, all in all, it's been a very rewarding day.'

There was no sign of the bucket now, and Aggie had a pair of scruffy slippers on her feet. 'I should have looked in the market for a pair of slippers for meself, 'cos these are Sam's and they're falling to pieces. I could probably have got a pair for two pence and they'd have been well worth the money.' Remembering the market, she remembered something else too. 'Ay, queen, what did yer do with the dress yer got? When yer'd gone, I looked high and low for the bag but I couldn't see it nowhere.'

'No, yer wouldn't, sunshine, 'cos I had a change of mind and took it with me. I knew yer wouldn't be able to keep yer hands off it. I thought we'd take everything over to Bessie's when she gets in from work, and she can see what we bought this morning. She has a right to know what we managed to get, and hear how much it cost, even though I know she trusts us not to diddle her.'

Aggie looked aggrieved at the mere thought. 'She knows we wouldn't do that, queen, not after she's been so good to us.'

'You should be going over to light her fire soon, so I'll come with yer,' Rita said. 'We can take everything over, including the coats and the children's things.'

Aggie's jaw dropped. 'I don't have to take me coat, do I? I was hoping I could start wearing that tomorrow.'

'Blimey, Aggie, ye're worse than a child! Can't yer let Bessie see it first? She can have a look-see at everything, then hide them away upstairs before Mrs Sinclair calls to pick Milly up.' Rita looked down at her friend's feet. 'I can take them over, sunshine, if yer feet are still sore. And I can light both fires, come to that, it won't kill me.'

Aggie wasn't having any of that. If there was anything going on, she wanted to be part of it. 'No, I'll do me whack, queen, as well as you, it's only fair. After all, I'm getting paid for it so it's like a proper job.'

'Yeah, ye're right, sunshine, we do get paid for it. So, 'cos ye're me mate, and not a bad old stick, I'll open the bag and let yer see me new dress.' Then Rita shook her head. 'No, I'll give you the privilege of opening the bag, and yer can tell me what yer think of me taste in high fashion.'

Grabbing the bag from her, Aggie chuckled. 'High fashion me backside, all for a dress what cost yer a tanner.' But her chuckle faded when she realised she was holding more than one dress. 'What's all this? How many bleeding dresses have yer bought yerself?'

'Only one, sunshine, I'm not greedy.' Rita felt very happy, the wait had been worth it to see her mate's face. 'There was one I thought would fit you, and I remembered your Kitty was the only one we hadn't got anything for, so there's one there for her as well. I hope they fit, it was just a case of guessing.' She leaned forward and pulled one of the dresses from Aggie's hand. It was a beige and brown short-sleeved cotton dress, more suitable for the summer than winter really, but it was very neat, and would look nice when it had been pressed. 'This is mine, and don't yer dare say it isn't high fashion because by the time I've finished with it, I could say I'd bought it at George Henry Lee and people would believe me. Now, don't sit staring down as though they're going to bite yer, and I don't think yer need me to tell yer which is yours and which is Kitty's.'

For a whole minute, Aggie was struck dumb. Then, in a tearful voice, she said, 'Honest, queen, this is the biggest surprise I've ever had. I'm not half bleeding lucky to have you for a neighbour.'

'Aggie Gordon, I do believe ye're going to cry! Well, don't yer dare let any tears fall on those dresses, not after paying sixpence and threepence for them.'

Rita had spotted the navy blue dress on the stall before she'd seen the one she liked for herself, and when she saw the size of it was sure it would fit her friend. 'Well, go on, sunshine, don't keep me in suspense. Have a look and see if it will fit yer. I know Kitty's will be all right, 'cos the woman on the stall has a girl her age and she picked it out for me.'

It wasn't often that Aggie prayed, but as she shook the dress out and held it against herself, she said a prayer. 'How does that look, queen?'

'I reckon it'll fit yer like a glove, same as the coat. But the only way to tell is to try it on. So come into the kitchen.'

Aggie put Kitty's dress down and lumbered to her feet. 'I ain't standing in no bleeding cold kitchen catching me death of cold, not when there's a fire in here. So if yer don't want to see me in all me glory, queen, I suggest you go and wait in the bleeding kitchen.'

'Have yer no modesty?' Rita asked as her friend pulled her dress up by the waist. 'I could no more get stripped in front of you than fly.' As the dress was pulled higher, an expanse of bare leg appeared, followed by blue fleecy-lined bloomers. 'Oh, I'm going to stand in the kitchen before I see any more of yer body.'

A muffled voice came from inside the dress. 'No, wait, queen, 'cos I need yer to help pull me dress over me bosom. And before yer start moaning, I know I have to do it meself every day, but it's murder getting the waist over these two bleeding big balloons I've got. So while you're here, yer may as well give me a hand. Just grab hold and pull, while I breathe in.'

The state of Aggie was such that Rita couldn't keep her laughter back. It wasn't so much the bulging tummy, or the rolls of fat on her legs, 'cos none of that could be helped. It was the huge safety pin keeping her bloomers up that was the last straw. Laughing as the tears rolled down her cheeks, Rita said, 'I'm sure if Laurel and Hardy could see yer, sunshine, they'd offer to make yer a partner. Laurel, Hardy and Gordon. Oh, what a scream it would be.'

'I'll give yer something to scream about if yer don't hurry up and get this bleeding dress off me. Ye're having the time of yer life while I'm suffocating. I can't get me breath.'

Rita gave one last tug, and Aggie's head appeared. She was bright red in the face and her chest was heaving. 'I'd have been a bloody sight quicker doing it meself,' she groaned. 'If me breasts weren't so firmly attached, yer'd have pulled the ruddy things off.'

Rita put a curled fist to the stitch in her side. 'It's a long time since I had such a good laugh, sunshine, but I wasn't making fun of yer, I think too much of yer for that. I know if yer could have seen yerself, yer'd have laughed louder than me.'

'I'll do a deal with yer,' Aggie said, keeping her face deadpan. 'If this dress fits me, I'll love yer till the day I die. If it doesn't go near me, I'll chase yer down the street with the stiff brush in me hand.'

Rita nodded. 'It's a deal, so let's be having yer. I really hope it fits yer, sunshine, 'cos it's a nice dress. But if it does, it's going over to Bessie's with the rest of the stuff. Nobody is allowed to have anything until Christmas Day. The kids have got to wait, otherwise they'll have nothing to wake up to on Christmas morning, and the same applies to us. So I want yer to say yer agree before yer try the dress on?'

Aggie made a grab for it and held it to her bosom. 'D'yer know what, Rita Wells, up till a minute ago I thought yer were as good as Cinderella's fairy godmother. But I've changed me mind, and now yer remind me of her wicked step-sisters.'

'That's too bad, sunshine, I'm sure I'll live. Now put that dress on, for heaven's sake, or Milly will be home from school and I don't want her to see anything. Not that there's anything here for her, but she might just let it slip to one of the kids. So put a move on, slow coach.'

The dress slipped over Aggie's head, over her bosom and then her tummy. She didn't have to tug or pull, and couldn't believe her luck. Even her chins were pleased for her when she shook her head in disbelief. 'I take every word back, queen, and once again ye're my fairy godmother. I'm beginning to think I'm dreaming and will wake up to a big disappointment. I'm not, am I, queen?'

'You are not!' Rita said, straightening the neat round collar on the navy dress. 'Right now yer look like a very attractive lady with a face like a film star and a figure like Mae West. Yer really look a treat, sunshine, and yer'll have your feller licking his lips when he sees yer on Christmas Day.'

Aggie's bosom swelled with pride. It was a long time since she'd heard compliments like that. Mind you, she wasn't daft, she knew her mate was only being kind, but she had to admit she did think she looked more than passable. And although it might be wishful thinking on her part, she'd swear it made her look thinner. Why, she could almost see her feet. She cast her eyes down again, then asked herself if she was seeing things. Was that her toes, or was it a dirty mark on the lino? Better not ask, 'cos ignorance was bliss.

When Milly came home from school she didn't need any persuading to stay in Rita's and play Snakes and Ladders with Jack. The girls in the street were more friendly with her now, and she could have played with them, but no, her best mate was Jack. So she was out of the house when Bessie came home from work to be greeted by a smiling Rita and Aggie.

'What is this, a welcoming committee?' Bessie walked straight to the fire to warm her hands. 'Yer both look like the cat what got the cream, so I presume yer've had a good day?'

'Well, we've a lot to tell yer, sunshine, but will have to make it quick because we've got our dinners on the go. Anyway, in a nutshell, we got the shoes for the boys and gave them to their mothers, who were absolutely delighted. I bet the lads are playing out in them right now.'

'Oh, that's grand, sweetheart, a job well done. And I bet the lads are blessing the pair of yer. Did yer manage to get them from the market, then?'

Rita nodded. 'We got everything we wanted from there. A lovely coat for Mrs Ponsonby, and Aggie got herself one which is a real smasher. Trousers for the three boys, a dress for Kitty, and a dress each for me and Aggie. And I've ordered the foodstuffs from the Maypole. I left the list with the manager and am picking it up tomorrow. I've paid for it, as well. I told Mr Lacy you'd been given some money to help out a few poor families over Christmas, and he's going to save as many card-board boxes as he can. I told him there'd be another big order for him Christmas week.' She shrugged her shoulders and added, 'I can't see him having enough boxes to spare, 'cos he'll have a lot of orders to be delivered. Still, we can ask the corner shop, I'm sure Sally and Alf will help out when they know what they're for.'

'Yer have been busy,' Bessie said. 'I'd have been lost without yer.'

'Ooh, ay, I can't take all the credit, it was team work. Aggie did just as much as me. In fact, she did most of the carrying. We work well together, don't we, sunshine?'

This compliment took Aggie's chubby cheeks on an upward journey which almost had her eyes disappearing from view. She was having some really nice things said about her today. 'Yeah, I bargained at the shoe stall, and Rita bargained at the next. We did really well, didn't we, queen?'

Rita nodded, knowing her mate would be tickled pink and feeling very important. 'We did that, sunshine, and next time we've got a few bob, we'll take a trip down there again. But now, down to business.' She passed two pieces of paper over to Bessie. 'One's the list of all the items we said we'd get – the prices are at the side. I couldn't get a receipt for anything from the market 'cos they don't give them. But the Maypole receipt is there, so yer can check the prices, and I've got the rest of the money here.' She put a hand in her pocket and brought out a large amount of coppers and silver. 'I think yer'll find the money will tally with the lists, Bessie, except yer'll have to take our tram fares into consideration.'

Bessie shook her head slowly. 'Yer don't really think I'm going to sit down and check, do yer, Rita? If I can't trust you two, then I can't trust anyone. I think yer've done wonders to have any money left out of five pounds. The way you two are going on, we'll have enough to put quite a lot in the hampers.' She suddenly remembered something. 'Oh, I nearly forgot again. I didn't put margarine down on the list, or bread. And if yer'd be angels could you order eighteen chickens from the butcher, and ask him to have them plucked and cleaned. It'll save anyone having to spend Christmas Eve with their hand up the backside of a chicken.'

Rita frowned. 'I thought it was fifteen hampers yer were making up, so why eighteen chickens?'

'To use in sandwiches for the two parties. And ask the butcher how much a decent-sized bird will be so I'll know where I'm working. And tell Stan not to worry, he'll get his money. I'll pay him a few days before the holiday. And seeing as it's a bloody good order for him, ask him to put a piece of dripping in with each one.'

'Are yer sure yer've got enough money for all this, sunshine?' Rita sounded doubtful. 'Yer won't get a chicken under three bob.'

'I'll sit and do a list tonight, and if yer find out roughly what the chickens are going to cost, I can pretty much work it out to the penny. Potatoes and veg will only be coppers, I'm almost sure I'll have money over. Enough to put a tangerine and an apple in each hamper to make the kids happy.' Bessie looked at the clock. 'Don't yer think yer'd better be on yer way, before yer husbands come in from work?'

Rita jumped to her feet. 'Yeah, come on, Aggie, the men will want feeding. But before we go, Bessie, yer've had the good news, but I'm afraid there's some bad news for yer.'

She was crafty enough to know that if it was really bad news, they'd have told her straight away. 'Oh, aye, what is it?'

'Well, we wanted yer to see what we'd bought, but we didn't want anyone else to see it 'cos it would spoil things for the kids. So it's all on your landing for yer to look through. We haven't just dumped it there, it's all neat and tidy. But d'yer think yer could keep it here until me and Aggie get a chance to take our stuff? The dresses and trousers will need washing and pressing, but we'll have to do it while the kids are at school.'

'Don't worry yer heads about it, I'll sort it out. I can put it in

380

the bottom of me wardrobe until ye're ready for it. Now get home and see to the family.'

Rita stepped down on to the pavement. 'The only big things that will take up a lot of room are the two coats, but I can take Mrs Ponsonby's tomorrow and that'll be out of the way. Aggie wants to wear hers now, but she's not getting it until Father Christmas brings it down her chimney. She's begged, and had a little weep, but I've put me foot down. Christmas Day and not before.'

Bessie made sure the clothes were off the landing and in her bedroom before Milly came over for her dinner. She was afraid that if the girl saw the boys' trousers she wouldn't be able to keep it to herself. The temptation to tell her best friend Jack would be too great.

They were eating their meal and not a word had been spoken for a while. This was unusual as Milly was a real chatterbox, never stopped talking usually during a meal. When Bessie shot a quick glance her way, she noticed the girl seemed preoccupied, as though there was something on her mind. She was soon proved right.

'Auntie Bessie, can I ask you something?' Milly kept her eyes down, her hand gripping the fork which was chasing a potato around her plate. 'You won't get mad at me, will you?'

'Now, Amelia Sinclair, when have I ever got mad with you? You can always talk to me, and I will always listen, yer should know that by now. Whatever it is yer want to ask, do it now and give that poor potato a rest, 'cos it's worn out running around that ruddy plate.'

Milly giggled, put the fork down and addressed the potato. 'I'm sorry, Mr Potato, but you can have a rest now while I talk to Auntie Bessie.' She laid down the fork and leaned her elbows on the table. 'Will I be here on Christmas Day, Auntie Bessie? Jack said there's going to be a party, and I would like to be here for that.'

Bessie wiped the back of a hand across her lips. 'I'm afraid I can't answer you, sweetheart, because I don't know. I would love you to be here, yer know that, but it's not up to me. Hasn't your mother mentioned it?'

Milly shook her head, looking downcast. 'Mother hasn't said anything about Christmas, and I don't like to ask her. But she might go to her friend's, I'm sure she'd like that better than being just the two of us.'

'I really don't know what to say, Milly, but yer know I'd love yer to be here. It's up to your mother, though, there's little I can do about it.' But the sadness on the pretty young face was more than Bessie could bear. 'Look, I'll tell yer what, sweetheart, I'll have a word with yer mother when she calls for yer. I can't promise anything, but I'll do me best.' And hoping to put a smile back where it belonged, she added, 'I'll get me guardian angel to have a word with her, too, 'cos she can be very persuasive when she's asked nicely to help me out.'

This cheered Milly up no end, and she giggled, 'Yer could ask the door and the fireplace as well. I bet they'd help if they could, being good friends of yours.'

'The door won't help, I'm afraid, 'cos it blames me for leaving it out in the cold all the time. I'm fed up telling it that every door is out in the cold, but I may as well talk to the wall.' Bessie leaned across the table, her face one big smile. 'Ay, I forgot about the wall, so there's another one to get on our side. Oh, I don't think we can lose with so many friends, it'll be a walkover.' She reached across for Milly's plate. 'Come on, sweetheart, let's get the dishes washed, 'cos yer mother will be here any minute.'

Evelyn's face was set when she came into Bessie's living room. She had made a decision and wanted to get it off her chest before she weakened. When she sat down, she addressed her daughter. 'Amelia, will you be a good girl and go home while I have a word with Miss Maudsley in private? I won't leave you on your own for long, and as the fire will be lit the room will be nice and warm. You could take the doll for company.'

'Yes, Mother.' Milly draped her coat over her arm. 'Shall I put the kettle on so you can have a cup of tea when you come in?'

Evelyn shook her head. 'I would rather you didn't light the gas, just in case of an accident. But I shan't be long.'

'Put that coat on, sweetheart, 'cos it's bitter out,' Bessie told her. 'I know it's only two or three steps, but yer could still catch cold.'

Evelyn sat nervously fingering her gloves as she waited for the door to close on her daughter. Then she wasted no time. 'I have thought over what you said about my late husband's family, Bessie, and intend doing what you suggested I should do. It is a drastic step for me, after eight years, and I risk being shunned. But I will not give Philip up without a fight. I love him dearly, and he returns my love. It remains to be seen if he will still feel the same when he knows I have lied to him about Amelia.' She screwed up her eyes and shook her head. 'No, I have not told him a deliberate lie, though I have acted one and that is as bad. But I believe there might be a way of keeping his love. After the holidays, I intend to visit Mr Lister-Sinclair with Amelia. When he sees the likeness between my daughter and his son, I don't think he could or indeed would want to deny she is truly his granddaughter. For Amelia is so like Charles it is uncanny. And if he accepts Amelia, then the hardest part of my battle will be over.'

'I think it is the best thing to do for everyone's sake. Amelia's grandfather would probably welcome yer both with open arms.' Bessie's heart went out to the woman she'd once thought of as a stuck-up snob, but who now looked sad and vulnerable. 'Yer'd never forgive yerself if yer didn't try.'

'My hope is that this time my father-in-law will believe me. It would make it so much easier for me to be truthful with Philip. You see, Bessie, my one fear is that, like Mr Lister-Sinclair,

Philip won't believe the man I married was the father of Amelia. After all, any man could have been, in fact, I could have been a woman who bestowed her favours freely.' Tears weren't far away, and she was quiet for a while until she composed herself. 'It doesn't automatically mean Philip will gather me to him and swear undying love for me. Rather than still wanting to marry me, he may turn me away for what he sees as my deceitfulness. But I love him so much I am prepared to throw myself at his mercy. And more than that I cannot do.'

'If he loves you as much as yer love him, then I'm sure he won't turn away from yer. Why should he? You are a married woman who had a baby by a husband killed in the war. Is there anything so terrible in that? Of course there isn't, and yer mustn't let anyone think you are ashamed. Keep that in mind and yer'll find the courage and the strength to do what yer have to do.'

Evelyn leaned forward and took both of Bessie's hands in hers. 'If I hadn't been so selfish all these years, thinking myself too good for anyone in this street, then what good friends we could have been. You would probably have talked sense into me years ago, making me confront Mr Lister-Sinclair with the truth. But then I would never have met Philip. I might have lived in luxury, and Amelia and I would have wanted for nothing. However, I would have missed two very important events in my life. One is meeting the man I adore, and the other is being brought down from my ivory tower to meet the most genuine people I'm ever likely to meet. I've been taught well by you and your friends, Bessie, and it's a lesson I will never forget. That money doesn't mean a thing if you haven't got good friends who are warm and compassionate.'

Bessie could feel a lump forming in her throat. 'I'm sorry meself that we left it so late to become friends, and I hope that now we are, we always will be. And I'm glad yer've decided to take the bull by the horns, for I do believe you will come through it a very happy woman. I hope so, for Amelia's sake. But I hope yer'll never stop me from seeing her? I have grown to love her very much.'

'That's a promise I will make, and which will be easy to keep. My daughter would never forget you, or allow me to either.' Evelyn stood up. 'I'd better go, I don't like leaving Amelia on her own too long. But I do thank you for making me see sense, and will keep you informed every step of the way.'

'Tomorrow night, when yer've got five minutes to spare, I'll tell yer what we've bought so far with the money. A lot of poor people in this street will bless you and your friend for giving them the chance to enjoy Christmas with food and warmth.' Bessie told herself now was the time. 'Oh, speaking of Christmas, will I be having Milly? That's if yer want to spend the time with yer friend, of course. If you are, I'd be very happy to have her for the two days.'

'Thank you, Bessie, I'd love to be with my friend. And I don't think I'm being selfish, I know my daughter would much prefer to spend Christmas with you and your friends.'

Chapter Twenty-Six

On the Monday of Christmas week, Bessie spent her dinner break going into town to buy material for the two dresses she had to make for the holidays. If she didn't put a move on they wouldn't be made in time, and then she'd have no present for Milly or a decent dress for herself. There was no time for her to dawdle in the big store, so she headed straight to the material department. Thankfully there were few customers, for most people who were able to make their own clothes would have allowed themselves more time than she had. Still, she was working every day and couldn't be in two places at once.

As she approached the long counter covered with bales of material of all colours, her eyes lighted on a roll of crêpe in a lovely warm deep wine colour. That's for me, she said to herself, just what I had in mind. She beckoned one of the assistants over and asked her for three yards, which was ample for her with her small, slim figure. While the assistant was busy, she walked along the counter, eyes searching for a colour which would suit Milly. And then she spotted it. A soft green, the same colour as Milly's eyes. It was in a linen material, medium thickness, which would be suitable for wear in summer or winter. She could make a small round collar in white, which would set it off nicely. So the assistant was asked to cut two yards off, and would she kindly wrap both materials together to make it easier for Bessie to carry?

Once out of the shop, she hurried to the tram stop. She'd be hard pushed to get back to her sewing machine before the buzzer sounded, but she wouldn't get into trouble for she was otherwise always punctual and never took time off. Her tummy was rumbling with hunger, but it would have to rumble until she got back to work. She'd brought two sandwiches in with her and had left them on her machine, covered by a roll of cloth. She'd have to wait until her boss had his back turned or was out of sight in his office before she could eat them. Anyway, she was feeling so pleased with her purchases she wouldn't be upset if she got told off.

Once settled on the tram, Bessie let her body sway from side to side with the movement, as her mind drifted over the latest events. Life was good right now with everything ordered for the hampers, which would be picked up by the very happy recipients on the morning of Christmas Eve, about ten o'clock, to give the butcher time to have them delivered. When Bessie had first told her neighbours in the street, a few days ago, their faces showed they didn't believe her. They took some convincing at first, for nobody had ever offered them a helping hand before. Then she'd been hugged and kissed so much she expected to be bruised all over. But it would have been worth it just to see a smile on the thin faces of these careworn women who had been dreading Christmas without even money for food, let alone presents for their children. And what mother doesn't want to see the happiness on their children's faces when they think Father Christmas has been and left them a present?

Bessie was brought out of her reverie by the conductor dinging the bell to warn the driver there were passengers wanting to alight at the next stop. When she glanced through the window she saw it was hers. She picked up the paper bag with the material in, and clung to the back of each of the seats between her and the platform. She swung herself down on to the pavement with a smile on her face when she remembered there were only five more days to go. She'd have to move fast to have the two dresses finished, but she'd get there. Once she started she'd go like the clappers.

Rita was taking a flat iron off the gas stove when she heard the entry door latch slotting into place. 'Oh, no,' she groaned aloud, 'I was hoping to get these finished and out of the way before the kids come in from school.' Putting the iron back on the gas ring, she lifted the net curtain and saw Aggie walking up the back yard. But it wasn't the same Aggie she was used to seeing, with untidy hair, stained pinny and stockings crumpled round her ankles. Oh, no, this Aggie was walking with the air of someone of note, her head held high and bust standing to attention. Rita didn't bother opening the door, she knew her neighbour would walk in without knocking. So she quickly picked up the iron, pretending she hadn't seen anything.

Aggie shut the door behind her and waited for her mate to notice her. 'Busy are yer, queen? I see yer pressing the boys' trousers.'

Rita didn't look up. 'Yeah, I want to get them out of the way before they come in from school. I've done the best I can with their shirts, and they look quite presentable, so that'll be them finished.' She was dying to look up, could imagine her mate getting all hot and bothered by this time. But Rita told herself to wait and see what Aggie would do to draw attention to herself.

'I've pressed Kenny's trousers and Kitty's dress, and put them away in the wardrobe so they won't see them. And I've done me own dress as well.' Aggie was indeed getting all hot and bothered. She'd gone to the trouble of dolling herself up to the nines, and her mate hadn't even looked at her! 'Have yer pressed your dress yet?'

'Yeah, I did mine first.' Rita didn't turn a hair, just kept on pressing even though she knew she wasn't making a ha'porth of difference to the trousers because the iron had gone cool. 'It's come up a treat, looks really nice on me.'

That did it for Aggie. 'Well, you miserable cow! I suppose yer've put yer dress away in the wardrobe without letting me see it on yer, have yer? That's dead mean of yer, that is, seeing as I've gone to the trouble of coming to show yer what mine looks like on.'

Rita was chuckling inside. 'It looks very nice on yer, sunshine, dead smart.'

'How would yer know that, smart arse, when yer can't even be bothered to turn yer head to see what I look like?'

'I heard the entry door go, sunshine, and lifted the curtain to see who it was. And, to my complete and utter amazement, I see a stranger walking up the yard.' Rita put the iron back on the stove. 'I had to look twice, and it was only seeing the blue fleecy-lined bloomers that I realised it was me mate and not Ethel Barrymore.'

Aggie bent down. 'My bloomers are not showing, clever clogs, 'cos I've put new elastic in the legs. So ye're not so smart, after all.'

'Take no notice of me, Aggie, 'cos I'm only jealous. Here's me, looking like a scullery maid, and you dressed to kill. I was taken aback, I can tell yer, jealousy eating at the very heart of me. In fact it was worse than jealousy, it was envy. And as yer know, envy is one of the deadly sins.'

'All right, all right, queen, yer've had yer twopennyworth of fun now so let's have a bit of honesty out of yer. How d'yer like me dress, and does it look nice on me?'

'Aggie, yer really look great. The dress suits yer, it fits yer curves as though it's been made for yer, and it makes yer look a lot thinner. Ye're never likely to get such a good bargain in yer life again. When yer go out in that, with yer new coat on, the neighbours will think there's a new family moved into the street.' Rita kissed her on the cheek. 'Just wait until Sam sees yer, his eyes will pop out of his head.'

Aggie's chuckle should have warned her neighbour. 'It's

not his eyes I'm after, queen, my thoughts are a bit lower down.'

'Don't you say another word, Aggie Gordon, or yer'll be sorry.' Rita wagged a stiffened finger under her friend's nose. 'Ye're likely to end up on yer backside in the yard, and that wouldn't do yer posh dress much good.'

Aggie managed to look aggrieved. 'I don't know what's wrong with you, Rita Wells. Ye're a married woman, like meself, have had two kids, like meself, and yer husband must have got the same parts to his body as mine has.' She stopped as a thought apparently entered her head, gave a little nod then went on, 'Mind you, your feller might have the same number of parts, but it doesn't mean his are the same size as my feller's. And I'm just beginning to see why yer haven't got no sense of humour, and never laugh when I tell yer a dirty joke. *That's* why there's never a smile on yer gob in the mornings when I come in full of the joys of spring after a night of passion.' Oh, how Aggie's thoughts ran ahead of her. She'd bring a smile to her mate's face if it killed her. 'Yer know, I always thought we were good friends, helping each other out in times of trouble. So it makes me feel really sad that yer have suffered in silence instead of sharing yer troubles with me.'

'What troubles?' Rita asked, while knowing full well she was walking into a trap. 'I haven't got no troubles, what are yer on about?'

'Yer can tell me, queen, yer know yer can trust me not to tell no one. And I'm the best person to ask about any problems ye're going through in the bedroom department. Yer shouldn't just lie there, gazing at the ceiling and thinking of England, when yer could be having the time of yer life. My feller sends thrills up and down me spine, has me crying out with desire, and takes me on a journey to heaven and back. Yer just don't know what ye're missing, queen, yer really don't.'

'Ah, but that's the point, sunshine, I don't miss it. Not one tiny cry or scream, not one plea for more, not one creak or twang of the bedsprings. And many's the night me and Reg have lain there listening to Sam pleading, "Ah, not again, girl, I'm worn out! It's all right for you, sitting on yer backside all day, but I've just put in a day's hard work, I haven't got the energy. Now turn on yer side and behave yerself until Saturday night." '

But Rita should have known she couldn't get the better of her mate. For as Aggie stood there with a look on her face that could have been anger or horror, she was actually using the time to think of a really good answer. 'D'yer mean you and Reg lie there and listen to our private conversation? Yer have no right to listen in, queen, that's being nosy.'

'Aggie, sunshine, once you get in yer bedroom, nothing is private because yer've got such a loud voice. If yer don't want to be heard, keep it down.'

'Ah, is that why we never hear you and Reg enjoying yerselves? D'yer put gags in yer mouth, so we can't hear yer?' Aggie dropped her head. 'It just goes to show, yer never really know who yer bleeding friends are.' She began to click her tongue. 'Yer've really taken me by surprise, queen, I'm cut to the quick. I mean, fancy your Reg lying there, listening to me pleading and not coming to my aid.'

Rita chuckled, 'How could he come to yer aid when yer were in bed with yer husband?'

'Yeah, I know all that, queen, but Reg knew my feller wasn't up to it, and knowing I was desperate, he could have come and taken over. I mean, he's a good mate of Sam's, he could have helped him out. Sam would have appreciated it.' Aggie saw Rita walking towards her with a very stern expression on her face, and tried to reason with her. 'One man is as good as another in a dark room, queen, and you would have gained from it, too! I've got a few tricks up me sleeve I could have taught Reg, and yer'd be surprised how much more exciting yer love life would have been. You and your feller wouldn't be lying there like dummies every night, listening to me and Sam enjoying ourselves, 'cos yer'd be too busy trying out the new tricks I'd taught him.'

Her face deadpan, Rita lifted the latch on the kitchen door. 'On yer way, sunshine, I've got too much to do to listen to what yer get up to in yer bedroom. So yer can just poppy off.'

Aggie's jaw dropped. 'Yer mean I get all dolled up in me new dress, comb me ruddy hair, and I don't even get asked if I want a cup of tea? Ye're taking yer spite out on me 'cos yer don't like hearing what goes on in me bedroom?'

Rita shook her head. 'No, that's not the reason I'm throwing yer out, sunshine, it's because yer were prepared to tell my Reg the secret of your fantastic love life, instead of telling me.' She couldn't keep her face straight any longer, her cheeks were aching. 'It's me what's supposed to be yer mate, not my Reg.'

Aggie pushed her friend aside and rushed into the living room before Rita could stop her. 'For one cup of tea, with a spoonful of sugar in, I will sit here and tell yer everything yer want to know about how to make your feller a happy man.'

Rita closed the back door and faced her mate. 'Yer know I don't like bad language or crude words, don't yer? So before yer get a cup of tea, I want yer to promise that what yer tell me will be really romantic, with no crude words about body parts.'

As she looked up at her neighbour, Aggie was thinking to herself that this cup of tea was going to be hard come by. How could she explain what went on in bed if she was stuck with making it romantic, and no crude words about body parts? Blimey, there was only one body part needed to give yer thrills of excitement, so if she couldn't be crude, what could she call it? Oh, she'd think of something while the kettle was boiling. 'All right, queen, yer've got yerself a deal.'

Rita was doubled up with silent laughter as she put the kettle on the stove. Many's the night her and Reg, lying in bed, had been convulsed as they listened to the antics of their neighbours. Not so much Sam as Aggie, who didn't know how to keep her voice down. And how she was going to tell Rita now about making love, without using crude words . . . well, she couldn't wait to find out. Particularly one part of Sam's anatomy that seemed to be Aggie's favourite, and for which she had several names.

The kettle began to whistle and Rita reached for a cloth to cover her hand from the steam as she poured the boiling water into the teapot. Perhaps she shouldn't encourage her friend, she might hear more than she'd bargained for. And it wouldn't be fair to encourage her then tell her off if her language, natural to her, was objectionable to Rita. No, it wasn't fair to do that to a good mate and neighbour.

'Here yer are, sunshine, a cup of nice, sweet tea. And I managed to find two biscuits, so there's one in yer saucer.' Rita put the cups down on the table. 'And I've decided not to charge yer, seeing as it's Christmas week. And I don't mean charge yer as in money, but as in yer telling me the story of yer love life. So drink up and enjoy yerself.'

When Aggie's bottom hit the chair, her bosom hit the table at the same time. 'Oh, thank God for that, queen, 'cos I've been racking me bleeding brain on how to tell yer something without using any bad words. And if I'd tried to describe things by using me hands instead of words, I know yer'd have clocked me one.' She took a deep breath. 'I can enjoy me cup of tea now, and me biscuit, even though it is two halves of a broken one. I'm not fussy, queen, I'm dead easy to please. And I'm not going to dunk the biscuit for long in case a piece drops off, like it usually does with me. I don't want to get a stain on me good dress 'cos I won't have time to wash it again before the big day.'

Rita watched with her heart in her mouth as Aggie picked up half a biscuit in her chubby hand and held it in the hot tea. Please God, don't let her ruin her dress, she hasn't got another one. I know she's not always as pure as she should be, but she doesn't mean no harm, she's really got a good heart. Then came a sigh of relief as the biscuit was taken from the tea and carried to Aggie's mouth with one hand, while her other was held below in case of an accident.

Aggie chuckled. 'Yer can breathe now, queen, the mission was accomplished with no accidents. But I don't think I'll dunk the other one, it's not worth the risk. It would break me bleeding heart if I messed me dress up before my feller sees it. It's only once in a blue moon he sees me looking decent, and I can't wait to see his face.'

'I'll bet yer a pound to a pinch of snuff he'll grab hold of yer and hug yer so close yer'll be gasping for breath.'

'D'yer think so, queen?' Aggie lowered her head a little so her friend wouldn't see her lips twitching. 'Ay, I don't suppose yer'd do us a favour on Christmas morning, would yer?'

'Oh, I don't think so, sunshine, there'll be too much to do here. Can't it wait for some other time, like Boxing Day?'

'Not really, queen, the mood would have worn off by then.'

Rita pursed her lips and wagged her head from side to side. 'I don't know why I always give in to yer, sunshine, but yer never fail to get round me. What is it yer want me to do for yer, and how long will it take? Don't forget I've got the dinner to see to.'

'Twenty minutes should do it, and I'd be really grateful to yer, queen.'

'What do yer want me to do in that twenty minutes?'

'Mind the kids for us. They wouldn't be in the way, they'd play with your two.'

'But where are you and Sam going? Yer didn't tell me yer were going out.'

'Oh, we wouldn't be going far, queen, only up the stairs to the bedroom.' Aggie banged the table so hard it lifted the cups out of the saucers. 'Oh, if yer could only see yer face, yer'd die laughing. And I can tell, without yer saying, that yer won't be minding the kids for us on Christmas morning. I'm surprised, really, 'cos I'd rather have twenty minutes with my feller, than the present yer've bought for me.'

'I haven't bought yer no present, Aggie Gordon, and well yer know it. Where would I get the money from to be buying you a present?'

Aggie spread her hands out as though asking for understanding, while inside she was having a good laugh. 'Yer couldn't buy me a better present than giving me twenty minutes alone with my feller. And it wouldn't cost yer a farthing either. Won't yer at least give it some thought? It would put me in a good mood for the rest of the day, and I'd go through me work like a dose of Andrews' Little Liver Pills.'

Rita looked in Aggie's cup to make sure it was empty before she spoke. Then she pushed her chair back and took her neighbour's elbow. 'I'll help yer up, sunshine, then let's see yer going through my kitchen door as fast as yer can, without the help of Andrews' Little Liver Pills. That'll get yer in practice for Christmas morning.'

With Rita helping her along, Aggie seemed to bounce across the living-room floor. 'Call yerself a friend! I bet I'd get more sympathy from her in number twenty-two.'

This statement pulled Rita up sharp. 'Mrs Finnigan? Yer can't stand the sight of the woman, yer call her all the names under the sun!'

'I know I don't like her, and I know I call her fit to burn.' Aggie was putting a fierce face on. 'But I bet if I asked her to do that little favour for me, she'd say she would.'

'Oh, I agree!' Rita glared back. 'She would say yes out of fear. The poor woman is terrified of yer.'

Aggie suddenly erupted. Her eyes receded into her cheeks, and her bosom and tummy shook with laughter. From between the folds of flesh, her eyes appeared for a second as she asked, 'So I take it yer won't have the kids on Christmas morning?'

Rita collapsed. Her arms went around Aggie's neck and they clung together, laughing so loud the neighbours could hear. The sound brought a smile to many faces. 'Aggie Gordon, what would I do without you?'

Between gasps, Aggie replied, 'Yer'd be bleeding miserable, queen, same as I would be without you.'

Bessie hurried up the street on her way home from work. But she wasn't on her own side, she wanted to ask a favour from Rita. When her friend opened the door, Bessie put a finger to her lips, telling Rita not to speak. If Milly heard her voice, she'd be out like a shot and that was what Bessie didn't want. 'I'm after a favour, Rita,' she said softly, holding up the paper bag. 'I've got the material in here for the dresses for Christmas and I don't want Milly to see it, I want it to be a surprise on Christmas morning. So will yer keep her here for a bit longer while I hide it?'

'Of course she can stay here, she's in the middle of a game with our Jack. But aren't yer cutting it a bit fine when there's only a couple of days to Christmas?'

'I know, but I don't seem to have had time to breathe the last few weeks. You and Aggie have sorted the hampers out, but I've had to keep check on the money every night, and by the time Evelyn calls and takes Milly home, I'm too tired for anything.' Bessie, red in the face from battling the wind, grinned. 'I'll not take long once I start. I can have Milly's dress cut out in half an hour. I'll do that tonight when she goes home. I don't need a pattern, 'cos it's something I do all day. I could cut a dress out with me eyes shut.'

'I wish I was that clever,' Rita said, 'but I'm ruddy hopeless. Anyway, yer'd better go before Milly hears yer. I'll keep her for half an hour, and perhaps yer can get her dress cut out in that time.'

'Ah, ye're a smasher, Rita, a real pal. I made a pan of stew last night, so I only have to put a match to the stove to warm it

through slowly. And I can have the dress done while I'm waiting.'
Bessie, as thin as a rake, was across the cobbles in no time. Rita
would have sworn her feet didn't touch the ground, The two
women waved to each other then disappeared into their own
houses.

Bessie went straight through to the kitchen and lit a match
under the pan. Then, still moving at the double, she went back
to the tiny hall to hang up her coat. Without stopping for breath,
she carried the plant from the centre of the table to the
sideboard, whipped the chenille cloth off and folded it up.
Then the green material was taken from the bag and spread on
the table, and a pair of scissors and a box of straight pins
brought out of one of the sideboard drawers. This was a job
Bessie was used to and good at. She'd been doing it every day
for about twenty years. With confidence and speed the scissors
snipped away until the skirt was cut and folded to one side,
followed by two parts of the bodice and the two short sleeves.
The old saying that the hands are sometimes quicker than the
eye was certainly true in Bessie's case. When Milly knocked
everything had been tidied away and the makings of her
Christmas present were lying on Bessie's bed, ready to sew
when she was on her own later. As she prepared to put their
dinners out, Bessie decided she would buy the small white
collar, it would save her time. She'd seen one in a haberdashery
shop nearby which would really set it off. It had a ticket on it
saying it was sixpence, but Bessie thought it would be worth it
because the white linen was edged with lace, and Milly would
be over the moon with it.

There was a rush to get the table cleared and the dishes washed
before Evelyn was due, and Milly giggled as the knock came
when she was reaching up to put the last plate on a shelf. 'Just in
time, Auntie Bessie, we were saved by the bell.'

Bessie gave her a big hug before hurrying through the living
room to open the door. 'Come in, Evelyn, it's bitter out there.

Winter has certainly come with a vengeance, I wouldn't be surprised if we have thick snow for Christmas.'

Evelyn shivered as she took her gloves off and went to stand near the fire. 'I don't mind if I'm indoors, I think snow looks so pretty seen through a window. It's when it turns to slush I don't like it. And I have to tell you that I don't know what I'd do if your friend didn't light my fire for me. It is such a pleasure to walk into a warm room. I often wonder how Amelia and I managed all those years of coming into a freezing cold house.'

Milly stood at the kitchen door, watching and listening. Her mother had changed such a lot in the last few months, and the girl was delighted that she and Bessie had become friends. But although Milly was pleased she was allowed to come to stay with Bessie so often, and her mother wasn't so distant with her, she knew she wasn't treated by her mother as Jack and Billy were treated by theirs. She saw there what a mother's love was, but had never experienced it for herself. Oh, things weren't as strict, and she didn't get told off so often now, but the girl knew that Bessie's love for her was genuine while her mother didn't show any love at all.

'Would you like me to go home and have a cup of tea ready for you, Mother? 'Milly asked. 'I will be very careful striking a match.'

This suited Evelyn, so she agreed. 'Yes, that would be nice. But you must promise to be very careful.'

Milly threw her arms around Bessie and gave her a big hug and kiss. 'I'll see you tomorrow, Auntie Bessie. It won't be long now to Christmas, will it?'

'No, sweetheart, only a few days now. And Father Christmas will be visiting all the children who have been good, and leaving them a present.'

'I've been good, haven't I, Auntie Bessie? I haven't been cheeky or naughty, and I always do as I'm told and say my prayers every night.'

'Oh, you've been very good.' Bessie felt uncomfortable talking to the child as though she was hers, when her own mother was sitting watching. But she couldn't force Evelyn into doing something that didn't come naturally to her. 'I think she's almost certain to get a visit from Father Christmas, don't you, Evelyn?'

'Oh, undoubtedly! And as you've been such a good girl, Amelia, I think we can safely say you will get a good present.'

Milly smiled, even though her mother still sounded distant, as though she was talking to a complete stranger. 'I'll go and put the kettle on.'

Evelyn listened to the door closing then said, 'I'm glad Amelia offered to make tea, I wanted to speak to you. I have bought her a new dress and coat for Christmas, but I don't want her to see them before. How am I going to manage that?'

'Where are they now?'

'Still in the shop. I've paid for them, they just need picking up. I can do that tomorrow when I leave the office, but if I take them home she's bound to see them.'

'Drop them off before yer come here. Put them in yer wardrobe, and I'll get them after work on Thursday. Don't worry, Milly won't see them, I'll make sure of that.'

Evelyn got to her feet. 'That's a load off my mind, thank you. And now I'd better get in to her.'

'Are yer still going to see yer father-in-law, or have yer changed yer mind?'

'I haven't changed my mind, no! It's my one hope of clearing up this mess. Amelia is off school for a couple of days after Christmas, and I'll take her on one of those days. And have no fear that I will back out, for I am determined.'

'I thought you were leaving it until the New Year, when all the holidays are over?'

'That was my intention, but I really can't wait that long, I have to get it sorted after Christmas, and hopefully start the New Year with my prayers and wishes granted. I may not be lucky, it's possible my father-in-law will not be at the office on the days before New Year, he may take an extended holiday. But as Amelia is off school then, I intend to take a chance. If I am unfortunate and my father-in-law isn't in the office, I will have to keep her off school one day in the first week of January.'

'I wish you all the luck in the world, Evelyn, I really do.'

Bessie closed the door on her neighbour and sighed as she leaned back against it. She meant what she'd said to her neighbour, she did wish her well. But was the time drawing near when she would no longer be able to see the young girl she'd grown to love? She sniffed up and pulled herself away from the door. Crying wouldn't get her anywhere, she should have known from the beginning that one day Amelia would be lost to her. And it was no good being miserable with Christmas on top of them. She wanted to give the girl the best Christmas she'd ever had, so she'd never forget her Auntie Bessie.

Chapter Twenty-Seven

Bessie's kitchen was as busy as a market on Christmas Eve morning with all the neighbours coming at five-minute intervals to pick up their precious hampers. Rita and Aggie were there to help, and there were many tears of happiness shed that morning as the women gazed down at the packets of tea, sugar, margarine, fruit, potatoes, veg, bread, biscuits and chicken, complete with dripping. Oh, and a couple of colourful crackers for the kids to pull. Bessie had put a piece of paper on the top of each box with a name on, so there were no mistakes made and every person on the list got their hamper.

Next door, in her kitchen, waiting for the kettle to boil so she could get washed, Evelyn could hear the commotion in the yard next door, and being curious hurried up to Amelia's bedroom to look down from the back window, with her daughter following close behind.

'What is it, Mother?' Milly asked as she watched a woman walking down her Auntie Bessie's yard carrying a box and looking very happy. 'Look, there's another lady coming into her yard. I wonder what's going on?'

'Let's be quiet for a while, Amelia, and we might see the reason for these women visiting Miss Maudsley.' It was after she'd seen four of them arrive empty-handed and five minutes later leave carrying a box that Evelyn realised what was happening. It was easy to see the chicken on the top of each one. The sight made Evelyn feel very humble. She wanted so much out of life, always had done, and these people asked for so little. 'Your

401

Auntie Bessie is a very kind person, Amelia, and so are Mrs Wells and Mrs Gordon. They're giving food to those women to help them give their families some festive cheer.'

'It must be costing them a lot of money 'cos, look, there's another lady coming in from the entry.'

'I did hear Miss Maudsley say that a very kind gentleman had given her a certain amount of money to help families who were very poor. I'm sure his heart would be warmed if he could see what was happening next door, and his own Christmas would feel extra special knowing he'd made so many people happy.'

'Won't Auntie Bessie tell him how happy the people were? I bet she will, 'cos I'm sure she'd like him to know.'

'Oh, she's bound to tell him,' Evelyn said, promising herself that as soon as she got to the apartment she would tell Philip of the scene she was now witnessing. And she would also tell him of the barefoot boys now wearing serviceable shoes that would see them through the winter. He would be so pleased. In her mind she could already see his smiling face.

'You can tell Miss Maudsley we saw the women and their hampers of food, and how much we both admire her, but you must not question her about where the money came from. Do you understand that, Amelia? You would be asking her to break a confidence, as the benefactor wishes to remain anonymous.'

Milly nodded. 'I won't ask her, Mother, but even if I did she wouldn't tell me. Auntie Bessie would never break a promise or tell a secret.' The girl was on pins, the time wasn't going fast enough for her. 'When am I going next door, Mother?'

'I said I would be leaving to go to my friend's at twelve o'clock and would call with you then so I could wish her the compliments of the season. I only have to get washed, I have my clothes all ready, so be patient for a little while longer.' A pang of guilt caused her to add, 'I have left Christmas presents for you, Amelia, I haven't forgotten you, but I'm not telling you any more, it would spoil the surprise.'

'Thank you, Mother.' Milly turned to leave the room. 'I'll get Daisy ready, she needs her hair combing.'

'Ta-ra, Sally, mind how yer go!' Rita closed the kitchen door and let out a long sigh. 'Thank God, that was the last one. Me feet are killing me, and I'm dying for a cuppa.'

'It's yer own bleeding fault, yer would insist on walking some of them down the yard in case they slipped.' Aggie turned the gas higher under the kettle. 'They would have made it under their own steam but, oh, no, yer had to do the job proper.'

'Stop moaning, the pair of yer,' Bessie said. 'Anyone would think yer'd done a day's hard work down a coal mine. Go and sit at the table and I'll bring yer a cup of tea through when the water's boiled. I'll have to put more water on, 'cos I've got thirty-six jelly creams to make.'

'Thirty-six!' Aggie put a hand to her cheek. 'What the bleeding hell d'yer want thirty-six jelly creams for?'

Bessie raised her brows. 'Don't yer like jelly creams, sweetheart?'

'Yeah, 'course I like jelly creams, queen, but not thirty bleeding six of them.'

'Have yer forgotten there's a kids' party here tomorrow afternoon, for eighteen kids what have probably never been to one in their lives? Surely yer don't expect to have a party without jelly creams, or trifle come to that.'

Aggie wasn't very good at adding up in her head, so she used her fingers. And when she found she ran out of fingers, she turned to Rita. 'Ay, queen, if the kids have one each, how many does that leave of the thirty-six?'

Rita gave Bessie a sly wink. 'Well, if they have one each there'll be eighteen over, sunshine, but they'll more than likely want two each. Which comes to thirty-six.'

'Well, the greedy little buggers! D'yer mean they'll eat 'em all, and there'll be none left over for us?'

'I thought yer weren't that fussy, sunshine,' Rita said. 'After all, yer seemed surprised when Bessie said how many she was making. And yer aren't wicked enough to pinch a jelly cream out of a kid's mouth, are yer?'

Aggie was going to nod her head, but her chins were disgusted with her and refused point blank to move upwards. Instead they swayed from side to side, which meant she meant one thing but was forced to say another. 'I wouldn't pinch one, no, but I'd ask in a nice way if they'd take their bleeding hands off and give someone else a chance.'

'I'll pour the tea out,' Bessie said, grinning at the hurt expression on Aggie's chubby face. 'Before you two come to blows.' She reached the kitchen, stopped, then turned around. 'Don't fall out, for God's sake, 'cos ye're supposed to be doing me shopping while I see to the jellies, trifles, make thirty-six fairy cakes, and on top of that get me veg done for tomorrow. I don't want to be running round like a scalded cat on Christmas morning getting the dinner on, when I've got eighteen kids coming at two-thirty.'

'Me and Aggie will be over to give yer a hand, sunshine, we won't leave yer swinging on yer lonesome. And while we're having a cup of tea now, yer can be making yer shopping list out. It won't take me and Aggie long to get round the shops.'

Aggie clicked her teeth. 'I bet she'll give us a list as long as me arm, and we'll be running round the shops like blue-arsed flies.'

Rita threw daggers at her mate. 'Yer know, sunshine, if ye're not that fussy on coming to help at the kids' party, and ye're also not fussy on the party for the grown-ups at night, then just say the word, and Bessie's shopping list will be a lot shorter.'

Aggie wagged a forefinger, inviting Rita to come closer. 'Why don't yer keep yer ruddy nose out of my business? And if yer insist on meddling, then make sure yer get it right. I didn't say I wouldn't help at the kids' party, and I didn't say I didn't want to come to the one for the grown-ups, either. I am dying to help with the party, 'cos yer know I love kids, especially eighteen of the little sods. And I'm looking forward to the company of grown-ups, too, and even more the company of six bottles of milk stout.' She tapped the side of her nose. 'So keep this out of it in future, queen, 'cos a black eye wouldn't go with the colour of yer new dress.'

While they were enjoying their well-earned cup of tea, Bessie had her notepad in front of her and the stub of pencil between her fingers. 'I think I'd better get three large tin loaves, to be on the safe side. It should be ample 'cos everyone will have had a big Christmas dinner.' She wrote that down at the top of the sheet of paper. 'I've already got the margarine in, and tea, sugar and connie-onnie. The milkman is filling me big jug, and that will well see me through.' She put the pencil between her teeth and rolled her eyes. 'If yer get twenty-four sausage rolls, Rita, that should be enough 'cos I'm going to cut them in two. But what to put in the sandwiches, though . . . have yer got any ideas?'

'Jars of paste are always handy, sunshine,' Rita said. 'There's salmon, chicken and meat. A jar of each would go a long way. Don't forget there'll be the jelly creams, the big trifle and fairy cakes. I don't think yer need much more.'

Bessie was busy writing. 'I've put down two jars of each of the pastes, 'cos I've got to think of feeding you and the men in the evening. I think I'll push the boat out and get a quarter of boiled ham too, it won't hurt to go mad and spoil ourselves for a change.'

'Is this yer own money ye're using, sunshine, 'cos if it is then yer can cut out the likes of boiled ham. Yer work hard for yer money and I don't want yer spending it on us.'

Aggie turned her head and glared at her neighbour. 'Speak for yerself, queen, 'cos I'm very partial to a nice boiled ham sandwich. Partickerly with a bit of mustard on.'

Rita returned her glare. 'Oh, and do yer often have boiled ham in your house? And is it partickerly spread with mustard?'

Aggie scratched her head. 'Well, I can't remember exactly when I had it last, queen, but I do remember how much I enjoyed it.'

'Perhaps I can jog yer memory, sunshine, wasn't it at yer wedding reception?'

'Ooh, er, was it that long ago, queen? It just goes to show how time flies when ye're having fun.'

'Well, since yer partickerly like it with mustard, I'll have to put a small jar of that on me list.' Bessie licked the end of the pencil. 'How do yer spell partickerly, sweetheart?'

Aggie snorted. 'How the hell do I know? I want to eat it, not spell it!'

Rita kept her face straight. 'D'yer think it's spelt the same way as particularly? Or is that a different word altogether?'

Aggie got the last word. 'Oh, it's a different word altogether, queen, and I wouldn't partickerly like it spread on me boiled ham sandwich.'

Bessie was thinking of all the work she had to do. She'd finished Milly's dress, but still needed to do some work on her own. 'To get to the question yer asked, Rita, I still had three pound left of the money I was given. So last night I took two pound notes to the corner shop and asked Alf to give me some two-shilling pieces. Every hamper that went out of here this morning had a two-bob piece in it, wrapped up in a piece of me notepad so it couldn't be missed. The rest is buying lemonade and food for the kids' party and ours, and I'm paying for drinks for the grown-ups' party. That, I think, takes care of everything, and I hope it answers your question, sunshine.'

'I think yer've done wonders, Bessie,' Rita said. 'I couldn't have organised things the way you have, I'd have been out of my mind.'

'I'll go along with that, queen, because if anyone had given me that much money I'd have spent the lot on meself.' Aggie had her arms folded under her bosom and for once was serious. 'Well, perhaps not all on meself, but I would have spent some on me house. And that's why I'll be needing a reference from both of yer to give to St Peter if I ever make it up that pathway to the pearly gates. At least I'm not lying. I would have been tempted by seeing so much money, and I'd have given in to temptation.'

Rita patted her arm. 'I think most people in our situation would have been tempted, sunshine. Trying to stretch the money every week, robbing Peter to pay Paul, and yet never quite managing to make ends meet. But when push came to shove, Aggie, yer wouldn't have used that money for yerself. I know yer well enough to know that. Tough on the outside yer may be, and a big mouth yer may have that puts the fear of God in most of our neighbours, but a thief, never!'

'I know what I would have done, though, queen, I would have sat up all night looking at it.'

'What!' Rita exclaimed. 'You what loves yer bedroom so much?'

Bessie held a hand up for silence. 'Right, that settles it. When the word bedroom is mentioned in Aggie's presence, then it's time to split up. Here's the list, Rita, and a ten-bob note. While you're doing that I'll get meself sorted out. And when the men come in from work, will yer ask one of them to go to the corner pub for the drinks? I'd say a bottle of port, six bottles of milk stout, and whatever beer the men drink. The pound I've got left should take care of that.'

Rita helped Aggie to her feet. 'Come on, sunshine, just listening to Bessie has me head in a whirl. She can have things done while you and me are thinking about it.'

'I'm expecting Evelyn to bring Milly in any minute, so I'd better get this table cleared.' Bessie only had to mention Milly's name and her spirits lifted. She'd have the girl for nearly three days this time, and they'd both love every minute of it.

* * *

Bessie shone the small torch she kept by her bed, and the light from it told her it was nearly half-past six. She hadn't slept well, she was too excited. She'd never had a child in the house for Christmas and didn't know whether they woke up very early. She had heard that some children woke their parents in the middle of the night, wanting to know if Father Christmas had been. But what time Milly would wake she had no idea. Perhaps she should go down and light the fire so the room would be nice and warm. She'd hung a few decorations last night, with Milly's help, and draped silver and gold tinsel over the pictures and mirror so at least the room looked a bit Chrismassy. After the girl had gone to bed, Bessie had hung a pillowcase from one end of the mantelpiece, in which she'd put some fruit and nuts, a Christmas stocking filled with chocolate bars, a new dress she'd made for Daisy, a book of drawings and coloured pencils to colour them with. The green dress with its pretty white lace-trimmed collar was hanging on a coat-hanger at the other end of the mantelpiece. The presents from her mother, which Evelyn had brought in already wrapped in Christmas paper, Bessie had left on the table so they would be the first thing Milly saw when she came into the room.

Clicking her tongue with impatience, she swung her legs over the side of the bed. She'd be better off downstairs lighting the fire instead of lying in bed. She never could stand being idle. She felt for the fleecy dressing gown which she'd had for so many years she'd lost track, and slipped her arms into the sleeves. Then, careful not to make a sound, she crept down the stairs and into the sitting room which was still warm from the fire she'd had roaring up the chimney last night. Once she'd raked the ashes out, it wouldn't take long for the sticks of firewood to catch because some of the coals were still glowing. Moving at the double as she always did, she soon had the ashes in the bin and fresh coal laid on top of the sticks which were crackling into life.

'Now for a hot cuppa,' Bessie told the grate. 'It's flipping freezing outside. I was only in the yard for a few seconds and I'm shivering, I'm glad I don't have to go to work.' Five minutes later she was sitting at the table with her hands around a cup, watching the flames dancing up the chimney. In the peace and silence of the room, her thoughts drifted. Would this be the last Christmas she'd see Milly? If her grandparents took her to their heart, as they surely would, and if they were very rich and could give her anything her heart desired, then it would be churlish not to be happy for her. But, human nature being what it is, Bessie couldn't help feeling sad.

She was so wrapped up in her thoughts she didn't hear the tell-tale creak of the stairs. It was only when Milly jumped down the last two, and there was a slight thud, that she came out of her reverie. Putting her cup down, Bessie held out her arms. 'A very happy Christmas, sweetheart, and I hope Santa has been good to you.'

'Merry Christmas, Auntie Bessie.' Milly held her tight and rained kisses on her face. 'It's going to be the best Christmas I've ever had.' The girl's eyes had already taken in the large parcel at the end of the table, and the pillow case and dress hanging from the mantelpiece. Milly had been told from an early age by her mother that there was no such person as Father Christmas, and even though all the shops were decorated with pictures of him, and the girls in school talked of nothing else for weeks, she still didn't believe there was such a person. That is, until her Auntie Bessie had come on the scene. If her beloved Auntie Bessie said there was a Father Christmas, then there must be.

Bessie removed the girl's arms from her neck. 'Aren't yer going to see what presents yer've got, sweetheart? The big parcel on the table is from your mother, and she's wrapped it in pretty paper, so d'yer want to open that first?'

'Which do you think I should look at first?'

'Oh, your mother's, definitely. I bet it's something really nice.' When Milly hesitated, Bessie said cheerfully, 'I'll give yer a hand, shall I?'

'I think it would be best if you open it, Auntie Bessie, I'm afraid of tearing the paper.'

'Don't worry about that, sweetheart, 'cos half the pleasure is ripping the paper off to see what goodies are inside. Look, get hold of my hand and we'll do it together.'

The dress inside was in a deep red wool, with long sleeves. Very serviceable for winter days. The accompanying neat, tailored coat, in deep red and grey checked pure wool, was of the finest standard. 'Oh, aren't you a lucky girl, sweetheart, they're lovely! Oh, my, ye're going to be quite the young lady in these. Your mother has such good taste. Both the dress and the coat really are beautiful. Don't yer think so, sweetheart?'

Milly put her hand on the coat and stroked it, not because she wanted to but because she thought it was what was expected of her. 'Yes, they are nice, I'll be able to wear them on a Sunday or if I'm going somewhere special.'

'We'll fold them up for now while you look to see what other presents Santa has brought for yer. Then I'll find a coat hanger and hang them in the wardrobe. We're going to have a houseful this afternoon, and I don't want them to get stains on them.'

'Is that green dress for me, Auntie Bessie?' Milly's heart was beginning to beat faster at the thought of the party. Just think, eighteen children, and one of them her friend Jack. 'It looks very pretty.'

'That's your present from me. I made it for yer, and I hope yer like it.'

Milly stood on tip toe to reach the top of the hanger. 'It's beautiful, Auntie Bessie. Can I wear it for the party? I promise I'll be careful and won't dirty it.'

'Of course yer can wear it, sweetheart, and it wouldn't matter if yer did make it a bit mucky, it's easy enough to wash.'

The girl's happiness knew no bounds. She threw her arms around Bessie's waist and cried, 'Oh, thank you, thank you, thank you! It's the prettiest dress I've ever had. You must be very clever to have made it.'

When Bessie smiled, she was once again hugged and kissed. 'You are the bestest auntie in the whole world.'

'I'll believe yer where thousands wouldn't.' Bessie stroked her hair. 'Now take the pillowcase down and see what other presents are in there for yer, while I make another pot of tea and some toast. And we'll have to have an early dinner, 'cos don't forget, today is going to be a very busy day and I'll need your help with the guests. After breakfast, you and me are going to have to move fast if we're to have everything ready on time.'

Bessie had worried herself to death when Reg and Sam carried Rita's dining table over. There wasn't enough room inside her house and the men had to stand in the street while the women made space for it by carrying the sideboard out through the kitchen and into the yard. 'I hope it doesn't rain or snow on me sideboard,' Bessie wailed. 'I must have been crazy to think we'd get eighteen children in here.'

'Calm down, sunshine, it isn't like you to panic,' Rita said. 'Once the table comes in, we can get everything organised. Give the men a shout, Aggie, then we'll have to move out of the way.'

'I'll go and get the chairs from our house.' Aggie saw the legs of Rita's table being manoeuvred round the door and decided to go out the back way. 'I'll carry them over two at a time and leave them under yer window until the men are finished.'

Rita had been right. When the men finally struggled down the narrow passage, they were quick to take in which way the new table and Bessie's should stand to give most space. Then, the job accomplished, they went out whistling happily. 'Ooh, that looks better,' Bessie said with relief, 'now we can get the cloths on and start bringing the food in. I'm glad Milly's over in your house, Rita, 'cos she'd only be in the way here.'

'She looks a treat in the dress yer made her, sunshine, yer did a good job on it. And, oh, boy, is she swanking in front of our Jack. There's a permanent look of disgust on our Billy's face. He's more determined than ever he'll never have a girlfriend. He looked horrified when Reg said he'd have daughters of his own one day.'

Aggie was dying to say that the day would surely come when young Billy realised there was more to girls than a mouth, but she thought better of it. It was Christmas Day, after all, and Bessie was on the religious side. Not that there was anything wrong with that, but being too pure meant yer missed out on a lot.

'Come on, Aggie, shift yerself,' Rita said. 'Start bringing the plates in, and a cracker to go on each one. And if ye're going to drop a plate, make it one of yer own, eh? I haven't got that many I can spare one.'

'Well, the bleeding cheek of you!' Aggie looked hurt. 'Another crack like that and I'll be telling yer to sod off and do the job yerself.'

Bessie puckered her lips and blew out. 'Will you two shut up and get on with the job in hand? I'm a nervous wreck without listening to you arguing.' She wiped the back of a hand across her brow. 'I'm sweating cobs and I'll be glad when it's over. I'm sorry I even thought of such a daft idea, I want me bumps feeling.'

Rita put an arm across her friend's shoulder. 'Yer won't say that when yer see the kids' faces when they set eyes on the table. Believe me, sunshine, yer won't regret it.'

Once again Rita was right. Bessie was paid back a hundredfold when she saw the wide eyes of eighteen children who had never seen such a well-laid table or the variety of food on offer.

Jelly creams in red, green and yellow, a huge bowl of trifle topped with cream and tiny silver balls, fairy cakes iced on top, sausage rolls, and several plates piled high with sandwiches. Some of the boys were giving each other sly nudges to make sure their mates had seen the Christmas cracker beside each plate. They'd never had one of those before and were longing to pull them, but they'd been warned by their parents to be quiet and well behaved.

Milly wasn't quiet, though, she was so excited she couldn't stop chattering. 'Can we pull the crackers, Auntie Bessie?'

'Yes, of course yer can. As soon as Mrs Gordon and Mrs Wells have poured lemonade out for yer, we ladies are going into the kitchen and leaving you to it. Everyone is equal here, it's everyone's party, so help yourselves. But I'm relying on the big boys, like Billy, to see that everyone gets a fair share. And Kitty will see to the girls.'

Once the three women had retired to the kitchen and closed the door, the racket started. Free to talk now, the boys' voices could be heard above the girls'. 'Ay, this is great, isn't it? I never expected nothing like this. I wish me mam and dad could see how much is on this table.' His mate answered, 'There won't be this much by the time we've finished. Ay, can yer eat those silver things?' A girl had the answer to that. 'Yeah, yer can eat them, but they're hard so yer'd be better off sucking them.'

Rita moved from one foot to the other. 'Let's go over to mine for an hour, what d'yer say? Me feet are dropping off, I couldn't stand for much longer. The kids will be all right, I can tell our Billy to keep an eye on them, and none of them are bad kids.'

Aggie nodded. 'My feet have had it too! And don't forget we've got to wash all the dishes for our little party tonight. I won't be in good form if me corns are acting up. Tell our Kitty and your Billy to keep an eye on the others, they're both sensible. Besides, it's their party, for heaven's sake, leave them to enjoy themselves.'

'Put yer head around the door then, Rita,' Bessie said, her own feet playing her up. 'I'll have to sit down meself, I'm bushed.'

As soon as Rita opened the living-room door the racket stopped and there was complete silence. 'We're going over to mine for a cup of tea, and we're trusting you to behave yerselves. We want yer to enjoy yerselves, as long as nothing gets broken. When yer've finished eating, yer could play some games. I was going to suggest Blind Man's Bluff, but as there's no room to breathe in here, yer couldn't play that. So ye're going to have to use yer imagination, I'm sure one of yer can think of a game.'

Several heads nodded, and two boys said they knew loads of games. 'And we'll behave ourselves, missus.'

Rita smiled and said to herself, Ah, God love them, they get very little in life. 'Yer better had behave yerselves, sunshine, or yer won't be asked back to next year's party.'

One boy piped up, 'How long can we stay here for, Mrs Wells?'

'Ooh, I'll have to ask the boss about that.' Rita backed into the kitchen and closed the door. 'They want to know when yer'll be chucking them out. But you go and tell them yerself, Bessie, and take a good look at them. That should tell yer whether it's been worth all the hard work yer've put in.'

Aggie gave her mate a dig. 'Ay, we helped as well. Let's all have a look-see at them.'

Eighteen children and eighteen happy faces. They were all wearing the cheap paper hats they'd got out of the crackers, some of which were too big and kept falling down over their eyes or hanging cock-eyed, giving the wearer the appearance of being drunk. On the older boys the hats were too small and looked like a pimple on a mountain. But who cared? The kids were having the time of their lives, and the sight was a tonic to Bessie. 'I'll have to throw you out at five o'clock, kids, 'cos I'm having visitors tonight. But the main thing is, are yer enjoying yerselves?'

The roar from eighteen voices must have been heard as far away as the Pier Head, and left the women in no doubt that Bessie's Christmas party was a huge success.

At eight o'clock that night, Rita and Reg Wells, and Aggie and Sam Gordon were enjoying a quiet drink with Bessie. Milly had gone to bed without any coaxing, dead beat from all the excitement. For years she'd had no friends to play with, and now she had so many. And she had someone to kiss her goodnight and tuck her into bed.

'Well, it didn't take long to get the place back to normal, Bessie,' Rita said. 'No one would believe yer had eighteen kids here this afternoon for a party.'

'It's thanks to the four of yer that it is back to normal, I'd never have managed it on me own.' She took a sip of her milk stout. 'What with the table to be carried over to yours, the mountain of dishes to be washed, and the floor swept and mopped, I wouldn't have known where to start. In fact, I'd have probably thrown me hands in the air and gone to bed.'

'Well, yer can sit back and relax now, queen,' Aggie said with the permission of her chins. 'When my feller gets a few more beers down him, he'll entertain yer with a song. And after another milk stout, I might even give yer one meself. I used to be noted for me clear voice. I was once told I should try and get on the Empire, or the Metropole in Bootle.'

Sam looked sideways at his wife. 'Who told yer this?'

Aggie waved a hand. 'Oh, some bloke what heard me sing.'

'How old were yer?'

'Don't be so bleeding nosy!' Aggie bristled. 'I was eighteen, if yer must know.'

'Yer were eighteen when I met yer, but I've never heard yer sing like a lark.' Sam was winding his wife up. 'This bloke what said yer had a good voice, was he sitting in a chair or lying on the floor, blind drunk?'

'It was before I met you, smart arse, and he was a proper gentleman, I'll have you know.' Aggie's tummy was thinking if she didn't laugh soon, it would burst. 'In fact, you wouldn't have stood a chance if this bloke hadn't been bandy-legged and cross-eyed. It took a lot of thought before I decided I'd be better off with you, because I never knew whether this feller, gent as he was, was looking at me or the person next to me.' Their smiles and titters egged her on. 'Another thing, something me mam said got me thinking. She said he was so bandy he'd never be able to stop a pig in an entry. I thought he'd be no good to me then, so I turned me charms on to you instead.'

Rita's husband, Reg, was chortling. 'Yer mam was right, yer know. He wouldn't have been no good to yer if he couldn't stop a pig in an entry. Not with all the pigs we see down these entries.'

And so for the next hour, the five friends enjoyed jokes and banter which put them in a good mood. It was nice to have neighbours you got on well with. Then, after the glasses had been topped up a few more times, Sam started the singing off. He had quite a good voice, and sang Paul Robeson's 'Old Man River' as well as the great man himself. Well, after so many drinks, anyone could have sounded like Paul Robeson. The women opted for Marie Lloyd songs, and they sang with gusto. The two men tried to out-sing the women, but at three to two they didn't stand a chance. They did try, God love them, but they'd drunk so much beer, they spent most of the time running down the yard.

'Men can't hold their drink.' Aggie thought she would impart this information to her mates in case they didn't know it. Her words slurred, she said, 'Not like us women.' She hiccupped several times, then passed her glass to Sam to hold while she pushed herself up. Slightly unsteady on her feet, she felt her way around the table. 'Yer'll have to heexcuse me, folks, I need to spend a penny.' She lurched from the table to grab hold of the door. 'I'll sing yer another song when I get back.'

'I'll go with her, just to make sure.' Rita took her mate's elbow. 'Come on, sunshine, and I'll sing "Look For A Silver Lining" with yer.' A few seconds later, 'No, that's not the lavatory door, sunshine, that's the entry door. Oh, okay, if you say so, then it's the lavatory door. I'll just stand here and wait for yer. But don't sit down, will yer, 'cos there's no seats in the entry.'

Bessie fell back in her chair and, with Sam and Reg, burst out laughing. Her tired feet and all the worry forgotten, she said, 'Oh, what a wonderful day this has been.'

Chapter Twenty-Eight

'Two whole days, my lovely Evelyn, with no interruptions at all.' Philip sighed with pleasure as he pulled her closer. 'I could ask for no finer Christmas gift than that.'

'But you must go and see your parents tomorrow, darling. I would not like to them to think I was keeping you away on the one day of the year when families should be together.'

'I will be going to see them. I have their presents, and certainly would not let such an important day pass without visiting them. You were invited, remember, they're longing to meet you. Will you not change your mind and accompany me on a short visit tomorrow? They would be so happy to meet you, and then I would not feel guilty about leaving you here alone.'

'But I wouldn't be alone, would I? Isn't Annie coming in to prepare and serve our meal? I'm not very good in the kitchen, I'm afraid, but giving her a hand would make the time pass quickly, and I can always potter around and help if I can.'

'It won't be for long, my lovely, perhaps an hour and a half. There'll be no traffic on the roads as the buses and trams are not running, it will only be fifteen minutes' drive each way and an hour spent with my parents. Can you survive for so long without me?'

'I will try, my darling.' There was tenderness in Evelyn's smile. She had never imagined a love such as she felt for this man, who was never far away from her thoughts. 'It will be hard, but I shall steel myself.'

'Let us forget tomorrow. We have the whole evening to

ourselves and I can lose myself in your beauty and my love for you. I shall open a bottle of wine, and when you are slightly inebriated, I shall lead you to the bedroom and make passionate love to you.'

Evelyn stayed him with her hand. 'Don't get up yet, my love. I want to tell you about something which touched my heart, and which I think will please you.' With the scene still in her mind, she told him of the women she had seen coming and going with boxes of food. 'All those poor families helped, thanks to you, and of course there were the shoes for the boys. And if you had seen the looks on the faces of those women as they carried their precious boxes, you would certainly have been moved to tears, as I was. Those women, so thin and gaunt through lack of nourishment, will be blessing you. With your help they will be able to feed their families this Christmas.'

There was astonishment on Philip's face. 'How could so many families be fed for just twenty pounds? Surely that would give them very little in the way of Christmas fare?'

She stroked his cheek. 'You live in a different world from them, my darling, as I did until my husband died. I had everything I wanted, never knew what hunger and hardship were. These people are so poor they barely exist, yet they have much more spirit than I. They love their children, and feed them while starving themselves. What I saw yesterday I found so uplifting, I thought I should tell you about the happiness you have put into their lives, your Christmas gift to them.'

Staring at the flames roaring up the chimney, Philip shook his head. 'You are making me see how very selfish I have been. I often drive past streets in the slums, but never think what life is like for people there. Oh, being a solicitor I find out many things, but never give a thought to the people who live in slums owned by clients of mine. I know many of them have no sanitation and must share an outside toilet with four or five other families, no running water in houses lived in by two or three families with children, and if they don't pay the rent on these hovels, they are turfed out on to the street.' He turned his eyes from the fire to look at her. 'I have acted for these landlords, but never once thought of the people I was evicting. And there are many other people, friends of mine, who don't give a thought to those who are less well off. We probably spend more in one day than these people earn in a year.'

'I only wished to tell you of the happiness you have given these families, my love, I didn't intend to make you sad. I certainly meant no criticism of your life-style or that of your friends. I am the last person to talk of selfishness, I have been selfish all my life.' Once again she stroked his face. 'It has taken two people to make me see myself for what I am. One is your dear self for showing me what true love is, and the other is a neighbour who has taught me humility.'

He squeezed her hand. 'This is the person who wrote out the list you showed me, isn't it?' When Evelyn nodded, Philip said, 'I want to meet her. In fact, insist on meeting her, she must be a very good person. And, she's a friend of yours.'

'Perhaps in the New Year, my darling.' Evelyn's happiness was blighted by the knowledge that there was much for her to do before the New Year came in. Her future, and that of Amelia, very much depended on the outcome of her visit to her father-in-law. 'Anyway, let's not talk of sadness. We have two whole days before us, let us make the most of them. Open that bottle of wine, my darling, and let us forget the outside world.'

This brought a smile to Philip's face and he was quickly on his feet. 'Your wish is my command.' He grinned down at her, his eyes twinkling. 'I can't quite remember now, my lovely Evelyn, how many glasses you need to make you so endearingly loving? Is it one glass or two?'

'I do believe that at this moment I would not need a single glass of wine to make me endearingly loving, my darling. You only have to touch me and my whole body comes alive.'

'Then go through to the bedroom, my sweet, and prepare yourself while I open a bottle. I want to make love to you slowly and sensually, until you purr with pleasure. When our appetites are appeased, we will indulge in a glass of wine and playful behaviour until our need is once again aroused. Remember, my lovely Evelyn, you do not have to leave tonight, so let our love for each other have its way.'

When Philip entered the bedroom, Evelyn was in bed, her head raised on two soft feather pillows. He placed two slender glasses and a bottle of wine on the bedside table, then with his face wearing the boyish grin that Evelyn found irresistible, whipped the bedclothes back to reveal her nakedness. His eyes never leaving her body, he untied the belt of his robe and let it fall from his shoulders. Then he slipped in beside her and took her in his arms. 'Every time I see how beautiful you are, I can't believe I had to wait so long to find someone so perfect. For ten years I've floated from one woman to another, looking for the perfect one, while at the same time you were a widow, with no man in your life.'

'I was eight years without a man in my life, my darling, but we won't gain anything by thinking what might have been. Let's be grateful we have found each other. If your uncle hadn't retired, and you hadn't taken over from him, we would never have met. So let's say that Lady Luck was on our side then and brought us together.'

'You make me very happy, my lovely,' Philip said, stroking her breasts. 'But I would be much happier if we were married and I was sure you were mine and no one could come along and take you from me. When are you going to make an honest man of me?'

'Very soon, darling. I am as anxious as you for us to be united in wedlock. I have made you a promise that very early in the New Year I will have my affairs sorted and then you can set the date for our wedding.'

'But what affairs do you have, my love, that are important enough to keep you from me?'

Evelyn put a finger to his lips. 'Trust me, all will be revealed in a week or so. Until then, we must both be patient.'

'I will try to be patient,' Philip said, moving his body to cover hers. 'But right now I have no patience, I can't wait to make love to you.' And as their two naked bodies met, both sighed with contentment and satisfaction.

The time passed quickly, far too quickly, and all too soon it was time for Philip to return to the office, while Evelyn had asked if she could have the remainder of the week off. 'I will ask someone to ring in and say I have a very bad cold and will be confined to my bed for the rest of the week.'

'I will not allow my future wife to tell lies.' Philip was adamant. 'I intend to tell them very soon that we are betrothed, and really have no interest in what they think. So do not bother making excuses, my love, you do what you have to do. The sooner your affairs are sorted out, the happier I shall be. But surely I don't have to wait for a week to hold you in my arms again? It is far too long, I shall pine away.'

'Give me two full days after today, my love. The day after that I'll meet you here in your lunch break. Perhaps you could take an extra half-hour to give us a little more time together?'

Philip pouted like a child. 'I feel as though someone has taken my favourite toy away and won't give it back to me.'

Evelyn kissed his cheek. 'You will soon have your favourite toy back, I promise. Anyway, when we are married you mustn't think you can always have your own way. I too can be very stubborn at times.'

He hugged her and grinned. 'You can be stubborn whenever you like, my love, but never in the bedroom. I am the master in that department.' After another hug, he said, 'I think you had better go before I change my mind and lock you in.'

'Yes, I must be on my way, darling, but the last two days have been heaven, and I thank you and love you. I'll see you very soon.'

Evelyn walked off in the opposite direction from the office, so she wouldn't be seen. It was quite busy in the city. For most people it was their first day back at work after the holiday. But she caught a tram without having to wait long, and the journey gave her time to empty her head of thoughts of Philip and her love for him, and concentrate on meeting her father-in-law after eight years. What would his reaction be? There was no point in trying to guess, she would have to meet him in person. She hoped he would be in the office today, so she could get it over with and not have to spend the day worrying. Amelia's school was closed so it would be an ideal time to try. If the office were closed, then she would have to wait until after the New Year holiday, but from what she remembered of Cyril Lister-Sinclair, he never missed a day at work. It was worth a try to put her mind at rest.

Rita opened the door and looked surprised when she saw Evelyn standing there. 'Hello, Mrs Sinclair, I wasn't expecting you until this afternoon. Bessie is at work so I'm minding Milly.' Too late she realised she'd slipped up on the name, then thought, Oh, blow it, why worry? 'Would yer like to come in? She's playing a game with my son.'

'Would you mind if I didn't?' Evelyn didn't want to offend, but her tummy was turning over with nerves and she knew if she didn't act quickly, then she never would. 'I have an important call to make this morning, and want to take Amelia with me.'

Milly had heard her mother's voice and come to the door. 'Do you want me, Mother?'

'Yes, dear. I have an errand to go on, and would like you to come with me.'

She tried not to let her disappointment show. 'My best clothes are over at Auntie Bessie's, do you want me to get them?'

'I'll fetch them,' Rita said. 'You go home with yer mother, and I'll bring the clothes to yer.' She pulled a face at Evelyn. 'I'm afraid yer'll be going into a cold house, Mrs Sinclair. I would have lit yer fire if I'd known.'

Evelyn smiled, thinking what she had missed over the years by not making friends with this woman and her neighbours. 'We won't be in the house long enough to feel the cold, I want to be away as quickly as possible. But if you would light my fire later, when you have time, I would really be most grateful.'

'Consider it done.' Rita stood aside to let Milly pass. The girl was struggling into her school coat, and her downcast expression revealed that she was not happy to be taken away from her game. 'The house will be nice and warm for yer to come back to.'

'Goodbye, Auntie Rita,' Milly called as she followed her mother across the cobbles. 'I'll see you later.'

'Yer'll see me in five minutes, sunshine, with yer best clothes.'

As soon as they were in the house, Amelia asked, 'Where are we going, Mother?'

'Wait until Mrs Wells has been with your clothes, dear, then I will tell you.'

The girl could see her mother was a little agitated, and wondered why. Young as she was, she connected her mother's nerves with the important call she'd heard her telling Auntie Rita about. But why did she need to take her daughter with her?

When Rita knocked, Evelyn opened the door quickly. 'Thank you so much.' She took the clothes, adding, 'Please don't think me rude, or ungrateful for your kindness to my daughter, but we must hurry to be off.'

'No need to apologise, Mrs Sinclair,' Rita said, turning to cross back to her own house, 'it is a pleasure to have your daughter, she's a little angel.'

Back in the living room, Evelyn handed the dress and coat to Amelia. 'Rinse your hands and face, dear, then put on your dress and comb your hair. When I have changed, I will sit down and tell you where we are going.'

'Couldn't Jack come with us, Mother? He would like that and he's my best friend.'

Evelyn shook her head. 'Not today, Amelia. You will understand why when we've had our talk. Something may happen today that will change our lives completely, yours and mine, so I'm afraid I can't allow Jack to come with us.'

Amelia had changed into her new dress when Evelyn came down the stairs wearing a dress she usually wore for the office. Her mass of dark hair had been brushed until it shone, but she wore no make-up apart from lipstick. With her flawless complexion, she didn't need to cover it with powder or rouge. 'Sit next to me on the couch, Amelia, and listen carefully. What I have to tell you will surprise you very much, and perhaps it was wrong of me not to tell you before this. But circumstances have changed, and I have no choice but to do what I am going to do today. A lot depends upon the outcome.' Evelyn crossed her legs and licked her dry lips. 'You know your father was killed in the war before you were born, don't you?'

'Yes, Mother, you told me.'

'But I didn't tell you that your father's parents are still alive, and you have a grandmother and a grandfather. After your father was killed, I had a falling-out with them. It is now nearly eight years since I have seen them. However, I think the time has come to make amends, if it isn't too late.'

Milly's eyes were like saucers. 'I have a granddad and grandmother?' She was finding it hard to take in, for she had often wondered why all the children in school had grannies and grandas and aunties, while she had no one except her mother. Now she would be like other children, with a big family and relatives. But there were questions in her head that dulled the happiness she was longing to feel. 'Didn't Granddad and Grandma want us? Did they send us away?'

'It's a long story, Amelia, and I can't answer it in a few words. Things were said that hurt, but the fault was on both sides. Today I want to find out if there is any regret on the part of your grandparents, and ask if the rift can be healed.'

'Oh, I would love to have a granddad and grandmother! That would make me the same as other children. Will they like me, Mother, d'you think?'

'I don't think they could help but like you, Amelia, for you were not responsible for the harsh words that were spoken. But I have to be honest with you and say I can't promise that your grandfather will even agree to see us. I intend to take you to his office, and if he is working today we can take it from there and see what happens.' Evelyn averted her eyes. She had robbed this young girl of so much. 'I will tell you that your father came from a very wealthy family, and your name is really Amelia Lister-Sinclair. It was I who dropped the "Lister", perhaps out of spite, or perhaps because I didn't want them to find us. It doesn't really matter now, it is all in the past. I would like to start again with a clean slate.'

For the first time in her life that she could remember, Milly touched her mother's hand. 'Can we go now, and see if Granddad likes me?'

Tears were stinging Evelyn's eyes. Oh, she had a lot of answer for, ruining this child's life. Please God, Cyril wouldn't turn them away. 'Yes, we can go now. Put your coat on, there's a good girl.'

Cyril Lister-Sinclair swivelled his deep leather chair as he faced Oscar Wentworth across the desk. 'We had a very quiet Christmas, just a few close friends for dinner. Matilda isn't one for socialising these days. But it was pleasant enough. The food was good and the wine plentiful. But I can't forget the Christmases of years ago, when the house would be filled with Charles' friends and merriment. I know I shouldn't dwell on the past, but

I can't help it. How was your Christmas? Did the children enjoy themselves?' He didn't mean to let a sigh escape but couldn't stop it. 'It really is a time for children. For the grown-ups it's just an excuse to buy new clothes and have parties.'

'You should have come to ours, Cyril, I did try to persuade you. You are right about children, though, it really is a time for them. Just seeing their eyes when they came downstairs and saw the presents under the tree was like magic. They are still too young to understand, and that is the beauty of it. They are so innocent they really believe Father Christmas came down the chimney and left the presents. Before Gwen had taken the boys to bed the night before, she had left a glass of wine and two mince pies on the table, telling them they were for Father Christmas as he got hungry working so hard.'

'Gwen is a wonderful mother,' Cyril said. 'Kind and loving, just as a mother should be. You are lucky in your marriage, Oscar, you should count your blessings.'

'I do every day, Cyril, believe me. I am the luckiest man alive.' Oscar was in two minds whether to tell his friend where he was off to when he left the office. He didn't want to build his hopes up, as he had done in the past only to disappoint him, but the lead he'd now been given in his quest to find Evelyn and Amelia looked very hopeful indeed, and would put some interest back in the life of the man who appeared to have everything but was sad and lonely, with little happiness in his life.

'I have some news which I think will interest you, Cyril, regarding the whereabouts of Evelyn and Amelia. I was intro-duced to someone a few days ago who has quite a high position in the Department of Education. I pretended to let it slip that I was trying to trace an old family friend and her daughter. During the long conversation, I asked him casually how I would find out if a child attended a school in the area, and he said he could do that quite easily if he had details such as surname and date of birth. As this conversation took place at a party, I didn't like to monopolise the man's time, so I said I would call to his office some time this week. I'll be on my way there when I leave here. If I have any news I will call this afternoon. If not I'll see you tomorrow.'

There was a spark of interest in Cyril's eyes. 'That sounds very promising, Oscar, the best lead so far. I would appreciate it if you kept me informed of any news. My thoughts are never far away from them, and the dreadful way I cast them aside.'

'No, Cyril, I will not have you shouldering all the blame when Gwen and I were of the same mind as yourself. If there is blame to be laid, then my wife and I must share it. However, I do not believe it was all one-sided, Evelyn did herself no favours by adopting the attitude she did. I only hope the years have mellowed her, and she'll realise there were faults all round.' Oscar pushed his chair back. 'I'll get off, old boy. I want to get to the Education Office before the staff have their lunch break. You can rest assured I will let you know the second I have news for you. It would please me no end to put a smile on your face again and hear the laughter that has been missing for so long.'

'You don't know how much your friendship has meant to me over the years, Oscar,' Cyril said. 'You have been like a son to me, and that is something I will never forget. Now, go about your business, and my prayers go with you.'

There were six steps up to the offices of C. LISTER-SINCLAIR LTD, and Evelyn and Milly were on the second step when the door opened and a man dashed out. He passed them without a glance, but some instinct made him turn back. He saw a slender woman holding the hand of a young girl.

'Evelyn?' Oscar climbed the steps to stand beside the couple. 'I don't believe it, Cyril and I have just been talking about you!'

Evelyn had recognised him as soon as he came out of the door, and the sight of him had stopped in her in her tracks. She told herself it was a mistake to have come. 'Oscar . . . what a coincidence.'

'It is more than that.' He looked down at the little girl and Evelyn heard his sharp intake of breath. For a few seconds he felt he was looking into the face of his old friend Charles. Then he pulled himself together. 'And this is Amelia, I take it?'

Milly looked up into the smiling face of the unknown man and smiled back. 'I'm going to see my grandfather. Do you know him?'

Evelyn's face flushed. 'We don't know that for sure, Amelia, he may not be in the office today.'

Oscar bent his knees so that his face was on a level with Milly's. 'I'm your Uncle Oscar.' He held out his hand. 'How do you do? I'm very pleased to meet you.'

She shook his hand, her pretty face aglow. 'Are you really my uncle?'

Oscar was tempted to hug her, but afraid it might frighten her. 'Let us say I'm a step-uncle who has been searching the city for you and your mother.'

Oblivious to the drama taking place, Milly asked, 'Do you think my grandfather will be pleased to see me and my mother, or will he send us away?'

'Far from sending you away, my dear, you will be welcomed with open arms. He will be most happy to see both of you.' Oscar stretched to his full height. 'Shall we go inside, Evelyn? It is far too cold to stand here.'

The entrance hall to the building was quite large with several doors off it, leading to the offices of the clerical staff. There was also an ornate winding staircase which led to Cyril's office, and those of his personal secretaries. 'Shall we talk here for a while before going upstairs?' Oscar asked. 'This is going to come as a shock to Cyril, and as his friend I care very much for his welfare. I am, therefore, concerned that the reason for your visit is not such that it will cause him further anguish, for he has suffered greatly over the last eight years?'

Evelyn shook her head. 'I have not come looking for trouble, far from it. I have come to ask for Mr Lister-Sinclair's help.' She glanced down at her daughter. 'I do not wish to explain right now, it would be a little awkward, but I will explain in detail to him the reason for my being here. I am hoping for his understanding.' She looked directly into Oscar's eyes. 'I believe you married Gwen, I saw the announcement in a paper. I hope she is well and happy, and would like you to convey my best wishes to her.' Her eyes dropped. 'We were very good friends at one time.'

'And there is no reason why you shouldn't be friends again. You have never been forgotten, Evelyn, but I hope we are all grown-up enough to realise that each of us must share part of the blame for the turn of events. Don't you agree?'

'Yes, I am more than prepared to admit I wasn't the most easy person to get along with. But someone has come into my life who has changed me greatly from the selfish person I once was.' With her daughter in mind, she added, 'You will hear all, eventually, but for now please take my word that I come not to make trouble, but to make peace.'

Oscar held out his hand and Evelyn took it with a tremulous smile. 'Welcome back, Evelyn, you and Amelia are going to make a lot of people happy. For months I have been scouring the schools in search of your daughter, and was on my way out now to visit the Office of Education. Now I am going to ask a really big favour of you. I would like to be the one to take Amelia into Cyril's office, without any warning. I have had to disappoint him so many times, I would like to be the one who unites him with his granddaughter. Would you allow me to do that, please?'

Evelyn nodded. Her heartbeat had slowed down now she knew she would be welcome. 'Of course you can, Oscar. I will wait here for you.'

'Certainly not! You must come upstairs and I will leave you in the capable hands of Cyril's secretary. He won't be able to see you, and Miss Williams is the soul of discretion so you need have no fear. She also makes a very good cup of tea.' Oscar gazed down at Amelia. 'You don't mind coming with me to meet your grandfather, do you? Your mother won't be far away and she will be in good hands.'

Milly felt as though she was dreaming. It was a lot for a young girl to take in, and she was afraid she was being shown something that would soon be snatched away from her. But the tall man looking down at her had such a kind face, she put her hand into his. 'I would like to see my grandfather now, please.'

When the rap came on his office door, without lifting his head from the ledger he was checking, Cyril called, 'Come in.'

'I've brought someone to meet you, Cyril, have you five minutes to spare?' Oscar was so happy, he could barely contain himself. He walked across the office floor with Amelia's hand held tightly in his, then pressed her close to the desk while he took a step back.

When Cyril looked up, he was perplexed, until he found himself looking into a pair of green eyes. At first he thought he was going to faint. He held his head in his hands for a few seconds, until he heard a soft voice asking, 'Don't you want to see me, Granddad?'

Wiping away tears, Cyril turned his chair sideways and held out his arms. Milly, seeing his tears, walked round the desk and into the outstretched arms. 'Don't cry, Granddad. Have you got a handkerchief and I'll dry your eyes for you?'

Cyril tried to compose himself, but he was far too emotional. The girl reminded him so strongly of the son he had lost. Her colouring, the shape of her nose, most of all the green eyes. To think he had turned his back on this child from the day she was born, calling her mother a liar. He had wasted eight years of both their lives.

'Granddad, aren't you going to give me a kiss and say you are glad to see me?' Milly wiped away the tear that was rolling down his cheek. 'I didn't want to make you cry.'

'I'm crying with happiness, my darling.' Cyril hugged her close, raining kisses on her face. 'And now I've found you, I'll never let you go again.' Over her shoulder he asked Oscar, 'How did this miracle come about?'

Oscar cleared his throat, for he was very touched by the scene. 'I was going down the steps while Amelia and Evelyn were coming up.'

'Where is Evelyn?'

'She's having a cup of tea with Miss Williams. I asked if I could bring Amelia in, I didn't want to miss the moment you found your granddaughter.'

Milly said quietly, 'I would like you to call me Milly, all my friends call me that. Except Mother, she always calls me Amelia.'

'Milly!' Cyril nodded his approval. 'Yes, I like that name, it suits you.'

'I'll have a cup of tea with Evelyn and Miss Williams while you two get acquainted.' Oscar said. 'I know Evelyn wants to have a serious talk with you later, Cyril, and I don't want to interfere so I think it would be best all round if I take Amelia . . . er, Milly . . . out for an hour or so. I could take her to meet Gwen, I know my wife would like that.'

'Then would you bring that chair around the desk so I can sit near my granddaughter for a few minutes first? We have a lot of years to make up.'

When a brown leather chair was placed next to Cyril's, Milly sat on it and giggled when she found she could swivel from side to side. The sound was like music to the two men listening, both of them remembering that Charles had been a giggler when he was a young boy.

'I'll leave you to it for a while. When Evelyn comes in, I'll take Milly to meet Gwen. I'll make it an hour, that should be long enough for you both to say what you need to, and to listen to each other.' As he was crossing the room, Oscar heard Milly asking, 'You do like me, don't you, Granddad, you won't send me away?'

'I don't like you, my darling, I love you. And I will never let you go now I've found you. And your grandmother will be so happy when she sees you, she will adore you.'

'I'm a very lucky girl, aren't I, Granddad?'

'It is I who am lucky, to have found you after all these years. Come and give your granddad a big kiss and a hug.'

Oscar closed the office door quietly, swallowing the lump in his throat.

Chapter Twenty-Nine

Evelyn stood at the top of the staircase, hands resting on the highly polished rail, and watched Amelia going down the outside steps with Oscar. She could hear her daughter's infectious giggle as she hopped down each step, and Oscar's laughter. He had been very kind and friendly, never once asking personal questions about her life since they'd last met. She had found it awkward at first being in Miss Williams' office, for they had met when she was courting Charles and he'd needed to call to the office one day to see his father. But although Miss Williams must have been filled with curiosity, like Oscar she was friendly without prying.

Taking her hand from the rail, Evelyn let out a deep sigh as she turned. She was on her way to face Cyril now, and was feeling nervous and apprehensive. The atmosphere was bound to be emotional, it couldn't be otherwise, but she hoped her father-in-law's reception of her would be as friendly as Oscar's, for her whole future depended on his reaction to what she had to tell him. The sooner she went in and faced him, the sooner her tummy would stop churning and her heartbeat would slow down. So, after running a hand down her skirt to smooth out any creases, and patting her hair, she straightened her shoulders and made for the door that bore his name in gold letters.

When the knock came Cyril jumped to his feet. He was crossing the floor when he called, 'Come in.' His arms were outstretched when Evelyn came through the door, and he gripped her shoulders and kissed her cheek. 'You are very welcome, my dear, it has been such a long time.'

Evelyn was reduced to tears. She really didn't deserve this kind of welcome. It was her fault this man had been without his granddaughter for so long. She had spent the last few days reviewing her actions, and knew now she had been a selfish bitch. She hadn't cared for anyone but herself and her greed for a life of luxury. When this man had lost his beloved son and was devastated, she hadn't tried to console him or even say she was sorry. Neither had she shed a tear for the man who was her husband, too busy feeling sorry for herself and worrying about her own comfort. And she'd kept on feeling sorry for herself for over eight years. It was Philip who'd made her take stock of the person she'd been, and she didn't like what she saw. She didn't deserve this man's kiss or his warm welcome.

'Sit down, my dear.' Cyril cupped her elbow until she was seated. 'Shall I ask my secretary to bring in some refreshment?'

Evelyn nodded. 'Miss Williams very kindly made me some tea, but I'm afraid my mouth is dry with nerves so another drink would be most welcome.'

Cyril picked up the phone and rang through to his secretary. 'A pot of tea and some biscuits, please, Miss Williams, and then I don't want to be disturbed for the rest of the day.' He replaced the receiver, and smiled. 'There is no need for nerves, Evelyn, I hope we meet up as friends, with the past forgotten. I cannot tell you how I felt seeing my granddaughter. She is so like Charles. I did you a grave wrong, my dear, and hope you can find it in your heart to forgive me?'

Evelyn shook her head vigorously. 'I know you have asked that we put the past behind us, but I want you to know that I do realise the type of person I was then, and that was a greedy and selfish woman. All I thought about was myself and my own comfort, and when circumstances changed I blamed everyone else for my plight. I haven't been a good mother to Amelia because I saw her as the reason I lost my status in society. I can see myself as I was then, and I don't like what I see. I knew you would want your granddaughter if you saw her, for she is so like Charles, but because I wasn't happy, I didn't want anyone else to be either.' She leaned forward and gripped his arm. 'But I have changed, Mr Lister-Sinclair, and I regret those lost years. The reason for the change is that I have met someone I have fallen in love with. The only man I have even looked at since Amelia was born. He returns my feelings and wants to marry me, and that is the reason for my coming to you today. I want you to help me.'

They were interrupted then as Miss Williams brought in the tray. 'Shall I pour, or would you rather do it yourself?'

Cyril smiled at his trusted secretary. 'You pour, if you will. You are much more efficient and will have the job done in half the time.'

As soon as they were alone again, he bent forward. 'Tell me about this man, and how I can help you?'

'I work as a secretary and he is my boss. All anyone in the office knew about me was that I was a war widow and my name was Mrs Sinclair. I made no friends, and no one knew I had a daughter. It was my boss who broke down the defences I had wrapped around myself, and gradually I fell in love with him. He is kind, thoughtful, humorous, and very much in love with me.' Evelyn sighed. 'But I haven't told him about Amelia, he doesn't know I have an eight-year-old daughter. It wasn't intentional to begin with. I never thought our feelings for each other would lead to anything. Then, when he asked me to marry him, I didn't have the courage to tell him about her. To be truthful, I'm afraid it will change his feelings for me. He will think I am deceitful for not telling him sooner.'

'If he really loves you, it won't change his feelings. Why should it?'

'Because I'm afraid then everything will have to come out in the open. That my name is really Lister-Sinclair and I was married to Charles, but his name is not on the birth certificate. If you remember, you advised me not to put Charles' name down as the father. Which means my friend will jump to the conclusion you and Gwen jumped to: that my baby was illegitimate. I couldn't bear to face him and have him think I was a loose woman, so I've come to ask if there is any way this whole sorry mess can be put right? Can the birth certificate be made right, or is it too late now?'

'Of course it can be put right. I will see to that as soon as possible, if you will let me have the original certificate with all the details on. And I have to hang my head in shame when I tell you I had the marriage annulled, on the grounds it had never been consummated.'

'I had an idea you would do that, and dropped the "Lister" from my name so people would not connect me with your family. I don't blame you for doing what you did. Although I was too wrapped up in myself at the time to appreciate how devastated you and your wife must have been, I can appreciate it now. The word "sorry" is totally inadequate, but it is the only one I can think of right now, and it comes from my heart.'

'Let the past be erased from our memories,' Cyril said, 'and look to the future. I will attend to the birth and marriage certificates immediately, that will be no problem for me and no one else will be told. Except for Oscar and Gwen, who have helped me so much over the years and who have for a long time questioned their own attitude towards you. They will both be overjoyed to have you back as their friend.' He sat back in his chair and held his chin in his hand. 'Now, about this man you have fallen in love with. Am I allowed to know his name?'

'He's a solicitor – Philip Astbury.'

Cyril sat forward to rest his arms on the desk. 'Philip Astbury! My dear Evelyn, I know Philip well! His family have been friends of ours for years, and they're friends of the Wentworths. Oscar knows Philip particularly well. He and Charles used to be in the same class at school as Philip.' He shook his head in disbelief. 'It's been such a marvellous day for me, meeting my granddaughter for the first time and seeing your good self again. And now, on top of that, comes the news that you and Philip Astbury are to wed! He's a wonderful chap, very popular with everyone, and comes from a good family. I'm so pleased for you.'

'I think perhaps you are taking too much for granted,' Evelyn told him. 'I can hardly face him and tell him I've been living a lie and have an eight-year-old daughter. I dread seeing the expression on his face which tells me I have lied to him and he no longer wants to marry me.'

'Then you won't have to tell him, I will.' Cyril left his chair and rounded the desk to where Evelyn sat. 'I did you a great wrong all those years ago, practically saying you were no better than a woman of the streets and leaving you to do your best with my son's child. I can only say that I was distraught with grief, and wanted to hurt someone. Now I want to right that wrong, so please let me?'

Evelyn shook her head. 'Much as I am dreading facing Philip, I feel I must do it myself. What a coward he would think me if I allowed you to do my dirty work.'

'My dear Evelyn, I have known Philip Astbury since he was a toddler. I know his parents well, and his Uncle Simon. We are all good friends. I firmly believe Philip will be more understanding when I tell him of my role in all this, and how very much I wronged you. And if you will allow me to do this one thing for you, it will ease some of the guilt I have carried around for a such a long time. Please, I beg you?'

Evelyn sighed. 'My fear is he may not want to take on an eight-year-old daughter. He has mentioned that his parents keep asking when he's going to wed and give them grandchildren, and I know he will want to have a child by me as soon as possible, for I am not young, I am twenty-nine.'

'How would Milly feel about you getting married? Would she feel left out?'

'Good heavens, no! I have not been cruel to Amelia, but neither have I been a good, loving mother. She thinks more of the woman who lives next door who is very good with her. In fact, the pair of them idolise each other.'

'Who is this woman next door? And where in Liverpool do you live?'

'Amelia and I live in a small two-up-two-down house, and the woman next door is called Bessie. She minds Amelia for me until I get home from work. She has a job herself, though, so only has Amelia for an hour or so every night and every weekend. They get on very well together, and although I should be ashamed to admit it, my daughter would far rather be with Bessie than with me.'

Cyril stared at her for several seconds before speaking. 'We can discuss these things another time, don't you think? The best person to solve your worries and put your mind at rest is Philip, and we can't guess what his thoughts will be on the matter. So, do I have your permission to speak to him?'

Evelyn nodded. 'If you think it would be for the best.'

Cyril opened an address book which lay by the phone, and leafed through the pages. Then he lifted the receiver from the hook at the side of the telephone and dialled. 'May I speak to Mr Philip Astbury, please? My name is Cyril Lister-Sinclair, and it is a personal call.' After a few seconds, Evelyn could hear Philip's voice and her heart turned over. She couldn't hear clearly, but it sounded as though he was very pleased by the call.

'Do you have a busy day ahead of you, my boy?' Cyril asked. Then, 'I was wondering if you could spare me an hour? No, it's not something I wish to discuss over the telephone, I need to see you. No, nothing is wrong, I was just thinking it's a long time since I saw you.' He smiled. 'Two o'clock will be fine, Philip, as long as I'm not taking you away from an important client. I look forward to seeing you.'

Evelyn jumped to her feet. 'What am I going to do? I don't want him to see me here, but Amelia isn't back yet . . .'

Cyril waved her to her seat before picking up the phone and dialling again. When he heard Gwen's voice, he asked, 'Gwen, my dear, is Oscar still there with Milly? Oh, would you ask him to drive back here straight away and pick up Evelyn? I am sure you would like to see her after all these years. There is no need for him to bring Milly unless you are busy. I'm sure Evelyn will explain all about the events that led up to today when she sees you. But it would be best if you could find something for my granddaughter to do while the explanations are going on. She has no inkling, and it would be better to leave it that way for now.' He suddenly burst out laughing. 'No, you may not keep my granddaughter, even though you think she is delightful! My wife and I have priority, and I can't wait for Matilda to see her. But right now, will you ask Oscar to make haste, please?'

Cyril was so happy he couldn't keep the smile from his face. It was like a dream come true, to have part of his beloved son back in his life.

'I know I have no right to ask any favours of you, Evelyn, but it means so much having a granddaughter in my life. It's as if my son will always be with Matilda and me. Every time we look at her, we will see his dear face. Would you allow me to take her home with me some time later today, when other matters important to you are settled? I don't want to ring my wife with the news, I want to walk into the room and watch her face when she looks at Milly. I won't even introduce them, I don't think it will be necessary.'

'I would be very happy for you to take Amelia home. You have been so generous today, with warmth, friendship and understanding. But if Amelia . . .' Evelyn smiled. 'It seems I'm going to have to give in, or be the only one calling my daughter Amelia. If Milly isn't home when Bessie gets in from work, she and two other neighbours will be concerned about her. But we have several hours yet, so I'll worry about that nearer the time.'

'I shall have to meet this Bessie sometime. If Milly is fond of her, then I must make sure I become her friend. When everything is settled, would you take me to meet her?'

'Yes, of course.' Evelyn turned her head as the door opened. 'Oh, here's Oscar, I'll get my coat from Miss Williams' office.' She hesitated then said, 'Mr Lister-Sinclair, would you ring me at Oscar's whatever the outcome? I shall be a bag of nerves, wondering what is being said in this office.'

'I shall ring you immediately my meeting with Philip is over, or even when he is still here, if that is what he wants. Have no fear, my dear, I feel certain that everything will turn out well for you. Now, go with Oscar and renew your friendship with Gwen. You both have lots to talk about.' His smile was one of encouragement. 'Oh, and most of my friends, young and old, call me Cyril. And I would like you to look upon me as a friend.'

Philip didn't wait for an answer to his rap on the office door but threw it open and strode across the room wearing a beaming smile, his hand outstretched. 'Hello, old boy, it's quite a while since we met. I hope you and Matilda are well?'

Cyril waved him to the chair opposite. 'We are both in good health, thank you. And I don't need to ask you, for you look remarkably well. Would you like some refreshment – a cup of tea or something stronger?'

'I had tea and a sandwich before I left the office, I couldn't cope with another cup.' Philip rubbed his hands together, smiling. 'I can still remember where you keep your stock of the finest wines and malt whisky in the city though, so shall I do the honours?'

'Yes, my boy, a whisky would go down very well.' Cyril watched as Philip opened the doors of the high cabinet which did indeed boast a fine selection of drinks. He was fond of Philip, and like all the people who knew him, had wondered why he had never married. It wasn't that the chances weren't there, for he was chased by every eligible female in their circle of friends. 'So, how is life treating you, my boy?'

'Life is excellent at the moment, Cyril, and I'm very happy.' Philip placed a glass in front of him, then sat down with his own glass in his hand. 'I'm delighted to see you, as ever, but rather intrigued by your telephone call. There is nothing I enjoy more than something with a hint of mystery to it.' He swirled the whisky round in the glass before taking a sip. 'Was there a reason for your call, or were you genuinely interested in my health?'

'There was a reason, Philip, and I think when you hear it you will be surprised.' Cyril was going to take things slowly and choose his words with care. 'I believe you know a woman called Evelyn Sinclair?'

Philip's brows shot up. 'Yes, I know her very well! We're courting! In fact, we will be getting married very shortly. It isn't general knowledge at the moment, except that my parents know of her though they have not met. Do you know Evelyn?'

Cyril sat back in his chair and drew a deep breath. 'I want you to listen without interruption for a short while, if you will. Evelyn Sinclair is really Evelyn Lister-Sinclair. She is Charles' widow.' He saw the shock on Philip's face and quickly went on, 'This is not to say she doesn't love you, nothing changes that, but there are things you should know. It is quite a long story, and I don't come out of it very well, but I think everything should be brought out into the open now and then you and Evelyn can start with a clean slate. So please be patient, dear boy, and listen to what I have to say.'

For half an hour Philip sat quietly, his expression changing at intervals. Cyril told him everything, kept nothing back. Except one thing, which was a little lie that would hurt no one: he told Philip that Evelyn conceived a child on the last day of her husband's leave before he was sent overseas. He was hard on himself, too, revealing how he had ordered Evelyn to leave the house in Princes Avenue, even though she was with child. The fact that she had a child brought Philip to the edge of his chair, but not once did he try to interrupt.

'Oscar and Gwen Wentworth were best man and maid of honour at Charles' marriage to Evelyn, which was held in a registry office because Charles only had a few days' leave and there was no time for the big society wedding my wife and I had envisaged for our son. Gwen was a friend of Evelyn's all those years ago, but lost touch with her just after the baby was born. Oscar has been trying to trace mother and child for a while now, without success. In fact today has been a day of coincidences and surprises. He was due to meet a man at the Department of Education this morning, in the hope he could pull a few strings and find the school Amelia attended. He was going down the front steps when Evelyn was coming up.' Cyril sat back in his chair. 'So there you have it, my boy, the full story.'

Philip sighed. 'Why didn't Evelyn tell me all this herself?'

'She wanted to. She loves you very much and is now terrified in case you think badly of her and walk away. She said you would think her a coward for not telling you face to face, but I talked her out of it. I took eight years of that woman's life by wrongfully accusing her of having another man's baby. I had just heard that Charles had been killed in action and was beside myself with grief. I couldn't believe she could possibly have been made pregnant by my son in that one day. I wasn't thinking clearly, Philip, and unfortunately Evelyn isn't given to showing any emotion. I thought her hard-hearted when she didn't grieve for Charles as I grieved.'

'I'm having a problem taking all this in, Cyril,' Philip said. 'I was hoping to marry Evelyn in the next month or so, even though I knew very little about her life. She wouldn't even tell me where she lived. None of that bothered me, I fell in love with her the minute I set eyes on her. Her being your daughter-in-law and the widow of Charles, I can live with. In fact, I would be delighted to be a close member of your family, and I know my parents would be pleased. They don't know anything about her really, not even her name. Evelyn asked me not to tell anyone until she'd sorted her affairs out. When I came here today I thought it was a friendly call, I certainly wasn't prepared for what you've told me. And, as I say, I can live with most of it. But for her not to tell me she has an eight-year-old daughter . . . well, I find that very hard to take.'

'Evelyn knows that, and it is her worst fear. She said your parents were keen for you to marry and give them grandchildren, and she knows they would be unhappy for you to take on an eight-year-old girl.' Cyril couldn't keep back what was in his heart and mind. 'Even though Milly is the most beautiful child imaginable. I am completely captivated by her, and she is the image of Charles. Now, there may be a solution to this, but I haven't mentioned it to Evelyn. She was very nervous when she left here, knowing you were coming. But I will test it on you, to see if you agree with what I have to say. I am going to ask Evelyn to let Milly come to live with Matilda and myself. We would dearly love to have her, she would bring happiness back into our lives. Evelyn could see her whenever she wished, while you could be her uncle. That would leave you free to lead the lives of newly-weds. To have your own children, your own family. How would that sit with you, Philip?'

'Cyril, I love that woman so much I will marry her no matter what her circumstances are. I admit I would like to start a family of our own, but I wouldn't make that part of the bargain. I would never take a mother away from her child.'

'Even if mother and child agree, and it is best for both of them?'

'Ah, I could live with that. But I can't see Evelyn doing so.'

'Then we must wait and ask her.' Cyril didn't want to mention the fact that there wasn't the closeness between Evelyn and her daughter there usually was between mother and child. Nor was he going to mention the neighbour, Bessie, whom he would very much like to meet.

'I am to ring Oscar's when you leave, and he will bring Evelyn and Milly back here.' Cyril was looking thoughtful as he tapped his fingers on the desk. 'Do you have any business to attend to, or would you like to see Evelyn today and clear the air? Or perhaps you'd like some time to think things through?'

Philip seemed to come alive. 'I don't have any clients, you know it is always quiet the week between Christmas and New Year. Even if I had, I would cancel their appointments. I desperately want to see Evelyn, tell her that no matter what obstacles are in the way, I intend to marry her as quickly as possible. My parents will no doubt be concerned, but when they get to know her, they will understand why I love her so much. When you said you were distraught when Charles died, and saddened that Evelyn showed no emotion, I could understand both sides. You see, from what little she has told me, her parents showed her no love. It took me a while to break down the wall she had built around herself, but it was well worth the effort. She is the most loving woman I have ever met. And in time, Cyril, you will find that out for yourself.'

He got to his feet and began to pace the room. 'I sound like a lovesick schoolboy, don't I? Who would ever have thought that Philip Astbury, the philanderer who attended every party with a different woman on his arm, would become so besotted, so head-over-heels in love, that he was prepared to do anything for the love of a special woman?'

'I should think all your friends will be very happy for you, Philip, for you are very well liked and have never spoken ill of any of your women friends.' Cyril was so happy he thought his heart would burst. This was one day in his life he would never forget. To see again the woman his son had married, and the granddaughter who was the fruit of that short marriage. Then to find out that Philip, the son of one of his best friends, was in love and wanted to marry Evelyn – well, it was like a storybook ending, where everyone lived happily ever after. But was he being over-optimistic?

Philip stopped his pacing and stood in front of Cyril's desk. 'Do you have a spare office where Evelyn and I could talk in private?'

'There is an office on the next floor which is furnished and comfortable, you are very welcome to use that. While I ring Oscar to ask him to bring Evelyn and her daughter, I suggest you help yourself to another whisky to steady your nerves.'

When Oscar answered the phone, he was asked to bring Evelyn and Milly back to the office. Cyril suggested that as soon as they arrived, Evelyn should be directed to the office on the top floor while Milly be brought into his office. 'It's been quite a memorable day, my boy, don't you agree? It is a long time since I have felt so happy and light-hearted. A great weight has been lifted from my shoulders.'

Oscar chuckled. 'It has certainly been a day of surprises. Gwen's eyes have been as round as saucers since Evelyn arrived. I know a little of what is happening but not all. I have been keeping Milly amused and out of the way. What a treasure the girl is! She is clever, without a doubt, but what I find most endearing is her sense of fun. When she laughs, it's catching. You can't help laughing with her. If she were mine, I would love her to bits.'

'I can't wait for Matilda to see her. And, as you know I love her dearly, you will not think I am making fun of her when I say the bottle of smelling salts will definitely be needed.'

'The door facing you at the top of the stairs is the one you need,' Oscar told Evelyn when they entered the lobby. 'You can't miss it.'

She was shaking visibly. 'I know it's silly of me, but I'm scared.'

'I'm quite sure there is nothing to be afraid of, my dear, so take a deep breath and run up those stairs as though you haven't a care in the world . . . which I'm sure you haven't.' He held on to Milly's hand and together they watched Evelyn mount the stairs.

'Why is Mother scared, Uncle Oscar? There's no bogeyman up there, is there?'

'Now, you don't believe in bogeymen, do you? You're a clever girl, and if you are clever, you will know there is no such thing. Come along and ask your granddad if I'm not telling the truth.'

Milly pulled her hand free. Giggling, she said, 'I'll race you to Granddad!' With that she took off like a shot, flung the office door open and ran across the floor to the desk.

Cyril looked up when the door burst open, to see Milly running towards him, her face aglow and her childish laughter filling the room. 'Well, I never, what have we here?'

'I bet Uncle Oscar I could beat him to get to you first.' She turned to Oscar, who was leaning on the back of a chair pretending to be out of breath. 'I won!'

'Ah, but did you win fairly?' Cyril asked. 'That is what you should ask yourself. Did you give Oscar a start because he is older than you and is carrying more weight?'

Milly's brow furrowed. 'I never thought of that, Granddad, because I've only ever raced the girls in school. But you are right, it wasn't fair, and I'm sorry, Uncle Oscar. So shall we call it evens?'

He dropped into a chair, chuckling. 'You weren't behind the door when they were giving brains out, my dear. I must remember never to play cards with you.'

Now this remark was of interest to Milly. 'Oh, I can play cards, I'm getting very good at it. I win more games than Jack does.'

'And might we ask who Jack is?' Cyril asked, eager to know as much as possible about his granddaughter's life. 'And where do you play cards?'

'Jack is my best friend, he lives in the house opposite ours. He is one year older than me so he is nine. Because he's older than me, wouldn't you think he'd win more games than me, Granddad?'

'Perhaps he likes you and lets you win?'

'Oh, he does like me, but he doesn't let me win. In fact, I have to keep my eye on him because if he gets the chance, he cheats.'

The two men exchanged glances. How refreshing it was to listen to a child who was too innocent to tell an untruth. 'Your grandmother is very fond of playing cards, Milly, so you would get along very well with her. Perhaps the games she plays are more grown-up than the ones you play, but she would love to teach you so you could play with her.'

Milly's eyes slid from side to side as she weighed up the situation. Then she asked, 'Does Grandma's table have a cloth on it that hangs right down over the sides?'

Cyril rubbed his chin. 'No, I don't think it does, my dear, but I'm not really sure. Why do you ask?'

'Well, if there was a cloth on the table that hung right over the sides, I'd have to keep my eye on her in case she tried to cheat.'

The hearty laughter of the two men reached the office of Miss Williams, and brought a smile to her face. She hadn't been told who the young girl was, but she didn't need telling. She remembered Evelyn from when she was courting Mr Charles, and as soon as she'd looked into Milly's face she saw the same features and the same green eyes as Mr Cyril's son. And there was the age of the girl. All the signs told the wise secretary that this was the granddaughter her boss had pined for for a long, long time. And because he was such a caring boss, and she had grown very fond of him over the years, Miss Williams was happy for him.

Chapter Thirty

Philip had pulled the two office chairs close together and, after holding Evelyn tight and smothering her with kisses, he pressed her gently down on to one of the chairs, still gripping her hands. 'My beloved Evelyn, why didn't you tell me all the things that were on your mind, and apparently worrying the life out of you? What sort of a man do you think I am, that you were afraid to confide in me?'

'I didn't think our relationship was going to become serious, and by the time it did, and I found myself in love with you, it was too late. I thought you would think badly of me, and couldn't bear for that to happen.' Evelyn stroked his cheek. 'I was afraid of losing you. If I had known your family were friends of the Lister-Sinclairs, then I would have been more open with you. But, as Cyril has probably told you, we didn't part on the best of terms.'

Philip nodded. 'He has been very open and honest, and I would expect nothing less of the man I have known and admired all my life. He wanted to be the one to tell me, so as to spare you. He has admitted that he did you a grave wrong, and by telling me of his involvement in your break from the family, is trying to put things right. He is so happy to have you back as part of the family, and his joy in seeing his granddaughter is beyond words. He is like a new man, now he has something to live for.'

'I would like to set the record straight, my darling, and tell you that all the fault does not lie on Cyril's shoulders, I was as much to blame. I wasn't a very nice person then. I was too selfish, and thought only of myself. Never once did I consider the anguish he and his wife must have gone through when they heard their son had been killed. As Charles' wife, I should have been a help to them in their grief.'

Philip raised her hand to his lips. 'It is all over now, my love, your worries are at an end. No need for any more secrecy, your life can be an open book.'

Still the frown was on Evelyn's face, for she couldn't believe life was going to be happy ever after. That would be too easy. 'What is going to happen now, Philip?'

'The only thing I am certain of at the moment, my lovely, is that you and I are going to be married as soon as possible.'

'I'm worried about your parents,' she told him. 'What are they going to think of me, and how will they feel about Amelia? I know they are longing for you to give them a grandchild, but I think it would be a great disappointment to them if they were asked to accept an eight-year-old child. It would be asking a great deal of them.'

Philip lowered his head. 'I'd be telling a lie if I said they wouldn't mind, for I agree with you that it would be a great disappointment to them. Given time, I'm sure they, and myself, would grow to love your daughter, but at the moment it is quite a lot to take in.' He raised his head, a half smile on his face. 'In any case, we don't have a house yet, and for a while after we marry we would have to live in the apartment which only has one bedroom.'

'Are you quite sure you want to marry me?' she asked. 'Is it not too much for you to take on? I would quite understand if you had second thoughts.'

'If there is one thing in my life of which I am certain, my lovely Evelyn, it is my intention to make you my wife. There could, however, be a short-term solution. Cyril has said he would love to have Milly living with him. He said it would be a joy for him and his wife to have Charles' daughter under his roof. I didn't make any comment on that, I was sure you wouldn't agree.'

Evelyn mulled this news over for a while then said, 'That could be a solution, darling. If Milly was with Cyril and Matilda, I could see her very often, and she would still be my daughter. And, quite honestly, I believe she would welcome it, for as I have told you, my daughter and I do not have a close relationship. That is my fault entirely, not hers, and something I intend to rectify now, if she will let me. It may take a while, but I have to make up for the years when I treated her like a stranger.' She squeezed his hand. 'You will like her, I know you will, and if everything turns out as we both wish, then it would be my hope that when we have children of our own she will be treated as their sister. I have left her out in the cold for so long, it has to end. I want to win my daughter's love.'

'Does she know about me,' Philip asked, 'or not?'

'Not until today, and not from me. Cyril said he would mention it to her casually, so it won't come as a surprise when she meets you.'

'And is that to be today?' Philip found himself wanting to meet the child who was born of the woman he loved and his old friend Charles. 'I am looking forward to meeting her, and I hope she likes me and we can become friends.'

'She is a very friendly girl, with winning ways. Which shows she has a strong character since I have done little to help her development. She will like you, and I have no doubt that you will like her. Would you like to go downstairs now and meet her?'

Philip pulled her to her feet. 'Let me hold you in my arms for a while, so I know you are real and our future together is sealed.'

Down in Cyril's office, Milly was entertaining Cyril and Oscar. A real chatterbox, with a keen sense of humour, she was telling them of the capers she got up to in school. When she mimicked her class mates and her teacher, her facial expressions and changes of voice had them roaring with laughter. Cyril wanted to hold her tight and never let her go, but was afraid of scaring her off. Then she surprised the men by asking, 'Who has my mother gone upstairs to see?'

Cyril cleared his throat. 'Your mother has met a man she has grown very fond of, and he is very fond of her. In fact, he would like her to marry him.'

Milly took the news very calmly. She had never really believed that her mother went to stay with an old school friend every weekend, but hadn't minded for it meant she could stay with her Auntie Bessie. 'Oh, I'm glad Mother has a friend. Will she bring him down to meet me, d'you think?'

'Would you like to meet him?' Oscar asked. 'He's very nice, I've known him since I was about your age and we were at school together, with your father.' He had given some thought as to whether he should mention Charles, in case it upset Cyril, but after careful consideration decided it was best to put the child in the picture.

Milly was standing at the side of Cyril's chair, and she put her arms around him. 'I didn't know my father, he was killed before I was born. But he was your son, and you must have been very sad.'

'I was, my dear, and so was my wife. And that is why I am so happy that you have come into our lives, for you look so like him, you will be a constant reminder. It will be like having him back again.'

There came a rap on the door, then it was opened and Evelyn and Philip came in. Oscar broke the silence by greeting Philip. 'Hello, old boy, it's a while since we met. Haven't seen you at any of the parties over the holidays.'

As they were shaking hands, Philip said, 'I have been off the social scene for reasons you have probably guessed. But it is nice to see you, and when you go home, please give my love and regards to Gwen.'

Milly watched the scene with interest, her hand clasped in one of her grandfather's. Then she asked, 'Are you my mother's friend?'

Philip walked over to the desk and held out his hand. 'I am a very good friend of your mother's, I hope you don't mind?'

Milly pursed her lips while shaking his hand. There were thoughts going round her head, the main one being that if her mother married this man, would she ever see her Auntie Bessie again? But he looked a nice man, and he was smiling at her so it would be rude not to smile back. 'You can't be a friend of my mother's without being a friend to me, can you? That would make us enemies and we'd have to fight each other with swords, in the park at dawn.' Suddenly she giggled and her face was transformed. 'I'm fast asleep in my bed at dawn, and I haven't got a sword anyway, so we'd better be friends.'

Philip was captivated. 'I wouldn't fight you, my darling, you are far too pretty.' He grinned, and that won Milly over. He's nice, she thought. And I'll really like him as long as he doesn't take me away from Auntie Bessie. 'Besides,' Philip went on, 'my sword has been sent away to be sharpened.'

'Thank goodness for that!' Cyril said. 'I wouldn't like any blood spilt on my floor, the cleaner would be very upset and think I'd murdered someone.' He raised his eyebrows and looked at Evelyn. 'Have you and Philip had a good talk?' When she nodded, he asked, 'And have all the problems been sorted out to your satisfaction?'

She looked to Philip. 'Would you say they have?'

'Most of them. There was never any doubt on my part, but there are others to consider.' He took a deep breath and decided to take the bull by the horns. 'Milly, I have asked your mother to marry me, but she won't give me an answer until she knows that I meet with your approval.' He dropped down on one knee and put his two hands on his heart. 'Please, Milly, will you allow me to take your mother's hand in marriage?'

Peals of childish laughter rang out and brought smiles to all those in the room. Even to Miss Williams in her office, but no one could see that. 'Oh, you are funny!' Her laughter turned to giggles, and her green eyes sparkled. She whispered to Cyril, 'Granddad, I do like him, so shall we let him marry Mother?'

'I think we should say he can, my dear, so he can get back on his feet. The wooden floor isn't very comfortable for his knees.'

Milly put a hand over her mouth and spluttered, 'It won't be very comfortable for his trousers, either, I bet they're not very happy.' She skipped round the desk and took hold of Philip's elbow. 'I'll help you up, then you can say sorry to your trousers.'

He was chuckling as he dusted his knees. 'Am I to take it that I have your approval to marry your mother?'

Milly nodded. 'I suppose so. Uncle Oscar has a very big house, and it's full of lovely things. Do you have a big house?'

'I don't have a house yet. I live with my parents part of the week, then spend some time in my apartment. But I will be buying a house when your mother and I marry.'

'Will it be as big as Uncle Oscar's?'

Evelyn gasped. 'Really, Amelia, it is rude to ask such questions.'

But Philip brushed her objection aside. 'It's only natural she should be curious. And to answer her question, I hope we will eventually have a house as big as Oscar's. But if you want to see a really big house, my dear, then you should see your grand-father's. It is probably the largest house in Liverpool.'

Milly's mouth and eyes widened at the same time. 'Is that true, Granddad? Do you live in a castle?'

'See what you have done now, my boy?' Cyril said, chortling. 'The child will expect to see a throne, and Matilda with a tiara on her head. The only thing I can do now is take her to see for herself. Would you like that, Milly?'

Evelyn spoke before her daughter could answer. 'I'm sorry,

Cyril, but I have to be getting home soon, or our friends will worry about us. Could we not leave it until tomorrow?'

Oscar saw the disappointment on Cyril's face and stepped in. 'I can run Milly and Cyril there in ten minutes, and that would give you and Philip time to talk some more. I promise to have Milly back here in an hour, then I could run you both as near to your home as you want me to. Does that suit you, Cyril?'

'It would be wonderful. I want to surprise Matilda, and couldn't keep this to myself until tomorrow.'

And Milly added her voice, because she wanted to see the house that was bigger than her Uncle Oscar's. And, most of all, she wanted to see her grandmother. 'Go on, Mother, give in, please?' So much had happened today, it was like being in a dream. She didn't want to go home to bed, wake up in the morning and find it had all disappeared. 'I want to see my grandmother.'

A few minutes later she was sitting on the back seat of Oscar's car, with her grandfather sitting next to her. 'It's been a lovely day, Granddad, the best I've ever had.' Then she remembered her friends, Aunties Bessie, Rita and Aggie. She must never forget how good they'd been to her. 'Well, one of the best, Granddad, 'cos I had a wonderful Christmas.'

When Oscar turned into the long drive, and the house came into view, Milly lost her tongue all of a sudden. It wasn't a palace, but it was nearly as big as one. 'Is this where you live, Granddad?'

'It is, my darling, and I hope you will spend many happy hours here with me and your grandmother. And I can tell you that this is going to be a shock to her, so we must be very careful now.'

Oscar opened the car door for them. 'I'll come in with you, Cyril. It might take the edge off the shock, don't you think?'

A maid in a black dress and white starched apron opened the door, and smiled when she saw the trio standing there. 'You're early, Mr Cyril, Madam will be surprised to see you. And you, Mr Oscar, shall I take your coat?' She looked at Milly with curiosity. 'Shall I take your coat, miss?'

Milly moved closer to her grandfather. 'This is my best coat, and my mother wouldn't like it if someone took it from me.'

Cyril and Oscar managed to hide their smiles. 'I wouldn't blame your mother for being annoyed if someone took it from you, my dear, but Maisie only wants to hang it up until you are ready to leave. Then she will give it back to you.'

'Oh, that's all right then.' Milly slipped off her coat and handed it to the maid who was having difficulty keeping the smile from her face. Then Milly remembered her manners, and said, 'Thank you very much.' But she still wasn't happy when she saw the maid walking away with the three coats over her arm. 'Will you hang it up by the tab, please, 'cos if you just hang it on a hook, it will put the coat out of shape.'

'Yes, miss,' the maid said, 'I will take really good care of it for you.'

The hall was massive, with a beautiful wide curved staircase. There were highly polished tables, gilt-framed pictures on the walls, several vases of flowers, and the most beautiful chandelier hanging down from the ceiling, its drops sending out flashes of colour. Milly's eyes were everywhere, she had never seen anything like it. But it was all so strange, she felt shy. 'Granddad, you won't let go of my hand, will you?'

'Of course I won't, my dear, and you have no need to be afraid or shy, for this is the house your father was born in. I'll show you his room later, but first I want to surprise your grandmother. She will be in the drawing room at this time of day, and I am not going to tell her who you are at first. Oscar will come in with us, and I want to see if your grandmother can tell who you are by looking at you.'

Milly had been looking forward to seeing her grandmother, but this house was so big it frightened her a little. 'You won't leave me, will you?' She looked up at Oscar. 'You'll stay with me, won't you, Uncle Oscar?'

'Your granddad and I will never be more than a yard from you, darling. In fact I will hold your hand all the time, I promise.' Oscar raised his brows and asked, 'Is that all right with you, Cyril?'

Milly didn't want to leave her granddad out though, 'cos he might be sad if he thought she didn't want him. She looked from one to the other. 'You can hold a hand each, then I'll have two men to protect me if there are any dragons hiding in cupboards.'

So it was a laughing trio who entered the drawing room. Matilda looked at them in surprise, it was far too early for her husband to be home. 'We've brought a visitor to see you.' Cyril let Milly's hand drop, and Oscar looked at him with a frown. But Cyril nodded as if to say, You go ahead, I want to see my wife's reaction from here. And Oscar understood. It was going to be a very emotional scene.

Matilda smiled at Oscar when he stood before her, Milly's hand in his. 'I didn't know you had a daughter, Oscar,' she said, eyeing Milly with curiosity. 'I thought your children were boys.'

'Oh, Milly is not my daughter. You're right, Matilda, my children are both boys and much younger. No, Milly is a friend of mine I thought you might like to meet.'

She looked at Milly and smiled. 'I am very happy to meet you, my dear. If you are a friend of Oscar's then you are a friend of mine.' She leaned forward when Milly smiled, and there was a strange expression on her face. 'You are a very pretty girl. You remind me of someone, but I can't think who.'

Standing in the background, Cyril could feel a lump forming in his throat. He wanted to tell his wife it was her granddaughter she was looking at, but he had lost the power of speech. He would have to leave it to Oscar to break the news, he himself was feeling far too emotional.

However, neither man was given the chance. Milly, young as she was, knew this was a very important moment in her life. And she felt sorry for her grandmother. Taking her hand from Oscar's, she moved to stand closer to the woman who was staring at her as though she was a ghost. 'Can't you think who I remind you of, Grandmother?'

It was when his wife fell back in her chair that Cyril was galvanised into action. He was by her side in seconds, his arm around her shoulders. 'Be brave, my darling, this is a wonderful day for both of us. This is Amelia, or Milly as she likes to be called, and she is Charles' daughter.' He was expecting her to faint, or ring for the smelling salts, but instead she pushed him aside and leaned forward to draw Milly towards her. And as Oscar was to tell his wife that evening, it was the most wonderful, yet sad scene he had ever witnessed. For Matilda was crushing the girl to her as though she'd never let go. The tears were running down her cheeks, and she began to rock Milly from side to side. She couldn't bring herself to speak, but her mind was reminding her that this girl was born from the seed of her beloved son, and while she lived, so did Charles.

It took Milly to break the tension. 'Grandmother, don't cry, 'cos you're making me feel sad. I thought you would be happy to see me?'

'Oh, I am, my darling, more happy than words can say. But where have you been all these years?'

'Granddad will tell you that, he's better at saying things than I am. But can you stop crying now, Grandmother, 'cos you're making my dress wet, and it's my very best one.'

Matilda sniffed and let her arms drop. 'I'm sorry, darling, but I am so happy I can't help crying. Now you are here, you won't ever leave us again, will you?'

Milly looked bewildered, so Cyril came to her aid. 'She has to leave us now, darling, for Evelyn is waiting for her in my office. I have so much to tell you, but I don't have the time to tell you now for I need go back to the office with Milly. Oscar was kind enough to bring us here, and he has promised to run Evelyn and Milly home. But you will see your granddaughter again very soon, I promise you. However, no more news for now, all will be revealed tonight.'

Matilda wiped a tear away and Milly reassured her, 'I do love you, Grandmother, and you'll see me loads of times, I promise. But now I want to ask you and Grandfather a favour. All the girls in school, and my friends, they call their grandparents Granda and Grandma. It sounds much nicer, doesn't it? So, please, can I call you the same?' When Matilda nodded, Milly gave her a big hug and kiss. 'I am a very lucky girl having a grandma and granda, and an Uncle Oscar and Auntie Gwen. And my friends in the street where I live, I love them too!'

Then something happened that Cyril had never seen before. His wife walked to the front door holding on tight to Milly's hand. She waved the maid aside. 'I'll see my granddaughter to the door, thank you, you may go.' She even walked to the car, waited on the path until it moved down to the double gates, then stood waving a handkerchief as Milly knelt on the back seat and waved back.

Cyril tapped Oscar on the back and chortled, 'Who was it said that miracles never happen? I think a certain little person is going to give my wife a new lease of life.'

Back at the office, Evelyn was on edge. 'My neighbour will worry herself sick if Milly isn't there when she gets home from work. I do hope they're not much longer.'

'The neighbour you are talking about, is it Bessie? The one I said I would like to meet?'

Evelyn nodded. 'And you will meet her, I promise. But everything can't happen in a day, it may take a few weeks.'

Just then they heard laughter in the corridor outside, and Evelyn let out a sigh of relief. 'Thank goodness, we'll make it home in time.'

The door opened and Milly ran towards her mother. 'You should see the size of the house Granda lives in, Mother. It's nearly as big as a castle.'

'Yes, I know, dear, I have been there. Was your grandmother pleased to see you?'

'Oh, yes, she gave me loads of kisses, and wanted me to stay there.'

Cyril thought this a good time to broach the matter that had been on his mind for a while. 'Have you and Philip made any plans?'

Philip nodded. 'I'm going to see my parents tonight, I think they should be told the news before they hear it from a stranger. Then tomorrow Evelyn and I will set a date for our wedding in the very near future. We will have to live in the apartment for a while until we find a suitable home, and that is the only drawback. There is only one bedroom.'

'Then Milly can come and live with us,' Cyril told them, 'we certainly have plenty of room and would love to have her.'

'I'll live with Auntie Bessie,' Milly said, surprising everyone but Evelyn. 'She has a room there for me.'

'But you can live with us, my dear,' Cyril protested. 'Your grandma and I would love to have you, and we have rooms to spare.'

Milly's face was set. 'No, I want to live with my Auntie Bessie. She is my very bestest friend and she'd be sad if she couldn't see me. And I wouldn't be able to see Jack, either.'

Evelyn shrugged her shoulders at Cyril. 'Shall we leave it for now and talk about it another day? I'm sure Milly will change her mind when she's had time to think about it.'

'I won't change my mind,' she said with a nod of her head for emphasis. 'I want to live with Auntie Bessie.'

When Evelyn tutted, Cyril held his hand up to silence her. He didn't want his granddaughter to be forced into living with him against her will. 'This Bessie must be a very fine person if you love her so much, Milly.'

'Oh, she is, Granda, she's lovely. And she is very funny when she talks to the door and the grate, she makes me laugh all the time.'

'She talks to the door and the grate, does she?' Cyril would have laughed if it hadn't been for Milly's expression, which said she didn't see anything wrong in talking to them. 'Do they answer her back?'

'Oh, yes, and she tells them off then for being cheeky.'

'Do you know, I would like to meet this Auntie Bessie of yours, I'm sure I'd like her. You see, I talk to my desk sometimes, and my paper basket if it trips me up.' He nodded. 'Yes, I'm sure I'd get on with her.'

'You are not the only one who wants to meet Bessie,' Philip informed him. 'Evelyn has told me a lot about her and I'm waiting to meet the lady I'm told is so kind and caring.'

Milly was delighted, for anyone who liked Auntie Bessie was a friend of hers. 'I'll ask her tonight when she can come to see you, Granda, shall I?'

Events were moving too fast for Evelyn. 'Miss Maudsley goes to work every day, Milly, don't forget. We'll have words with her tonight, and see when it would be suitable for her.'

Milly wasn't going to be put off so easily, though. 'She doesn't work on a Sunday, Granda, would you like to see her then?'

Cyril could see by Evelyn's face she didn't like the way the conversation was going, and guessed she was worried in case her daughter invited them all to her house. He knew from Milly that it was a two-up-two-down, and while that didn't bother him, it might bother Evelyn. So he found a solution which he thought would suit everyone. 'Why don't you all come to my home on Sunday for dinner? A sort of celebration. Evelyn, you could bring Milly and Bessie. And Philip is invited, of course, and Oscar and Gwen. You could make your peace with Matilda, who would love to welcome you back into the family. What do you say?'

Milly clapped her hands with glee. 'Oh, yes, Granda, that would be lovely.' She turned to Evelyn. 'Ooh, I can't wait until Sunday, Mother, we'll all have a wonderful time.'

Chapter Thirty-One

Evelyn lay in bed on the Sunday morning going over the whirlwind events of the last three days. So much had happened she hadn't been able to take it all in, but now, in the still of an early Sunday morning, with Milly fast asleep in the next room, her mind was able to catch up on events. Philip had taken her to meet his parents and they had welcomed her with warmth and friendliness, instantly putting her at ease. She hadn't been asked difficult questions or made to feel awkward, for Philip had already told them everything from start to finish. They discussed the wedding, and both his parents were pleased that at last their son was to settle down. They instantly got involved in planning things, when it should be, where it should take place, and where to hold the reception. And they were sincere in the pleasure they showed at their son's choice of wife. It was Mrs Astbury who first brought Milly into the conversation, by saying she must be looking forward to being a bridesmaid. Even though Evelyn wouldn't be wearing white, Philip's parents still wanted their son to have a wedding he would remember for the rest of his life.

Evelyn sighed, but it was a sigh of relief and happiness. All her fears about facing Cyril had been groundless. The meeting had gone so smoothly, with not a word of reproach from him. As for Oscar and Gwen, it was lovely to see them again and renew their friendship. She had such a lot to be thankful for, and no one realised that more than herself. But the fears and apprehension she'd suffered before meeting all these people had taken their toll, with a constant headache and tummy taut with tension. And although she'd had a smile fixed on her face most of the time, the first real, genuine belly laugh had come last night, and Bessie was the cause of it. Evelyn stretched her legs and relived the scene in her head.

'Ay, Evelyn, let's be serious for a minute while I get something off me chest.' Bessie was sitting on the couch with Milly beside her, while Evelyn sat in the fireside chair. 'Milly tells me that her granda's house is nearly as big as a palace, and filled with beautiful things. And he's got a maid, a housekeeper, a cleaner and a gardener. Now is she pulling me leg or is she telling the truth?'

'She's telling the truth, Bessie, I did tell you that the Lister-Sinclairs were very wealthy. They have a beautiful home. Why?'

'Why! Because I can't go to a place like that, I'd make a holy show of meself, and you into the bargain. I'd be frightened to open me mouth in case I put me ruddy foot in it.' She leaned forward to poke the fire. 'No, you two go and enjoy yerselves, I won't bother. I don't know why I was asked in the first place, I'd be well out of me depth.'

'Oh, you've got to come, Auntie Bessie, 'cos Granda and Uncle Philip are dying to meet you. I told them you were my bestest friend, and they want to be your friend as well. You've got to come or I'll cry and I won't go either.'

Bessie returned the poker back to the companion set then leaned back on the couch. 'Listen to me, sweetheart, I don't speak posh so I'd be frightened to open my mouth, and I don't have fancy clothes so I'd feel uncomfortable.'

'They're not snobs, Bessie,' Evelyn told her. 'I used to be a snob, as you well know, but I was only pretending to be something I wasn't, which is what snobs do. People who really have money aren't a bit like that. You would be made very welcome, I can assure you, and wouldn't feel uncomfortable at all.'

Bessie snorted. 'Oh, no, in me home-made dress and me Marcel-waved hair, I'd be the belle of the ruddy ball! And I can't afford to go out and pay a fortune for another dress, even if the shops were open, which they're not.'

Milly was pouting, very near to tears. 'I'm going in the dress you made me, Auntie Bessie, so that's a home-made dress, and I love it. And I'll tell everyone that you made it for me, so they'll all think you are very clever. I bet none of them could make a dress.'

'That's different, sweetheart, 'cos you're family. If you turned up in a sack, they'd still love yer. But I'm not family, yer see.'

Milly folded her arms, her face set. 'If you don't go, then I won't go either, so there!'

'Don't start behaving like a baby, Milly,' Evelyn said. 'You can't always have your own way. If Miss Maudsley doesn't want to come, we can't make her. I'll be very disappointed, though, because I've told Cyril and Philip so much about her they really do want to meet her.' She suddenly had a brain wave. 'It's a pity, Bessie, because you said you would like to thank the man who gave the donation at Christmas, and if you don't come with us tomorrow night, you'll miss the chance of meeting him.'

Bessie chuckled. 'Nice try, Evelyn, but it won't work.'

Milly had shuffled to the edge of the couch. 'Which man is that, Mother, do I know him?'

'Yes, dear, it's Uncle Philip, the man I am going to marry.'

Bessie's eyes narrowed. 'Are you having me on, Evelyn, 'cos if yer are, I'll set the poker on yer. In fact, I won't bother with the poker, I'll have a word with the front door and tell it not to let yer in any more.'

Evelyn let her head drop back and laughter filled the room. 'Oh, if you don't come, Bessie, you'll miss out on a lot. Milly's granddad is like you, he talks to his desk, and the waste-paper basket. You would have so much in common.'

Bessie viewed her through narrowed lids. 'Is this another try, Evelyn? If it is, yer must be getting desperate, sweetheart, 'cos I could do better meself.'

'Mother isn't telling fibs, Auntie Bessie,' Milly said. 'She is going to marry Uncle Philip, and Granda does talk to his desk and the waste-paper basket, he told us.'

Bessie stroked her cheek. 'It's no use, sweetheart, I'm sure they are the nicest people in the world, but it doesn't alter the fact I'm not in the same class as them, and I really would be embarrassed. My clothes wouldn't fit, me accent would go down like a lead balloon, and I'd be dead miserable. You and yer mother go, and have a nice time. You can tell me all about it after. It'll be a New Year then, nineteen hundred and twenty-six.'

But nothing would move Milly. 'If you don't go, then I'm not going. I'll stay with you.'

Bessie lifted her hands in defeat. 'Okay, okay! I'll go with yer and spend the night in the kitchen helping the servants. Are yer satisfied now?'

They were sitting in a taxi on Sunday when Evelyn said, 'You look very smart, Bessie, I must say. Your hair looks very glamorous.'

'And so it ruddy well should do!' she said. 'I've had dinky curlers in all night, and I haven't slept a flaming wink. I don't know, the things we women go through. If a burglar had broke into my house last night, he'd have taken one look at me and scarpered hell for leather down the ruddy street. The things we women have to put up with, it's nothing but flaming torture.'

'Well, I think you look lovely, Auntie Bessie. Nobody will look as nice as you.'

Bessie was feeling very nervous, and would much rather have been sitting in her little house, with a fire roaring up the chimney, than in a taxi on her way to a house as big as a castle. At least in her own place she could talk to the furniture without feeling embarrassed because it was used to her Liverpool accent. Another thing, this was the first time she'd been in a taxi in her whole life and she felt uncomfortable enough, so how was she going to feel in a house as big as a ruddy castle, with a maid and a housekeeper? She gave a sigh and promised herself she'd find a chair in a corner somewhere and sit out of sight for the night. Or else find the kitchen and give the cook a hand. That would be more up her street than sitting with a group of people who had more money than they knew what to do with.

'It's the next house, driver,' Evelyn said, leaning forward to tap on the glass partition. 'You can drive straight into the driveway.'

While she was paying the man, Bessie was taking stock of the house and gardens, and felt like either getting back in the taxi and asking the driver to take her home, or taking to her heels and running as fast as she could. This was no place for her, she should never have given in to Milly.

'Come along,' Evelyn said, taking Bessie's elbow, 'Maisie has the door open.'

Bessie took one look at the uniformed maid and her heart dropped even further as she asked herself what she was doing here. But when the maid smiled as she asked if she could take her coat, Bessie found she could smile back. And she was soon thinking to herself that she'd have a good look around the enormous hall so she could describe everything to Rita and Aggie. She had barely got as far as the winding staircase, with the gilt-framed pictures spaced at intervals on the wall, when by her side she heard a deep voice saying, 'So, this is the Bessie I've heard so much about?'

After nearly jumping out of her skin with fright, she turned her head to see a man who appeared to be about the same age as herself. He was holding out his hand. 'I'm Cyril Lister-Sinclair, Milly's grandfather, and she's told me so much about you, I feel I know you.'

Bessie looked at the outstretched hand, then at the smiling, kindly face, and her hand went to join his. 'I'm pleased to meet yer, er, sir,' she said, pumping his hand enthusiastically. 'But Milly exaggerates something terrible, so don't believe everything she tells yer.'

Cyril saw before him a woman who was small and thin, with a face as honest as the day is long and eyes full of humour. 'Ah, yes, I can well imagine my granddaughter has a very vivid imagination, but I don't believe she exaggerates her feelings for you. She tells me you are her bestest friend, and I find myself a little jealous of you. I'm hoping in the near future to become another of her bestest friends.'

Bessie looked around for Evelyn and Milly, but they had disappeared. She was alone in the hall with this man she found she was at ease with. 'Oh, Milly is your friend already, she has told me so. You are very lucky, she's a child anyone would be proud of. Clever, caring, loving and with a sense of humour. She's also a very pretty girl, and I have to admit I love the bones of her.'

'Here you are, old boy,' a man's voice boomed, 'Evelyn said I would find you here.'

'Ah, Philip, may I introduce you to Miss Bessie? She is a neighbour and friend of Evelyn and Milly's.' Cyril made the introductions, and Bessie weighed Philip up as they shook hands. 'You are one of the reasons I came tonight, Mr Philip, 'cos I wanted to thank yer for being so kind. There are a lot of people in our street who would like to thank yer as well, so I'll do it for them.'

Cyril frowned. 'What is this about, Philip? I didn't know you knew Miss Maudsley?

'I have never met the dear lady until this minute, Cyril, but I know a lot about her. And when the chance comes, I would like to have a private conversation with her.'

'This is all very mysterious,' Cyril said. 'Would I be allowed to sit in on this conversation? I am now very intrigued.'

The sound of childish laughter had three pairs of eyes turning towards the sound. They saw Milly pulling on her grandmother's arm, her face creased in laughter. 'Come on, Grandma, here she is. This is my Auntie Bessie.'

Cyril couldn't believe his eyes. His wife looked twenty years younger as she laughed while being pulled towards the group. 'Auntie Bessie, this is my grandma and I've told her all about you.'

Without a word being exchanged, Cyril and Philip stepped back. Both men were interested in how this meeting would go, for it could affect their own lives. Matilda was smiling when she stopped in front of Bessie. 'My granddaughter has never stopped talking about you. You have certainly made an impression on her.'

Milly dropped her grandmother's hand and reached for Bessie's. 'She's my bestest friend in the whole world, Grandma, and I do love her.' She gazed up at Bessie, her green eyes shining. 'Aren't you my bestest friend, Auntie Bessie, and don't you love the bones of me?'

There was no need to say it, for it was plain to those watching that Bessie adored the girl, but she confirmed it by saying, 'Yes, sweetheart, ye're me bestest mate, and I love the bones of yer.'

'I was telling Milly how much I liked her dress, it is so pretty,' Matilda said. 'And she tells me you made it for her. Is this true?'

Bessie didn't know how to address these people, so decided to use no names. 'Yes, that is my job, I'm a seamstress by trade.'

'That is wonderful! Did you hear that, Cyril, Bessie is a seamstress. I have said for years we should employ a seamstress, it would be so useful.'

'I'm sure Bessie is already gainfully employed, my dear.' But while he was speaking an idea was forming in Cyril's head. Part of the idea had been there since he'd first known of Milly's love for this woman, and now his wife had given him a way of taking it further. 'Don't you think you should go back to the drawing room, my dear, and take Milly with you? Evelyn and our guests will think it rude of us to both to disappear. Philip and I will be with you shortly, but we both wish to have a word with Bessie.'

'My husband is right, I should get back to our guests.' Matilda was not usually a demonstrative person but, wonder of wonders, she put her hand on Bessie's arm and squeezed it. 'We will talk later. My granddaughter said we should be friends, and I would like that very much.'

Milly escaped from her grandmother's hand and put her arms around Bessie's waist. 'Aren't you glad you came now, Auntie Bessie? I told you they would love you.'

Bessie smiled and stroked her hair. 'Yes, I'm glad I came, sweetheart, but you run along with your grandma now, and I'll see you soon.'

'Can I have a kiss first, please, 'cos you haven't given me one today. And then I'll be a good girl and go with Grandma.' When Bessie bent down to kiss her, the girl's arms went around her neck, and those watching could hear her say, 'I do love you, Auntie Bessie.'

Bessie smiled. 'I know yer do, 'cos yer told the shovel, and the shovel told me.'

Milly put her hands on her hips and feigned indignation. 'I'm going to tell that shovel off when I see it, it had no right to tell tales.'

Bessie pushed her towards Matilda, who was watching with great interest. 'You go with yer grandma now, I'll see yer in a bit.'

Cyril turned to Philip. 'I wish to talk to Bessie. Would you like to join us, or would you prefer to join our guests?'

'I'll tag along with you, if you have no objection?' Philip winked at Bessie. 'I can't leave you and Bessie alone in the study, what would people think!'

The two men took an arm each, and led her in the direction of Cyril's study. When they reached the door, she burst out laughing.

'Two male escorts no less. Wait until I tell me mates, they won't believe me. I know what one of them will say. "Oh, aye, two bleeding coppers taking yer in for being drunk." '

Both men roared with laughter. And although they couldn't read each other's mind, they were both thinking it wasn't hard to like this little lady. 'Oh, are you known for getting drunk and being escorted by policemen to the nearest police station?' Philip asked.

'Oh, yes, every Saturday night without fail. I have me usual six bottles of milk stout, then the landlord throws me out for being drunk, and I sit in the gutter singing me head off until the local bobbies take me to sleep it off in a cell in the police station.'

Cyril looked at Philip and opened the study door. 'We've got quite a character here, my boy, I think we will have to go easy on the brandy and port. There are no gutters around here, and the nearest police station is a mile away.'

Philip winked. 'I will take responsibility, old boy, I'll keep my eye on her all night.'

'Which eye will that be, sir, so I can dodge it?' Bessie was beginning to enjoy herself. Okay, so they were rolling in money while she was as poor as a church mouse, but that didn't make them any different. And these two seemed happy enough, they were laughing their heads off.

Cyril pointed to a comfortable leather chair. 'Make yourself at home, my dear. What I have to say is very important to me, my wife and Milly.'

Philip stood up. 'Would you prefer I joined the other guests then, Cyril? I don't want to intrude.'

'No, you stay, dear boy. This matter concerns Evelyn, and as her husband to be, it also concerns you. I will try to make it as brief as possible, or if we're not back with our guests when the bell goes for dinner, my dear wife will not be too happy.' He waited until Philip had seated himself, then looked across the desk at Bessie. 'I believe Evelyn has told you most of the story, up to last week when she and Milly came back into our lives, so I won't go over that ground again. What I have to say concerns you, and my granddaughter. While Milly appears pleased to have us in her life, to be part of a family, and seems fond of my wife and myself, it is you she loves. She talks of you constantly, you are her bestest friend and she loves you. Of course I would like her to love my wife and me too, but I am not stupid enough to think love is something immediate, that you can take for granted. You have to work at love, to earn it.'

'Oh, Milly will come to love you in time,' Bessie said. 'She is a lovable child, with a heart full of love to give. It just takes time, Mr . . . er . . . Mr Cyril.' Bessie shook her head. 'I'm sorry, I'm at a loss as to what to call yer. But don't worry about Milly, she'll come to love yer, I know she will.'

Cyril lifted a pencil from a stand on his desk and started to scribble on a large blotting pad. 'I've asked Milly to come and live with Matilda and me while Evelyn and Philip begin married life together. We want her so much, for after all, she is the daughter of our beloved son. But Milly was quite definite that it was you she wanted to live with, and I would never force her against her will. I want her to love me, not hate me. So I wondered if you would consider the post of nanny to her?'

'But I have a job, and me own little house. And me two best mates are my neighbours, I couldn't leave all that to be a nanny. I don't know the first thing about being one, I'm not qualified.'

It was Philip who said, 'I don't want to interfere, but I think love is the best quality anyone can have. And you only have to listen to Milly, and Evelyn, to know love is something you have in abundance. I think it is a marvellous idea. I'm sure you want to be with Milly as much as she wants to be with you. If you were suddenly to be taken out of her life, she would fret dreadfully and be very miserable.'

'And I'd be broken-hearted,' Bessie said with feeling. 'I knew it would happen one day, it had to, for she wasn't mine to love and to hold. But I haven't the faintest idea what a nanny does! I'm not well educated or clever, so I wouldn't be up to the job!'

'Let me explain what it would entail, Bessie,' Cyril said, 'then you can take the idea home with you and give it some thought. All you would be required to do is be a companion to Milly. Accompany her to school and back, help with her clothes, take her for walks to the shops or to the park, do the things you already do together now. This is a huge house, far too big for Matilda and myself, but we will never leave it because our son was born here and it holds memories of him. There are many rooms which are not used, so you would have your own separate accommodation. Your own entrance, sitting room, bedroom and bathroom. And my wife and I would appreciate it if you had your meals with us, as a family. You would have days off, and could have your friends visit you whenever you wished.' Cyril smiled. 'One who would be very welcome is a young boy named Jack. Next to you, he is Amelia's bestest friend, even though he does try and cheat at cards.'

When he paused to consider his next words, he caught Philip's eye and was rewarded with a slight nod and a smile of encouragement. 'Of course you would receive a salary, to be mutually agreed, and would be treated by the staff as a member of the family. But what is most important, you wouldn't be parted from Milly, and she would have her bestest friend here all the time.'

For a few seconds Bessie bowed her head in thought. Then asked, 'But what if I give me house up, pack my job in, and then find the arrangement you talk of isn't suitable? I'd have lost everything, and at my age I can't afford to take a chance. Apart from me two mates in the street, I don't have a soul in the world to turn to.' Her voice thick with emotion, she went on, 'I love the bones of Milly, but what would happen to me if I didn't get on with yer wife and the atmosphere wasn't a happy one?'

Philip left his chair to sit on the top of the desk, where he could look her in the face. 'I hope Cyril will forgive me for butting in, but I have an idea which may put all your fears to rest, my dear. You see, your future is of great interest to me also, for Evelyn admires you very much and has told me she will never forget how you helped her and will always remain friends with you. So listen to my idea and tell me what you think.' He gave her a smile of encouragement. 'Why not take a week off work, move in here and take on the role of nanny, as Cyril sees it? We all know you get on like a house on fire with Milly, but you are worried you may not fit in with Matilda and the staff. A week of living with the family would help you make a decision on whether you feel you would fit in. How does that appeal to you?'

'Take a week off work? I've never taken time off in all the twenty-odd years I've worked there. What would I tell the boss?'

Cyril felt like slapping Philip on the back for coming up with such a good idea. 'You would not have to worry about that, my dear. I will ring your employer if you would give me the name of the firm. I think we should have a trial run, as Philip suggests. If you turn it down out of hand, you may come to regret it. Please give it a try.'

All that was going through Bessie's mind was the thought of never seeing Milly again. And that didn't bear thinking about. And it wasn't as though she would be going to people who would look down on her, for she had been treated with great respect and friendliness by everyone she'd met. And like Cyril said, if she turned the offer down she may live to regret it. She nodded her head. 'I'll give it a week's trial, as yer said. And I want to thank yer both for the nice welcome yer gave me, and being so kind.'

Cyril was beside himself with happiness. 'You will not regret it, Bessie, I promise you that. And Milly won't be the only one to be delighted when she's told, I believe you will be a valuable addition to this household. Now, if you will write the name of your employer down, Bessie, and your full name and address, we can join our other guests. There are only two you haven't met already, that is Oscar and Gwen, but they know all about you.'

As Bessie wrote out her full name and address, and that of her employer, they heard her muttering through the side of her mouth, 'You two would charm the birds off a ruddy tree. I'm going to have to keep a close watch on yer.'

Rita showed her surprise when she opened the door the next morning and saw Bessie standing on her front step. 'My God, Bessie, the streets are not aired off yet! Why are yer up and about so early, and where's Milly?'

Bessie grinned. 'And a Happy New Year to you as well, Rita Wells. That's a marvellous greeting, I must say.'

'Well, I didn't expect yer so early, sunshine, I thought yer'd be having a lie in after being out late last night.'

'I've got something important to tell you and Aggie, and as Milly is still fast asleep, and me fire's lit and the kettle on, I wondered if yer were both decent enough to come across for half an hour?'

'I'm dressed, as yer can see, but I don't know about Aggie, I haven't heard her this morning, she might still be in bed.'

The next door opened and Aggie's head appeared, her hair tousled and a smudge of soot on her face. 'Yer might not have heard me, queen, but I heard you raking the ashes out.' She eyed Bessie. 'Did I hear yer say yer had something to tell us, queen? I'll just slip me coat on and come across, seeing as yer've got the kettle on for a cuppa.' Her head popped out a bit further so she could see Rita. 'Get yer coat on, queen, and let's hear what she's got to tell us about how the other half live. I hope yer haven't gone all stuck-up on us, Bessie, and expect us to wipe our feet?'

Bessie started to cross the street. 'The tea will be on the table in five minutes, and don't make a sound. What I've got to tell yer is not for Milly's ears.'

Ten minutes later the three women were sitting around Bessie's table and she was telling them that Evelyn was getting married in four weeks' time. The man she was marrying was called Philip, and he was the one who had given them all that money at Christmas. They were getting married in a church in Mossley Hill, and Evelyn was saying she would be buying a wedding dress in ivory, with her being a widow. Milly was going to be bridesmaid, and a friend of Evelyn's called Gwen had been asked to be maid-of-honour. It sounded like a big posh affair, and she wouldn't mind going to see it. Then she told her mates a little about the Lister-Sinclairs' house. How they had carpets in every room, pictures and chandeliers. 'Yer might get to see it for yerselves one of these days, yer never know.'

Aggie huffed. 'A snowball stands more chance in hell than we ever do of getting inside a posh house like that! They'd think we were beggars and chase us.'

'Well, it all depends.' Bessie sounded mysterious. 'I've got something to tell yer, and I want yer to give me yer honest opinion on what yer think I should do for the best.' She raised her thumb to the ceiling. 'Keep yer voices down, for heaven's sake, or I won't be able to tell yer if Milly comes down.'

Bessie went over everything that had been said in Cyril's office, and as the story was unfolding the expressions on the faces of her two best mates changed every few seconds. Aggie nudged Rita so many times her side would be black and blue. But although there were gasps of surprise, they didn't once interrupt.

'So there yer have it, and I don't know what to do for the best. It's kept me awake half the night. First I think I should go, then the next minute I think I couldn't leave this little house after living here all me life. So what do yer think I should do for the best?'

'I'd give it a try,' Rita said without hesitation. 'Yer'd be a fool to turn down an offer like that, especially as yer say everyone was friendly and they treated yer like one of their own. I don't know why yer didn't agree right away, knowing yer'd be with Milly. Yer'd break yer heart if yer didn't see her every day, yer know that.'

'She's right,' Aggie said. 'Yer'd be living in the lap of luxury, with yer own rooms and a bathroom as well.' She hoisted her bosom and leaned her elbows on the table. 'Did they really say yer could invite me and Rita?'

'As often as yer want to come. Mr Cyril knew about yer, 'cos Milly had told him. Oh, and Jack as well.' Bessie sighed. 'I think it might be too good to be true. Perhaps I wouldn't fit in. I can't speak posh, I don't know which knife to use first at the dinner table . . . oh, there's all sorts of things to think about.'

'Yer had yer dinner with them last night, didn't yer?' Rita asked. 'Then yer didn't eat with yer fingers, surely, so yer must have learnt something.'

'I just followed what everyone else did. Nobody sat watching me, they're far too nice for that, and not a bit stuck up.'

'It's up to you, sunshine, but I think yer'd be mad to turn down an offer like that. Don't yer agree with me, Aggie?'

'Yeah, I do! And she'd be selfish, as well. I mean, like, how else are you and me ever going to get into a toff's house? And to be able to go to the lavvy without having to go down the bleeding yard! I bet they've got that posh toilet paper we see in rolls in the shops.' Aggie's chins swept from side to side as she told Bessie, 'I think it would be selfish of yer to turn it down. Ye're not thinking about us two, are yer? Don't yer think we'd like to swan up the driveway what yer told us about, in our best secondhand clothes? Don't be so bleeding miserable and grab the offer with both hands.'

'That's something ye're going to have to learn not to do,' Bessie said. 'Yer don't use any bad language when yer come to visit me.'

Rita smiled. 'So yer are taking the job?' When Bessie nodded, she said, 'I'm glad for yer, sunshine, I know ye're doing the right thing. Me and Aggie will give yer a week to settle in, then we'll pay our first visit. And I'll bring a gag with me to stick in her mouth if she forgets to watch her language.'

Bessie had been living with the Lister-Sinclairs for three days. Although Matilda had told Cyril things were going very well, he decided on the fourth day to come home at lunchtime and see for himself. He knew his wife could be difficult sometimes, having been spoilt by him since the day they wed. He didn't tell her he would be back, wanting to surprise her and to see for himself how Bessie was fitting in. Milly had gone back to school, but would be leaving it the following week to go to a private school which was nearer her new home. She spent a lot of time in Bessie's room, and Cyril was hoping that would change when the trial week was over and she'd agreed to stay on. She seemed to be happy enough whenever he saw her and he was keeping his fingers crossed. He would be very upset if she told him she wanted to go back to her own house.

Cyril let himself in the front door and put a finger to his mouth when the maid came to take his coat. 'I will have some lunch, Maisie,' he said softly, 'a sandwich will do. This is a surprise visit to see how Miss Bessie is settling in.'

The maid grinned. 'She's settling in very well, Mr Cyril. Everyone likes her. She's very funny, always laughing.'

Cyril nodded and turned away, hoping Matilda appreciated Bessie's humour too. 'They're in the drawing room, are they?'

'Yes, they finished their lunch some time ago.'

He stood outside the door, listening, and heard Bessie's voice saying, 'My mother's name was Matilda.'

'Oh, what a coincidence!' his wife said. 'I'm surprised they didn't call you Matilda then, instead of Bessie.'

'I wasn't christened Bessie, my real name is Elizabeth. But my mam said it was too much of a mouthful, so from then on I got Bessie.'

Cyril was about to knock when Bessie spoke again. 'My mam didn't get Matilda either, she was always called Tilly. It suited her, too, like a pet name.'

'Tilly!' Matilda laughed. 'That's a funny name!'

'I didn't think so, I liked it. It was more friendly, 'cos all our neighbours had pet names for people they liked. Margaret was shortened to Maggie, Clementine to Clemmie, and so on.'

'Would I suit Tilly, do you think?'

'Ooh, don't ask me, sweetheart, I don't want yer husband giving me down the banks.'

Cyril smiled and turned away from the door. He wouldn't intrude, not when they seemed to be on such friendly terms. He'd have his sandwich in the kitchen and then go back to the office.

On Friday morning, Oscar called to see him. 'My wife is curious to know if Bessie has made up her mind yet?' He sat down in a chair facing Cyril. 'We are both of the opinion that you have a gem in her, and agree you should do your best to hang on to her. She is down-to-earth, honest, practical, and with a very sunny disposition. The very qualities that will help Milly grow into a sensible girl with her feet firmly on the ground.'

Cyril nodded. 'She seems to have found favour with everyone, and I'm hoping we have found favour with her. Milly would be devastated if Bessie went back to her own house. In fact, I think she would pine and make herself ill if they were parted. But there's little we can do, it is up to Bessie. Tomorrow sees her week's trial over, and I am really keeping my fingers crossed. It's not only Milly, either. Matilda gets on really well with Bessie, and you know how hard to please my wife is! However, there is little I can do but hope.'

'Why don't we bring the matter forward and then you'll have your mind put at rest?' Oscar asked. 'I could come with you, on some pretext, so Bessie won't feel she's being ambushed. And if push came to shove, I could always add my plea to yours. I'm quite good at pleading. What do you say, old boy?'

'I think it would be a good idea, but it would have to be this afternoon after lunch. Evelyn will be there then. She's visited Bessie a few times this week, they seem to be fast friends. I'd be so glad if Matilda could be close to them too.' Cyril closed the folder he'd been going through and placed it at the side of the desk. 'Have you any business to attend to or shall we have a drink at the club and an early lunch? I'd say two o'clock would be a good time to arrive home. Bessie has to leave at three to pick Milly up from school.'

'So Evelyn calls to see Milly too, does she?'

Cyril nodded. 'Usually Philip is with her, he wants Milly to get to know him.'

Oscar smiled at him across the desk. 'Life has changed radically for you over the last few weeks, hasn't it? And all to the good.'

'I feel a new man, my boy, and a much younger man. My dear wife and I can't believe how lucky we are. The house has come alive with Milly and Bessie there. There is a homely feel about it, and when Milly's laughter fills the rooms, it's like music to my ears.' Cyril pushed his chair back. 'To the club, dear boy, we can pass an hour away talking of how life was, and how it is today.'

'Hello, Mr Oscar.' Maisie smiled as she took his coat. 'It is nice to see you.'

'Where are the ladies?' Cyril asked. 'In the drawing room?'

'Yes, Mr Cyril. They finished their lunch half an hour ago. Shall I bring a tray in?'

'No, my dear, Oscar and I have just come from the club.' He walked towards the drawing room with Oscar close on his heels. Cyril opened the door to hear Bessie say, 'I think a colour like hyacinth blue would suit Milly, and it would look nice with your ivory.'

The men had entered quietly, and the women started when Cyril said, 'Do you think I would suit hyacinth blue, Bessie?'

She shook her head. 'No, Mr Cyril, it wouldn't go with yer complexion at all. Far better stick with the grey top hat and tails that Matilda was saying yer'll be wearing.'

Oscar kissed each of the ladies in turn. 'Plans for the wedding going well, are they, Evelyn? Gwen and I are looking forward to it. Her parents have agreed to have the two boys for the day.'

When Evelyn smiled, he thought how much she had mellowed. All from her love of Philip, who clearly adored her in return. 'Yes, we seem to be organised. Invitations have gone out, the reception has been booked, flowers ordered and cars attended to. I have had a fitting for my dress, and you probably know that Gwen had hers at the same time. There is only Milly to worry about now. She is being very stubborn, insisting that Bessie should make her dress.'

'I don't mind, Evelyn, as long as you show me a pattern and get the same material as Gwen's. I'd need three yards, 'cos I wouldn't want to skimp it. And there's no need to worry, I'll make sure she looks as lovely as she is.' Then she said something that brought a smile to every face. 'I'll see if I can manage to get me sewing machine up here tomorrow so I can make a start as soon as I have the material. It's only a hand machine, I think I could manage it on the tram.'

'Does that mean you've decided to stay with us?' Cyril asked. 'To make this your home?'

'Of course it does, yer daft thing! There was never any doubt of that. I'm happy here, I get on with everyone. That is, if you're satisfied with me?'

There was a chorus of approval and Oscar said, 'I'll take you home tomorrow and help you with the sewing machine. And there must be other things you want from your home?'

'I don't need any furniture, seeing as my rooms here are already furnished, but there are a few things I must have, sentimental things that belonged to my parents. I wouldn't part with them. And I'll have to ask me two mates to give the rent collector a week's notice for me, and pay him the two weeks' rent. Oh, and they'll stop the coalman and the milkman too, and that's the lot.'

'What about your furniture?' Oscar asked. 'Won't you try and sell it?'

'I'll let my two mates do it. It isn't worth much, but they'd get a few bob for it and they'd be grateful 'cos they aren't well off. One of the local secondhand shops will empty the house so the landlord won't have any complaints.'

'That's something I'll have to think about, too,' Evelyn said. 'I'll come with you to meet Milly, and we can talk about it on the way.'

Cyril put his hand on Bessie's shoulder. 'We'll leave you ladies now, but I'm delighted you are going to stay with us. I shall go back to my office a very happy man.'

Oscar went as far as kissing Bessie's cheek. 'I'll pick you up at ten o'clock in the morning and we'll sort out your affairs then. And for now, welcome to our circle of friends.'

Chapter Thirty-Two

'I'll make us a cup of tea to warm us up,' Bessie said, 'it's freezing in here 'cos the fire hasn't been lit all week. Would yer rather just take the sewing machine and I can come back another day for the other things?'

Oscar shook his head as he looked around the small room. 'No, Bessie, this is a very warm overcoat, I don't feel the cold. We may as well get it all done in the one journey.'

She had seen his eyes going around the room, and chuckled. 'Bit of a difference to the Lister-Sinclairs', eh? But it was home to me mam and dad, and it's been home to me all me life. I'll miss it, for the memories it holds, but we can't have everything we want in life, can we? Being with Milly is the best thing in my life.' Bessie took a deep breath then blew it out slowly. 'The sewing machine is on the floor in the bedroom on the right. While you're doing that, I'll make us a drink.'

Oscar came down with the Singer hand-sewing machine, which was housed in a wooden case with a handle on top for carrying. 'You would never have managed this on the tram, Bessie, it's heavy.'

'I would have had a go. I might be little and thin, but I'm quite strong.' She grinned up into his face. 'I'm glad I didn't have to, though, 'cos it would have been hard going lifting it on to the tram. So thank you, Mr Oscar, I'm beholden to yer.'

He placed the sewing machine on the floor before asking, 'Why "Mr" Oscar? We're getting very formal, aren't we?'

Bessie scratched her head. 'To tell yer the truth, I don't

know what to call anybody! All the servants call yer Mr Oscar, and they say Mr Cyril, and address Matilda as Madam. And I'm only a servant, so I should do the same, I suppose.' A picture came into her head and she put a hand over her mouth to try and keep the laughter back. But it didn't work and she began to chuckle. 'Can yer imagine it, Oscar. I'm sitting at the dining table, and as yer know it's a very long table, almost as long as from here to the Pier Head. Anyway, Cyril sits at one end, Matilda at the other, and I'm somewhere about halfway down. And I want the cruet set. Do I leave my chair and fetch it myself, or do I call, "Ay, Madam, would yer pass the cruet set down, please?" Or perhaps, "Shove the salt down, Matilda, there's a good girl". Or do I keep me mouth shut and do without the ruddy salt?'

Oscar was shaking with laughter. 'Oh, Bessie, you are absolutely priceless. I can quite see why Milly won't be parted from you. You are really going to be an asset to everyone in that house.'

'Ay, ay, ay! It's all right for you laughing, but that doesn't help me, does it? I want you to tell me how to address people, before I get the sack after only being there a week.'

'You are treated as one of the family, so you address them by their first names. They don't call you Miss Maudsley or Miss Bessie, do they? And for friends like myself and Philip, it is the same, strictly first names.'

'Right, that solves that little problem.' Bessie's grin appeared. 'If I get the sack for being too familiar, I'll expect yer to find me another job, okay?'

He moved towards her and put his arm across her shoulders. 'I think you can safely say that your home will always be with the Lister-Sinclairs. They know how lucky they are to have you. However, if it will make you feel any better and put your mind at rest, you will always find a job with my family.'

The kettle began to whistle and Bessie made haste towards it, shouting over the noise of the kettle, 'Yer can always put an offer in, yer know. I'll go to the highest bidder.'

Thinking there would never be a dull moment in the Lister-Sinclair household while Bessie was there, Oscar followed her in to the kitchen. 'I'll put the machine in the car out of the way, then you can see what else you wish to take with you.'

Bessie poured the hot water into the teapot before following him. And, sure enough, there were dozens of kids around the car. It was so unusual to see one in the street, particularly a big posh one, they were curious. But they weren't touching it, and moved out of the way to let Oscar put the machine on the back seat. 'Ay, mister, that's a smashing car, what make is it?' one lad asked, eagerly eyeing the leather upholstery and the clocks on the polished wooden dashboard. 'I bet that cost a lot of money.'

Oscar noted the holes in the boy's woollen jumper, and the trousers which were far too small for the size of the lad. His shoes were well worn, and he was without socks. 'It's a Bentley, made in this country,' Oscar told him. 'And one day, when you're a man, you might have one.'

'I wish I could,' another boy said, wistfully, 'but I never will, 'cos I'll never have that much money.'

A front door on the opposite side of the street opened and Rita appeared. She'd seen the car, and her two sons were among the crowd of boys. 'Bessie, if my two are in the way, chase them.'

'They're not doing any harm, Rita, don't be worrying.' Bessie waved her friend over. 'Rita, this is Oscar, he's helping me take some of me things. Oscar, this is Rita, one of me best mates.'

Rita shook his outstretched hand. 'Pleased to meet yer. Yer'll have to excuse the way I look, I'm up to me neck in housework.'

Bessie tutted and huffed. 'Rita Wells, will yer stop making excuses for yerself? Oscar isn't a snob, and he's not daft either. He knows yer can't do housework without getting dirty. I was going to come over to see you and Aggie, 'cos I want yer to do me a couple of favours. But seeing as ye're here now, yer might as well come in.' Bessie's keen eyes spotted Kenny Gordon, and she called, 'Kenny, go and ask yer mam to come over too. Tell her not to bother putting an evening dress on, or her tiara, it's only an informal cup of tea.'

Oscar looked on with mixed feelings. All these children were poorly dressed, it was a narrow mean street, yet not one of them had put so much as a finger on the car or been cheeky. It made him feel quite sad when he thought of his own children who wanted for nothing. He was deep in thought when he heard a loud voice shouting, 'Get out of the way, the lot of yer, anyone would think yer'd never seen a bleeding car before.' And crossing the street, he saw a woman with enormous breasts and stomach, untidy hair, and wearing a dirty pinny which had clearly seen better days. She pushed the children out of her way and stood before him with a beaming smile on her face. 'They won't hurt yer car, mister, they're not bad kids.' She nearly pulled his arm out of its socket with her hearty handshake, then she rubbed her hands together. 'Now, our Kenny said something about a cup of tea, and unless me ears were deceiving me, he said something about a custard cream biscuit too.'

Bessie smiled. 'I wish I had ears like yours, Aggie, they only hear what they want to hear. But ye're going to be disappointed 'cos I've only got ginger snaps. Anyway, come on in or I'll never get everything done I wanted to do.'

Oscar was given a china cup and saucer which brought knowing looks and nudges from Aggie. 'Blimey, she's only been living with the toffs for a week, and she's already forgotten herself. Another week and she won't even remember you and me, Rita.'

Bessie's eyes went to the ceiling. 'Aggie, if I live to be a hundred I'll never forget you. For ye're one of those "once seen, never forgotten" people. And I wouldn't trust yer with a china cup 'cos yer'd break the ruddy thing with those ham shanks yer call hands. I've only got three china cups and saucers, they were me mam's and I treasure them. I don't even use them meself.'

'Take no notice of her, sunshine, yer know how she likes having yer on. If yer'd given her a gobstopper instead of a biscuit, it would have kept her quiet for an hour. So let's pretend she's not here and tell us what favour yer want from us?' Rita suggested.

'I'd like yer to tell the rent collector I'm giving a week's notice and he can take over the house from next weekend. I'll leave yer the money for the two weeks' rent.'

Rita pulled a face. 'I'm not half going to miss you, sunshine, after all these years of us being friends. It won't seem the same with a new family living facing me.'

'The same goes for me, too, queen,' Aggie said. 'We've had some good laughs together and we'll miss that.' For once Aggie showed her soft side, her voice full of emotion. 'And yer've been a good pal to me and Rita, always there to help out when we were stuck for money to buy food. We'd have been in Queer Street many a time without yer.'

'The three of us have helped each other, Aggie, it hasn't been all one-sided.' Bessie's heart strings were being pulled. It wasn't going to be easy to move out of this house and away from her two mates. 'Anyway, can we get back to business? I'm only taking a few small things with me, like photos, ornaments and pictures, things that belonged to me parents. So what I want yer to do is, have a look around yerselves and see if there's anything yer'd like. The beds and bedding should be worth having, but yer can decide that. I'm leaving the key with yer. Anything yer don't want, get the man from that secondhand shop on the main road to come and have a look at it, and ask him what he'll give for it. And any money yer get I want yer to share between yer.'

'Don't be so daft!' Rita said. 'We'll get the best price we can for it and we'll give you the money. I wouldn't dream of keeping it. We've always been the ones to take off you, and never been in a position to give you anything back, so the least we can do is help yer out now. But we don't want the money, we'll hand it over to you.'

Aggie's chins, which fascinated Oscar, swung up and down. 'Hear, hear! I'll second that, queen. It'll be our pleasure to do something for you. Especially after what yer did for us at Christmas, and half of the ruddy street too. A flipping hero, that's what yer are.'

Bessie swivelled round in her chair to face the visitor, who was sitting in the fireside chair, greatly interested in the goings-on. 'Oscar, if yer hear anything that's not meant for your ears, yer won't repeat it, will yer? Not that anything is a matter of life or death, and yer'd find out eventually anyway, but for now keep it to yerself.'

Oscar grinned. 'Bessie, don't you know I'm as deaf as a door post?'

She grinned back. 'Anything yer don't understand, I'll explain to yer on the way home.' She swivelled herself round again and leaned her elbows on the table. 'Now, ladies, listen carefully. Evelyn will be coming down this afternoon, and a van will be calling to pick up what she wants from next door. Milly will be with her, and she wanted me to tell yer to make sure Jack's in, 'cos she wants to see him. And now, don't say a word until I've finished, let me get it all off me chest – Evelyn wants to know if you would be kind enough, next week, to give her notice in to the rent collector as well as mine. She's given me the money to cover two weeks' rent, so I'll give it to yer before I leave. And when the man from the secondhand shop comes here, she would very much like you to get him to look at the furniture and bedding she'll be leaving behind and she wants you to share the money between you.'

Rita shook her head. 'Ah, come off it, Bessie, we can't do that! We hardly know the woman!'

'No one regrets that more than Evelyn. She knows yer used to call her all the stuck-up cows going, and says you had every right 'cos that's exactly what she was. But yer haven't heard it all yet, so will yer keep quiet and let me get on? What I'm going to say next might have yer thinking she feels sorry for yer and is giving you her hand-me-downs, but that would be far from the truth. She's getting married in three weeks, as yer know, and she'd like you to come to the wedding.' Bessie ignored their gasps of astonishment and carried on. 'Yer will be getting an invitation through the post in the next few days.'

'Huh!' Aggie's face was a picture. 'This is a bleeding joke, Bessie Maudsley, and I'm surprised at yer, playing a trick like this on us.' Then the table rocked as her tummy shook with laughter. 'Can yer imagine me and you at a toff's wedding, Rita? In a sixpenny dress from Great Homer Street Market, a scarf on our head 'cos ye're not allowed in church without yer head being covered. We'd be a laughing stock. Folk would move away from us in case they caught something.'

But Rita wasn't listening, she was studying Bessie's face. 'It's not a joke, is it, sunshine?'

She shook her head. 'No, it's not, and I'm surprised at yer for thinking I'd stoop so low as to pull a stunt like that. And another thing: if you two aren't good enough to be invited then neither am I! D'yer think because I've moved to be with Milly, I've suddenly joined the ranks of the well-off? I haven't changed, yer silly nits, and I never will. And, what's more, the people I live with now, and the likes of Oscar here, and Philip who Evelyn is marrying, they treat me as an equal. I get on like a house on fire with all of them. I don't try and be something I'm not, and I never will. So if I'm good enough for the wedding, then so are me best mates.'

Rita said quietly, 'I believe yer, sunshine, and it's very thoughtful of Evelyn. But we've got no clothes for a posh wedding, we'd stick out like sore thumbs and that really would be embarrassing for us.'

'You'd have enough money from the sale of the contents of

both houses to buy yerselves some really classy clothes. There's a shop in a lane off Church Street where they sell good secondhand clothes. Yer'd get a smashing dress and hat from there 'cos they mostly deal in wedding outfits. For the money yer get for the furniture, bedding and kitchen equipment, yer could doll yerselves up to the nines. And it would be a day yer'd enjoy, one to look back on.' Bessie looked from one to the other. 'Before yer say anything, there's another reason yer should give some thought to it. The groom will have all his family and friends at the church, while Evelyn will have very few sitting in the pews on her side. I'm not asking yer to feel sorry for her, like, it was just a passing thought.'

Aggie gave Rita a sly kick. 'What d'yer say, queen, have yer made up yer mind? Meself, I'd like to go 'cos I might never get another chance to go to a posh wedding. And I quite fancy meself in a big picture hat.'

Rita stared at her, straight-faced. 'You in a wedding outfit . . . now that would be something to see.' She suddenly burst out laughing, 'I wouldn't miss that for the world!'

'Are yer both game for it then?' Bessie asked. And when they both nodded, she said, 'Thank God for that, one problem solved. So I'll give yer the rent money now for both houses, and my front door key. Milly will give yer next door's when the van has been and Evelyn has taken all she wants from there. But don't hand the keys over to the collector on Monday 'cos yer'll need them to let the man from the secondhand shop in. Give them to the collector the following week, we'll have paid up till then.'

Bessie closed her eyes and held her forehead in her hand. 'Is there anything else now? Oh, yeah, two things. I'm expecting yer to come and visit me next week, so how would Tuesday be, say about twelve? Yer can have some lunch with me. Then I'll bring Milly down on Saturday, 'cos I know she'll have me motheaten, wanting to see Jack.' She rubbed her forehead again, but it was all a pretence. 'What else was there? Oh, yeah, on the day of the wedding, yer won't have to worry about how to get to the church, they're sending a car to pick you up. And that wasn't Evelyn's idea, it was Philip's, her fiancé's. That's because she had told him how good yer were helping me with giving the Christmas hampers and things out. He wants to meet yer so he can thank you himself.'

Aggie was so flabbergasted she didn't know what to do or say. She folded her arms, hitched her bosom and sat back quickly in her chair. Now the chair wasn't used to being sat on by a person of Aggie's weight, it was only used to Bessie and Milly, so it creaked like mad to let them know it objected. But Aggie didn't hear it, her mind was on other things. 'If we're going to get in a car, I'll have to make sure I don't buy a hat with a bleeding big brim or I won't be able to get through the door.'

Rita was excited inside but keeping it under control until she was in her own house. She looked at her neighbour now, put an arm across her shoulders and said, 'I don't think getting in the car with a hat on is yer biggest worry, sunshine, I'd be inclined to be more worried about yer blue fleecy-lined drawers and yer elastic garters. I mean, if yer hat fell off yer could always run after it, but if yer knickers fell down – well, it doesn't bear thinking about.'

Oscar couldn't stop talking and laughing as they drove back to the Lister-Sinclairs'. 'What a pair of personalities your friends are, Bessie, I could have sat listening to them all day. You will miss them, for they are everything you need in friends. Warm, loyal and funny.'

She nodded. 'Yes, I will miss them, but I certainly won't lose touch with them. I have seen those two laughing their heads off when they haven't had two ha'pennies to rub together. It's when times are hard that yer find out what people are really like, and Rita and Aggie are the salt of the earth.'

'I'm intrigued as to where Philip fits in. How did he come to hear of these ladies?'

Bessie told him about the donation, Evelyn's part in it, and how she, with the help of Rita and Aggie, had been able to help so many poor people in the street. 'It was hard going, 'cos I worked every day, but it was worth it to see the faces of women who hadn't had a decent meal in years. Husbands out of work, kids to feed and clothe, they were really living on the breadline. Philip was very kind, and although those people will probably never meet him, they will be eternally grateful to him.'

Oscar was really moved by what he'd heard. 'I wish I had known, my father and I would have helped. Cyril too, he would have been the first to put his hand in his pocket. Well, we will all be there to help next year. Or even now, if your friends know of any families who are really in trouble, I can get help for them. My family and my friends are very fortunate, but I'm afraid perhaps we don't always appreciate it. This afternoon has been an eye-opener for me, and a lesson I won't forget in a hurry.' He took his eyes from the road for a second to glance at Bessie and to smile. 'I like your friends. Thank you for letting me meet them.'

It was a week before the wedding and Matilda was in her bedroom trying on one of three dresses brought for her inspection by an assistant from one of the best shops in the city. She was helping her client pull the dress down over her hips. It was a navy blue dress, in stiff shot silk, with full skirt, high neck and raglan sleeves. 'Would Madam care to look in the mirror?' the assistant asked. 'I think it suits you beautifully.'

Matilda turned several times to inspect her appearance in the full-length mirror. Then she looked over to where Bessie was sitting on a delicate antique chair. 'What do you think, Bessie, does it suit me?'

In the four weeks she had lived in the house, she had often felt like asking Matilda why she always wore such old-fashioned clothes that made her look much older. But she hadn't liked to be so forward. Now, though, Matilda wanted a dress for Evelyn's wedding, and that dark one didn't do a thing for her, only made her look old and faded. It wouldn't be truthful or fair if Bessie didn't say so. 'I wonder if the assistant would kindly leave us alone for ten minutes, to give you time to make up your mind? This wedding is an important occasion, and the choosing of a dress for it is not something to be decided in a hurry.'

Matilda nodded. 'I think that's wise. Would you go down to the drawing room for a short while, please? I'll ring for the maid when we have finished our discussion.'

When the young lady had left the room, Matilda asked, 'Do you not like the dress, Bessie?'

'D'yer want my true opinion?'

'Yes, of course. I would expect nothing less than the truth from you.'

'In that case, don't say I didn't warn yer. That dress makes yer look old, colourless and drab. In fact, most of your clothes don't do yer justice. Ye're not an old woman, Tilly, so why do yer dress like one? And yer've got beautiful hair, but yer comb it right back into a bun which makes yer look older and is a waste of such an asset.' Afraid she'd gone too far, Bessie said, 'I'm sorry, I'm maybe speaking out of turn. But I'm also speaking as a friend who thinks yer could be a knock-out in the right clothes and a different hair style. And I'm sorry I called yer Tilly, that was out of order too.'

Matilda bit the inside of her lip to keep a smile at bay. She was getting used to Bessie being outspoken, and really appreciated it. Most of the staff fawned over her, always saying what they thought she wanted to hear. 'What about the other two dresses? Do they not find favour with you?'

Bessie told herself she may as well be hung for a sheep as a lamb. 'No, they're the wrong colour and style for you. Yer need something younger, so Cyril can see in you the young girl he fell in love with and married.'

Without saying a word, Matilda crossed the room and pulled on the bell cord. She waited for Maisie to come into the room then asked her to tell the shop assistant that unfortunately none of the dresses had found favour with her, and would she take them back to the shop with apologies? 'Tell her I will ring her supervisor to say she has been very pleasant and efficient, so she won't get into trouble. And now Miss Bessie and I are going to her room and I am to be shown how I should wear my hair so I look like a young girl again. That should be very interesting, I have never seen magic performed before.'

When Bessie brought Milly home from school that night, the young girl stood at the door of the drawing room and gazed at her grandmother with eyes and mouth wide. Then she ran to her. 'Grandma, you look beautiful! Have you been to the shop to have your hair done? It makes you look very pretty.'

Matilda took the girl in her arms. 'As pretty as you, would you say?'

'Oh, yes, Grandma, much prettier than me. Have you been to a hairdresser's?'

'I have my own private hairdresser, my darling, and that is your Auntie Bessie.'

Milly ran to fling her arms around Bessie's waist next. 'Oh, you are clever, Auntie Bessie. My dress for the wedding is the most beautifulest dress in the whole world, and now you've made Grandma look beautiful. I love you, love you, love you.'

'And guess what?' Matilda asked, looking very self-satisfied. 'Your Auntie Bessie has offered to make me a dress for the wedding.'

'Ay, Tilly Mint, I didn't offer, I was talked into it.'

Cyril happened to walk into the room at that moment. He

often came home early now there was something for him to come home to. 'What were you talked into, Bessie?'

She knew he hadn't looked in his wife's direction yet, and she also knew Matilda was anxious to know what his reaction would be to the change in her appearance. 'Ask yer wife, she's the one who causes all the trouble around here.'

Cyril was speechless when he glanced at Matilda. It was a few seconds before he could move. 'My darling, you look wonderful, about twenty years younger. You look like you did the day we got married.' He kissed her on the lips. 'I have told you often you should visit a hairdressing salon. They have worked wonders.'

'I haven't been over the door, my darling, and the wonders were performed by Bessie. Who, incidentally, didn't like any of the dresses Cripps sent for my inspection, and sent the girl packing with them. She said they made me look old and staid, so I worked my charms on her and now she is to make me a dress for the wedding. She hasn't been given much time, but she said as soon as she gets the material, and a pattern I like, she will have it cut out and tacked in no time, ready for me to try on. Oh, and I am to be called Tilly from now on, and that is also down to Bessie.'

Milly's giggle joined Cyril's hearty laughter and the two women smiled at each other, knowing in that moment they had each found a friend for life.

It was the day of the wedding, and the Lister-Sinclairs' house was all hustle and bustle. There was excitement in the air, smiles on every face. Evelyn had spent the night there before leaving for the church with Cyril, who was giving her away. She had written to her parents telling them she was to be married and hoping they would make an attempt at a reconciliation. But if they were to be reconciled, it had to be because they wanted to make amends to her, not because she was marrying into a very wealthy family. So in her letter she hadn't said who she was marrying, just told them the name of the church and the date and time. She had asked if they would kindly reply to Philip's address within the week. But there had been no reply. Evelyn knew if she had told them who she was marrying they would have been to see her the day they received the letter. She was sad, but it proved they had never really loved her. Their only love was for money.

'Evelyn, ye're miles away!' Bessie said, coming into the dressing room. 'But I'm glad to see ye're not a nervous wreck, I'd hate to have yer fainting on me.'

'I was thinking how lucky I am, Bessie. My life has changed so much I sometimes wonder if I'm dreaming.'

'Yer've got the rest of yer life to dream, sweetheart. Right now it's time to put your dress on. I've just finished getting Milly ready – she was so excited she couldn't stand still, and I have to say she looks a picture. I know I'm biased when it comes to your daughter, but she looks good enough to eat.' Bessie stopped to draw breath. She'd been on the go since she got out of bed, seeing to herself first, then dressing Matilda and doing her hair. And, wonder of wonders, Matilda had even asked her to put some powder and rouge on her face. She was a different woman these days, preferred to be called Tilly, laughed a lot and was more outgoing. And she looked a real beauty today in a dress of soft silk which fitted her to perfection. She had allowed Bessie to choose the material and colour, and not been disappointed. The dress was a pale beige, and she'd bought a wide-brimmed hat in a deeper shade, with gloves and shoes to match.

'Well, that's my bit of dreaming done, sweetheart, so let's get you ready.' Bessie reached for the dress which was hanging outside the large wardrobe. 'Lift yer arms up so I can get it on without creasing it.' Five minutes later, Bessie stood back and sighed with pleasure. The dress was a dream of beautiful ivory-coloured soft silk. There were yards of it in the skirt, and the nipped-in waist showed Evelyn's figure off to perfection. It had long sleeves which tapered off to the wrist, and the low round neck was set off by the link of pearls Philip had bought her as a wedding present. Bessie filled up, and a tear trickled down her face. 'Oh, sweetheart, you look lovely, and I'm so proud of yer. If it weren't for mucking yer dress up, I'd squeeze yer to death.'

'Will you do my hair, please, Bessie? You're much better at it than I am. And then all I need is a touch of rouge because I look a little pale. I'll leave the hat until it's time to leave for the church.'

The door opened and in came Matilda and Milly. The girl was hanging on to her grandmother's hand until she saw her mother. Then she ran forward. 'You look like a fairy, Mother, really beautiful.' She did a twirl. 'And hasn't Auntie Bessie made me the most lovely dress? I wish Jack was going to the church so he could see me.'

Bessie's mind flashed back a few months, to the day Milly had dressed in her mother's clothes and had the street out. 'There's nothing to stop you putting it on for him one day, sweetheart. Remember, yer like getting dressed up?'

Milly smiled, knowing right away what her Auntie Bessie was talking about. 'Mother, what have you done with the trunk that was in your bedroom? I often wondered what was in it.'

'It's in Philip's apartment at the moment, I had nowhere else to put it. Why do you ask?'

'If you don't want it, could I have it, please?'

'Of course you can, dear, but why would you want it?'

'Because then I'll have something of yours, and I'd like that.'

Bessie turned her head so she couldn't see the tears that welled up in Evelyn's eyes. It wasn't sadness the two women felt, it was happiness, for although Milly might never again live with her mother, she had now let it be known she would always think of her as her mother.

'Come on, let's get moving,' Bessie said, 'we've got a wedding to go to.'

Philip sat in the front pew with his best friend Clive, who was acting as his best man. 'She's late, isn't she?'

'Calm down, old boy, we were very early, at your insistence. Anyway, it's a bride's prerogative to keep the groom waiting.' Clive glanced sideways at his friend. He'd never thought to see Philip as nervous as he was today. Mind you, having met Evelyn he could understand why. Clive was happy his friend had found the woman of his dreams and was settling down.

Philip turned in his seat to see the church was filling up. He was about to turn back when he saw two women sitting in a pew at the very back of the church. They were on Evelyn's side, but he had never seen them before. Then a thought struck him. 'I've just seen someone I want to speak to, Clive, I won't be a minute.'

Clive frowned. 'This is most unusual, old boy, the bride could be here at any moment.'

'I'll be back before then, I promise.' With that, Philip walked towards the back of the church, surprising guests who were already seated. All heads were turned as he walked into the next to last pew, where he bent to talk to two women who were strangers to everyone except Bessie.

'Would I be wrong in saying you are Rita and Aggie?' Philip smiled when he saw the women look at each other, surprise on their faces. 'It's all right, ladies, I'm Philip.'

In a daze Rita and Aggie shook his hand. 'Ay, lad, shouldn't yer be down by the altar?' Aggie asked. 'Yer don't want to miss yer own wedding, do yer?'

'I have wanted to meet you for some time now, and I was hoping I could talk to you at the reception. However, Evelyn said she had a feeling you might not come to it, that you may sneak away from the church after the service.'

'I won't say we didn't think about it,' Rita said, truthfully. 'Yer see, me and Aggie would feel like fish out of water, not knowing anyone and . . . well, we wouldn't fit in.'

'What nonsense,' he said. 'You have been invited as our friends and I would be disappointed if you let me down. In fact, I won't go back to my best man, who will be tearing his hair out by now, until you promise faithfully you'll come to the reception? A car has been booked to take you with Bessie.'

Rita heard one car draw up outside just then. 'Here's Evelyn! Quick, get down to the altar. We'll come, cross my heart and hope to die.'

Oscar waited until Philip was standing by his best man, then whispered, 'Are they coming to the reception?'

Philip nodded just as the organ started to play and all eyes turned to see Evelyn on Cyril's arm, walking down the aisle. She looked so elegant and beautiful. Cyril felt proud as he smiled at his friends. Gwen followed behind with Milly, looking very pretty in matching dresses, their bouquets of pink flowers matching the floral headdresses. Milly was smiling, not in the least shy. She was happy, and proud that her mother looked so beautiful. And she was glad her mother had Uncle Philip, 'cos he was nice. Then she saw her Auntie Bessie and waved, mouthing the words, 'I love you,' and blew a kiss to her grandma. She was a very lucky girl having so many people to love her.

Philip thought his heart would stop as he saw the woman he adored walking towards him with a faint smile on her face. She was the picture of perfection and he felt he must be the luckiest man in the world to have won her love. He stepped from the front pew as the couple came abreast, and took Evelyn's elbow when Cyril smiled and released her arm before taking his seat next to his wife and Bessie. 'My darling Evelyn, you look so beautiful,' Philip told her quietly. 'I will love you for the rest of my life.'

There were tears shed, but once the service was over and the guests spilled into the church yard for photographs there was much jostling and laughing. The first to be photographed were the bride and groom, standing in the arched entrance to the church and looking the very picture of happiness. Evelyn was a radiant bride, Philip a very handsome groom. Then there was another photograph of bride and groom with Milly standing between them. This was followed by close family, then a group photograph which Rita and Aggie were pulled into by Oscar at the request of Evelyn. Then Oscar asked for one to be taken, away from the crowd, of the three friends, Bessie, Rita and Aggie.

'Ooh, er, I wasn't expecting that, Oscar,' Aggie said, her bosom rising high with pride. 'Thanks very much.'

'I'll make sure you all get a copy,' he promised them, 'and that they're framed for you.'

'Yes, thank yer, Oscar,' Rita said, 'it'll take pride of place on me sideboard.'

Aggie and her chins were thinking ahead. 'We'll get all the neighbours in to see us all dolled up. But they better hadn't pick the photie up, though, and get all fingermarks on it, or I'll marmalise them.' The day had been one that she and her mate would never forget, and it had all been down to Bessie.

The reception was beautifully laid out, the food delicious. Poor Rita's side must have been sore with the constant digs she was getting from Aggie. In the end, she said, 'Aggie, I've got eyes in me head, sunshine, I can see what you can see.'

As the meal progressed there was a lot of laughter, most of it provided by Bessie, Rita, Aggie and Milly. Many friendships were formed that day. As Rita and Aggie realised, not every toff was a snob. And Milly reminded them some friendships would go on forever when she said to Rita, 'Don't forget to tell Jack how nice I look.' Then she grinned. 'I'll tell him myself next Saturday.'

The Sunshine
Of Your Smile

Joan Jonker

Molly Bennett and Nellie McDonough have been best mates for over twenty years. When times were bad and money scarce, they kept their families together with love and laughter.

Now, their children are grown up, and Molly is a grandma. This doesn't go down well with Nellie, who likes to have everything her mate has. But when she finds her daughter Lily is making wedding plans, Nellie is determined to have the biggest and poshest hat in Liverpool.

But, before that, the friends have a job to do. They want to reunite a mother with a son she hasn't seen for years and a grandson she doesn't even know she has . . .

Praise for Joan Jonker's previous Liverpool sagas:

'You can rely on our Joan to provide a cosy, reassuring read with a heartwarming ending' *Liverpool Echo*

'Look out for large dollops of fun and emotion. There's something for everyone' *Middlesborough Evening Gazette*

'A happy and wholesome read' *Coventry Evening Telegraph*

0 7553 0317 2

headline

Strolling With
The One I Love

Joan Jonker

Kate Spencer and her best friend Monica Parry have plenty to keep them busy – their boisterous young families seem to need constant supervision, and it's not easy running their Liverpool households on the meagre wages their husbands bring in. But the plight of a neighbour's teenage daughter soon brings home to them just how lucky they are. Seventeen-year-old Margaret Blackmore is pregnant, and her boyfriend insists he can't be the father.

Unable to stand by and watch while a young life is ruined, Kate and Monica determine to help poor Margaret if they can. Is her boyfriend telling the truth? And if so, who on earth is responsible? The local busybody, Winnie Cartwright, may be able to provide the answer . . .

Praise for Joan Jonker's previous Liverpool sagas:

'Another of her endearing home-spun sagas . . . convincing plotting and characters who touch the heart' *Liverpool Echo*

'A happy and wholesome read' *Coventry Evening Telegraph*

'Look out for large dollops of fun and emotion. There's something for everyone' *Middlesbrough Evening Gazette*

0 7472 6798 7

headline

Now you can buy any of these other bestselling books by **Joan Jonker** from your bookshop or *direct from her publisher*.

FREE P&P AND UK DELIVERY
(Overseas and Ireland £3.50 per book)

Victims of Violence	£6.99
The Sunshine of Your Smile	£6.99
Strolling With the One I Love	£5.99
Taking a Chance on Love	£5.99
After the Dance is Over	£5.99
Many a Tear Has to Fall	£6.99
Dream a Little Dream	£6.99
Down Our Street	£5.99
Stay as Sweet as You Are	£6.99
Try a Little Tenderness	£6.99
Walking My Baby Back Home	£5.99
Sadie was a Lady	£6.99
The Pride of Polly Perkins	£5.99
Sweet Rosie O'Grady	£6.99

TO ORDER SIMPLY CALL THIS NUMBER

01235 400 414

or visit our website: www.madaboutbooks.com

Prices and availability subject to change without notice.